ACKNOWLEDGEMENTS

Thanks go to . . .

My wife, Jane for putting up with me as I ventured into another world on a regular and frequent basis while engrossed at the iMac.

My daughter, Laura for the illustration of Oliver Markland.

The Black Buoy for providing warmth and comfort like no other pub, and for supporting this project.

Jay Stapley *(www.jaystapley.co.uk)* for composing 'Damn My Luck', the theme to *Florida Key* and for performing it at the book launch.

Janet Roberts for clearing the kitchen table to make way for my weekly 'meeting' with publisher and editor David.

Chase Kimball for enthusiastically reading through my initial manuscript and pointing out the many mistakes I'd made.

Adrian Mould for supplying me with one or two nice fruity Corbières in Montolieu while I chewed my proverbial pencil during the writing of *Florida Key*.

D1927868

CAST OF CHARACTERS

An acknowledgements list would not be complete without all the characters who lent their names and were happy to pay for the privilege of appearing in *Florida Key*, enabling me to complete the book.

Cast of Characters, in order of appearance:

Mark Osborne, as bad man Marc Ozborn
Sarah Beech, as murder victim Sandy Beach
Phil Booth, as the Cincinnati traffic cop, with wife Lou and dog Bertie
Annie Morris, aka Mrs. Baltzwinik-Toporofski, as the murder victim's neighbour
John Moores, as the Police Chief heading the hunt for Yushi Yakamoto
Graham Staples, as the Police Sergeant working with Moores
Katie Barnes-Copeland, as the forensic scientist
Mark Emanuele, as prison cellmate M.J. Emanuele, aka *The Assassin*
Chris Dickinson and Kerry Greenland, as Oliver's hosts in Indianapolis
Audrey and Bob Needham, as the helpful couple at the Black Buoy pub
Ursula O'Mahoney, as the Editor of the *Terre Haute Daily Times*
Melody Goddard Rhode with her dog, Blaise-Pascal, as Coldplay's aunt
Lorraine Mills, as the Police Patrolwoman
Theresa Ashley, as the British expat Police Officer
William Wheatley, as the Police Officer working with Theresa Ashley
Zac Brightmore, as the Post Room boy at the newspaper offices
Miss Alberta Louise Baudet, as the owner of the boat *Miss Baudet*

INTRODUCTION
By the Author

This could have been that difficult 'second album' period for me. Following on from *Muddy Water*, I daren't have dreamed that I'd be lucky enough to have a second crack of the whip. But I did. I was invited to write a second novel, and this is it– *Florida Key*.

The other day, I was searching through old papers and found something that I'd drawn up at the start of the creative process. It was a mind map, I think they call it, with lines and squiggles, crossings-out and arrows, underlinings and circles. This finished book bears little resemblance to the plans I formulated at the beginning. I admit, there was hardly a plan at all, just the premise for a tale based on a personal experience I had while on holiday in Florida.

Any thoughts about writing a book during that American vacation were embryonic. It was more about swimming in the ocean, or having a beer at *Skinny's*, where they serve their renowned 'Number 1' burgers. I visited a flea market and found an old key for sale. As I held it in my hand, contemplating its purchase for $17, I immediately knew that this object would become the subject of my next book.

I, like *Florida Key*'s central character, Oliver Markland, pondered the question of where the key originated from. When the seller informed me it might be from a prison, my imagination went into overdrive. Where was the prison? Who was held captive there? Why? When? What happened to him?

For me, there was only one way to find out. I'd let my imagination run wild and let it feed me the answers. Then, another thought occurred to me–what if the inmate had been executed? And what if he hadn't committed the crime?

All these questions bombarded me while I was standing in the hot Florida sunshine.

To help me write the book, I went on an imaginary journey. The character became me–or rather I became the character. Apart from those initial mind maps, I didn't know where Oliver Markland would take me.

Each day I began writing, I couldn't wait to find out what would happen to central characters Yushi Yakamoto and Oliver Markland.

So, although *Florida Key* is a work of fiction, to me it's as real as if it all actually happened.

Poor Yushi. Lucky Oliver. Fortunate me.

How it all Began

(MONDAY, 13TH APRIL, 1981)
PARIS, ILLINOIS, MIDWEST USA

The crash of plastic coming down on a human head was like nothing else he'd ever heard. She shouldn't have ridiculed him. That was his justification for what he had done to her.

What he hadn't expected was for the red and black plastic object to disintegrate into so many pieces. Obviously, he hadn't known his own strength. Obviously, at that moment when she fell, he wished he could have turned the clock back and decided not to return to her house. He should have simply moved on, but now that was easy to think. Everything is easy in hindsight.

Still with a head full of confused rage, as he moved his right foot back into a position where he could make a good strike, he saw her eye open slightly—only one, before it flickered and convulsed—and then when her eyeball turned upwards, he took a swipe. He couldn't control himself, such were his repressed feelings, as if possessed by the devil himself. And now she was dead. Of that there was no doubt in his mind.

For a few seconds, he stood motionless, wondering what her final thoughts had been as she took her last breaths.

(FIFTEEN YEARS LATER)
JOLIET CORRECTIONAL CENTER, ILLINOIS, USA

Only 21 when he was taken to Joliet, Yushi Yakamoto was as American as they come. For him, life was all about living the American Dream, about Taco Bell fast-food, Mountain Dew soda drinks and Hershey's chocolate bars. He had toyed with the idea of changing his name to make it more American-sounding, and when he was twenty he even got as far as going to a lawyer who had promised to handle everything on his behalf for 'only' $199.

It was funny how, in these circumstances, Yushi now thought about such details. He recalled that it hadn't been the amount of money that had made him change his mind, even though the cost, in his opinion, was a rip-off just for a few forms to be filed. No, in the end, it was out of respect for his parents, who had come to live and work tirelessly in what had once been a wonderful nation in the 1950s. They had been proud of their Japanese heritage, and proud to be making a good life for themselves in a country that, only a few years previously, had had their national differences with Japan, to put it mildly. Yes, he was glad to have honoured his parents' good name, and decided at the last minute to cancel his application to become 'Mr. Stephen Josh Mote'. Instead, he settled for only paying his lawyer's $25 initial consultation fee, continuing with his original birth name.

Now, aged 36, Yushi was led out of his cell, on the fourth floor of Block A. As he sat, strapped in position, helplessly watching the lethal concoction of drugs being injected into his arm, he reflected on how his decision to remain in the United States as Yushi Yakamoto had been a big mistake.

PREVIOUSLY, SOMEWHERE IN MIDWEST AMERICA

Mark Osborne had been born in 1943, the fourth son of a soldier of the United States military. He never knew his father, who was stationed in Tunisia in 1942 to do his bit for Uncle Sam, and never returned. As Osborne grew up, constantly being bullied by his older brothers, and outraged that his pa could have so selfishly left him, the chip on his shoulder became a growth that refused to diminish. With his father no longer around, his mom began drinking to quell the pain of her loss, but that soon became the least of the family's worries.

Uncles and aunts were ever-present in the tenement block where they lived, on the rough side of town, for the first year or so—which saw his mother struggling to raise the family on very little money. For a while, things were just about tolerable, although Mark constantly had to hit back at his brothers when his mom wasn't looking. By the time he was five, the visits from uncles and aunts had all but dried up, and even by that young age he had learnt the meaning of being poor.

He loved his mom, really he did, but he hated it when she left him at home with his brothers, and then heard her returning home late at night, each time accompanied by the sound of a different man's voice. When he'd ask his mom the following morning who the stranger was, she just shrugged and said that it was what she had to do to put food in his belly. All his fault, then, he thought.

He remembered rebelling, in his own small way, as soon as he could, when being taught to read and write. The infant pupils would take it in turns to chalk their names on the blackboard in class for the teacher, and Mark would deliberately spell his first name with a C instead of K, and 'Osborne' was also changed to suit his whim. Eventually, the teachers gave up trying to correct the boy, and soon 'Marc Ozborn' gained his first victory over authority. In that small way, it helped to make him feel less helpless, but unfortunately the anger was ever-present, and still growing.

On the occasions when he wasn't playing truant and Ozborn actually attended his junior school, he paid hardly any attention in class—with the notable exception of anything related to the Second World War, and particularly what led the United States to become involved. He lapped up historical facts to do with the events at Pearl Harbor, and how, prior to that fateful day in December 1941, Churchill repeatedly attempted to persuade Roosevelt to join the Allies in their fight against Germany. "Damned Japs", he thought, damned Krauts, and damned Brits, too. If it weren't for Churchill, his pa might still be alive today.

Ozborn was proud that he'd decided to misspell his name—'Osborne' looked too British, whereas 'Ozborn' appeared more individual, in his mind, and more American. Either way, no figures of officialdom ever checked, and the name stuck.

Over the years, his anger grew at how his pa had left him—for that was the way Ozborn saw it. His anger grew at how his brothers tormented him—to the point where he lashed out to protect himself against their spitefulness. At least he was learning to fight, with a well-placed punch here, and a kick there. His anger grew at how his mom behaved with the drink bottle. He became rude to her men friends when they tried making small talk with him, sometimes kicking them in the shins if he thought he could get away with it without his mom noticing. Usually, he succeeded with the quieter ones who chose not to react and cause a scene, especially when they hadn't yet got what they'd come for. They were the ones he hated the most. 'Spineless shits', he called them, sometimes to their face when Mom was out of earshot.

By the time he was 12, he hated the world, and everyone around him. His own life sucked, but in his own eyes it wasn't his fault, was it? By 13, he'd discovered where his mom stashed her bottles of vodka and whisky, and it didn't take long before he learned how their contents eased his own pain, just like they did for her. By the time he'd reached 14, he was off, taking his brother's car and driving it into a ditch a few miles out of town. No matter, he'd take another from the parking lot at the mall—it was surprising how many there were to choose from with their doors unlocked and keys left in the ignition. It served the owners right for being such lazy bastards, he thought, and gleefully watched in the rear-view mirror as they'd come out, scratching their heads as they looked at the now vacant space between the lines on the ground.

Inevitably, time was served at the Youth Detention Center, and that was where Marc Ozborn acquired a new interest, along with the associated skills needed to obtain, and use them—narcotics.

(WEDNESDAY, 8TH APRIL, 1981)
PARIS, ILLINOIS

Every morning when she arrived at the practice, dental assistant Sandy Beach had already slipped on her appropriate, flat, black shoes, and she would already be wearing her crisp, white tunic with its thin, navy-blue lines around the collar and pockets. Dressed smartly prior to making the short journey to work from her home, she made sure she had every button fastened all the way to the top, so as never to reveal any of her cleavage. Despite this, when she was leaning over to place various pieces of oral apparatus into the mouths of the clients, Mr. Edgar, the dentist, couldn't fail to fantasise about the fine figure so obviously lurking beneath his assistant's formal attire.

Although Sandy was acutely aware of the sensuality that she exuded, she would never intentionally let it be shown—at least as far as being at the dentist's was concerned. Although she'd always quite fancied Mr. Edgar, she'd never imagined him to be rough enough to satisfy her secret desires.

But at The Old Parlor Tavern on Main Street, Paris, it was, however, a completely different matter. Out came Sandy's hairpins, and down came her long, auburn locks. Her flat shoes were substituted for high-heeled cowboy boots, and her smart and proper uniform swapped for a low-cut halter-neck top, the black clingy fabric of which left nothing to the imagination, especially when she provocatively chose to wear no bra, as was the case on this particular evening.

Just like when she was 'entertaining' her guests at home on her waterbed, she was in control, and she liked that feeling. When she strutted, deliberately slowly, to the bar, practically all the men, as well as a good number of the women, stopped their conversations mid-flow to ogle her self-assured stride as she walked towards them. Eyes glued to her tight jeans that could have been sprayed on, they continued gazing as she confidently strode past.

Once at the bar, Sandy needn't wait a moment before being offered any number of drinks, but she was choosey before accepting the first. Preferring instead to initially be served directly by the bartender, she coolly brushed aside all advances with a warm, gracious smile, and began her evening with a Bud Light, eyeing up whoever she'd most fancy taking home with her that night to satisfy her sexual energy.

A string of expletives spouted from the mouth of 38-year old Marc Ozborn, as he battled to contain his anger at the poor young guy who'd inadvertently spilled a couple of drops of beer on his arm. The fact that it was Ozborn himself who'd caused the spillage didn't matter, as far as he was concerned.

"Damned retard. Be more careful next time," Ozborn spat as he made his way through the crowded space.

"But . . ." the young guy began to defend himself, to no avail. It was too late.

The man with no manners had all but disappeared into the throng of people on his way through to the bar. The young guy considered following in order to extract an apology, but decided against it, having read the drunk expression of anger on the perpetrator's face. "People like that are best left alone," he thought, and wisely decided to let the matter go.

Sandy had been sitting sideways-on with her back in perfect posture at one of the tall stools, sipping the beer occasionally as she held the bottle elegantly, caressing its neck suggestively with her fingers. She enjoyed observing the crowd, and although she'd already been offered at least four drinks from eager suitors, so far she'd been disappointed with the type of man that had approached her.

She liked variety. Sometimes she liked to be treated gently, but tonight she was in a different mood. This time she wanted someone experienced and rugged, someone to pull at her hair and slap her—'a bit of rough', as she called it. As if the gods had read her mind, a tall, unshaven but attractive man came pushing his way through the crowd towards the bar. He looked angry and full of testosterone, as he turned behind him shouting some expletives while brushing his arm dry.

She decided there and then that he would be the one going home with her that night, no matter how out of his head on booze, and maybe more, he clearly was.

PART ONE

YUSHI'S BIKE RIDE

CHAPTER 1

ALLENTOWN, PENNSYLVANIA, USA
(SUNDAY, 22ND FEBRUARY, 1981)

Yushi's Light Bulb Moment

Yushi would be approaching his twenty-first birthday in only two months. He sat in his bedroom, feeling as depressed as he had done when coming up to his twentieth. And his nineteenth, eighteenth, and all the years back for as long as he could remember. He felt that his life wasn't exactly setting any fires alight. Not even any cinders.

True, he was doing quite well in his job taking telephone calls in the sales office at the factory that made electrical connectors. He was always polite to the customers who enquired as to whether they had twenty-two-pin male quarter-inch variants in stock, or what the price would be for, say, half a dozen single-flange steel couplers. He efficiently dealt with each enquiry, he always called back when he said he was going to, and precisely replaced the telephone receiver after each call, before carefully picking it up again the next time it rang, answering with a polite "Good afternoon, Yushi speaking, how may I help you?"

Since leaving college and starting work, Yushi had had great expectations that 'something great and good' was going to happen to him, but it never seemed to. Sure, he got on well with his colleagues at the sales desk, and the three women in the typing pool seemed to like him enough when he asked politely if they'd mind completing some paperwork or other. But, in short, he was bored out of his mind.

That was his work life. Things were pretty much the same in his home life too. He lived comfortably, and he had no complaints about how his mom cooked his dinners and washed his clothes, or how his dad engaged him in conversation about his work life, or his social life. "What social life?" he thought to himself, as he sat in his bedroom, literally twiddling his thumbs in a circular motion whilst contemplating the nothingness that lay before him. Maybe that could be part of his problem, the fact that he had no social life.

And by social life, what he actually meant was love life. He knew that he wasn't bad-looking, and he did have a few friends after all, and some of them were in fact girls. He was able to engage comfortably in conversation about his favourite movies and records, about his hobby of cycling, and about topical issues of the day, but only when he was in a group. When it came to being in the company of a girl on his own, his basic problem was that he was shy. And so, he avoided failing in the heterosexual relationship department by not attempting one in the first place. Instead, he concentrated on his hobby, which at least made him athletic and strong. He could be good at being athletic and strong without the fear of clamming up through not knowing what to say next.

As his thumbs turned in circular motion, he wondered what he could do to reduce his feelings of sadness and frustration—before it was too late. Soon to be 21 and never been kissed, at least not in the way he wanted. If he weren't careful, his life would be over before he knew it, and his love life wouldn't even have begun, so he had to do something. But what, exactly?

Whether it was the pressure caused by his impending, significant coming-of-age birthday, or whether it really was one of those 'light bulb' moments, Yushi somehow came up with the answer. Of course! He would leave. Leave home, leave his job—and go. He could afford to. Living at home was quite cheap—free, in fact—and so he'd built up a fair amount of savings that should last a while. For the first time in his life, Yushi Yakamoto became truly excited and leapt to his feet, putting an LP on his stereo—"ah yes", he thought—Bowie's *Aladdin Sane*—until sinking back on to his bed, deflated with the realisation that he had nowhere specifically in mind to go. But a seed had been sown, and as he went downstairs to his mom calling dinner-time, Yushi was determined to pick up his thoughts later where he'd left off, and work out a plan. A plan of escape, and a plan for the rest of his life—or at least for the next few months.

CHAPTER 2

(MONDAY, 2ND MARCH, 1981)

Yushi's Preparation

On Monday, 2nd March 1981, having had the whole of the weekend to really think his plans through, Yushi went to work with a spring in his step, inconsistent with his normal, unenthusiastic trudge. He waited until everyone except his boss had gone home at five o'clock, before knocking at the door—politely—of the glass-partitioned office belonging to Mr. Jim Pursey, the Manager of the Sales Office, in order to tender his resignation. Conscientious and conscious of his position of minor responsibility towards his co-workers, customers, and Mr. Pursey, Yushi had decided to work more than his contractual notice period right through to the end of the month, instead of the obligatory one week. That would no doubt help Mr. Pursey, and would also bring in three more weeks' wages to fund his travels.

It was time, decided Yushi, to grow up, to leave home, meet people and to explore his country—and maybe, just maybe, get a girlfriend. That was how it happened in the movies, wasn't it? Surely, the possibility may lend itself, at least once perhaps, during his epic bike ride. It was a trip that he'd been fastidiously planning, poring over detailed American Automobile Association maps spread over the floor of his bedroom, red marker pen poised to plot his route.

His parents, while initially expressing concern when his intentions were first proposed to them, eventually capitulated and gave Yushi their blessing. After all, they themselves had shown courage when they had decided to come to the Land of Opportunity, so perhaps some of their sense of adventure had rubbed off on Yushi. A good idea, they thought. It might help their only son become less introverted.

Mr. Yakamoto senior even pledged to give $100 to his son's cause. He didn't know that Mrs. Yakamoto would be secretly stashing double that amount into Yushi's wallet—"just to be on the safe side," she whispered in Yushi's ear. She wanted to be sure that, as Yushi cycled off in a westerly direction across the country towards the Golden State of California, he would always be able to afford a room in a motel, a hot meal, and have enough money to phone home at least every other day to let her know he was safe and well. And for certain to clean his clothes at the Laundromat. "Always have pride in your appearance," she advised, or rather commanded.

But clean clothes were less on Yushi's mind than the preparation of his bicycle. Twenty-one gears, a firm, leather saddle, lightweight aluminium frame, and thin, 26-inch wheels were well engineered to make up his pride and joy. All he was uncertain about, in the end, was whether to swap his tubeless tyres for more practical tubed versions—but that would involve spending some of his limited savings on wider wheels, and what would be the point, when he'd already got a large number of spare tubeless tyres hanging up in his parents' garage? So he opted to use what he had.

Next on his mind was the question of whether to take a rucksack or panniers, or both. And, if panniers, should they be front- or rear-mounted? And another dilemma: how would he record his adventure? He would like to take his full-bodied Pentax camera with long-range and wide-angle lenses, but that would add weight. And what about a compass? And maps? Some proper cycling shoes would surely be essential. . . The organisation began to bother him, and as the end of March approached, he became more and more nervous about the challenge he'd set himself. Yushi was even considering backing out. It was his father who, having wished he'd done something like this when he was young and unencumbered, encouraged him to go through with what he hoped would be a trip of a lifetime. "Travel broadens the mind, son," he said.

So that was it, Yushi thought. There was no going back now. He decided to get some final advice about what equipment to take, so on the Saturday two weeks before his planned departure, he arrived at Cycle City, the best bike shop in Allentown, to browse the accessories on offer and, if the store manager wasn't too busy, he would politely pick his brains.

Satisfied with the answers to all his technical questions, and about to leave the shop, Yushi noticed one accessory in the glass cabinet that he hadn't previously thought of buying. He wasn't even aware that such a thing existed. He stared at the radio on display, and it was not just any radio. This one, priced at $29.99, was just what he hadn't realised he needed—until now. It was specifically designed for fixing onto his bike's handlebars with a bracket that enabled it to be removed with ease and speed. Supplied with batteries that the store owner threw in for free, the sound was good too, clearly picking up AM stations, and it was waterproof. It even had a horn and built-in reflector on the front, and with its bright-red and shiny-black body, it looked just great. Yushi was very pleased indeed with his impulse purchase.

The next two weeks flew by, as he finalised his tasks at work, and busied himself with his preparations at home. A few of his sales-desk colleagues had signed a good-luck card and had bought him a present—a pair of cycling gloves and a Timex watch—but there was no big leaving party for Mr. Yakamoto junior. Mr. Pursey kindly allowed him to leave at lunchtime instead of the normal 4.30p.m. and, as Yushi left the building for the last time, he reflected on what a waste his life had been selling boring electrical connectors during his employment at the company. As he walked through the reception area, he noticed the replacement recruit waiting to be ushered in to take his seat in the telephone sales office. The same seat that was still warm from Yushi's backside, occupied for three uneventful and dull years of his life.

That was all about to change, Yushi thought, when his backside would soon be sitting on a very different seat. Excited more than at any time he could remember, he hurried home to the garage where his prized bike was awaiting its final preparation. The tyres would be checked, and the brakes, the chain and the gears. Everything was now ready for his departure and the next day his mother, father and sister would be presenting him with a farewell traditional Japanese breakfast of steamed rice, miso soup, and grilled fish.

Yushi would have much preferred bacon, eggs, and maple syrup, but this would be no time to add to his mother's angst and sadness. He knew she would find it hard to hold back her tears, and he wondered if he'd be equally able. Before taking to his bed for an early night, Yushi went in the garage to put the finishing touches to his bike—to fix his handlebar-radio, now with batteries fitted, and two national flags on a long wooden stick attached to the rear of the bike's frame. That would please his mom, he thought, as he stood back to admire them; symbolically, one of them sported stars and stripes, and the other a red circle on white.

CHAPTER 3

(WEDNESDAY, 8TH APRIL, 1981)
PARIS, ILLINOIS, USA

Ozborn's Failing

Marc Ozborn staggered his way to the bar to get a bottle of beer and a whisky chaser, the first of several from that establishment that evening. He didn't notice the attention that he'd gained from a woman sitting on a stool, elegantly holding her bottle of Bud Light, and observing him with interest. Still brushing off some spilt beer from his arm, he had already had two or three swigs of liquor from the bottle he kept wrapped in brown paper on the parcel shelf under his Dodge pickup truck's dashboard. He was pleased with how smart he was, keeping it there, out of sight from prying road-cops' eyes. He was pleased with the way that he could lean across the passenger seat, shift his body in a certain position, and swig from the bottle beneath the sight-line of the windows—even when he was driving. Yeah, he was smart alright, he thought. He must have been—he'd never been caught for that particular offence.

He'd just strayed into town, and the neon-signed Old Parlor was the first brightly-lit tavern he'd come to, so he pulled into the parking lot, finished his joint before flicking the remaining stub to the dusty ground, and made his way inside. Positioning himself at the bar, he pulled a packet of Marlboro Unfiltered from his top pocket. "Shi-it," he murmured, when he realised there were none left. He crumpled up the empty packet and threw it in disgust across the wooden bar, wondering what to do next, whether to make his way all the way back through the crowded room, past the guy who had spilled beer on him, to his pickup where he knew he had more cigarettes. He'd at least get a pop at the punk that had knocked into him, he considered, but he really didn't want the bother of going anywhere, now that he'd got to his position by the bar.

Then he heard sweet music to his ears from a few feet further along the counter.

"Hey there, Marlboro Man. Help yourself." An almost full pack of smokes came sliding along the wooden surface towards him, and he looked in the direction of where they, and the woman's voice, had come from. Despite the effects of the recent inhalation of his joint, as well as the plentiful alcohol consumption, he was still able to recognise a pretty lady when he saw one. And this lady was no exception. "Why, thank you, Ma'am," he responded in his usual low, gravelly voice, doing his best to reduce the slur in his voice to a minimum, while touching the rim of his hat.

"You're very welcome," the lady in the black halter-neck top mouthed sexily, turning up the charm a notch, as the gruff voice that matched his rugged good looks confirmed to her that tonight this man would be the one going home with her, if she had her way.

"Why don't you move over here so I can light it for you too?" She beckoned Ozborn to take up her offer—while he attempted to disguise that his legs weren't exactly coordinating with his brain.

For Sandy, the usual small talk followed, but she found herself more captivated than usual with this particular man's conversation. For Ozborn however, it would just be good to sleep in more pleasant surroundings than his pickup truck or at the trailer park, and if he were to get laid, that would be an added bonus. Less than one hour later he was being offered more than just a bed for the night.

Sandy went outside, with Ozborn in tow, who followed her to her Volvo estate. She was already anticipating what would be happening on her waterbed when they got back to her place, and the fantasies that were running through her brain were causing much excitement and anticipation. Stone-sober, she remembered exactly where the handcuffs were in the bedroom that she'd bought especially for such occasions. It was true that this guy could do with a shower before they got down to business, but, such was her eagerness to commence proceedings, she wasn't even sure if she could wait for that.

After pulling up at the drive of her neat bungalow, they both got out of the car and giggled as they made their way, arms around each other, to the front door. Once inside, Ozborn found himself being eagerly stripped, his clothes being discarded here and there as he was led to the bedroom. The bedroom, he noticed, even in his stupor, had the most grotesque, flecked-green wallpaper adorning it. The next thing he knew, his hands were being cuffed to the bed posts behind him, and this unique woman was straddling him, riding him as if he were a horse and she were a cow-girl swinging a lasso in the air. The waterbed squelched as the mattress rose and fell like waves at a theme park, making him feel sick. The interior decor didn't help matters, and was hardly what he should have been focussing on to prevent himself puking, but that goddamn awful colour was the last thing he remembered seeing after prematurely climaxing, and promptly passing out.

Sandy Beach wasn't happy, and she made it perfectly clear to Ozborn that that was the case when she awoke with her alarm clock going off the following morning at 7.30a.m.

"Come on. Get up, you! I've gotta go to work, and you've gotta get outta here," she commanded.

There was hardly any movement from the side of the bed where Ozborn was still out cold. All he could manage was a feeble groan. Sandy proceeded to get dressed in her prim and proper dentist's uniform. She looked over at the unlocked handcuffs still dangling from where she'd given up on having any pleasure the night before. Well, that had been a complete waste of time, she thought, as she pulled back the bed sheets in the hope that that would get this guy out of her bed. As she did so, she couldn't help but admire his body—lean, muscular and tanned. The admiration just added to her pain of unfulfilled satisfaction. His rough and rugged facial features still attracted her, but not half as much as the sight of his manhood—

although limp now—and his perfectly-formed buttocks, still offering promise of a better time to be had than during last night's disastrous failure.

"Look, you can come back again this evening if you want, and I'll be home from work by around four!" exclaimed Sandy. "You can even stay here all day if you don't have anywhere else you need to be, and maybe we can have a more successful time tonight. There's coffee in the kitchen for now, and I can give you a ride back to the Parlor on my way to work so that you can get your truck. How does that sound?" she asked, hoping he'd agree. Sandy wasn't finished with him yet, and was keen for him to finally satisfy her cravings at the second attempt. A slight smile appeared at the edges of her neatly lipsticked mouth as the man in her bed nodded 'yes'.

All that day, while staring into the wide-open mouths of men, women and children, professionally concentrating on the oral hygiene tasks she was being paid to do, Sandy's mind wandered elsewhere. She was looking forward to getting home to continue the unfinished business with her Marlboro Man. She wasn't even sure of his name. Mark, she thought he'd told her, but no matter what it was—she wasn't too bothered about getting on first-name terms with him—she just wanted long, sensual, exciting and rough sex with him. That was all.

The end of the working day came and Sandy said 'good evening' to Mr. Edgar, and made her way home-but not before stopping at the grocery store to pick up some things for dinner. The least she could do was to feed Marlboro Man's belly later, after she'd had her fun. She then pulled up outside her bungalow, hoping to see the pickup truck there, but it wasn't. At least three hours went by until she heard the growly sound of a car engine, tyres skidding to a halt and loud country music blaring out of the car's window. Then she heard the truck door slam shut and footsteps. "At last!" she thought.

During the day, Ozborn hadn't had an awful lot to do. Having recently moved to Illinois, he was in an unfamiliar town in an unfamiliar part of the county. After being dropped off by Sandy to collect his truck from the tavern's parking lot, he thought about going inside for a morning hair of the dog. He hadn't needed to think too long and hard about it, and by the time mid-morning had brought in the bar's regular farmers for their beer and breakfast, he was already on his third solitary drink while the owner busied himself with glass-washing and other such chores. By the time Ozborn reached into his pocket to pay for his fourth beer, he was still sober enough to calculate that he was nearly out of cash.

"If you wanna do something around here for some beer money, I've got plenty of jobs for you," offered the owner, keen to take his seat at the other side of the bar, and read the newspaper.

"Don't mind if I do," replied Ozborn. And so, the two men swapped places, and it remained that way for the rest of the day. In between serving beer and washing glasses, Ozborn would occasionally converse with customers, while taking swigs from his constantly-replaced Corona bottles, but rarely speaking more than a few words. He was used to working behind a bar, but not used to making small talk at any hour before dusk, and woe betide anyone whose attitude didn't agree with him, especially if they appeared to be anything other than what he termed '100% American'.

By the time he pulled up at Sandy's later that evening, once again he was hardly in any fit state to perform what she was expecting. Drunk he might have been, but his brain still imagined groping those delicious breasts of hers. He stumbled in through the front door—only to be greeted by a look of disgusted and frustrated disappointment once more from his hostess.

CHAPTER 4

(WEDNESDAY, 8TH APRIL, 1981)

Yushi's Wrong Turning

Two days into his endurance-testing cycle ride, Yushi was feeling pleased with himself. His beloved bike was, so far, performing brilliantly. He was enjoying the challenge of achieving his 90-mile-a-day goal. The first day had been tough when he rode away from home at midday, waving goodbye to his family, trying not to shed a tear and noticing the false bravery on the faces of his parents, particularly his mom, as they in turn did everything to hide their melancholy emotions.

The previous night, the first on his own, staying in a motel room about 40 miles heading out west from Allentown, was unusual for him to say the least. He'd never stayed the night in a building other than his home on his own before, not least a hotel or motel. By late afternoon he had already begun feeling tired, so he decided to call it a day early, find somewhere to stay, take an evening meal, watch TV and get an early night. Only 40 miles covered was well below his target of at least double that distance if he had any chance of reaching California before his money ran out, but yesterday had been an exception due to the late set-off time, he told himself.

Yushi anticipated that usually he'd be off and away before 8.00a.m. And sure enough, by his third day on the road he had worked out a routine that would enable him to reach his self-imposed daily mileage quota. His routine was to study his AAA map the night before, and plot a destination target 90 miles ahead, and then break the planned route into three sections of 30 miles each—allowing himself a snack break at 30 miles, and lunch at 60. Although Yushi was fit, he struggled initially to get his stamina up to the necessary level to do the full 90 miles, but it was the mental fatigue more than the physical that was his biggest handicap during his first few days. At the beginning of each day, and at each 30-mile stretch, he very nearly gave up and turned back to the comfort of home and his mom's cooking.

However, being the somewhat introverted thinker that he was, he devised a strategy that would help him reach each 30-mile position—with the help of his old, wise grandfather's words entrenched in his memory.

"Yushi," his beloved grandfather used to say. "Whenever you face a seemingly insurmountable task ahead of you, remember that the journey of a thousand miles begins with a single step." And so Yushi bore that advice in mind and simply divided each 30-mile section into three further 10-mile sub-sections. It was a simple idea, but for Yushi it worked, and by his fourth day on the road he felt more confident than ever that he'd be able to complete all 3,000 miles of his adventurous trip.

He began to relax into the journey, joyfully observing the wonderful nature and magnificent surroundings. As well as enjoying the visual treats, he also loved listening to his handlebar radio. He found that the pop stations on the AM band were perfect for listening to his favourite songs, and he spent many happy hours fine-tuning the little knob to see what programmes he could pick up as he rode along. He even sang along to the hits that were played on rotation from any place he was able to receive a strong enough signal. 'Being With You' by Smokey Robinson was a good one, as was Kim Carnes's 'Bette Davis Eyes'. His voice didn't do much justice to 'Nine to Five (Morning Train)' by Sheena Easton, but he was very happy with his rendition of George Harrison's 'All Those Years Ago'. Yes, thought Yushi, he really loved anything by any of The Beatles. He sure was glad of his bike radio—it was the best $30 investment he could have made.

By day five, Yushi was able to settle back in his saddle and worry less about the physical challenge ahead of him, and more about the mental torment that troubled his soul. With a normal soon-to-be 21-year-old's hormones rushing around his body, and so much time to think, he pondered the big question. How, up to this point in his comfortable but dull existence, had he not managed to have a relationship with anyone he could call a girlfriend? So, during the planning stages of his trip, when he joined the Youth Hostel Association, he wasn't only thinking ahead toward his sleeping accommodation. By staying in a hostel, he hoped he might get the perfect opportunity to, in the words of one of his musical heroes, 'Lay, lady, lay'.

***

That morning, he called ahead from the room of his motel to the Youth Hostel in Cincinnati, enquiring whether there might be a bed available that night. "Why, sure!" the administrator confirmed, with gusto. "That will be $12, and perfect timing for you. Why don't you join us for our street party? I'm sure if you're travelling all that way by bicycle, you'll be wanting some food and company by the time you get here," the woman at the end of the phone line continued, with an infectious friendliness present in her voice that Yushi was most impressed and attracted by.

"Well, thank you. I'd sure like that," replied Yushi, giving his name to her so she could book his bed in the dormitory. The woman told him to ask for her by name—Megan—when he arrived, and he was convinced that she had been flirting with him. For the first 60 miles of that day's cycling, he wondered what the street party would be like, and who he might meet there. With growing confidence in himself, he hopefully daydreamed that tonight could be his lucky night, perhaps even with the flirtatious Megan.

It was around 2.00p.m. when Yushi set off on the final 30-mile section of the day, anticipating it should take him around three hours along the relatively flat tarmac of Route 50. As he approached the outskirts of Cincinnati, the traffic became busier than he had ever been used to, and it took him by surprise. This was by far the largest city or town that he had so far encountered, so the volume of traffic matched the city size accordingly, and he wasn't even downtown yet. Yushi put all thoughts about street parties and girls to the back of his mind, and concentrated on reaching the hostel in one piece. A road that just a short while ago was quiet and peaceful had now become a loud and frightening roar, full of huge articulated trucks with their chrome funnels billowing exhaust fumes into the sky, and speeding cars of all shapes and sizes whizzing past and towards him.

He didn't like it. He was scared. And he was confused. His confusion arose from the fact that, although his route should have been straightforward, and there were many signposts guiding road-users towards Cincinnati, those signs were aimed at modes of transport bearing more than two wheels and two pedals. It was a fact that the large green 'exit' signs were meant primarily for vehicles travelling at 50 miles per hour, and were therefore situated at least a mile before the actual turning was reached: obvious to those truck and car drivers, but not to poor Yushi. He wasn't to know that the small lane directly after the green signpost was actually a slip-road for emergency vehicles needing quick access onto Interstate 275, a massively busy, eight-lane highway circling the city. Not noticing the tall 'EMERGENCY ACCESS ONLY' sign that was way above his line of sight, after cycling for five minutes along this deafeningly loud road he realised he'd made a mistake, but by now it was too late. It would be too dangerous to turn around and go back against the oncoming traffic, even on the emergency lane, so his only option was to continue as fast as he could until he reached the next possible turnoff. But before he could reach one, he heard the distinctive sound of a siren wailing in the distance behind him, which was growing louder and louder, until the police car from where it was emanating pulled to a stop in front of him. The oblong, red flashing lights on its roof were intimidating enough, but that was nothing compared to the clearly disgruntled Officer of the Law who got out of his patrol car and walked back towards Yushi, gun in his holster. Yushi could see his own image clearly reflected in the mirrored gold-rimmed shades that the policeman was wearing. As he suddenly became a rather frightened young man, Yushi's heart, already beating heavily from the physical demands made upon it from cycling, began thumping a whole lot more. His earlier daydreaming about meeting Megan was quickly replaced by an ominous thudding from within his rib cage he was certain could be heard out loud. He'd never been stopped by the law before.

CHAPTER 5

(FRIDAY, 10TH APRIL, 1981)

Sandy's Frustration

Sandy couldn't believe it. She'd been looking forward to slipping into her alter-ego self all day, and had very generously, in her opinion, decided to give the man a second chance. And now, here he was, once again drunk to the point of hardly being able to walk at all, let alone in a straight line, and expecting to grab at her body for a quick fumble. Well, she thought, he's got another thing coming if that's what he's expecting.

"Don't you dare touch me!" she angrily warned him as he made an unsuccessful lunge at the top half of her clothing. "You'd better go in there and cool off, otherwise you can get the fuck out of here," she said, coldly, pointing to the other room while trying to control her voice's quiver and to disguise her disappointment and annoyance—not that Ozborn had the capacity to recognise it anyway.

What Sandy hadn't expected though was that, despite Ozborn's inebriated state, he was still very strong, as he made a second attempt to grab hold of her arm with one hand and push her head back with the other to go in for a slobbery kiss to the mouth. This time, as she retracted her head, she made it clear that she wasn't going to accept his advances, no matter how much she had been keenly anticipating them only moments earlier. "Get the fuck *off* me," she shouted at him, followed by a swiftly aimed knee where it would hurt the most. Ozborn finally got the message, and staggered indignantly to the other room to calm down, but not before swiping a plate off the kitchen table so that it hit against the adjacent cupboard.

Miraculously, it didn't break. But it was enough for Sandy to regret ever setting eyes on the man, who, to all intents and purposes, was still a complete stranger to her. She didn't know anything about him, and while reprimanding herself for stupidly letting him into her home, she glanced though the half-open door to see him out for the count on her bed. The emotion of sexual excitement and anticipation had long since evaporated. Sandy Beach now felt a new emotion—fear.

The only thing she could think of doing was to let the guy sleep off his alcohol intake, avoiding any conflict when he awoke—maybe cook him some of the food she'd bought, and optimistically hope he'd calmly leave of his own accord. As it happened, he remained asleep on her bed for the rest of the evening, she ate her meal alone, and eventually went to sleep on the pull-out bed she kept for guests in the spare room.

CHAPTER 6

(FRIDAY, 10TH APRIL, 1981)

Yushi's Disappointment

"What the hell d'ya think you're doin', boy?" asked the voice from behind the gold-rimmed sunglasses. Yushi looked in silence at the six-foot tall man while he was being addressed. Unusually for a policeman, and against normal policy, he had a beard, which the cop continuously ruffled with his hand as he spoke. "Ya know you're committing a traffic violation on that cycle of yours, don't ya? Well? I'm waiting for your answer, boy, and I haven't got all day," the gum-chewing traffic cop barked. He clearly wasn't a man to be messed with. Yushi, feeling intimidated as the officer towered over him, did his best to explain how he'd inadvertently found himself breaking the law by riding on Interstate Highway 275, but his tongue became more and more tied as he scrambled to find his words. Fortunately for him, Phil Booth, the policeman with six years' service in the Cincinnati Traffic Unit, was beginning to show a small amount of leniency, probably realising that the cyclist was genuinely sorry for his mistake.

"Well, I can't leave you here to fend for yourself, it's far too dangerous. I'll have to lift your cycle into the trunk and escort you off the freeway at the next exit," decided Booth.

With that, he opened the lid of the patrol car's huge, empty trunk, large enough to take one, or perhaps even two bikes, as long as the front wheels could be removed and placed alongside the frames. Thanks to Yushi's bike having quick-release forks, that was no problem, with no need for a spanner. Inside the car, Officer Booth wrote down Yushi's name and address, and with a smile, decided to write 'ADVISORY ONLY' on the triplicated report form, before tearing off and handing Yushi a copy.

Only a few moments later, the policeman was driving away from the scene, with his 'criminal' passenger being allowed to sit upfront next to him as they engaged in conversation. By now, the traffic cop had dropped his guard and had become quite inquisitive about his passenger's adventure. A feeling of envy came over Booth, who had never followed his own dream to travel when young.

"So, where ya headed?" asked Booth, who was becoming increasingly fascinated by the young cyclist's adventure. Booth had never ventured outside the Midwest and by this time the policeman chose to continue the car journey beyond the first exit point so that they could continue talking. He asked all the obvious questions like, "don't you get tired?" and "where do you sleep?" and, before he knew it, he ended up offering to take the brave adventurer the whole way to that evening's Youth Hostel accommodation. "That way I'll be sure that you've arrived safely and haven't gotten back on the freeway again, okay?" he teased.

Yushi was actually grateful for the ride. That whole episode had upset his equilibrium and he was pleased that he wouldn't have to negotiate the busy inner-city roads. He began thinking ahead again towards the street party—and meeting Megan. Plus, it was quite fun being driven in an officer's car, with the police radio constantly squawking news of various crimes and misdemeanours taking place across the county.

His driver, extremely familiar with the whole area, was clearly sure of the best route to Brushwood Avenue, where the hostel was situated. As they turned left into the street, they could see the many tables being set up along the middle of the cordoned-off road. Each table was covered with a bright orange cloth, and people were milling around with smiles on their faces as they carried plates and cups, and trays full of all sorts of delicious-looking food.

Yushi looked for the house number, 1284, and discovered it was facing the hub of the activity, with people constantly coming in and out of the building.

"Well, Yushi," began the policeman, "this looks like as far as I can take you. We'll just get your cycle out, and I'll be on my way back to the freeway, to check there ain't no more cyclists getting lost like you." He smiled at his little joke as he pulled over to stop, got out and opened the trunk, then lifted the bike, its front wheel and Yushi's rucksack and pannier, and placed them on the sidewalk.

In his eagerness to reassemble the bike without using up the officer's time any longer than necessary, Yushi hastily gathered his things and said goodbye, and watched the policeman do a U-turn and drive off into the distance. For good measure, Officer Booth turned on the car's siren for a couple of seconds, his way of saying goodbye, causing some of the folks preparing the party to turn around, curious to see what was going on. They were used to hearing police sirens in the city, but not at this close range in leafy Brushwood Avenue.

Megan from the hostel was one of them, and she instantly guessed that this must be the hostel-guest she'd been expecting. She waved at Yushi, and walked towards him, with welcoming, open arms. "You're here already. That's great. I'll show you the dorm and where you can store your bike. What happened? Did you get arrested?" she jokingly asked, with a gorgeous twinkle in her eye that Yushi was instantly attracted to. As he pushed his bike along the sidewalk to the imposing building with its pillars and front porch he was struck by how pretty Megan was.

As he thought to himself how well the day was now turning out, he failed to notice that his precious red and black radio must have become detached from his bike's handlebar, and was now residing in the far-left corner of the police car's cavernous trunk.

With the street party in full swing, a live bluegrass band belted out some fine tunes. Amid the laughter and fun, dancing and talking, Yushi was enjoying himself, and he was convinced that Megan's friendliness towards him must be a sign that she liked him just as much as he liked her. Naively, he thought she surely fancied him. It might even be love at first sight, he convinced himself, as his mind raced ahead to more carnal thoughts.

Poor Yushi—he really wasn't very worldly-wise when it came to women. The party atmosphere, as well as the balmy warm air, and no doubt the ice-cold bottles of Coors, combined with Megan's sexy figure, made a far greater impact on Yushi than was normally the case for an inexperienced young man. Megan and Yushi spent at least a couple of hours in each other's company, and as the evening fell to dusk, night came and the pretty tree lights were turned on, Yushi was absolutely convinced that tonight may be his lucky night. The first such lucky night of his entire inexperienced and naïve life up to that point.

But unfortunately for Yushi, Megan was merely being her natural friendly, warm and giving self, showing the youth-hostel guest the hospitality she'd be offering to all her guests, male or female, young or old, single or in a group. In fact, the truth was that she couldn't wait for her boyfriend to return from work so that she could really get into the party spirit, and properly dance the night away until the early hours. In fact, she was beginning to find Yushi a bit, well, clingy, and she tried to encourage him to chat with some of her neighbours so that she could go off, smoke a few cigarettes and socialise—without her hostel guest constantly at her side.

Not wishing to appear rude, Megan continued to engage in polite conversation with Yushi, who in turn continued to read the signs wrongly. If she had known what was going on in Yushi's head, she would have immediately put him straight, but unfortunately, as she'd never been very aware of her effect on the opposite sex—apart from when her boyfriend flattered her—she just carried on regardless.

Making an excuse about needing to go to the bathroom, the beautiful Megan disappeared inside the hostel, leaving Yushi to chat to some of the other party guests. While he was engaged in conversation,

Megan's boyfriend arrived and went inside to find her. When Yushi later looked across the way, he glimpsed the couple cuddling and kissing on the building's porch like the happy young lovers that they were. Feeling what seemed to him like a giant punch to the guts, he was devastated. All of a sudden, his good mood changed to one of bitterness and depression. How could she do this to him? he thought. They had been getting on so well together, and he'd been convinced that this night was going to be a very special one indeed. Feeling utterly dejected, he sorrowfully removed himself from the party and decided he should go to bed. Trying to avoid eye contact with Megan so that she wouldn't detect his sadness, he walked past her and her boyfriend and into the hostel, just managing to utter the word "goodnight" from the side of his mouth. Despite Yushi's age, he was still an unworldly individual when it came to relationships with girls.

Feeling happy that this somewhat immature hostel guest wouldn't be demanding any further small-talk from her, Megan tugged at her boyfriend's arm to get him to join her in dancing into the small hours. Her infectious smile and love of life made it impossible, despite his two left feet, for her boyfriend to refuse.

If Yushi hadn't gone to bed so early, he would have been reacquainted with Police Officer Booth when the patrolman decided to drive miles out of his way, and on his own time, in order to return the small handlebar radio to its owner, after he had discovered it to be still in the patrol car. It wasn't until the following morning that Yushi came down to breakfast and Megan informed him of the policeman's kind action: "Beyond the call of duty," remarked Megan, and Yushi nodded.

Awkwardly embarrassed at even thinking that Megan might have had affectionate feelings for him, Yushi quickly gathered his things together, re-attached the radio to the bike, loaded his panniers and set off on his way, but not before politely thanking Megan for her kind hospitality and invitation to the street party. He realised it wasn't her fault that she hadn't fancied him—it was his fault for being a frustrated idiot. There was no reason to part on anything other than good terms. As he weaved his way determinedly through the morning Cincinnati rush-hour for at least 50 minutes until reaching the outskirts of town, he vowed to forget about girls for a while and concentrate on his cycling.

As he rode along, he looked up at the cloudy sky. With his head also cloudy, Yushi forgot, for the moment at least, all thoughts about his ambition of meeting someone with whom the prospect of losing his virginity might become a reality. Heavy-hearted, he instead concentrated once more on his beloved grandfather's 'Thousand Mile' theory, as he set off to reach that day's first 30 miles.

CHAPTER 7

(SATURDAY, 11TH APRIL, 1981)

Sandy's Invitation

On the same morning that Yushi was physically distancing himself from Cincinnati and his unsuccessful liaison with Megan, Sandy was also distancing herself metaphorically from her ill-fated carnal affair with Marc Ozborn. When she awoke in the early dawn hours and looked out of the window to see the sun rising above the cornfields in the distance, she decided she had to tell Ozborn, in no uncertain terms, to leave.

She woke him roughly and informed him that she'd be going off soon, and that she'd appreciate it if he would leave her house after he'd finished the coffee and the doughnuts she'd thoughtfully bought at Kmart especially for him the previous day. She was polite but firm, and as Ozborn wasn't yet fully wide awake, he simply rubbed his eyes, grunted and nodded his head. Getting out of bed and stuffing two doughnuts in his mouth, leaving a trail of icing sugar across his stubbled chin and upon the kitchen floor, his head throbbed, and he was in no mood to protest or argue.

Sandy had all but given up on Ozborn, which was a shame as far as she was concerned, for she still felt an attraction for his rugged physique, but she wasn't prepared to tolerate any more of his failings. "Let go and move on" was her philosophy, even though she couldn't deny being more than a little wistful that her thrill-seeking hadn't been fulfilled. However, now that she'd made her decision, she'd simply have to wait until the next man caught her eye down at The Old Parlor Tavern. Unbeknown to her that morning, it would turn out that she wouldn't need to go anywhere near the place before she would meet him.

While Ozborn used her bathroom facilities, Sandy busied herself with preparing for her day ahead, which was to consist of a few hours at work in the afternoon and, before that, a shopping trip combined with a lunch-time meet-up with Cynthia Morton, an old school friend, near Cincinnati. When she was ready to leave the house, she beckoned Ozborn to the front door and held it open for him. He made a few gruff noises, but accepting his fate, he reluctantly walked out and, after a feeble attempt at a kiss on Sandy's lips that she pulled away from, he climbed into his pickup, turned the ignition key and roared away to a destination unknown. Sandy sighed with disappointment; she still hadn't lost that craving for the roughness of his attractive body and handsome features.

For Ozborn, another day of drifting, drinking in bars, maybe smoking a few joints, lay ahead. Aiming his vehicle in any direction, none in particular, he hit the gas, leaned across to grab his whisky bottle from the ledge, and bent down out of sight to take a swig as he veered across the lane. Lucky for him there was no oncoming traffic. Although he had no idea where he was headed, he felt sure he'd be back sometime soon—he still fancied the ass off Sandy and was determined to have his way with her next time.

Sandy's meeting with Cynthia went well. They enjoyed lunch at China Palace—a fairly new diner specialising in Asian cuisine just about 80 miles away. After they gorged themselves on a feast of mouth-watering sweet and sour chicken and spring rolls, discussing family, work and the latest fashion in boots, it was time for Sandy to head off back to the dental practice. She mustn't be late–Mr. Edgar had booked in an appointment with Chase Kimball, a patient of many years standing, for the fitting of a new porcelain crown. Being a lawyer of long-standing, Mr. Kimball wasn't short of a few dollars, and Mr. Edgar wanted to justify his high charges by making his client feel very special, so Sandy's full attention was required.

After hugging her friend farewell, and promising to catch up again "real soon", Sandy pointed her car back towards Paris, Illinois. As she drove along the long, straight and flat road that stretched miles ahead, her thoughts drifted from her rendezvous with Cynthia and returned to the rendezvous that never actually got properly underway with Ozborn. As she tapped her hands on the steering wheel in sync with the beat emanating from the car radio, she hardly noticed the weather taking a turn for the worse, but sure enough, after a few miles, the dark clouds began offloading their contents.

Within seconds, huge raindrops danced in the air, feet from the ground, as they splashed heavily against the road surface. Headlights of cars and trucks reflected on the road surface as their wheels sent torrents of spray upwards. Up ahead, she could see what seemed like a black object, moving slowly forward. As her own vehicle approached, the object became more clearly defined, and it became apparent that the object was actually a person riding a bicycle, struggling against the elements that were most certainly not being too kind to him or her.

She slowed down and pulled in front of the rider, and as she did so she pressed the button to lower her window, so that when the cyclist caught up alongside her, she'd be able to engage in conversation without getting too wet herself.

"Hey there, can I give you and your bike a ride?" Sandy shouted above the noise of the rain, twisting her head around in order to indicate the huge space in the rear of her Volvo. "You must be soaked to the skin."

Yushi was indeed already wet through, and was very grateful for the kind offer from this complete stranger. He figured it must be something to do with his national flags flying on his bike that extracted a certain kindness from many people's characters. And this lady did appear pretty kind, and kind of pretty too. He chuckled under his breath at the way his mind worked, and accepted the lift with gratitude. "That's very good of you, and thank you for stopping," he said as he got off his bike and began detaching the quick-release wheel so that it would fit more easily in the woman's car.

Once the bike was in the back, Yushi got in the passenger seat and held out his hand to shake the woman's. "I'm Yushi. It's nice to meet you."

Sandy was naturally curious to discover more about her passenger. "So, what's a guy like you doing on a cycle with two national flags flying in the wind behind you? Where are you headed? Where did you set off from?"

Normal pleasantries followed, with exchanges back and forth and explanations about his journey—very similar to his banter the previous night with patrolman Booth, Megan, and the other attendees of the Cincinnati street party. The conversation flowed quite naturally, and Yushi found himself enjoying their chat and talking about his journey. But as the rain persisted, he couldn't help feeling a slight pang of guilt that he wasn't actually cycling. At this rate, he could probably hitch across the whole United States by car–but that wasn't quite his objective, was it? After all, anyone could do that.

So, as they drove along and the weather cleared as quickly as it had worsened, Yushi asked if he could be dropped off at the next convenient stopping place, so that he could continue under his own pedal power.

"It looks like the weather's clearing up now. I guess I should get out and continue by bike," he said.

Obligingly, Sandy pulled over, but also slightly reluctantly. She admitted to herself that she found this young lad to be intriguingly attractive. Clearly, he was an interesting character—it wasn't every day she met someone cycling the breadth of the country solo.

"That's a shame, Yushi. I was really interested in hearing more about your story. But I guess a man's gotta do what a man's gotta do," she grinned as she turned towards him and gave him an endearing smile.

There was also something else about him, she thought. He was fit, toned and muscular, and his dark, straight hair blended perfectly with the smooth skin on his face. Although his accent was American through and through, he had an Asian look about him that she found to be quite, well, beautiful, and she didn't want this to be the last time she saw him. She figured out that his route would take him near her home town. "How about I give you my address in Paris, Yushi? And then when you reach Marshall, you'd only need to make a small detour to the right, and you can call by," she volunteered. "I've always got plenty of food in the refrigerator, and if you need a bed for the night, that would save you the cost of a motel room."

Pleasantly surprised by this stranger's generous invitation, Yushi was very happy with Sandy's offer, and they said their goodbyes at the roadside. He estimated his arrival time based on his average 10 miles an hour speed. "That's wonderful, thank you, and I'd love to take you up on it, please. I reckon I'll probably be arriving by early afternoon tomorrow. Would that suit you?" he asked with enthusiasm. He was thrilled that he'd get another chance to meet his saviour from the deluge, although he reprimanded himself for thinking about anything other than getting a free bed for the night.

The timing of Yushi's expected arrival suited Sandy too, as she was only due for a morning shift at the dentist that day. "That's perfect," she said, as she scribbled her address on a small sheet of notepaper and handed it to him. "I'll be home from work by two in the afternoon tomorrow, so come by any time after that. It'll be nice to see you again."

As she drove off, watching Yushi in her rear-view mirror as his strong legs began to power him along the road with ease, she wondered whether he'd ever seen a waterbed like hers before. She also wondered how experienced, or otherwise, he was in the bedroom, judging by the innocent look he had about him. This could be kind of interesting, she thought to herself. All the previous night's frustration with Marc Ozborn began to disappear into the distance.

CHAPTER 8

(SUNDAY, 12TH APRIL, 1981)

Yushi's Love Lesson

The previous evening, Yushi had checked into the Sunlight Roadside Motel. It was by now becoming routine for him to either phone ahead to a youth hostel and enquire if they had a vacancy, or alternatively just stop at a small town when he was feeling tired, usually by around five o'clock, and call in at whichever hotel or motel he came across. He'd firstly check the price—usually there would be a neon sign outside, but sometimes not. If it were under $20, he would take the room without hesitation. If it were over that sum, he'd continue to another establishment and try there.

For last night's accommodation, he didn't need to look any further than his first destination in town, and after he paid his $18 to the proprietor he pushed his bike into his room, got changed out of his cycling gear, and then went off in search of a burger-and-fries eatery, preferably take-out, so that he could consume his meal in his room while resting up his weary legs on the bed, watching an old episode of *Happy Days*, followed by *Star Trek*. He could never get enough of Lieutenant Uhura.

He soon found a Wendy's Old Fashioned Hamburgers restaurant on the next block, and a few minutes later was tucking into his meal back at his room. After that, he spread his AAA map on the bed in order to plan his route for the following day, and where exactly he'd be turning off the main road in Marshall for his detour up to Sandy's place in Paris. He was pleased with himself that his estimation of arriving there by around 3.00p.m. should be easily achievable, given his progress earlier that day. Yushi took a shower, then settled back on the bed to watch still more re-runs of Arthur 'Fonzie' Fonzarelli's antics, followed by more of James T. Kirk and the Starship crew, until drifting towards sleep, wondering how he'd be getting along with his hostess the next evening.

Was it his imagination, or did he detect a certain electricity between her and him? He liked the idea that perhaps there was, but after feeling so deflated by reading the signals wrongly with Megan last night, he decided not to get his hopes too high this time. How many more good opportunities would he get to get laid on this trip? he thought. He was becoming almost desperate to, in his own words, become a 'real man'.

That morning he awoke early, at 6.17a.m. to be precise, according to the small digital clock-radio at his bedside, and after getting out of bed at 7.00a.m. he showered again–after all, he was paying $18 for all the hot water he wanted, inclusive with the room-rate, so why not? Feeling fresh and ready for the day ahead, by eight o'clock he had wheeled his bike outside, returned the room key to the motel office, and then set off on his way out of town and on to the next, where he'd stop for some breakfast. Maybe some waffles and syrup—and definitely much coffee.

What his examination of the map the previous evening hadn't made obvious was the almost sudden change of land contour from relative flatness to rolling hills and, to make matters worse, the light breeze had become much stronger and was blowing completely against him. And so, his estimation of progress soon became way out, and by the time he reached the next town, Yushi's body was already feeling the strain. By the time he found a diner, he was for sure in need of that breakfast and a welcome sit-down. After quickly padlocking his bike against a down-pipe outside of the café, he staggered toward the entrance, wobbly-legged from the exertion of the previous couple of hours, turning his head round to confirm all was safe and secure with the bike.

Once inside the building, he was grateful to be ushered by the waitress to a space at the busy counter, where almost instantaneously a mug of hot coffee was placed in front of him. For Yushi, it hadn't come a moment too soon. As he took his first gulp, he relaxed into the backrest of his cushioned stool and contemplated whether he did want only a waffle, or whether he should treat himself to a full American breakfast instead—including waffles piled high.

The waitress at the counter leaned across to take his order. The young cyclist failed to take notice of the unshaven man, clearly inebriated even at this early hour of the day, as he lurched between the tables on his way to the exit. If he had paid attention to him, he would have clearly seen that the man was not in a good mood. Marc Ozborn was still feeling pretty angry for having been turfed out by Sandy at some ungodly hour of the morning before he'd had the chance to yet shake off his throbbing headache developed the night before. If Yushi had been sitting any closer to the glass-fronted door, he would have also seen the man walk out into the morning sunshine, put on his shades and walk towards his pickup truck, past the bicycle that was leant against the building's drainpipe.

Ozborn, for no reason in particular, kicked a mound of stones and gravel at a nearby dog, causing it to howl and instinctively dart away back toward the cycle. It was then that he was drawn to turn and see the bright red and black object fixed on the bike's handlebar. He meandered over to it and observed what he thought was a small transistor radio, one like he'd never seen before. He twisted the top dial, and after the initial click, it came to life with some country tune that he liked. How cool. Amused, and without giving a second thought, he tugged at the device and could tell straight away that to remove it from the handlebar, he merely needed to slide it forward, which is exactly what he did.

When reaching his truck, he brazenly tossed the radio in through the open window, where it fell onto the seat, bouncing off and onto the floor. Ozborn climbed in and, before driving off again to nowhere in particular, he leant down to pick up the radio and placed it on the seat next to him, pleased with his new acquisition. Noticing his bottle, he thought he may as well take another swig of his Bourbon, before stepping on the gas and leaving a plume of dust behind his spinning tyres.

It took a while before Yushi felt nourished and refreshed enough to embark once again on his journey. But with his stamina now returned, it was time to leave $4 on the counter, sling his rucksack strap across his shoulder, and move on to his next ten-mile target as shown on the map. As he pushed open the door and walked to his bike, he immediately noticed that his radio was no longer attached to the handlebar.

"Ah, shit, Shit, shit, *shit!*" spewed from his mouth. Even he was surprised at his own fury. As if in denial about what had happened, he looked around the car park in case it had miraculously come loose and fallen off somewhere. How could he have been so *stupid* to forget to remove it, especially with it being so easy to do so? Eventually, he couldn't deny the fact that it had been stolen, and that he should have been more security-conscious in the first place.

As he mounted his bike and rode away from the diner, his anger with the perpetrator as well as himself for having left the radio on the bike, turned to sadness. Incredibly downhearted, Yushi spent the whole of the next ten miles in a dreamlike state of mind, going over and over what had happened, feeling more and more sorry for himself and hardly paying any attention to the road ahead. He cycled through the next town without paying any attention to it, such was his feeling of melancholy. A further period of three hours of solid riding elapsed, and it was only by good chance that he happened to look up when he did, seeing the signpost for Paris. Why did that name ring a bell, he wondered? And then he remembered, of course, about his accommodation for the night at Sandy's.

"Okay, Yushi," he conversed with himself under his breath, "Forget about the radio. What's done is done. You'll just have to buy another one when you see a cycle store." Conscious of his finite budget, he told himself that he should work for the money—maybe something like picking fruit on a farm somewhere. Perhaps that would make up—financially at least—for his own, completely avoidable, misfortune.

So, with a plan in his head for his own redemption, angry and sad as he was, he concentrated instead on finding his way, with the help of Sandy's directions that she'd scribbled down, to her address. Perhaps he may be able to put the bad day he'd been having so far well behind him, and enjoy the rest of it—in her company.

Turning into her road, he saw—a few hundred yards ahead—her bungalow exactly as she'd described it. One of a pair of properties set back from all the others in the street, and with a distinctive tree growing in the front yard next to the drive. As he approached, he could see her Volvo parked up against the door of the double garage, and he knew for certain that he'd arrived at the correct house. As he got off his bike and pushed it the few remaining yards along the drive, the fly-screen on the porch flew open, and Sandy stood there, beaming a welcoming smile at him. She looked amazing—even more glamorous than on their first meeting yesterday, and she'd looked pretty darn hot then, he thought. As she stood there dressed in high boots and tight jeans, with one hand perched on her hip, he felt her eyes follow his every movement as he approached.

"Hi there!" Sandy called out in a welcoming tone. "Glad you made it. I can't believe that you actually cycled all that way since I saw you yesterday. That's one heck of a long ride. Come on in and make yourself at home. You must be exhausted, and starved as well, I bet!"

Without giving much of a chance for Yushi to get a word in edgeways, she went on to say that she'd got them both a dinner of chicken stew bubbling away in the slow-cooker, if he'd care to join her later. But meanwhile she'd open up the garage so he could store his bike away for the night, and then she'd show him his room, and where the bathroom was so he could take a shower if he wished to.

"That's real kind of you, Sandy, and I'm very grateful," Yushi politely replied, expressing his appreciation for her hospitality.

Although feeling a little shy, he managed to ask whether she might have a cold drink he could have.

"Why, yes, of course," she replied. "No wonder you're thirsty in this heat, and I think I may even join you." And with that, they returned outside and sat on the porch drinking one Bud after the other, and picking up from where they'd left their conversation the day before. All the while, Sandy was becoming quite mesmerised by her guest. She found his apparent lack of any self-confidence, his naivety and his softly-spoken demeanour surprisingly attractive.

The attraction was definitely mutual. Yushi was having some difficulty in not staring at the upper half of Sandy's body, her cleavage in particular. He didn't realise that her posture was a deliberate ploy to create maximum impact. He also didn't pick up on the fact that she was enjoying subtly teasing the poor shy guy, and then catching him squirm with embarrassment at being caught gazing trance-like at her. Sandy wondered what more games she might be able to persuade him to play with her later.

"Why don't you go and get comfortable now, take a shower, unwind, while I make us a green salad to go with the chicken?" she suggested, with a little plan up her sleeve. Yushi was glad of the offer. He was admittedly weary, and also very sweaty and probably quite smelly from his day's hard riding, as well as being hungry. He was looking forward to getting out of his cycling gear and putting some fresh clothes on. He obediently followed Sandy through to the room that she'd prepared for him.

"Only one bathroom, I'm afraid," she indicated to the room across the hallway. Although Yushi's legs and arms were understandably aching, he was in much finer spirits now than earlier. It wasn't possible to feel otherwise, such was Sandy's way of making him feel so welcome and relaxed. And she was incredibly gorgeous, too, he couldn't help noticing. Remembering back to Cincinnati, he realised how stupid he'd been to misread the signs from Megan—but this was so different.

He was sensing a sure-fire chemistry with Sandy, of that there was no doubt.

As Sandy meandered back to the kitchen, she felt glad that she'd never gotten around to fixing that rusty old bathroom lock that didn't quite latch properly. After tossing some pre-washed salad leaves around in a bowl with some balsamic vinegar and olive oil, only taking a few minutes if that, she uncorked a nice bottle of her favourite Ernest and Julio Gallo Zinfandel from the wine rack, settled back in her sofa, and waited. She waited until she could hear her guest exit his room and enter the bathroom, closing the door behind him. And then she waited a further few minutes until she could hear the distinctive sound of the glass shower door being pulled to, and the swoosh of the water being turned on. She waited, as she took a few more sips from her glass, and then got up to make her move. She knew exactly how to open the bathroom door completely silently, so that she could step inside the room and be seated on her old Lloyd Loom chair, to watch Yushi standing in the cubicle while he soaped and shampooed himself, eyes shut and oblivious to her presence. This could go one of two ways, she thought. She'd do her best to ensure it went the way she wanted.

Yushi was shocked with self-consciousness after he'd washed the soap from his eyes and saw his hostess brazenly sitting there, unabashed. He instinctively crouched his body, covering his privates with his hands.

"Take no notice of me, Yushi," breathed Sandy. "I only came in to put a fresh towel out for you. I'm sorry to have startled you—I didn't realise you were already in here," she lied. "But I gotta say, I liked what I saw, so I stayed!"

Deliberately, she stood up to hand him a towel, necessitating him to raise his arms to open the door with one hand, and take the towel with the other. With him now fully exposed in front of her, Sandy felt an electrifying tingle pass through her entire body.

Confident she had read the signs correctly, she made her big move.

"Yushi, have you ever been on a waterbed with a woman before? You have been with a woman before, haven't you?" she baited. Before waiting for his answer, she held out her hand for Yushi to take, as he tried to dry himself, at the same time clumsily hopping along, as she assertively led him through to her room.

Yushi felt as though he were in a trance. "Can this actually be happening?" he asked himself. "Have I had too many beers? Have I fallen asleep, and is this all just a wonderful dream?" He pinched himself hard, quite literally, and the pain confirmed the scenario was indeed all very real. Well, if this is what happens when you go cycling across the country, I may as well get to LA and turn right back to do it all over again, he concluded. Rather than protest against Sandy's invitation, he allowed her to take control of the situation. Besides, he didn't really know what to do anyway. Luckily for him, Sandy did.

"So Yushi, have you ever been on a waterbed before?" she repeated. "Come, you should try it," she beckoned, patting the bed next to where she now lay. As he nervously but excitedly climbed onto the bed, its surface flowed back and forth while making an unusual but sensual 'glup, glup' noise as it did so. The more he moved, the more waves he created, and it was an altogether strange, but rather pleasant, sensation.

"What do you think?" asked Sandy, eager to impress her young guest.

"Well," began Yushi. "It's a bit like laying on top of an air-mattress in a swimming pool, but with much more movement up and down."

He tried continuing with his comparison, but Sandy eased herself across, and gently placed two fingers on his mouth. "Enough talk," she said. "Let's see how it feels when we do this . . ." And with that, she certainly did take complete control of the situation, sitting cross-legged in front of him so that she was able to lean forward and lift up his t-shirt, remove it and toss it across the room. Her own instinct told her that this might be his first full encounter with a woman, and the thrill it was giving her was greater than she could have imagined. She hoped it would be an encounter that this shy young man would remember for ever. It was also a first time for her too, of a different kind. The first time she'd ever seduced a virgin—and she was loving every minute of it.

As far as Yushi was concerned, he wasn't sure what he should be doing next, so he thought he'd better let his teacher do whatever she wanted. It was as though all his dreams had been answered in one go. His head felt dizzy when she undid the buttons on her own shirt, revealing her incredible breasts only inches away from his eyes. They were as good as any he'd seen in the magazines he hid in his bedroom at home. And when Sandy stepped off the bed in order to remove her jeans, creating a tidal wave—in body and mind—it was all too much for him. As he climaxed at the sight of Sandy standing there, facing him, in only her panties and open blouse, he felt incredibly embarrassed. But he needn't have. Sandy knew exactly what she was doing.

"That's okay, you sweet innocent thing, you needed to let out all that tension, didn't you?" As Sandy whispered her reassuring words, Yushi was too mesmerised to answer. He'd waited a heck of a long time to experience a situation like this, and he was more than happy to let his tutor guide him all the way. The ecstasy he felt left him breathless but he was soon ready for more. "It's quite alright and nothing to worry about," Sandy continued. "Now we can carry on and have some serious fun."

Convinced that Sandy was enjoying the liaison as much as he was, Yushi was unfortunately unable to differentiate between her basic carnal lust, and love, whatever love was. He imagined he must be falling in love with this stunning older woman, and he presumed that the feelings must surely be mutual. Yushi had a lot to learn about women in general, and certainly this one in particular. But for now, like the cliché, he lay back on the bed, letting the motion of the waterbed beneath him add to the sensation, closed his eyes, and thought of America. This had now turned into the best day of his life, and he would never forget it, all thanks to Sandy Beach of Paris, Illinois.

Later, after a very pleasant meal together, they spent the rest of the evening watching TV, playing some records and chatting about this and that, including Yushi's forthcoming journey on his bike to the next major city of St. Louis, Missouri. According to his calculations, the city with its famous arch, the 'Gateway to the West' was about 180 miles away, so it should take him two days to reach. As well as loving the sex, Sandy was also enjoying Yushi's company, and expressed sadness as she remembered he was supposed to be leaving in the morning. Not only that, she had more bedroom tricks she wanted to teach him and fantasies of her own to fulfil. "Why not stay one more day?" she suggested. "I have to go to work, but afterward we could go for a cycle together—I have my own bike in the garage. It looks like we're in for another hot day, and we could go down to the creek, take a swim . . . and who knows what might happen?" she suggested provocatively.

Well, Yushi wasn't going to turn down such an offer, and his imagination already began running away with him. Besides, he had been making good mileage so far on his journey, and while he was staying at Sandy's it wasn't costing him a dime, so what was stopping him? Nothing, he concluded, as he enthusiastically agreed to stay.

But for now, all the cycling—and not to mention the other more exceptional exertions of the day—had taken their toll on him. He yawned heavily, and although he tried to cover it up, Sandy noticed, and it set her off too.

"Come on," she said. "You've had a long day, sweet thing. It's time to turn in. I guess you'd prefer to have your own room . . ." Yushi feigned tears, and Sandy picked up on them, joining in with the little game. " . . . But of course, if you prefer . . ." She got up off the couch and ushered Yushi into her bedroom for the second time in the space of a few hours. They slept naked together, both of them content.

Relieved as well; they had both achieved the experience they'd been craving.

CHAPTER 9

(MONDAY, 13TH APRIL, 1981)

Ozborn's Return

As was normal for Marc Ozborn's mornings, he awoke with a headache. After driving away from the diner the previous day, he, as usual, had nothing much to do except find a bar and get wasted. By the afternoon, he'd decided to go home, smoke some weed and fall heavily asleep, not waking again until 9.00a.m., with the usual barks of mongrel dogs roaming around outside. Home was a 25-foot aluminium, single-skinned mobile house-on-wheels, situated in a trailer-park on the outskirts of a run-down industrial town that had seen better times. Some days he'd turn on the TV to watch James Garner solve another case, and wish his trailer could be more like Jim Rockford's—at least clean and relatively tidy. Instead, Ozborn's was in a permanent state of filth, with dirty dishes, discarded clothes everywhere, and beer cans overflowing the trashcan. While he was drinking some strong coffee, his peace was disturbed by a banging at his door, that initially he ignored. The banging continued, and it was easy to recognise his landlord hollering. The thin walls weren't exactly good sound insulators.

"Ozborn, I know you're in there. Your rent's way overdue, sir. You know the rules. I've got a dozen others like you on social, queuing up for a place like this. If you don't pay up by tomorrow, you're on your way, okay?"

"Fuck off. I'll get your money," was the only response Ozborn could be bothered to make.

"Make sure you do, Mr. Ozborn. By tomorrow, y'hear?" shouted the trailer owner, issuing a final bash against the door, before going on his way to other tenants on the site who were also late with their dues. Ozborn looked around for the document he'd need in order to collect his welfare money. There it was, under an old *National Enquirer* magazine. He'd have to go to Terre Haute, the main town of the county, to cash it. While there, he may as well enquire whether the owner would give him another stint in The Old Parlor Tavern in Paris—not far away—to gain a few extra dollars and down some more free beers. Doing his best to look respectable, splashing some water on his face and smoothing it over his greasy hair, he stepped outside into the hot sunshine.

While driving along, he glanced down at the radio that he'd dishonestly acquired the day before, deciding not to take a swig from the nearby Bourbon until after collecting his money. Some weeks he'd be asked into the back office for a compulsory meeting with his job liaison officer, who would update him on any fresh vacancies that had arisen since their previous meeting—all of which Ozborn had no intention of pursuing. But he needed to go through the motions, and at least appear interested, in order to keep getting those payments. And best to be sober too, so there'd be no arguments, he decided reluctantly.

Today turned out to be one of those type of days. Ozborn reflected for a moment on how he hated those "dumb interrogations", as he called them. He couldn't understand why he would possibly want to work his balls off, for just a few dollars an hour in some factory or grocery store or farm. Sure, he thought, he could just about manage bar-work at a push, but having to be polite to stupid opinionated a-hole customers wasn't his idea of fun. At least The Old Parlor in Paris wasn't too bad though—Dean, the proprietor, was kind of okay, and it was also kind of easy to slip a few bills from the cash register into his back pocket when Dean's back was turned. And of course, he could drink a few free beers there.

Following his job meeting, his route into Paris took him past Sandy's house that afternoon. Her car wasn't there, so he guessed she must be at work. "Hmmm, I never did get that piece of ass, did I?"

he mumbled to himself as he recalled his previous attempts to get it together with her that led nowhere. “Don’t mind if I do,” he thought, deciding to try again to consummate their ‘relationship’, and call by later that evening.

As Ozborn entered The Old Parlor, Dean looked up and was actually glad to see him, having had a particularly heavy night with a new rock band he’d been trying out. The band was really lively, and all he now wanted was some downtime before things got busy again later. “You wanna do a few hours behind the bar? Same arrangement as before?” he asked Ozborn.

“Yep, sure thing,” was all that Ozborn needed to say, and once again Dean swapped his place *behind* the bar with a stool *at* the bar.

While Ozborn was busy washing glasses, wiping tables and pouring draft beers, Sandy was a few miles away, preparing to leave Mr. Edgar’s dental practice, and looking forward to going for a swim at the creek with Yushi. Sure, she was quite fond of him, but really he had merely relieved her sexual tension, probably caused by that guy Mark’s repeated inability to fulfil her needs, she thought. But the thrill she’d had from being a teacher to her virgin student, obviously could now no longer apply. Yushi was sweet enough, and had a nice lean body that he eventually found the courage to do something with, but his shyness and inexperience was, how could she put it, a little boring. He was, after all, just a boy, and Sandy preferred a ‘real’ man—who understood exactly how to satisfy a woman without any prompting. Someone with experience of being with women. Someone like Mark, whose body, if she was really honest with herself, she still craved. Still, she knew Yushi would be moving on the following morning, so for now they could simply have a skinny dip at the creek, enjoy the sunshine, and maybe have a barbecue later back at home.

Yushi, on the other hand, was completely fired up, eager to gain a repeat performance in the arms of his new girlfriend, for that was how, in his mind he now described Sandy. Ecstatic at his unbelievable success the previous evening, and also seeing her beautiful nude body this morning as she prepared herself for her working day ahead, he couldn't wait for this afternoon to come. He was certain she also felt the same way. Love was in the air, he thought.

During the morning while Sandy was at work, he busied himself with some bike maintenance, adjusting the gear changers, the brakes, tightening the spokes, and pumping the tyres. And after that he did the same for Sandy's bike. It was the least he could do.

Then he had a brainwave that he would put to Sandy later; why doesn't she drive out to meet him in St. Louis at the weekend? He would ask her. He'd have reached the city by then, and it would be so cool if she came. He would wait until they get to the creek before presenting his idea. Should he do it before or after they'd made love? Whatever. Either way, he was so looking forward to seeing the thrilled expression on her face later when he would offer his invitation.

Yushi heard Sandy's car pull up outside the house, where he waited to greet her, smiling, with both bicycles propped up by the garage door. Sandy was pleased. She hated pumping up bike tyres, and she knew hers would need air. So, after she'd changed into her trainers, shorts and t-shirt, she emerged from the house, ready to go. Yushi looked adoringly at her sexy attire as they mounted their bikes and set off along the road, then up a small lane for twenty minutes or so to the creek. Chatting away to her, he was very happy. Once there, it was quiet and peaceful, and they were completely alone. "Come on, then! Last one in's a chicken," Sandy challenged, stripping off everything and running into the shallow water, waving her arms around to create splashes as big as she could.

Yushi excitedly stripped off too. When he caught up with Sandy, after attempting to dodge all the splashing, he embraced her. He went in for a kiss, expecting that it would be reciprocated eagerly, but he was mistaken. Sandy instead turned away from him, diving under the water and emerging several feet away. Confused, he swam over to her, this time managing to hold on to her more tightly. Not wishing to be impolite, Sandy did offer him a kiss, but not the long, lingering one he was hoping for—it was a quick peck on the cheek, and then she was off again, swimming for only a few more moments before getting back out onto dry land and immediately drying herself down with one of the towels she'd brought along. That left Yushi standing waist high in water, puzzling over what was happening. By the time he joined her, she was lying on the grass, but no longer the naked woman he'd anticipated being with.

"There, what did you think? It's a lovely spot here, isn't it?" Sandy began apprehensively, having made up her mind not to lead him on unfairly. "I adore coming here so much," she continued.

Yushi had to agree, but he wasn't picking up any of the same vibes from her as he had done the night before. Confused, he tentatively answered. "It's great here, yes. But Sandy, I've been thinking. We were so right for each other last night, I'd like that to continue, wouldn't you?" and then he introduced his proposal for her to join him in St. Louis. Instead of his suggestion being received positively like he'd hoped, there was instead silence. "Sandy? Did you hear me?"

"You are so sweet, Yushi, and what happened between us yesterday was truly wonderful, but I wouldn't want you falling for me. For one thing I'm much too old for you anyway. You'd make a girl your age very happy, I'm sure, but I don't think I'm the one for you. I'm sorry. I won't be coming to St. Louis, but you're really lovely for asking. Come on, let's not spoil a nice time—we can go home and have us a nice barbecue in the back yard. How about that?"

Despite a barbecue being the last thing on Yushi's mind right now, he reluctantly agreed, and they pedalled back to the house, this time in silence. He was so crestfallen, he actually had tears welling up—but not wishing to admit to them, when they reached Sandy's road, he pretended that it was the breeze that had caused his eyes to water. He wasn't sure whether he'd be able to remain composed, such were his feelings of sadness, disappointment—and confusion. He had been certain that they had had mutual feelings for each other, and yes, maybe even love. He dwelled on his own stupidity. After the disappointment with Megan, then the theft of his radio, and now practically being dumped by Sandy after only one day, he was feeling very upset with himself, and even a little cross with her. Ah, the radio, he remembered. That would take his mind off things. He'd go into town, find a bike shop and buy a replacement for the one he'd had stolen.

Trying to sound more cheerful than he actually was, he told Sandy he was going to sort something out with his bike in town, and that he'd be back later for the barbecue. With a definite tension developing in his head, he rode aimlessly around town for at least an hour, going methodically up and down each street in the grid system, sometimes completely forgetting what he was meant to be doing.

Meanwhile, at The Old Parlor, the evening customers began pouring in, and to coincide with that, so did the regular bar staff. "Okay, Marc," said Dean. "You can go now. Take $20 out the register, and I'll see you next time, whenever that may be." Ozborn, already having had at least seven beers, took the $20, plus an extra twenty just because he could. If Dean was too darned lazy to keep a close eye on his cash register, then he could hardly be blamed for taking a little bonus, could he? he justified.

Remaining in the tavern, his wallet now containing more than it did when he'd arrived, Ozborn had a certain business arrangement to conclude. "Alright if I help myself to a beer, Dean?" he asked of the owner. Dean nodded, and with the bottle in hand, Ozborn looked around in search of the punter he'd been conversing with earlier. Seeing him sitting alone in the corner on a curved, red, plastic-cushioned seat, shaded from the ceiling fan that doubled as a light, Ozborn approached the man's table and sat opposite him.

"I promise you," said the man with his Stetson low over his face, "this is real good shit, man." As Ozborn passed a $20 bill under the table, a tiny plastic bag was pushed into his open hand. Rising from the seat and stuffing the bag in his jeans back pocket, and without any further words spoken, Ozborn left the table and finished his beer as he sauntered through the establishment toward the exit door. Once outside and in his pickup, he tipped some of the bag's white powdery contents on to the back of his hand, and with one big sniff it was up his nose. He grimaced, his eyes tightly shut. Man, that sure was strong stuff, concluded Ozborn.

Turning the ignition key, he put his foot down and sped out from the parking lot and onto the road, tyres screeching. "Maybe a little too quick, Marc," he said to himself. "Don't wanna bring unwanted attention, now." He turned the truck's radio on—full blast. Then he remembered in his stupor, Sandy's place wasn't far, and she was one cool chick. "Let's see if I can't get in between those lovely tits *this* time, hell yeah!" thought the man who was by now riding high on cocaine and booze.

Oblivious to whatever speed he was doing, he weaved along the, thankfully not busy, road to her house. His head now completely spinning, he spotted up ahead the misshapen tree at the front of her yard and sped towards it. Turning sharply into her drive, he skidded to a halt just in time not to hit the tree, causing half the gravel to rise into the air and land on the neatly-cut lawn. Reaching down to take a swig from his Bourbon bottle, he caught sight of the little bike radio, that had fallen back on the cab floor. He remembered how much it had amused him, and thought Sandy would like it too. Grabbing it, he then almost fell out of his truck's door.

Sandy, out in the back yard, tending to the barbecue she'd recently lit, had no doubt about who the driver was once she was able to peer over the fence and see Ozborn's truck. With the truck's radio still blaring country songs, Sandy felt real anger. How dare he just turn up uninvited like this? But as well as feeling anger, was she a little excited, too. Well, when she came round to the front and saw the state of her lawn, and how close Ozborn's truck had been to hitting the tree and her garage door, she concluded it was only anger. "What the hell do you think you're doing, just coming here like this? Who the fuck do you think you are?" she shouted.

"Oh, baby! Aam shorry. C'm 'ere and let me kissh you bedder," was the only semi-coherent slurred response Ozborn was capable of making, as he staggered from his rusty old vehicle towards her, trying to put one arm around her so that he could get a squeeze of her breasts with the other.

"Get your hands off me! You weren't capable of performing the other night, and you're definitely in no fit state now. Look at you!" Sandy cried out, now quite frightened. She didn't know Marc, and certainly hadn't seen him this bad before. Despite clearly being off his head and not only drunk, he was still a big and powerful man, and when she saw his eyes rolling upwards and a look of fierce determination in them, she backed away. But the more she backed away, the more he came at her, lunging out to grope her wherever he could reach. It was his feeble attempt at showing her he was able to satisfy her this time. With his dirty jeans revealing a large piss stain around the crotch area, Sandy couldn't believe that she'd ever contemplated entertaining this man.

Her comments had clearly riled him, and she could see the fury in his face. She found herself backed against the garden wall, with nowhere to go. As he came nearer, spittle forming at the corners of his mouth, she had no choice but to lash out any way she could. And the only way was by raising her knee firmly upwards into his groin. She thanked God that she hadn't yet opened another bottle of Gallo, and that she was fully in possession of her faculties. Wham! That got him where it hurt, but instead of him backing away, he just came back for more. Now she was really scared. Then, just as he raised his left hand, she darted away from him and ran into the house. Still clutching the little radio in his right hand, he went staggering after her, literally frothing at the mouth, unable to string two words together. Having no chance to shut and lock the door behind her,

Sandy ran, screaming, into the kitchen, now quite terrified of the man who appeared to be completely out of control.

Once inside the kitchen, he suddenly appeared to calm down, a vacant glaze in his eyes replacing the fierce fury that was there only moments earlier. Despite being previously so scared and disgusted by his physical appearance, Sandy was surprised to discover she still found something strangely attractive about this crazed man. Now, *she* was the one in control.

CHAPTER 10

(MONDAY, 13TH APRIL, 1981)

Sandy's Murder

Yushi eventually found the Two-Wheels bike shop, but he was unlucky. They didn't stock handlebar radios. "Not much call for them round here," he was informed. "But we can order one in for you if you want. It'll be here Wednesday or Thursday." Not very useful when he should be around 300 miles away by then, Yushi thought. He dejectedly left the store and rode slowly back to Sandy's, hoping that he'd have more chance of buying a radio in the city of St. Louis at the weekend. He really did miss tuning into the local stations as he passed through each small town, and the lack of success at Two-Wheels of course did nothing to break his sombre mood. He was still brooding about Sandy's surprising change of behaviour towards him.

A couple of hours later, Yushi would be sitting on a bed, head in his hands, sobbing his heart out in the De-Lux Country Motel on the other side of town.

After leaving the bike shop, and having returned to Sandy's house at least expecting a nice barbecue to help cheer him up, he was utterly perplexed to find his rucksack propped up against the front porch, with a roughly scrawled note attached with sticky tape. About to leave Sandy's for the last time, with his rucksack loosely strapped across his back, glancing again at the rusty old pickup truck in the drive before cycling off, he reread the letter one last time.

Sweet Yushi. Sorry, but I think it's best that we don't see each other again. I've reserved a room for you at the De-Lux on the road out of town towards St. Louis. It's paid for on my card by way of apology. Sandy

Without thinking, Yushi angrily screwed the paper into a ball and tossed it to the ground. Confused, he pushed open the front door and went inside. He physically shook at what he saw, and a kind of bewildered rage swept over him, an emotion he'd never experienced in his life before. Ten minutes later, he was cycling away from the premises for good, incredulous at how someone could have been so mean to him.

It was already seven o'clock and the sun was setting. He'd need to cycle fast to get to the motel before it was dark. Sure enough, when he reached his accommodation, panting hard, Room 15 had already been allocated to him. The proprietor had been expecting a Mr. Yushi to arrive sometime that evening, according to Ms. Beach, who'd phoned earlier to book, and pay with her MasterCard. He asked the young man to sign for the room key, and screwed up his eyes to attempt to read the signature. "Thank you, Mr.—err, Mr. Kamoto. Enjoy your stay."

Yushi was still too dazed to engage in any conversation, and simply took the key and left the reception office, pushing his bike along the forecourt until he reached his cabin. Although he hadn't eaten in hours, he was hardly able to concentrate on going out to get a meal, regardless of his hunger. Instead, he put some coins in the vending machine outside his room, and then sat on his bed, slowly stuffing potato chips into his mouth. Picking up the TV remote by its curly black cable, he then spent the rest of the evening indifferently skipping back and forth between *Happy Days* and *Star Trek*. He was so miserable, he couldn't raise a single smile at the Fonz, nor any interest whatsoever for Lieutenant Uhura.

Sandy, on the other hand, wasn't even capable of feeling miserable. She was lying on the floor of her kitchen, stone dead. Tiny fragments of red and black plastic, as well as some larger pieces, were strewn all around her, some stuck in the blood that had oozed from her head, the dark red liquid now congealing around them. Some electrical components could be found nearby. Two batteries remained in their casing, with thin red and blue wires still attached, while the small loudspeaker, once pumping out great tunes, was now silent. All that night, only the television on the wall, showing more minutes of advertisements than actual programmes, offered any sound from within the house. But, listening very carefully, one would just about be able to make out an occasional snort and snore emanating from somewhere outside. The patio doors leading from the kitchen to the terrace at the rear of the bungalow were half open. The barbecue's dull embers still had a faint red glow, but the rib-eye steaks on the griddle were as burnt as the charcoal beneath them.

(TUESDAY, 14th APRIL 1981)

Before the sun rose the following morning, the man who'd been snorting and snoring on the terrace awoke and looked around in a daze, unfamiliar with his surroundings. Gradually, he came to and, after shaking his head and rubbing his eyes a number of times, he pulled himself up, holding onto the now-cold barbecue kettle. Where in hell on earth was he? And more importantly, why was he naked? Doing his best to establish the answers to his own questions, he did vaguely recall leaving The Old Parlor, but that was about all. When that had been was impossible for him to remember. He tried his best to piece together the various recollections swarming around his head—a head that was pummelling him relentlessly like a jackhammer on full power.

Gradually, some things came to him. Yeah, he thought. Hadn't he gone to Sandy's house after drinking at the bar? But never having previously stepped out into her back yard, his present surroundings were alien to him. It was dark and cold, only a glow from the window next-door and a bright light from indoors afforded him any further clue. As he stumbled around on the patio, he was drawn to the brightness inside the house. He squeezed his way through the gap of the glazed patio doors, hoping to find his clothes. The light caused his head to nearly explode with pain, as he stepped into the kitchen, where he abruptly stopped in his tracks.

"Jeez! What the . . .?" He stood there, staring at the woman's body, sprawled out and face down on the floor in front of him. For what seemed like hours, but in fact were only seconds, the memories suddenly came flooding back, with the now familiarity of Sandy's kitchen confirming where he was. He remembered when he almost fell out his truck, clutching his new prized possession to show off, then chasing the woman into the house, and he remembered raising his hand to her—but that was about all. The rest was now self-evident.

"Well, I'll be a sonofa. . ." he thought. Staring around at the pieces of 'his' red and black radio, he looked up at the large wall-clock that told him it was 5.13a.m. Ozborn worked out his plan, and it wasn't very complicated. "I'd better get the fuck outta here, hadn't I?" he muttered under his breath as he finally fully worked out the potentially grave situation he was in. Noticing his hat, shoes and clothes randomly discarded around the room, he gathered them together and got dressed. Buckling his belt and telling himself to be smart and use his brain, he concluded that he mustn't panic, but should instead look around carefully and make sure not to leave any incriminating evidence.

After all, he'd watched *The Rockford Files*, and he knew how the police liked dusting things down for fingerprints. Apart from the bike radio, there was nothing else that caught his eye that could possibly link him to ever being there. Very calmly, he began gathering all the small parts of radio from every nook and cranny, depositing them in a paper grocery bag he found on the marble counter-top. Convinced he'd retrieved them all, he scrunched the bag up, then casually stepped over Sandy's body and the spread of blood, and left by the front door as calmly as if he were the milkman delivering two pints and a carton of juice.

Inside the cab, Ozborn donned his Stetson and tipped its brim just so. Then he carefully turned the truck's ignition, just letting the engine tick over without revving it. He gently slipped the column-shift into gear and reversed the vehicle with a low growl, as quietly as possible. Once backed out of the drive, he lit a Marlboro and proceeded as slowly and quietly as he could, waiting until he was fully at the end of Sandy's road. Stopping at the T-junction, he wound down the window to let in the balmy, early morning air, and switched on his favourite country station. A few miles later, as well as tossing his cigarette butt in the air, he also threw out the paper bag, aiming at a ditch, wriggled in his seat to make himself more comfortable, and sped off, thanking the Lord he'd been so smart.

If he'd noticed the twitch of curtains at Sandy's neighbours, he may not have been so pleased with himself.

"He's gone," announced the kind but formidable lady known locally as Mrs. Baltop, as she pulled her curtains together with a gentle tug.

"That's good, Han," replied her husband, feigning interest. "Now best to come away from the window, my love, and try to get back to sleep. It's still very early."

The lady's full name, Hannah Baltzwinik-Toporofski was a little too difficult and long-winded for most American folks to pronounce, so when she and her husband Daniel settled in America, she adapted the family name for ease, combining the first syllables from each part, but still preferring to at least keep using the name Toporofski whenever possible.

Daniel was usually the one to stay up all night, fixing sewing machines on the dining room table, and it had been his profession since entering the country, first getting an apprenticeship to learn the trade when they'd arrived. Like so many East European immigrants with similar work ethics and values, he eventually took the plunge and broadened out on his own with a little money borrowed from the National Bank and Trust Company, and soon he had a flourishing business. After being given the opportunity to sell his company many hard-working years later, mending sewing machines was now just a hobby to keep him occupied. Spending his retirement days on a golf course had never interested him.

It was Hannah who was still bringing in a tidy sum, thanks to her expert knowledge of the antiques trade. Regularly, usually the last Sunday of the month, she would hold yard sales outside their bungalow to sell off the unwanted pieces that held little value. That was how she first got to know Sandy, who would often come over to browse. The rather large, feisty lady, now in her early fifties, kept hold of the more valuable items to take into one of the Chicago auction houses a couple of times a year, and it was her meticulous attention to detail, and great observational skills, that helped her to be as successful as she was.

However, despite being rather good at what she did, Mrs. Toporofski's real ambition was to be on television. She dreamed of being interviewed as an expert in her chosen category of antiques. Or, if not that, maybe a chat-show hostess. Alternatively, a newsreader reporting an incident. Anything would do—she wasn't fussy, but she acknowledged that her age and white hair were now against her in this day when only glamorous models were chosen to present the TV shows. Standing at the window of her bungalow, she imagined what on earth the man in the pickup truck next door was doing so early. And why she'd heard shouts and screams the night before. But she didn't want to cause a fuss with Sandy, so she blanked it from her mind, and got back into bed.

Although Mrs. Toporofski didn't exactly approve of the various men-friends she saw coming and going next door, nonetheless she liked her neighbour, and thought Sandy to be a very pleasant, and beautiful, young lady. If only she had Sandy's youth and good looks, the TV stations would be clamouring for her services for certain, she daydreamed.

Whatever had been going on next door was none of her business, Mrs. Toporofski concluded. Besides, Sandy was always very professional when it came to caring for her teeth at Mr. Edgar's. She was due to have a check-up that very morning, so her neighbour could discuss it with her when she saw her at the practice if the appropriate opportunity arose.

CHAPTER 11

(TUESDAY, 14TH APRIL, 1981)

Moores' Investigation

Although it was highly irregular for Sandy not to arrive punctually at the dental practice, Mr. Edgar wasn't overly concerned. His first patient of the day was Hannah Baltop, and as it was only to be for a check-up, he could easily manage without Sandy's assistance. He expected Sandy would turn up anytime soon, with a genuine reason for being late. Perhaps her car hadn't started, or the washing machine man was coming, or she was simply feeling a little unwell.

By the time he had completed the routine examination of his patient, he concluded that she needed one small filling on her upper left molar, but because he had no one to mix the cement paste, he concluded that he'd have to ask Mrs. Baltop to return the following week. "Why, of course, that's alright, Mr. Edgar," agreed Hannah. "But I was sure Sandy would be here today. She only told me the other day that she'd be seeing me for my check-up."

"Well, I expect she had good reason not to show. I am sorry to you, Mrs. Baltop, for the inconvenience this has caused you," apologised Mr. Edgar. "Perhaps she had car trouble, or maybe she was feeling a little under the weather," he went on. "But I must say that it is indeed somewhat unusual of her not to at least call."

Hannah took the card that indicated the time and date of her new appointment, and suggested to Mr. Edgar that she pop round to Sandy's later, just to make sure she was okay. "You do know that we're neighbours, don't you, Mr Edgar?" she said, by way of explanation.

Almost as soon as Hannah began driving home, her mind became distracted when she noticed a garage sale in full flow by the side of the road. Not one to risk missing some golden trinket that she might purchase for a song from a seller unaware of its true worth, she pulled over to have a rummage, spending an enjoyable half an hour there. She cannily picked up an item of jewellery that should easily make a ten-fold return on her outlay–and, very pleased with her lucrative bounty, she continued back to her house, thinking ahead as to which Chicago auctioneer would be best to sell it through.

It wasn't until she pulled into her drive that she noticed Sandy's Volvo next door. "Oh yes," she thought, as she remembered her intention to check on her neighbour. Before going into her own home, she went straight to Sandy's front porch and rang the doorbell. She waited a minute before ringing it again, and waited some more. She tried the handle, but it was locked. She began walking around the path in order to try at the back. As she reached the patio, she heard her name being called.

"Oh, Hannah," cried her husband. "It's for you. The telephone. It's Hindleman Auctioneers in Chicago for you, darling. Shall I tell them you'll call back?".

With Hindleman's being the very dealer she'd considered using for today's little windfall, she hollered back over the fence to Daniel. "Coming! I'm coming. Please tell them to wait." A minute later, she was deep in conversation with Mr. Hindleman himself, completely forgetting what she was about to do earlier. While she was arranging to take a trip up to Chicago in the next few days, Daniel prepared the soup for their lunch. Today it was carrot and coriander with croutons, which they ate as they watched their favourite midday soap on TV. That always sent them to sleep after they'd finished. They'd grown accustomed to their little afternoon nap, and they rather looked forward to it every day.

***

(TUESDAY, 14TH APRIL, 1981)

Over at Route 40 on his way to crossing the state line into Missouri,

Yushi was now having a much better time than the previous day. He'd eventually slept like a log at the De-Lux Motel, after tossing and turning for a while, mulling things over and over about Sandy's change of heart, her peculiar note and what he'd seen in the house. While trying to get to sleep, he'd decided it best to put everything behind him, forget all about Sandy and move on.

He concluded that members of the opposite sex were just trouble, and he could do without that kind of trouble—at least until the next time.

Nevertheless, he acknowledged it was thanks to Sandy that he was now more worldly-wise, and he should always be grateful to her for that. And that waterbed sure was a lot of fun, he mused, smiling to himself. But remembering his last sight of that ugly old truck on her driveway, and what it represented, sent a shiver of disdain through him. Yushi was upset alright. But if Sandy had chosen to two-time him, then she didn't deserve his company anyway. No, in hindsight she'd been right to suggest they shouldn't see each other again.

Now feeling well and refreshed, he left his motel at a good, early hour. The perfectly flat road ran parallel to the interstate highway, enabling him to reach speeds of over twenty miles an hour for long periods. He focused on the practicalities of his journey. Probably at this rate, even after a Big Mac stop, he may even reach the outer suburbs of St. Louis by dusk. And then, if he made equally good progress tomorrow morning, he could be at the famous giant arch by midday—it was a landmark high on his agenda to visit.

Thinking about where to stay next, and thanks to last night's free accommodation, courtesy of Sandy Beach, he didn't feel too guilty about dipping into his savings and paying for another motel.

Perhaps tomorrow night he should be more frugal with his money, and go back to using the cheaper youth hostels instead. There would be plenty to choose from in the city, according to his national directory.

***

(WEDNESDAY, 15TH APRIL, 1981)

A whole twenty-four hours had gone by since Hannah Toporofski had last thought about checking on her neighbour. She glanced out of her window and noticed that Sandy's car was still parked in her drive. It was a little odd, she thought, to see it in exactly the same position as yesterday. Then, she suddenly remembered about her auctioneer's distracting phone call. "Silly me," she scolded herself. "Daniel, I'm just popping next door to see if Sandy's alright. Maybe she's sick and needs something brought for her."

"Okay, darling. Don't be too long. We've got pea and ham soup today, and I'll be pouring it out soon," replied her husband.

Hannah didn't bother trying Sandy's front door bell this time, instead going straight round to the back yard. The patio doors were half open, so Sandy must be at home, she thought, but before Hannah reached them she was able to see that, rather strangely, the kitchen light was on, even though the dazzling midday sun was streaming through. She tapped on the patio door and called out.

"Sandy, dear, are you home? Can I get you anything? Sandy, can I come in, honey?" There was no answer, only the sound from the TV greeted Hannah as she stepped into the kitchen. A number of flies buzzed around her head, and, still blinded by the brightness of the sun reflecting on the shiny marble worktops, it took a while before her eyes could adjust. When they eventually did, the scream she let out could have pierced Daniel's eardrums right across the yard fence. Hannah's stomach churned violently, she gagged and choked, turning her head away towards the sink just in time to catch nearly all the jet of vomit as it retched forth from her mouth. Some also splashed down her fresh, pale-yellow blouse, clean on only that morning.

As soon as she'd recovered enough, she ran out of the door as quickly as her legs would carry her, not even taking a second look at the body and dark mess surrounding it. Having never seen what a pool of blood really looks like, except for the fake stuff on TV detective shows, Hannah couldn't be sure it was in fact blood. She certainly wasn't going to stay around to examine it further. Shaking hysterically, she stumbled over the ledge by the patio and fell flat on her face on the grass, shouting wildly for Daniel to come. And come quickly he did, almost dropping the saucepan of soup from his grasp.

"Oh my!" was all he could utter, as he took in the horrific scene in Sandy's kitchen. He helped his wife to her feet and led her back to the sanctuary of their home, where first he tried to soothe her nerves with a glass of ice tea, before reaching for the phone and calling 911.

It seemed like only minutes before there was a cavalcade of three police vehicles, lights flashing and sirens blaring, pulling into the road and screeching to a halt outside both houses. An ambulance slowly reversed into Sandy's drive and stopped next to her Volvo. Half an hour later, while various professionals milled about, in and around Sandy's house, all doing their specialised jobs, an unmarked Buick sedan car arrived, and the fresh-faced police chief, with neatly cut hair and wearing a smart suit and tie, stepped out, steadily chewing gum.

"Okay, what do we have here?" John Moores asked, speaking to no one in particular. "Who found the body?" He knew these lines off by heart. They happened in the movies, so as far as he was concerned, they should happen in real life too.

Sergeant Graham Staples, who was one of the policemen closest, nodded with his head to the house next door. "A Mrs. Hannah Baltzwinik-Toporofski, Sir," he offered, looking down at his notes as he did so. She's the neighbour."

"You don't say," retorted Moores. "Jeez, who has a name like that? You gotta be kidding me!" The chief shook his head as he walked towards the neighbour's house.

As he rang the doorbell, he called back to the older and more weather-beaten sergeant. "What did you say her name was?"

"She's also known as Mrs. Baltop, Sir," Staples shouted in reply.

"Why didn't you say that before? Jeez!" Moores mumbled under his breath. It was Daniel who answered the door and led the chief through to his wife, who was looking very pale as she sat on the sofa, still shaking.

Moores was well-experienced in dealing with homicides, having previously served in the Chicago Police Department for five years before he relocated the 200 miles south to the relative peace and quiet of the area he now worked. Thankfully, not a great deal happened here, at least not in comparison with Chicago. That suited him. Plain ol', hard-working American farmland types were more his ideal.

Moores was a racist. The way he saw things, for too long he'd had to contend with an ever-increasing ethnic population back in the Windy City—although he reckoned the Irish weren't so bad. He'd say at least you could understand them, just about, and their black beer with a frothy cream top was really good. But those Asians, particularly the Chinese, the Taiwanese, and the goddamn Japanese—well! "Jeez. What the hell's gone wrong with this country? And now I've come all the way over here to interview someone whose name I can't even say properly. Jeez!" mumbled the chief under his breath. But professional conduct ensured he kept his thoughts to himself. "There, Mrs, err..." he began, trying to recall the name that Sergeant Staples had told him.

"You can call me Hannah," said Hannah.

Police Chief Moores liked his clichés: "Okay Hannah. Let's take it from the top..."

CHAPTER 12

(WEDNESDAY, 15TH APRIL, 1981)

Police Hunt

A youthful and energetic Katie Copeland, with a clear complexion and infectious smile, was the recently-appointed head of the forensics team, and had been dispatched from the nearby city of Terre Haute, just across the Illinois state border with Indiana, and this was to be one of the first cases where she would be in charge.

What she was to deal with today was nothing out of the ordinary, according to her more seasoned colleagues, who Katie could sense were somewhat envious of her quick promotion since leaving university. For as long as she could remember, she'd had ambitions to work in forensics, and now her dreams had come true. But with any dead body, a search in and around the property, the collecting of fingerprints, with methodical photography and meticulous note-taking, Katie was also astutely aware that all victims were someone's son or daughter, and she made it her business to treat the situation with great respect. And she'd leave no stone unturned in order to determine how any such tragedy had occurred.

After staring at the body for a few minutes, the young woman searched thoroughly around the rest of the house, including the bedroom. She had learned that usually sex or money, sometimes both, were the root causes in murder cases. And this was, in her opinion, certainly a murder—although at first sight she wasn't able to second-guess the cause of death. Judging by the bloodstain on the kitchen counter-top, the victim's head must have hit it prior to falling to the floor.

But what caused her to collapse in the first place? Had she been hit, and if so, with what? She peered again at the corpse, and at the mass of thick blood surrounding it. In fact, it was so thick that she nearly missed the raised profile of some objects from within it. She called out to one of her co-workers. "Get over here, please. We need to take a look at this before the CSC's come in." Copeland was aware that once the Crime Scene Cleaner agency began doing its job, there would be no more opportunities to afford her further detailed examinations of the room.

"Okay Katie. I'm onto it," responded her Number Two. While the grisly task of separating the small solid objects from the now-brown, sticky goo was being carried out, Copeland studied the bedroom. She stood there and ran her left hand through her straight, shoulder-length blonde hair, as if the action helped her to think. With the other hand, she prodded the unmade bed, and the glup-glup sound that only waterbeds made as their content swished back and forth, could be heard. "Nice," she thought. She looked closer at the pale white marks against the blue mattress sheet. "Okay, so it appears a male has been enjoying her bed, too," she deduced, having found dried semen stains at a few previous homicide investigations she'd worked on before. "Any news from the kitchen yet?" she shouted, on her way back to where the ambulance crew were on standby, waiting for her to give the all-clear to remove the body.

Her colleague was standing at the sink, still stained by the neighbour's smelly vomit, washing the small objects under the faucet, and holding them up to the light to examine them more closely. "Well, we have pieces of plastic, and a knob of some sort, Ma'am, that I can tell you. But what they're from is anyone's guess."

***

Still at the Toporofskis' house, the police chief was just wrapping things up with Hannah. Apart from detailed accounts regarding antiques and dental appointments, she hadn't offered an awful lot of useful information, with the exception of one mildly possible lead.

Mrs. Baltop said she remembered seeing an old pickup truck being driven past her house very early the day before. Unfortunately, she didn't know what make of vehicle it was, nor could she describe the driver well as she could only make out the profile. "It was very dark," she explained. "And I'm not very good with cars. As for the driver, I think it was a man wearing a hat."

"That narrows the possibilities down to several million," thought Moores, as he stood up to leave and thank the lady for her help. As he was leaving, he turned to ask one last question. "If you don't mind me asking, where on earth does a name like, err, err . . ." he struggled to remember, " . . . Baltzwinik-Toporofski come from?" His enquiry was music to Hannah's ears. It was an opportunity to explain her family's name to someone who, at last, showed interest.

"Well, where we came from, to begin with we had no family name," she started to explain. "Then we were required to take a surname when we lived in little *shtetls*—village ghettos to you. In my country we would simply use the patronymic names of our trade. '*Topor*' is the word for axe, and my family used axes to collect turpentine by cutting grooves in trees. And if you want, I can tell you how we got the name Baltzwinik . . ." Hannah would have continued enthusiastically, but Moores interrupted, as politely as he could.

"Perhaps another time, Mrs Baltop, but for now, as much as I'd like to stay longer, I have to be getting along."

Hannah understood.

"Yes, indeed you must. That poor, dear Sandy. I do hope you find the answers you're looking for."

As Moores returned to Sandy's drive, he was approached by Sergeant Staples, who was holding a crumpled piece of paper that he'd found screwed up on the ground, and which he handed to his boss. Moores read it and reread it. "So, who the hell—or what—is 'Sweet Yushi'? Sounds like one of those foreign rice dishes you get up in Chicago. Okay, you'd better get on over to the De-Lux, *now!*" he commanded Staples. Staples had worked under his Chief for some time, and had become used to being bossed around without so much as a 'please' or 'thank you'. It didn't faze him—he merely saw it as part of the job, and chose to simply "accept the status quo", as he put it.

Moores walked across the gravel drive to the Forensics' station wagon, where the team were just finishing up. Judging by the number of small stones on the lawn, Sandy Beach must have been a pretty careless driver, he thought. "Okay, what have you got for me?" demanded Moores of Copeland. The pieces of red and black plastic that had been recovered from the congealed blood were held out to him in a clear polythene bag. "Is that all?" he asked, dismissively. "What are they?"

"Well, I'm not sure, Sir," answered Katie. "Most are broken pieces of plastic from an unidentified object, but there's also what appears to be a knob from some kind of apparatus. It's quite tiny—maybe it's from a kitchen gadget—like a food mixer. But we couldn't find anything else in the room to match it. Whatever it's from, it was used to strike the woman. We found a cut to her head of a similar size, and another fragment of the same red plastic embedded in her scalp."

"Did it kill her?" asked Moores.

"We can't say at this point, Chief. She may have struck her head on the counter top, or the stone floor, and that may have finished her. Or she may have been hit after she'd fallen. We'd need to wait for the lab report to come back." That was all Katie could offer for now.

Over at the De-Lux, Staples was also gathering important information. The proprietor handed his register over and, sure enough it looked like someone by the name of 'Y. Kamoto' had stayed two nights ago, according to the almost illegibly-scribbled signature. With a description given of a male in his twenties, dark hair and of Asian appearance, Staples headed back to police headquarters in Marshall, mildly pleased with himself. He had a name, and a description. And the room had been reserved in the name of 'Yushi', and paid for by Ms. Beach herself. But what was lacking was the crucial ID of Kamoto's vehicle. The motel owner said he hadn't noticed any car pull in to the parking lot around the time of the guest's arrival, but he admitted he hadn't particularly been looking either. Kamoto had failed to enter his plate number in the book, and unfortunately the motel owner hadn't insisted he did so either.

"Don't you have a camera outside?" asked Staples, enthusiastically anticipating returning to base with pictures of the main suspect.

"We do," the owner answered, slowly. "But it's been down a week now—we're still waiting for the technician. He should be coming tomorrow to fix it."

By the time Staples had returned to Police HQ, Moores was sitting back in his office chair, with his feet up on the desk. It had been a long day, and the chief was tired. Once Staples had relayed what he'd found out at the motel, Moores went over the information they had so far managed to obtain: "So, we're looking for a male, name of Yushi Kamoto, Asian, probably a goddamn Jap with a name like that, in his twenties, and the murder weapon probably being a kitchen appliance striking a blow to the head of Sandy Beach. Semen on her bed too. She pays for Kamoto's motel room, but we don't know why. We don't know what he was driving, but the nosey neighbour next door remembers seeing a pickup truck before dawn of the morning after the murder. The truck may have nothing to do with it, but it's all we've got for now. Okay, Staples. Let's turn in. It shouldn't be too difficult to find this sonofabitch. We'll get him tomorrow, no problem. I'll see you here sharp at nine."

Moores couldn't let his racist tendencies be seen publicly, but to himself he admitted that he had them, and he had good reason as far as he was concerned.

Ever since his father had died a sad old man, bent double and racked with pain as a result of his beatings as a prisoner-of-war at the hands of the Japanese, the police chief just couldn't help how he felt. His father had told him time and time again how he'd suffered so badly, so it was understandable that he still felt the way he did, wasn't it? That's how Moores justified the ingrained feelings of hatred he had towards all Japanese, even twenty years after his father's passing. And now, already convinced of Yushi Kamoto's guilt, he went home satisfied that before long one less "Nip", as he referred to them derogatorily, would be freely roaming the streets of the America he was so proud of.

(THURSDAY, 16TH APRIL, 1981)

When Moores arrived at the precinct the following morning, the busy open-plan area was already buzzing with the usual din of ringing phones, people talking loudly, and typewriters clattering. Staples was already seated in the chief's office, waiting, with a brown paper bag in front of him. "What's this? Doughnuts already?" Moores asked.

Before he had the chance to peek inside, Staples took the bag and emptied its contents all over the desk. "This was brought in by one of our guys out on routine patrol—everyone was told to look out for anything suspicious within a three-mile radius of Beach's house." The pile of bits consisted of a number of red and black plastic pieces, a small loudspeaker, a couple of batteries and some wires. "And look at this," he went on, picking up something else in particular and holding it forth. "A silver-coloured knob just like the one we've already got."

"Bingo! But what the hell is all this? It's no way a kitchen appliance. Looks more like the parts to a goddamn radio, but I ain't never seen a radio looking like this," said Moores. There were so many tiny pieces, it would have been like trying to put together an impossible jigsaw puzzle in 3D to work out what it had once looked like. He went out from his office into the main area. "Listen up, everybody. Does anyone recognise what kind of radio these pieces are from?" he asked, holding up the largest pieces and the loudspeaker in the air for all to see.

"Sure, Chief," answered one of the sergeants. "I got me one of those for my bicycle. It attaches on the handlebar."

The cogs in Moores' head were turning ten to the dozen. "What if this Kamoto guy didn't have a pickup truck, or any other motor vehicle for that matter? Maybe the truck that Mrs. Toper-what's-her-name reported has got nothing to do with the murder. What if Kamoto used a cycle for his getaway?"

"Yeah, and that would explain why there was no record of any license plate numbers in the motel register," added Staples.

"Okay," continued Moores. "So we're looking for a goddamn Jap on a bike. Forget the pickup truck from now on." He turned to the other sergeant. "How far can you cycle in a day?"

"Well, it depends on wind, land contours, road condit . . ." he began.

"I don't wanna goddamn lecture—just a rough number of miles. I've no idea—I've not ridden a bike in years. Is it 20, 50, 100, 200? Just give me an approximate number," said Moores, impatiently. He finally got the number he'd been waiting for. "It could be up to 100," said the sergeant.

"Okay," said Moores, going over to the map on the wall. "Our friend Makoto started from Beach's house three days ago in Paris and goes in this direction," pointing to the motel's location.

"Kamoto," corrected Staples.

"Jeez, whatever. They're all the goddamn same," the chief said quietly to himself. "Thank you, Staples," he said, rather patronisingly. "If he's going in that direction, my hunch is he's heading west. And if he cycles a hundred miles a day, he'll be past St. Louis and halfway to Kansas by now."

"But that's if he stays on his bike," Staples pointed out. "Maybe he'd get a ride, or take a train or a Greyhound? And why wouldn't he just head home, wherever that may be?"

"Because he's smart. He's going around in broad daylight on a pushbike for all to see. He's right under everyone's noses. He thinks he's the last guy we'd be looking for. But he's so wrong. Put out an

APB for a cycling Asian gentleman. Yushi Kamoto, we're coming to get you!"

"But, Chief. We're still drawing a blank with that, as well. No record of anyone by the name of Yushi Kamoto so far."

(THURSDAY, 16TH APRIL 1981)

Meanwhile, oblivious to the frantic activity that was taking place 150 miles away, Yushi's prediction of arriving at the Gateway Arch by midday was perfectly correct, and as he crossed the mighty Mississippi River he could see the colossal Gateway Arch structure towering to the sky in front of him. "Wow! That's just how it looks in the pictures—but even more impressive," he marvelled, as he padlocked his machine to the bike rack after riding up to the entrance. Gazing upwards, he could just about make out the 16 observation windows at the top, and he could hardly wait to ride up there on the special internal tram that he'd read about.

But first, he would do what he assumed may be the boring bit—a visit to the arch's museum in the basement, and a viewing of the movie about the building's construction.

As he entered the site, and walked towards the ticket booth, he was absolutely devastated to see a large A-board displaying some very unwelcome words.

"*Due to maintenance work being carried out, today, the tram to the top is temporarily out of service. . . It will reopen at 10.00 hrs, Friday 17th*"

Yushi just stood and stared at the sign, and couldn't quite believe his unfortunate timing. "What to do? What to do?" he asked himself, trying to make a decision on the spur of the moment. After weighing up his options, there was obviously only one thing he could think of. He'd simply have to stay at the nearest hostel tonight and return in the morning. Meanwhile, he could at least do "the boring bit". As it turned out, it wasn't boring at all. Relaxing back in his theatre seat and stretching out his legs, he actually found the half-hour film very fascinating indeed.

While Yushi was completely absorbed by the documentary, events were developing at a very fast pace back in Paris, Illinois.

CHAPTER 13

(THURSDAY, 16TH APRIL, 1981)

Booth's Tip-Off

Philip Booth was getting himself ready for his shift that was due to begin at two o'clock that afternoon. With the morning free, he'd spent a very enjoyable time with the love of his life. In fact all three loves of his life, if you counted the dog and the motorbike. First, he went for a long walk with his wife Lou and their adorable Shar-Pei cross Staffy dog they'd named Bert. Phil, being somewhat of an anglophile, really liked those PG Woodhouse tales of Bertie Wooster, and so had named the dog they'd owned ever since it was a day-old puppy, after the very British character. Following the walk, the ever-smiling Lou and he had coffee and breakfast together at the new deli in town. Very nice it was, and great waffles too. And then, while Lou went off to work as a nurse at the local hospital, Philip enjoyed a couple of pleasant hours in his garage, tinkering with his Harley Davidson, taking things apart, cleaning them up, and putting them back together again.

Thursdays were usually good, and so far today this one had been no exception. As usual, when it was time, he'd collect his patrol car from the precinct, and check inside the office to see if there were any notices pinned to the wall. Sometimes, there might be an APB—All-Points Bulletin—meaning all law enforcement officers, including him, should be on the lookout for an individual who was wanted for having committed an offence, or who might also be a danger to the public.

Today, there were three such bulletins, containing the names and brief details of the alleged perpetrators. Tim Fort, Caucasian male, 54, in the Boston area. Leroy Williams, black male, 37, Silver

Springs, Colorado. Yushi Kamoto, Asian male, early twenties, Marshall, Illinois. "Hmm, why does that name mean something?" pondered Booth. His curiosity got the better of him, so he read on, slowly grooming his beard and moustache while deep in thought. Of course! Yushi was that guy he'd picked up last week for cycling on the freeway. And there's a mention here also of a bike radio—the very same radio he'd retrieved from the car trunk and returned to Yushi at the Cincinnati hostel. What? Wanted for murder? The radio was the weapon? "But Yushi was such a nice guy. I'll be darned," exclaimed Booth generally to whoever was nearby. He flipped the page over to see who was investigating the case. "Okay, I'd better call and tell Chief Moores what I know." Booth shook his head in disbelief about young Yushi, as he muttered to himself. "It just goes to show, you sure never can tell with some folks."

As he picked up the phone and dialled, he also began flipping through the large lever-arched file where all traffic violation reports were stored, and went straight to the letter 'K' tab, looking for the 'Kamoto' page. There was no relevant report. "That's odd," he thought. He was sure he'd given out an advisory ticket to the cyclist, but where was it? The switchboard at the Marshall precinct answered his call, and Booth asked to be put through to Chief Moores.

After hanging on the line, and hearing a few clicks, he finally heard a voice.

"Moores here."

Booth went through his account with the chief, who was extremely interested in everything that he was being told, while all the time Booth was now thumbing through his own handwritten duplicate book, searching for some explanation as to why the main report wasn't where it was supposed to be.

"Well, I thank you for calling, Officer Booth. You've been a big help to us," said a grateful Moores. He could see this crime soon becoming one of the quickest he'd ever solved, having the confirmation from Booth about the young man on his cycle, travelling west from

Cincinnati. Just as he was about to hang up, he heard Booth shout down the phone at him.

"Wait! You've made a mistake!" Booth had reached the page he was looking for, and continued. "You're after the wrong man! Well, maybe he is the right man, I don't know—he struck me as incapable of harming a fly, let alone killing a human being—but anyway, that's your business. No, you see Sir, you've got the wrong *name*. It's not 'Kamoto'. It's 'Yakamoto'!"

Booth's call did seem convincingly thorough, and Moores wasted no time, knowing what he had to do. Immediately, he instructed his department to get to work, gathering all information on the wanted man, now that the correct surname had been established. Within minutes, the APB was altered, and in less than an hour, Moores received yet another call, this time from a police officer based in the St. Louis eastern suburbs.

The officer had been called to an unrelated minor theft at a motel eight miles from downtown, and when he had gone to investigate, he began by looking through the large leather-bound guest-book on the desk, reading all the names, one by one, some of them so poorly written that only a few were legible—including that of Yushi's. But luckily for this officer, the young manageress was very particular about following the rules of the management.

She always demanded a form of identification from every patron—like a passport, driving licence, credit card, or anything with their name on—and she always efficiently typed out receipts for every one of them, including their names in full, cross-referred with the formal ID to ensure correct spelling. This practice dramatically reduced the theft-rate from the rooms, once the patrons realised that there was a full record of them held on the motel's system. From the pile of dockets she handed over, the astute officer noticed the name of 'Yakamoto'. He immediately radioed in to his HQ, who then got on the phone to Moores.

It was early afternoon when Moores took that call. He looked at the map. He and Sergeant Staples could be in St. Louis in two hours if they left right away, he calculated. Better to be "hands on" there than stuck behind a desk in Marshall. "Come on, Staples. We're going for a little ride to catch this S.O.B.," he called to his colleague.

With the magnetised blue light on the roof of Moores's police Buick flashing, they sped west along Interstate Highway 70, taking the exit before they reached downtown. Moores wanted to stop at the motel where the observant officer had called from, in case there was anything showing up on the motel's CCTV tapes—assuming they had cameras actually working at this establishment, unlike at the De-Lux. If only they could get a picture of Yakamoto and, if possible, the bike, that would be the icing on the cake, he thought. At last, an easy-to-wrap-up homicide. He was already looking forward to receiving a promotion and a higher pay scale.

When the two officers arrived, they were pleased to see that this motel was efficiently run, and the cameras were all operating as they should be. The motel manageress, savvy as usual, had already been checking the footage before Moores and Staples arrived. She was able to present them with images of not only Yakamoto entering the reception office, but also of the bike being pushed by him to the room in which he'd stayed. Even though Moores wasn't a cyclist himself, he was able to recognise the machine as a racing model, with its characteristic drop handlebars. And as well as its panniers on the rack, the image of two distinctive flags at the rear could also be made out—one American and the other Japanese. "We're getting closer!" he said, turning to Staples, who nodded in agreement.

Surely, it must only be a matter of time before someone spots a guy riding a bike along the road with flags on it. It's not the sort of thing you see every day, thought Moores. He turned to thank the manageress as they were leaving. "There's one last thing I can tell you," said the woman. "Mr. Yakamoto told me he was headed straight for Saint Lou when he handed back the room key to collect his deposit."

***

Following his unsuccessful attempt to visit the Gateway Arch the previous day, Yushi had stayed the night at the Huckleberry Hostel only three blocks away. It was very popular with back-packers, and free-spirited travellers like himself. It was the largest hostel he'd stayed at so far, with an eight-bedded dormitory on each of the four floors, and two single-sex shower blocks in the basement. He'd prefer, if one was available, to have a room and shower to himself, but at only $8.75 a night, he couldn't complain. What he hadn't counted on was that there was a rota of chores to be carried out by all guests in the morning. The jobs could be anything, maybe mopping floors, cooking breakfasts, doing laundry, or any other tasks necessary for the smooth-running of such a busy hostel. Each floor had its own 'team leader', delegating the duty roster.

With breakfast being served at 9.00a.m. sharp, and Yushi's designated chore—folding hundreds of bed sheets, a task that would take at least an hour—he was aware that he wouldn't make it to the Gateway Arch by today's ten o'clock opening time. He could opt out from doing his chore, but if he did so he would then have to pay $20 for his accommodation—more than many motels even.

He concluded that as he probably wouldn't get to the Arch until midday now, that would make it too late in the day to set off on his travels after completing his visit. So he reserved a bed for a second night, got on with his chores, and then made the short ride to the arch, locking his bike to the same rack as he'd done the day before.

At the ticket booth, the A-board was still in position, but with a change of notice: *'Due to the over-running of essential maintenance work, the observation area will unfortunately remain closed until three o'clock today'.*

"What the . . .?" Yushi groaned, disappointed and not just a little annoyed too. Well, he wasn't going to give up, and he bought his ticket for later. "Are you positive the tram will be working this afternoon?"

he asked the clerk behind the glass screen. "I came yesterday and stayed over in town especially. I don't want to be let down a second time," he said, rather curtly. After being apologised to and assured that the engineering would definitely be completed by three o'clock, Yushi decided to spend his time wisely. He'd ride around downtown, take in the sights, and, ah yes, find a bike shop from which at last he could buy his replacement radio. Then maybe he'd go and sit in the sunshine on the banks of the Mississippi until opening time.

So, off he went, across the Gateway's park area and straight into the bustling city. Pulling up at the sidewalk, he asked someone if they knew where a bike store was. They did. It was at the other end of the street he was on, which was over three miles long. "No matter," he thought. "I've got the time," and he cycled along the busy road, quite sure that in a city this big, the shop was bound to stock handlebar radios.

When he reached the store, he wasn't disappointed. And in fact they had the very same model as the one he'd had stolen, and at the same price. "Great!" he thought. He'd never forget to remove it again, even when he was exhausted. Things were looking up.

"First time in the city, pal?" asked the shop assistant, nodding towards the giveaway rucksack, as Yushi was retrieving $30 from his wallet in one of its pockets. "Where ya headed?" The assistant, with his name badge stating 'I'm Paul, and I'm pleased to help', was well-used to seeing backpackers and long-distance cyclists coming into the shop. His boss had trained him to make conversation with the customers—they tended to browse longer and spend more money that way. Yushi explained that he was going to California, and Paul pretended to be super-impressed, but in fact had heard it all before.

"Wow, man, that's a mighty long way! Have you been to the Arch while you're in town? You must go. It's real cool too! You can go all the way to the top," he went on, a little too enthusiastically, Yushi thought.

"It was closed earlier, so I'm going there this afternoon," replied

Yushi, on his way out. Disappointed that his sales technique wasn't successful today, Paul just said the obligatory "You have a nice day now", as he turned to serve the next customer.

Outside, in the heat of the afternoon sun, once back at the river near the Arch, Yushi sat and ate a sandwich, and waited patiently until three o'clock. He looked at his watch, and it was nearing that time. Before going to the Arch's kiosk for a third time, he padlocked his bike yet again to the metal racks outside.

Inside the foyer, he was glad to find that all the facilities were at last now open, including the much-heralded tram to the top. There were dozens of other people all milling around, buying their tickets, eager to experience the ride up inside the structure.

Waiting in line, Yushi eventually boarded one of the eight tram pods, each able to carry five passengers. When he finally reached the observation gallery, he was stunned by the magnificent view of the city far below. His ticket allowed unlimited time up there, and he was intending to take full advantage of that fact, bearing in mind this was his third attempt to be there. He was completely mesmerised by the sights afforded from each window. It was better than he could have hoped for, and he'd be happy to stay there until closing time. And that was exactly what he would have done, had it not been for Moores and Staples.

Unbeknown to Yushi, down below on firm ground, Moores and Staples had just arrived in the city, and headed straight for the police headquarters on Jefferson Street, only two miles from the Arch. At the precinct, the news of the hunt was already the topic of the day. "He could be anywhere, if he hasn't already moved on, that is. It's like looking for a needle in a haystack in a city this large," said Staples to Moores, rather despondently.

He was overheard. "Don't worry—with an APB out on him, I bet it won't take too long till we get a tipoff," assured one of the officers present. "We've got his name, we've got his picture, and we've even got what his cycle looks like. If he's in the city, we'll find him, I can guarantee," the officer went on. "The whole Metropolitan force is on the lookout, and right now we're checking all the motels, hotels, hostels and even bike shops. Someone will have seen him," he said, doing his best to reassure the colleagues who'd just arrived from the neighbouring state.

As suggested, Moores and Staples sat tight and waited. They didn't need to wait too long before the switchboard lights began flashing, as officers from around the city called in. Moores listened intently to a call, scribbling down the information he'd just been given, and then turned to Staples.

"Come on!" shouted Moores to Staples. "This is the news we've been waiting for. We've had positive IDs from the Huckleberry Hostel, as well as from a downtown cycle store. Yakamoto was there earlier, and said he was heading to the Gateway Arch. Let's go!"

Despite the heavy traffic, now in rush hour, it took only a few minutes for their police car to screech to a halt at the base of the enormous structure. Running towards the entrance, they went past the many bikes in the rack, with one in particular standing out with its two flags flapping in the breeze. "He's here, Chief!" wheezed Staples, already out of breath. As they raced up to the kiosk counter, past the queuing visitors, Moores held up the picture of Yakamoto in front of the teller, along with his police badge.

"Do you recognise this man's face?" he demanded, urgently, almost rudely. "Is he still here?"

"Err, it's possible, Sir," the uniformed, rather large, black lady said, flustered. "But I see so many faces, I don't get paid enough to study them. I just sell the tickets. Let me look closer," she continued, now more composed. "Yeah, I think I saw him. He was a little off with me because we was shut earlier, but I think he came back if I remember rightly. He may still be up top, I don't know—I only see them going up, not coming back down, Sir."

Moores and Staples pushed past all the people waiting to board the next tram compartment, and as soon as the sliding doors opened, they jumped in. "Wait!" shouted Moores. "We can't both go up. What if we miss him coming down in another tram car and he gets away?"

"Good point, Chief," agreed Staples, who immediately turned to one of the security officials patrolling the foyer. "You, Sir," he demanded, flashing his police badge. "Close the doors, and don't let anyone out until we say so. And if you see this man..." he continued, while shoving a picture of Yakamoto in front of the official, "... arrest him!"

Then they had to wait impatiently for everyone else to board the train compartments, and for the machinery to jolt into motion, slowly at first. "Jeez. Can't this thing go any faster?" Moores complained, once they were inside. Staples was still too out of breath to reply. Near the top, the doors slid open, and Staples groaned as he saw there was a final flight of stairs they had to climb. Pushing his way through the throng of sightseers, the fitter Chief Moores leapt up the steps, two at a time. Staples followed behind, more slowly, climbing each step individually. As they reached the 65-foot-long observation room, it was already filled to capacity with over a hundred people moving around between all the windows on both sides.

The policemen stood still and looked around. There, over in the far right-hand corner, staring out at the St. Louis city landscape, they saw the unmistakeable profile of Yushi Yakamoto. They weaved their way over through the crowd and stood either side of him. As he was grabbed by the arm, Yushi looked up in surprise as Moores said one word to him: "Gotcha!"

CHAPTER 14

(FRIDAY, 24TH APRIL, 1981)

Yushi's Conviction

With the whole nation dismayed by increased crime rates, the police were under pressure from the political establishment to show that their crime-solving record was keeping pace with the times. The 'encouragement' filtered down to federal, state, county and municipal forces across the land, and none more so than in the areas around Paris, Illinois, where the case of Yushi Yakamoto had become notorious.

John Moores was all too aware of the need for him to achieve positive arrest and conviction results, especially as he was eager to gain promotion. He wanted to make it easy for his bosses to choose him over other candidates for any positive career move, maybe even a pathway to the world of politics where he had a chance of making much more money than his current pay level allowed.

The public was understandably appalled by the brutal killing of Sandy Beach, and the press capitalised on the case's notoriety. Copy-editors looked for a hook that would sell newspapers, and unanimously settled on dubbing the story 'The Bike Radio Murder'.

With the four-word strap-line catching on, it wasn't long before it became the story that everyone wanted to read. As the coverage of the crime grew, Moores had felt under even greater pressure to conclude the case and gain a conviction, sooner rather than later. It was true that Yushi Yakamoto was his main, and only, suspect.

He had carefully considered all the basic elements of the Sandy Beach case—although not over much time. Certainly, Moores couldn't help agreeing with Officer Booth's sentiments that Yakamoto had come across as an okay kind of individual, but despite protesting his innocence throughout all questioning, the facts spoke for themselves, indicating that he was the killer.

A week after a surprised Yushi had been apprehended, Moores churned the facts over in his biased mind. One: Yakamoto had been present at Ms. Beach's house—his fingerprints were all over the place. Two: the bike radio used to hit her belonged to him. Detective work uncovered that he'd purchased it from his home town of Allentown the week before he set off on his aborted cross-country journey. And there were a number of fingerprints on the broken pieces of plastic, including his. Three: there was semen on Beach's bed, and matching traces in her body. They were likely to be Yakamoto's, according to the autopsy report that forensics expert Copeland had written, again confirming his presence at the house.

The chief left his office for a moment to get a coffee from the vending machine in the corridor, then returned to his desk. Opening Katie Copeland's report, he continued with his summation of the circumstantial evidence. Four: the report also said the woman's body was badly bruised at the top of her thigh. With Yakamoto's legs so strong, he was easily capable of causing such an injury. He probably gave Beach a hard kick for good measure after smashing her head with the radio. Five: they found no hard evidence of anyone else being present at the house at the time. Six: Yakamoto's profile; he was a loner, he had few friends, and no job. He was just a no-good bum, travelling through Paris at the wrong time for Sandy Beach.

Then Moores' bias went into overdrive; "And what sort of crazy guy drifts across the country on a pedal bicycle? My guess is that he happened by chance upon the vulnerable woman, he screwed her, they had an argument, she told him to leave, and then he lost the plot and killed her in a fit. Then the bastard casually goes to the motel she'd booked for him after departing the scene and leaves her for dead in a pool of blood."

Moores had made his mind up, talking to himself in the sanctity of his glass-screened office. "Yakamoto's a goddamn, schizophrenic, psychopathic killer, counting on us to believe he's as sweet as apple pie. He's a damned Jap as well. Sweet Yushi, indeed! Jeez." Despite his privately-confessed racist tendencies, Moores had been trying hard to concentrate on only the facts of the case, and to condemn his contemptuous opinion of the Japanese to the back of his mind, but try as he might, he found it impossible.

***

(TUESDAY, 17TH NOVEMBER, 1981)

Yakamoto was held in custody for seven long months after he'd been arrested, until the day of his trial in mid-November. After the initial flurry of excitement directly following the murder and subsequent manhunt, the newspaper activity had inevitably died down during the period following the crime. But with the trial looming on the horizon, once again the 'Bike Radio Murder' became the focus of everyone's attention.

No one had been following the case in the media more closely than Hannah Baltzwinik-Toporofski. Naturally, she was terribly upset by what had happened to her unfortunate neighbour, but she was ashamed to admit that she had quite enjoyed the attention accorded her, especially by the television news crews who interviewed her on no fewer than five separate occasions. She was filmed outside her own house, outside Sandy's front door, in Sandy's back yard, and twice inside Sandy's kitchen. With each reporter's interview, she found a new way to describe the same event—the discovery of Sandy's body.

When the local stations and newspapers began ramping up their coverage in advance of the upcoming court activity, Hannah became excited that she may have more opportunities to appear on TV. But alas for her, it wasn't to be. Reporters had now moved on to film outside the courthouse, and only still photographs of Sandy's house were used. Hannah's disappointment turned to remorse and some shame at her own selfishness; it dawned on her that while she was being denied the chance of another TV appearance, poor Sandy had been denied her life. Churning over her memories of what had actually happened that horrible day when she'd discovered Sandy's lifeless body, Hannah drifted into a kind of sub-consciousness.

As she replayed the events in her mind's eye, slowly, the fuzzy image came to her of the old pickup truck she'd seen edging along the road on that early morning. Then she gradually realised that she may have seen a similar truck in Sandy's drive once or twice in the days before she was killed. Maybe it was the same one? "Oh, I'm so useless when it comes to cars, I barely know what my own looks like," she thought. But as she reflected some more, she quizzed herself; hadn't she heard some shouting as well? When had that been exactly? Two days before she'd discovered poor Sandy? The day she'd been murdered? It could have been either–or even both. "Oh my, I just can't be sure. I'm becoming so confused and forgetful these days," she puzzled. "But oh, my Lord, this could be important." She wished she could have talked it all over with Daniel, but he was out collecting sewing machines. She ought to make a call. "Now where did I put that policeman's card? I know it's here somewhere." After finding it, she nervously picked up the phone and dialled the number printed on it.

It was the morning before the trial when Moores was contacted by the woman he found easier to remember as 'Mrs. Baltop'. She hadn't been particularly articulate on the phone, but he reluctantly went over to Paris to see her. Now back at his office, he pondered some more. To be blunt, he was annoyed that Baltop had left it this long to call, but anyhow what she'd told him was of not much use anyway. She may have seen a vehicle, and she may well have heard raised voices.

Investigating this further would undoubtedly lead nowhere, decided Moores. He had nothing firm to go on, it would delay proceedings unnecessarily. "And, besides, we already know who did it," he justified his inaction to himself. He ran things through in his head, concluding that Mrs. Baltop was probably pissed off that she hadn't been asked to appear in court—she's just missing being in the limelight. Moores remembered how she had repeatedly asked him whether he'd seen her on the television news, like she was some goddamn film star! "I bet she'd been going through her wardrobe, picking what to wear outside the courthouse for the reporters."

In truth, Moores really wanted to come away from the courtroom at the end of the trial with another conviction under his belt, and today's interview with Mrs. Baltop was just a distraction he could do without. He gently closed the folder containing his meeting notes, bent down and slipped it in between a stack of other folders piled high on the floor next to his desk.

The next day, at the courtroom in the town of Decatur, south-central Illinois, on a rainy afternoon, the Prosecution summarised the police evidence to the jury. Yushi's parents and sister were in the visitors' gallery, sobbing. The alleged perpetrator stood in the dock, head hung low as the judge finally received the verdict and read it out, passing sentence.

"Yushi Yakamoto, you have been found guilty of murder, and you will remain at Joliet Correctional Center until such time as when you will be put to death by lethal injection. Take him down."

Yushi had already predicted that there would be no fairy godmother coming to aid him in his hour of need, but nevertheless, the judge's words broke him. It had been his grave misfortune, as had been outlined to him by his lawyer, that although the US Supreme Court had halted all death sentences in 1972, that decision had been reversed in 1974. The Illinois legislature had reinstated the death penalty by lethal injection that same year. Yushi sank to his knees, whispering prayers in Japanese words that his grandfather had taught him, as he was lifted to his feet by the courthouse assistants, and led away.

The newspapers were euphoric in their headlines. '*BIKE RADIO*

KILLER IS SWITCHED OFF', was one. '*CAUGHT BIKE-RADIO HANDED*', read another. But '*JUDGE TURNS DOWN THE RADIO KILLER*', was Moores' favourite.

The papers were spread neatly upon his desk like trophies. Leaning back in his chair and with a wry smile, he clasped his hands behind his head, anticipating the promotion that would surely follow.

How It All Ended

As often as they possibly could, Yushi's family visited him at Joliet, although the journey from their home in Allentown was a tiring 1,500 mile round trip and took days to travel by car. It was easier to take a domestic flight, but as one year went in to the next, whatever means of transport had been chosen, the stress and strain for his father was becoming intolerable, and failing health eventually prevented him from visiting his son. Yushi's mother, although with physical strength greater than her husband's, found the visits terribly traumatic, and eventually had to pass the duty to Mitori—Yushi's younger sister by five years.

Yushi continued protesting his innocence to anyone who might be prepared to listen. Finally, he came to the conclusion that it wasn't doing much good. "Everybody's innocent in here," remarked one of his fellow inmates nonchalantly, shrugging his shoulders when Yushi tried to engage him in conversation.

Birthdays, Thanksgivings and Christmases continued to pass by without celebration. Even his sister Mitori's wedding to her fiancé Jerry had to be missed. Another milestone in Yushi's life came and went, when he was informed of the passing of his parents within months of each other, seven years following his incarceration. Now there was only one living soul who truly believed him to be innocent of murdering Sandy Beach. And that was Mitori, now 23 years old.

In the confines of prison, Yushi did his best to make the most of the life he had while remaining on so-called Death Row, cruelly never knowing when his time was going to be up. As the years went by, he began to believe that this would remain his fate forever, and that his execution date may never come. That would at least be something, he thought, remembering his beloved grandfather's teachings about respecting the value of all life.

Taking advantage of the prison facilities that were available to those who behaved well, Yushi did his best to conform to the rules so that he could enjoy using the gym, the library, the games room and the television room. Remaining always a loner, he had only one inmate who he considered to be anyone more than just an enforced acquaintance, his cellmate M.J. Emanuele, who liked to call himself '*The Assassin*'.

Yushi developed an interest in politics and current affairs, and one afternoon, while in the Television Room watching the regional news, he recognised a face on the screen. Bolting upright to pay greater attention, he saw that the bulletin was about Governor John Moores. The same Moores who had been his arresting police chief ten years previous. Although the sound on the TV set was turned down too low for Yushi to catch every word of the commentary, the images showed Moores being led away by a number of other men. Underneath the TV pictures, the words scrolling along the bottom read 'GOVERNOR ARRESTED IN CORRUPTION AND RACISM SCANDAL . . . SOME PREVIOUS CONVICTIONS TO BE REVIEWED'.

The next time he had a visit from his sister he told her what he'd seen on the news that day, and asked her to find out all she could so that he might argue that he'd been a victim of Moores's racist bias against him. Yushi knew all along for a fact that there had been another man at Sandy's house when she was killed. And it was his bet that Moores probably knew it as well.

Unfortunately for Yushi, Mitori's attempts to link Moores's anti-Japanese behaviour with Yushi's conviction were fruitless. The state authorities, many of who were in office during Moores's heyday, wanted no further embarrassing miscarriages of justice to come to the fore. The Review Board decided there was insufficient evidence to warrant re-opening the notorious 'Bike Radio Murder' case. Without him knowing it, time for Yushi was beginning to run out.

Seven months later, on Friday, 14th June, 1996, as he helplessly watched the lethal concoction of drugs being injected into his arm, Yushi Yakamoto reflected on whether his decision to keep his

Japanese name had perhaps been an unfortunate one. Perhaps, if he'd changed it to the all-American-sounding Stephen Josh Mote, just as he'd contemplated doing when he was younger, his fate may have had a different outcome.

PART TWO

OLIVER GOES TO AMERICA

CHAPTER 15

(MONDAY, 6TH APRIL, 2015)
WIVENHOE, ESSEX, UK

Island Vacation

America. Oliver couldn't believe it. So far, the furthest he'd ever been on holiday was to Spain. And that trip hardly counted because it was with school when he was 13, and he didn't enjoy it at all, thanks to a grotty overnight stop near Dover and a 20-hour coach journey, with the ferry crossing so rough it made him sick the whole way. And then there was the one family trip to France a year later but, at that time, they were such a dysfunctional unit, it was more like an endurance test than a holiday.

Nowadays, his family life was more settled, and Oliver's father was trying to make up for his son's unhappy childhood. After demonstratively clicking the final keys on his laptop computer, he announced with a big grin that he'd booked them a two-week summer holiday in Florida.

Thoughts of sunshine, beaches, palm trees and swimming filled Oliver's head. He couldn't concentrate on much else as he counted down the days towards the time when they'd be setting off on their British Airways flight to Tampa. He'd methodically Googled everything he could, and spent further hours viewing YouTube films of Anna Maria Island—the place off the west coast where his dad had arranged to rent a house, complete with its own private swimming pool, no less. He enthusiastically imagined in *his* mind's eye all the oversized, overpowered cars that were commonplace in the videos. To say he was excited was an understatement.

He hoped that he'd be able to indulge in his passion there—cycling—an activity that he could proudly claim to be very good at. After all, he'd been practising a lot around his home town of Wivenhoe, near Colchester in Essex. If he went out early enough in the mornings, before the dog-walkers were about, he'd power himself along the river path to Alresford Creek, reaching some impressively high speeds, according to the Garmin tracker fitted on his bike. Oliver liked his gadgets.

Oliver, by now a 17-year old student, was enjoying living in Essex. Primarily, his life was wrapped up in his academic work, as he had studied hard at school for his exams in a number of subjects, managing to pass several GCSEs. His dad had encouraged him to continue his education with A level studies at college, which he was now doing. He had chosen English Literature and Sociology, and liked them both, but not equally. English was by far his favourite.

Perhaps this was on account of his father. Just a few years previously, his dad had indulged his own passion for writing when his autobiographical book *Muddy Water* was published. Maybe, because of *Muddy Water* and the exposure to the literary world, Oliver now harboured a desire to become a journalist. He even dreamed of one day having his own newspaper column, perhaps editing a magazine, maybe even writing his own book. Very often, when in an everyday situation, his mind would conjure up some fictitious tale to fit the reality; he relished developing the characters and plots, weaving his ideas into a number of short stories.

He began submitting various essays and stories to newspapers and magazines, local and national. From most of them, he heard nothing, but occasionally he would get a reply from a features editor here, or a publisher's secretary there. Usually, the letter or email contained a polite 'thanks but no thanks', suggesting that he contact them again in the future after having gained some further practical experience. "Very helpful. Not!" thought a frustrated Oliver. But he did receive a couple of much more encouraging replies, with one even enquiring whether he had any other work that could be submitted. "Your work is 'quite promising'," was the exact phrase used in the email he received. Of course, Oliver did enthusiastically send more, and waited patiently for an answer that unfortunately never came.

Oliver maturely told himself that he had his whole life ahead of him. He philosophically reasoned that he'd be receiving many more rejections before getting that one lucky break that mattered. Meanwhile, he would concentrate on his studies, and with his holiday to Florida looming, for now he would look forward to enjoying his 2015 summer break from college, while continuing to research the cycle-ways of Anna Maria Island.

During this extensive Florida research, he discovered to his delight that, yes, he'd be able to hire a bike, and not just any old bike at that. As he scrolled the pages on his iPhone, he found there were a number of bike shops situated along the Anna Maria Island coast road. For only $35 a day, Oliver could rent a Cannondale, one of the best bikes he knew of. He pictured himself riding along that very road, and had to pinch himself that it would soon all be a reality.

There were only a few short weeks to go. Oliver counted down the days.

***

(SATURDAY, 6TH JUNE, 2015)
ANNA MARIA ISLAND, FLORIDA, USA

The day Oliver had been waiting impatiently for finally came on the first Saturday of June. For Oliver, who had never flown previously, the sheer size of the British Airways 747 was overwhelming. He understood the basic theory of aircraft thrust and lift, but was still astounded that something so huge could possibly remain above the clouds, transporting hundreds of passengers so smoothly, and in complete comfort, to a destination on the other side of the world.

Relaxing into his seat, he watched three whole movies back to back. *Godzilla* kept him amused, *Snakes on a Plane* kept him looking across the aisle, and *The Blues Brothers* kept him laughing all the way through. Then he flicked through the various in-flight music channels that were on offer. A self-imposed country-music initiation came via the songs of Dwight Yoakham and Tim McGraw, and he concluded that he didn't much care for either. Nevertheless, viewing the accompanying pictures, he figured that as he would soon be in the land of the Stetson hat, he'd better grow to like it.

En-route from Tampa airport in the very cool, yellow, open-topped Mustang his dad had rented, more country sounds blared from every station on the stereo, and this time Oliver got what the American way was all about—a sense of freedom. They cruised along Freeway 75 towards the massive bridge that would carry them onto the island, with the sun shining brightly behind them. The cloud-free sky was clear blue, the car's air-conditioning blasted out cold air—and the whole experience of seeing this country for the first time was truly exhilarating for the impressionable young Oliver.

One hour later, their built-in satnav had guided them to the front door of the large house that would become their home for the next 14 days. "Wow! Is this where we'll be staying?" Oliver asked, not quite believing his eyes, being more used to the density of the small houses packed into the narrow streets of his Wivenhoe home town. He tried to hold back his elation as his dad turned the key in the front door. Once inside the large hallway leading to a massive open-plan kitchen and lounge, Oliver gazed at the TV screen, larger than any he'd ever seen. As he walked around the room, taking in his surroundings, he pressed a button on the wall. First there was a click, then the low hum of a motor, as the ceiling-to-floor vertical blind swished slowly to the right, revealing a window the width and height of the whole room.

Having seen pictures of the house on the internet, he already knew that there was a swimming pool, but the photos didn't do it justice. Oliver's jaw dropped at what he saw. The garden was surrounded by palm trees, and there was a barbecue and outdoor kitchen at one end, with the pool at the other. There were steps leading down into the clear water, past a fountain constantly cascading a gentle trickle into the pool. Surrounding the pool were chairs, tables and more sun-loungers than he could count at first sight—and all this was for just the two of them! He reckoned this was going to be some holiday, as he stepped outside to immerse himself in the sounds, the humid heat and the ambiance.

"Right," said his father. "Let's go and see the sea!" Oliver nodded his approval, especially as he recalled that the local bike rental shop was just across the street from the house, near the entrance to Holmes Beach.

Less than ten minutes later, Oliver was standing among at least twenty bicycles; drop-handlebar lightweight racers, tough fat-tyred mountain bikes, and hybrids with their upright seating position and medium-sized wheels. He decided on a hybrid, and made arrangements with the proprietor to return the following morning to collect it. Being reminded that he should also bring his passport "for the paperwork," he loved the man's deep American drawl. Of course he'd heard the accent plenty of times in films and TV shows at home, but somehow this was different. It was real.

On exiting the shop, having been instructed by the man to "have a good day now," Oliver and his dad wandered slowly in the heat towards the beach entrance, past a café-bar built of bamboo selling 'HOT-DOG AND COLA FOR $5', according to the placard outside, which they both settled on having while staring out towards the ocean. The sea was a light blue, and the soft sand pure white. And with a 17-year-old's hormones rushing around his body, it was impossible for Oliver not to notice the many beautiful, bikini-clad, golden-tanned beach babes that could be observed in every direction. Was he in paradise? He wondered whether cycling and swimming mightn't be his only holiday activities.

After their long flight, father and son were both feeling tired, and the heat didn't help. "Let's go back to the house now, get settled and take a quick nap," suggested his father. "Then we can go to the shop to pick up some things for dinner. How do you fancy if we barbecue some burgers by the pool?" His dad's idea suited Oliver very well, and they left the beach to trudge in the heat back to the welcome lower air-conditioned temperature inside their temporary new home.

After unpacking cases and generally familiarizing themselves with their new surroundings, feeling refreshed after their short rest, it was time to venture out again to the shop, this time in the Mustang. After pulling into the Publix Supermarket car park, they headed to the shop's entrance to buy provisions for the next few days. Oliver was in awe at the variety of food products in brightly-coloured packaging, many of which he never even knew existed. With Oliver grabbing items off the shelf in a mild frenzy, his father eventually urged him to control his enthusiasm, and they left the shop carrying only two bags full, although Oliver could easily have filled ten. He reached inside the brown paper sack and pulled out one of his purchases to try—a packet of Combos. "I'll be coming back for more of these, Dad," he said with a smile, after biting into the cheese-filled pretzel pieces. "Here—try one!"

While munching on Combos, they stood in front of an area outside where the supermarket trollies were stored, looking at a large community board on the wall, with various advertisements pinned to it informing patrons of upcoming local events. Oliver's father, eager to explore the area in the days to come, noticed one particular sign. 'FLEA-MARKET. THIS SUNDAY, 10AM. *SKINNY'S* PARKING LOT, 39TH ST'

"That's tomorrow. What do you think, Oli?" asked his dad, keen to persuade his son to go with him, but knowing he was unlikely to be interested in looking through piles of other people's junk.

"Hmm, I think I might rest in, Dad. You know, jet-lag and all that," came the answer that his dad preferred not to hear.

Deciding not to push it for now, Oliver's dad opted to just get home and start the barbecue—but not before saying a few words that he knew would get under Oliver's skin. "Okay, son. But whatever *Skinny's* is, it could be fun. And don't forget the FOMO!"

CHAPTER 16

(SUNDAY, 7TH JUNE, 2015)

Key Bargain

Oliver's father had known exactly that any mention of FOMO, or the 'Fear of Missing Out' would render his son unable to resist joining him that Sunday morning. Having woken earlier than anticipated, they were both relieved. Thankfully, the different time zone they were now in appeared to have had little adverse effect on their personal body clocks. Being greeted by another beautiful, cloudless sky, over breakfast Oliver's father was met with a very unusual request.

"Dad. I've been thinking . . ." Oliver began cautiously. "When we're out, can I call you by your name, and not 'Dad'? It would make me feel older than I am, and . . ." Although initially surprised by Oliver's request, his father was positively flattered by what his son said next. ". . . and I'd feel like we were more, err, you know, kind of, sort of, mates!"

Not being able to come up with any off-the-cuff objections, Leslie Markland nodded slowly and agreed. "Okay son," he said.

"Thanks, Dad," Oliver replied, relieved that that small discussion had gone so well. He was already imagining chatting up those tanned girls on the beach, or anywhere else for that matter, and he hadn't wanted to come across like the schoolboy that he actually still was.

"Right then," Leslie prompted, clearing up the cereal bowls. "Let's go and find where or what *Skinny's* is. And also see what interesting things we might pick up from the flea-market." Despite Oliver over-emphasising his false sigh, he was looking forward to going there, especially now that he'd satisfactorily resolved the little awkward question he'd been afraid of asking.

Checking the tourist map, they discovered that 39th Street was only a short walk from the house, almost opposite the bike shop. "Well, we may as well collect the bike while we're out," suggested Oliver, and off they went, dressed in shorts, t-shirts and trainers. Having completed all the necessary paperwork at the shop, Oliver was soon pushing his new machine along the pavement, hardly able to contain his urge to leap on it and ride off along the beachside path. Instead, he walked along with his dad until they reached *Skinny*'s.

There was a large wooden board outside a ramshackle house proclaiming its full name, '*SKINNY'S PLACE*', serving their so-called 'Number 1 Burgers'. Rough and ready tables and chairs, pots, umbrellas, palm trees and a menu blackboard were dotted around the bright blue-painted exterior. Leslie peeked inside. Huge ceiling fans whirred around slowly, hardly creating any draft, but nevertheless the interior provided welcome shade from the scorching sun. Even at this early hour, a number of sunglass-wearing men and women stood or sat at the bar counter, protectively holding their ice-cold beers, hands wrapped around the frosty glasses, as they chatted, laughed and generally passed their Sunday morning doing nothing too energetic.

Making a mental note that they should go there later for lunch, Leslie was still none the wiser about the location of the flea-market. He was informed by one of the waitresses that they needed only to continue a few yards past *Skinny's* and they would see its location in the car park at the side of the building. So, they stepped outside and, sure enough, there it was, thronging with people busily setting up their stalls and preparing the displays of their many items for sale.

Curious passers-by mingled with the more serious collectors, as they browsed the bric-a-brac, posters, second-hand clothes, watches, coins, embroidered tablecloths, and a host of other handcrafted items. This was exactly what Leslie had been hoping for, and Oliver was surprised to find himself equally interested in having a good look at what was on offer. Whereas his dad was specifically seeking some presents to take home for friends, Oliver was more keen on finding something for himself—something American, maybe something historic, definitely something that would remind him of his visit.

Carefully locking his bike to a lamppost, using the long, heavy-duty chain provided by the shop, he began his search by meticulously leafing through every poster in the rack of one stall, before moving on to sift through the pre-worn t-shirts of another. Then he came to an area that specialised in old car parts, but as much as he'd like to own a grill from an old Chevy, or a tail-light cluster from an Oldsmobile, he had to bear in mind the practical implications of transporting any such purchase on the plane home.

Very happy just looking around and soaking up the pleasant atmosphere, Oliver moved along to another seller's pitch where a lady had a number of flat glass cases spread out on her trestle tables. One of the cases housed thirty or forty medals, another contained hunting knives and a third had a collection of handguns. Oliver was fascinated—he'd never actually seen a real gun before, except the ones worn in the holsters of the policemen patrolling in and around Tampa Airport.

This was more like it, he thought. True to form, he began imagining the circumstances in which the medals, knives and guns had been used in their days of old. As he peered through the glass top, the lady stall-holder with silver hair and rimmed spectacles spotted his interest and came up to talk to the young man who looked intently at what she had on offer.

Apart from the bike-shop man, this was the first American that Oliver had engaged in conversation with, and he found himself drawn again to the accent. But the stallholder was equally fascinated to listen to Oliver speak. They began to chat, with Oliver explaining he was visiting the island on holiday from England. "Oh, gee!" said the lady, turning to her friend working at the next table. "Did you hear that, Jean? This young man is all the way from Engerland!" Then addressing Oliver again, she asked a question that made Oliver laugh. "Now tell me, is that anywhere near Scartland? I've always wan-ned to go there."

Jean then came over to join them, and Oliver found he enjoyed being the centre of their attention. "Oh my, have you been to Bucking-haam Palace? Now that's in London, isn't that so?" asked Jean.

"Yes, it is. And yes, I have been there, but only to see the Changing of the Guard," he admitted, although sorely tempted to say 'yes' to Jean's next question about whether he'd met the Queen. As he continued lapping up the inquisition, he casually looked along the length of Jean's table at the wooden boxes and more glass cases on it. One particular display cabinet caught his attention more than the others, and he moved over to it.

"You can open it, if you want," said Jean. "Have a good look at them. They've all got a story to tell."

That was exactly the same sentiment he'd been thinking himself, as Oliver delicately lifted the glass lid until it was resting back on its hinges. Inside were perhaps as many as a hundred different old keys of all shapes, colours and sizes. Some were in bunches, held together with wire rings, but most were singular, laying in a jumbled mess on top of each other. Oliver picked some up at random and examined each one in turn. Where were they from? What was behind the doors that they locked? Some of the largest appeared quite ancient, made of iron or other metal, now rusted and pitted, perhaps used on gates at some slave trader's mansion, or maybe to secure bank vaults in the Wild West. Oliver was drifting into his imaginary world, thinking up any number of possible yarns to match each of the keys in his hand.

As he pondered more and more, he wondered if any keys had identifying letters or numbers on them. He rummaged through the entire collection, individually turning them to scrutinise further. Curiously, there was only one single key in the entire collection that had any identification markings, and Oliver began examining it with great curiosity. It was at least 15 centimetres in length, almost completely flat except for some grooves cut along the shaft, and the handle was almost as large as Oliver's palm. Not only was it one of the largest keys in the cabinet, it was perhaps also the shiniest and, as if possessed by the key itself, Oliver felt a wave of euphoria flow through him. He knew immediately that he wanted to buy it, but he didn't have a clue why. Maybe it was simply because it looked good, and would be a cool souvenir to take home with him back to Essex.

Oliver was also mildly curious to learn more about the key, its history and where it was from. As the journalistic, inquisitorial person in him came to the fore, his mind raced. What if he could actually discover which lock this key opened? Perhaps the key had an interesting story to tell. Maybe something he might write about, he pondered. An essay, a short story—or even a book? He was dancing cartwheels in his head!

Noticing the trance-like state the young man now appeared to be in, Jean brought her potential customer firmly back to the real world. "I'm not entirely sure what that one is, but you're welcome to have it for only $35." Oliver gulped, and reluctantly began returning it with the others. Observing the sad look on his face, Jean was nevertheless eager to make a sale, her first of the day. She rarely sold any of her keys ever, and had vowed never to buy a job lot of them again, as was the case with this load. To her it wasn't a collection, it was an encumbrance.

"How much have you got? Why don't you make me a sensible offer?" she suggested. Oliver was aware that he actually had $25 in notes in his right pocket, and a handful of coins in the other. He thought he'd try his luck, picking a number from the air less than twenty. "I've got $17," he said, not actually telling a lie. Jean held the back of her hand to her forehead feigning a nervous attack, but with a friendly smile as well. "I wouldn't normally do this, but as you've been so charming, it's a deal!"

Oliver, extremely pleased with his excellent negotiating skill he never knew he possessed, paid up, and shook Jean's hand. She certainly had a firm grasp. "I don't suppose you can tell me anything about the key, can you?" he asked, somewhat timidly. It would take him a while, he thought, to become as forthright as people like Jean. "Anything at all would be really useful," he went on, not overly expecting to obtain any further information from the lady.

But, keen to help her customer, Jean surprised him by calling across to her friend from the first memorabilia stall, as she retrieved the key from Oliver's hand, and inspected it some more. "Pat, have you got any clue what these words might mean? Our young man here wants to know."

Pat came over and took her turn at studying the flat, brass-coloured piece of metal. The rounded oval shape at the top contained a large letter 'A' in the centre, with the words 'FOLGER ADAM CO.' engraved above. "Well, let's see," said Pat, who seemed to know more about keys than Jean did. "I'm afraid I don't have any inkling about 'Folger Adam'," she said, but went on.

Oliver was enthralled by what he heard next, and he had no doubt that he'd just spent the best $17 possible. Pat continued; "See this here?" she said, pointing at the engraving beneath the 'A'. "I know this place—my cousin lived there when he worked as a guard before he passed. The letters 'ILL' are short for the state of 'Illinois', and 'JOLIET' is the name of the town. I think you've just bought yourself a prison key!"

CHAPTER 17

(SUNDAY, 7TH – WEDNESDAY, 10TH JUNE, 2015)

Beach Baby

Leslie and Oliver both agreed that the burger at *Skinny's* really was 'NUMBER 1', as the sign outside had claimed. While Oliver was devouring his meal, he was unsure what he most wanted to do afterwards. He'd been eagerly waiting for what seemed like ages to take a ride on his Cannondale, but now he was also very keen to return to the unlimited broadband connection in the house, so that he could research his new acquisition. He settled on doing the ride first, then returning to his dad later, who he'd spend the remaining part of the day with at the poolside.

In some ways, the terrain along the coast road was similar to the one on the Wivenhoe track back home. Both were flat and straight, running parallel to water, and both were equally exhilarating. The big difference was the heat and humidity in Florida. In Wivenhoe, although often in its own pleasant microclimate, the temperature averaged 22 degrees in the summer. But here, it was a whole ten degrees higher. Even cycling at a steady ten miles an hour and creating his own breeze, within minutes, sweat would be covering him from head to toe. But who cares? thought Oliver, as he weaved his way along the beach paths. With incredible views of the sea, the sand, and wonderful bird-life, the excessive heat didn't bother him.

After completing several miles and arriving back at the pool, he found that his dad had fallen asleep on one of the loungers, a contented and relaxed look on his face. Not wishing to disturb him from his nap, Oliver fetched his iPad, changed into his swimming shorts and quietly joined his dad on an adjacent sunbed. The only sound that could be heard was the trickle of the water cascade.

Oliver began researching keys, and quickly disturbed the peace with a yell that instantly woke his father. "Huh? Uh? What's going on? What's the matter?" Sitting bolt upright, for an instant, Leslie didn't know where he was, or what was happening.

Oliver didn't answer at first, but just carried on scrolling through various web pages, engrossed in what he was reading. Eventually, he answered slowly while still taking in the details of his search for 'Joliet prison' on Google. "Sorry, Dad. I didn't mean to wake you up," he apologised. "But I'm amazed about the old key I bought at the flea market. Coincidence or what?"

Not knowing what his son was talking about, Leslie asked him to at least give him a clue. "Dad, on the plane I watched three films, one of them was *The Blues Brothers*," Oliver slowly began explaining, while continuing to read. "Well . . . you just wouldn't believe it . . . hang on a minute . . . it's incredible . . ."

"*What?* What's incredible?" demanded Leslie, now slightly peeved at having his sleep interrupted by this blather, and listening to yet another very long drawn out pause. "Son. Spit it out!"

"Well. In the film, Elwood Blues comes out of prison, to be met by his brother Jake," Oliver began thoughtfully. "No, hang on, it was Jake that came out, and Elwood was waiting outside," he paused, hesitating.

"*Get on with it!*" his dad demanded, half joking, half serious.

Oliver took the hint. "Okay, Dad, keep your hair on," he laughed, before holding up his flea-market bargain as if it would explain all. "At the beginning of the story, Jake comes out of prison. It's the very-same actual prison that this key comes from!" He'd finally managed to convey his discovery to his dad, who now paid greater attention.

"Let me see that thing," Leslie said, stretching out his arm and beckoning for the key to be passed to him. Analysing it closely, he looked carefully at the top part of the key, now as curious as Oliver. Reading 'JOLIET. ILL.' and guessing 'ILL.' meant 'Illinois', he then looked further down the key's blade. "I wonder what these markings mean. '410A'? Maybe it's a cell number or something?" he said, with raised eyebrows.

"I don't know, Dad," taking back the key and screwing up his eyes to look at the tiny engraved markings. "But I'm going to do my best to find out," he asserted.

"I'm sure you will, son. I'm sure you will," replied Leslie, knowing fully well that once Oliver got the bit between his teeth, he rarely let go. He guessed that next his son would be requesting that they actually go to Joliet. Laying back to soak up some more rays, Leslie already knew what his answer was going to be. He hoped it wouldn't cause a conflict between them, but aware that Illinois was such a long way from Florida, it would have to be a firm 'No!' The warm sun finally took control and he drifted back to the pleasant dream he was living in a few minutes earlier.

Later, while Leslie cooked their poolside meal, and Oliver quietly prepared the salad, the question Leslie was expecting was sure enough posed by his son. "Oliver, where exactly is Joliet?" Leslie began to respond.

Not wanting to discourage Oliver's natural interest, but equally appreciating that a journey of such distance would not be a practical possibility, he continued: "Hmm, so it's near Chicago, is it? Have you any idea how far that is? It must be over a thousand miles from here. It may not look far on a Google map, but this is a big country. It would take us days to get there, and we're only here for a two-week holiday!"

Oliver, although mildly disappointed, accepted his dad's logic without further argument, much to the surprise of Leslie. Being honest, he also didn't really want to spend most of their holiday in a car, even as nice as the Mustang was. "I know. You're right, Dad," conceded Oliver. "But maybe I could come back after I've finished my A levels."

"Yes, maybe you could, son." Leslie returned to the business of evenly browning the chicken wings, and wondered whether

Oliver would remember this conversation once they were back in Wivenhoe. Knowing his son as he did, he guessed that he would.

***

As they settled nicely into their holiday, their mornings would alternate between having breakfast at home by the pool and going out to eat at one of the many restaurants on the island serving huge dishes that would keep them going until their evening meal. Then, they might go their separate ways, with Oliver cycling off to explore another section of the island. Leslie was simply content just to relax by the pool, maybe walk across to Holmes Beach and swim in the ocean, have a beer, and listen to the sounds of crashing waves intermingling with the cries of the egrets that could be seen all along the sand. He'd had a tough couple of years, what with one thing and another back home, and he felt he really needed this break to unwind and do very little else.

Oliver, on the other hand, was energetic and restless, keen to fill his time with as much activity as he could. This of course meant cycling dozens of miles, the length and breadth of the island, sometimes rather enviously watching the groups of people his age on the beaches, as they chatted and laughed, some of them throwing a Frisbee between them, some of them playing volleyball on a makeshift court. He couldn't imagine how they were able to dart about in the sweltering heat, but nevertheless they did. He wished he had the courage to openly engage in conversation with strangers, just like Jean and Pat had done with him at the flea market. In truth, he felt a little, well, lonely.

Oliver needn't have worried. A minor miracle happened and his wish was granted! "Hey! Wanna join in? We need one more," called out one of the girls to him as she held up a volleyball from where she stood on the beach.

At first, Oliver looked behind him, assuming her question was being addressed to someone else. "No. I mean you, stupid!" she scorned, in fun.

"I'd love to. Thank you," Oliver replied, leaning his bike against a palm tree and walking towards them.

"*Thank you!!!*" falsely mocked the girl. "How frightfully proper! I do say, are you British by any chance?" she asked, imitating his accent that she recognised from the TV. "I do so love your *Downton Abbey* show, it's one of my favourites of *all* time!" she giggled.

After the grunts, groans and shrieks that emanated from their match, lasting all of ten minutes, Oliver collapsed under the shade of a tree, and was quickly joined by the *Downton Abbey* girl and her friends, all keen to listen to their guest talk to them. Being somewhat more in tune with world affairs than the two women at the flea market, they didn't ask whether Oliver had met the Queen—but they did want to hear about life in England and its capital city, its politics, culture, media and music. Oliver was introduced to all of them in turn, and he took on board the names of the girls more easily than the boys—particularly the very beautiful Sam, the one who'd persuaded him to join them.

Oliver was delighted to have made some new friends, and was hopeful that they might meet again, especially Sam, who didn't appear to be partnered with any of the boys. "Sure thing—we'll be here again tomorrow, same time. Come down if you're free," offered one of the guys, whose name Oliver had already forgotten and was too shy to ask again.

That evening, while Oliver was watching the giant TV after dinner, Leslie noticed that his son was even chirpier and more laid-back than previously. Then, when the words on the television read 'COMING NEXT ON PBS: *DOWNTON ABBEY*', Oliver laughed out loud, and told his dad why.

In bed later, Oliver was excited about the following day and the chance to see Sam again. As was his habit before turning off the light, he picked up his tablet to check his emails, Facebook and Instagram.

It was still open at the internet page on which he'd been researching Joliet prison earlier. He glanced across at the key situated on his bedside cabinet, his very own Florida Key, and he felt a very positive sixth sense feeling. He knew without doubt that the key would be the reason why he'd be returning to America. He just wasn't certain about when, or how, that might be.

CHAPTER 18

(THURSDAY, 11TH – FRIDAY, 12TH JUNE, 2015)

Blossoming Romance

The sun shone in through the bedroom window and woke Oliver even before his 7.00a.m. iPhone alarm, as he'd forgotten to close the curtains the night before. He immediately visualised the day ahead, hoping that, as promised, Sam and the others would be on the beach again. Feeling something cold brush against his arm, he felt around to discover that the Florida Key, as he now called it, had remained on the bed with him throughout the night. Though thoughts of Sam were on his mind, his key and his bike came a close second.

Having arranged to go with his dad to the nearby Peaches Restaurant for breakfast, he waited patiently for his father to rise, and continued with his research as he did so. It was amazing what was on the internet, he thought to himself. From the comfort of his bed, he was able to look up various facts and figures about the institution that first housed inmates in 1858, and finally closed its doors for the last time as an active prison at the turn of the millennium, with many of its former 'guests' being transferred to nearby Stateville Correctional Center. The building had then been left to fall into disrepair, but nowadays, after extensive renovation, it had been turned into a tourist attraction. While the repairs were being carried out, site construction workers would have enjoyed easy pickings of souvenirs to sell on to collectors, who in turn were eager to snap up a piece of the prison's history. Oliver guessed this was how his key had eventually found its way to a Florida flea market several years later.

During its operational years, it would have housed thousands of people, many of them 'lifers'. Once again, Oliver's mind drifted into another space and time, as he speculated what some of these people had served, or were still serving, time for. What were the cells like? What were conditions like?

As he tapped his iPad and scrolled the pages, his fingers held the key's 'bow', the name of the section used to turn the blade, according to the diagram he was looking at. He wondered how many times the guards had turned this particular bow, locking their prisoners behind them? Perhaps even Pat's cousin had!

Each question answered led to another unanswered, and Oliver only had access to some general information that was freely available to the public. But one thing became clear as he continued reading the websites and their statistics about the people who'd lived there, incarcerated for days, months or years—all would have had their own story to tell. Just like Jean had said about the hundreds of different keys in her glass cabinet.

Startled by a knock at the door and the call of his dad alerting him to be ready soon, Oliver closed the cover on his iPad and quickly dressed. Here in Florida, on holiday, it only took seconds to find a t-shirt to go with his shorts and sandals. Grabbing his phone, he took a rushed photo of his key, planning to show it to Sam later, assuming she'd show up. Hoping very much that she would.

At Peaches, he and his dad enjoyed a very large, and probably quite unhealthy breakfast. Regardless, they both casually ate with abandon—at least this would set them up for the rest of the day. As they ploughed through the bacon, fried egg, hash browns, maple syrup and cream—all piled on the same plates—Oliver told his dad he'd be meeting his volleyball friends later. Leslie couldn't have been more pleased, having hoped that his son might make some friends sooner or later, for one simple reason. Oliver's news alleviated his guilt. All Leslie wanted to do was much the same as he'd done yesterday, and hopefully tomorrow and the next day—absolutely nothing.

Under the same palm tree where he'd sat the day before, Oliver waited for the volleyball players to show up, anxious that they might not. But he needn't have worried, and after playing another exhausting match, they all collapsed on to the sand, and shared out chilled fruit juices and bottled water from their cool bag, including one of each for Oliver.

They chatted some more, revealing more details about themselves. It transpired that they'd all grown up either on Anna Maria, or in nearby Tampa or Sarasota, and they were all students currently on holiday on Anna Maria. Although Sam no longer lived in Florida full-time, her family still owned a house on the other side of the island that they visited every year for their summer vacations. "Why don't you come on over?" she asked Oliver. "It's not far, maybe twenty minutes on your bike. We are close by an inland waterway that you can paddle on, and we've got two kayaks we can take out. It'll be fun, and you can get to meet my folks."

As Oliver was thinking things couldn't be getting any better, they just had, and he gratefully accepted Sam's invitation. "What's your number? I'll text you where it is," she asked, smiling. Seconds later, Oliver's phone went 'ting', and he was looking at a text message from Samantha Dickinson containing a Google map that pinpointed the exact location of her family's house. "Come over around eleven tomorrow and I'll have the kayaks ready."

As he closed the map app on his phone, the photo of his key showed up on the screen. Deciding to save telling Sam about it until tomorrow, he spent the rest of a pleasant afternoon with her and the others, before returning home to his dad, who didn't look like he'd moved since going home after breakfast.

***

Oliver had never kayaked before, even though he lived in Wivenhoe, by the River Colne. When the tide was up, he'd often see canoeists and kayakers paddling, while he cycled along the riverside path, but it had never occurred to him until now that he might like to give it a try. It must have been the holiday air, he told himself, but more likely it was Sam. When he arrived at her house, he was still a little apprehensive as to whether he'd manage okay on the water. Sam sensed his anxiety and did her best to dispel it. "Just follow what I do, and you'll be fine. Come on in the house first, and meet my mother and father," she warmly invited her guest.

Sam had been waiting for him with the same broad smile she always wore, and was keen to introduce her new English friend to her parents, who were standing together in the kitchen. Oliver could see where Sam got her good looks from, observing her mum's beautiful straight, brown hair.

Her father, with bushy black eyebrows and a tall frame, probably a foot taller than his wife, had a rather endearing, permanent friendly grin that made Oliver feel instantly at ease. As they politely shook hands, Sam's mum smiled warmly and demanded that Oliver call them by their first names, Kerry and Chris. Kerry suggested he join them for lunch later on the veranda. "Sometimes, you can sit outside and see the manatees swim. They're just beautiful to watch," she continued.

Oliver didn't know what a manatee was, but not wishing to appear ignorant, he simply said "Really? Wow!" and made a mental note to ask Sam for a 'manatee explanation' later.

Another mental note he made later, after clambering out of his kayak at the end of their paddle, was that he should join the Wivenhoe Canoe and Kayak Club as soon as he returned home. The experience of paddling had been such great fun, and much easier than he'd thought it would be. Not only that, Sam didn't need to explain what a manatee was, because they were lucky enough to have witnessed one in the sea. The slow-moving creature that resembled a small elephant without a trunk, was swimming gracefully under the surface, minding its own business, within just a few yards of their boats. Oliver hadn't expected that an underwater mammal would have made such an impact on his emotions—but he suspected it was more to do with the person he was with than the animal itself.

Sam was also very happy to be with her new companion, and listened attentively as Oliver engagingly answered her parents' questions at the dining table over lunch. Perhaps it was his English accent that she found so charming and attractive, but she also recognised a kind-natured quality in Oliver that she really admired. She hoped that their meeting might lead to more than just the kind of short-lived holiday romance she'd experienced before.

Her parents may as well have been reading her mind, based on how the conversation developed at a rate of knots. There had been something Oliver was plainly keen to talk to Sam about, and the opportunity came up perfectly when asked by Chris about what he wanted to do with his life after completing college. Explaining that his ambition was to become a journalist or writer, Oliver then went on to describe his story of purchasing the key from the flea market. Everyone around the table was fascinated with his account of how he'd felt compelled to buy it, and his subsequent discovery of its origin.

"Well, my! Isn't that a wonder?" exclaimed Kerry. "You know, Joliet isn't too far away from where we live near Indianapolis, Oliver. Probably only about 200 miles. You could come stay with us if you wanted to research more." Chris nodded in agreement. Absolutely delighted with Chris and Kerry's kind offer, Oliver was fast learning that long distances in America meant less than back at home. To travel two hundred miles from Wivenhoe would have been considered a real trek, but here a journey of that distance was just a casual trip up the road, so to speak. He thanked Mr. and Mrs. Dickinson for their invitation, telling them that he would love to do that one day.

That night, Oliver recounted the brilliant day he'd had with Sam and her parents to his dad, while at the same time Googling where exactly Indianapolis was in proximity to other large cities that he'd heard of, like Kansas City, Columbus, St. Louis, Chicago and Cincinnati. Oliver's mind raced ahead, quicker than he could speak, concluding excitedly that he should definitely take up his girlfriend's parents' offer. "Woah! Come on!" Did he just hear himself describe Sam as his '*girlfriend*'? "Don't get ahead of the situation here," he maturely checked himself. "Indianapolis is a world apart from Wivenhoe."

America was indeed an enormous country, he considered, and to have met some people who lived only two hundred miles from where his Florida Key came from must surely be fate. And it would definitely be no hardship spending more time with Sam. As he chuckled happily to himself, he couldn't believe his luck. Now, as well as knowing that he would be coming back, although not knowing precisely when, he at least had a firm idea of how.

CHAPTER 19

(SATURDAY, 13TH – SATURDAY, 20TH JUNE, 2015)

Studious Research

For the rest of the holiday, Sam and Oliver became inseparable. It was a relationship neither of them could have dreamed of. They were good for one another, and the more worldly-wise Sam had an immediate effect on Oliver, who soon stepped up to the mark, quickly maturing far beyond his 17 years of age. They would spend every one of their remaining days together until it was sadly time for Oliver and his dad to leave. Leslie also became a guest of the family as well, having been invited, with Oliver, over for dinner with the Dickinsons on the penultimate evening of their holiday before flying back to London. Oliver had already introduced Sam to his dad when she'd been over for a barbecue by the pool, but Leslie hadn't yet met her parents, and to the relief of the loved-up teenagers, they all got on extremely well.

After a delicious meal on the Dickinson's veranda, with Oliver and Sam pointing out the manatees swimming only yards away, the conversation flowed comfortably. "Leslie," Chris began, puffing on his cigarette. "We, that's Kerry and I, have told Oliver that he's welcome to come back to stay with us whenever he wants, of course with your agreement. We understand he needs to complete his college studies over there in England, but he's also told us so much about his ambition to become a writer, and we'd like to help in any way we can, maybe with his prison key project—it could become a great story, you know. Anyway, it's been a pleasure to get to know him over the last week or so. He's a great kid! And as Sam's parents, it's been real nice to see our daughter so happy." Sam and Oliver went bright red in equal measure.

"Well, I've seen him become quite obsessed with his key, and I know what he's like once he gets a bee in his bonnet. It would be really good for him to have an assignment to work on," Leslie replied.

"A bee in his bonnet, Leslie? Whatever's that?" laughed Kerry, never having heard the expression before.

"Well, you know," Leslie tried to explain, but with the effects of a few glasses of his hosts' rather excellent Napa Valley Merlot running through his veins, he was having some difficulty. "You know, when someone gets a scratch under their skin, and can't stop itching until it's gone. . .no, I didn't mean that. . .when someone can't let a puzzle go until they've solved it. That sort of thing. You know?" Kerry and Chris did know, having heard about Oliver's prison key on several occasions now.

"Well," said Chris, moving on. "As we say, he's always welcome at our home in Plainfield. That's where we live, just outside Indianapolis in the state of Indiana."

"You're very kind. And Sam may like to visit us in Wivenhoe," reciprocated Leslie. That's near London. And of course you're very welcome too," was the most he was able to say without slurring too badly, the effect of the wine nicely dancing around inside his head. Sam looked up, her smile even broader than normal, as she turned expectantly to her mother. Kerry in turn looked at her husband, eyebrows raised, asking the same question but without any words.

"Why, sure!" Mr. Dickinson responded positively to his wife's notion. "Maybe we can figure something out. Christmas shopping in London Town sounds like it could be a lotta fun." Sam and Kerry beamed, and Oliver was thrilled.

It was eleven o'clock and time for Oliver and his father to depart. Wisely having decided beforehand to leave the Mustang at home, after saying their polite goodbyes, they called for the Magic Bus to come, using Oliver's iPhone. They stood outside in the warm night air at the beachside stop, waiting for the free community transportation to arrive.

"What a brilliant idea this is!" said Leslie. "We should have one of these in Wivenhoe, son."

"Yes, but Dad..." a sober Oliver replied. "... In Wivenhoe you can walk everywhere anyway."

"You gotta *point* there!" exclaimed Leslie, laughing at his own non-existent joke, a vague reference to his love of the singer Harry Nilsson that no one else would have understood, except perhaps Oliver. Oliver did get it, and chuckled. Eventually, the multi-coloured hippie-style bus came, and with no fixed fare, its driver only accepted donations in payment. The two Wivenhoe passengers shared the journey with a number of drunken Anna Maria women on their way to a party. For them, the night was just beginning, but for Oliver and Leslie their evening was coming to an end.

Much of Leslie's last day on the island was spent with a hangover, and for Oliver it was a day of sedate sadness. Unfortunately, Sam and her parents had gone away for the day, so last night he'd had to say goodbye to a girlfriend he wouldn't see again in quite a while. He thought back to when he'd first met her, and now there could be no doubt that she was in fact his girlfriend. Until the next time they could be together, they'd just have to make do with seeing each other two-dimensionally, using FaceTime and Skype, and although upset at the prospect of being apart for what seemed forever, Oliver knew philosophically that Christmas would come around soon. He hoped beyond hope that Sam and her parents would be making that shopping trip to London.

Meanwhile, Oliver would use his last day to concentrate on surfing the net for his prevailing Florida Key project. His brain had become like blotting paper, absorbing anything and everything that might be of potential relevance. Each page he read about the prison in Joliet had links to more multiple-page sites containing further information and, before long, his head was spinning. But as he delved deeper and deeper, a thought occurred to him. Could it be remotely possible, he wondered, to learn about any of the inmates housed in the actual cell appertaining to his particular 'Florida Key'. Their names, their crimes, their sentences, even their fate? Were they out of prison now? On parole? Leading new lives?

Oliver was fascinated to think that the real lives of real people had been held in a cell during years gone by, locked by the very key he was holding in his hand today. With only the tiny engraved markings on his key to go on, he knew his quest for this kind of information would be difficult to fulfil. But he was on a true mission now—and one day he would write his book chronicling his findings. Off he went again on another tangent.

As usual, his mind wandered while he flipped between one page and the next. He visualised coming across some deep, dark website containing details of the criminals incarcerated day after day, month after month, year after year. What sort of a life would that be, he speculated? What had their crime been? How old were they when they first entered the jail? And when were they released? If they in fact were released. There were so many questions to be answered. He imagined how awful it must be to lose one's freedom, something he took for granted. Although intrigued beyond words, Oliver decided that for today at least, his last on Anna Maria Island, those thoughts were too depressing, and he forced himself out of his trance-like state. Deciding that he should continue with his internet research back at home in Wivenhoe, he pulled the cover over his iPad and switched it off.

Apart from returning his bike to the shop, and looking forward to going for their last *Skinny*'s burger that evening, Oliver had little else to do except laze by the pool and cast his mind back over what a great holiday he'd had. Every aspect had been perfect. The house, the car, the beaches, the food, the restaurants. His Cannondale had undoubtedly been a great success. He'd even grown to like country music.

But best of all, he'd met a special girl—and he'd also bought a special key.

And none of this would have been possible had it not been for his dad having chosen Anna Maria Island as their holiday destination.

That evening, with Leslie's hangover thankfully gone, he raised his ice-cold beer mug and clinked it with his son's glass of Coke. For him, he'd managed to get the rest and relaxation that he'd sorely needed. It was rewarding to see his son so happy, at last, and he was pleased with how well the two of them had got on together.

"These *Skinny's* burgers really are the Number 1!" Leslie mumbled, almost incoherently, with his mouth full, grinning at the same time. Oliver guessed what his dad was trying to say, and nodded. While waiting to empty his mouth so that he could reply, he suddenly felt a wave of regret come over him, as he remembered asking to call his dad by his name when in public.

"They certainly are number one," Oliver said softly, raising his glass. "Thanks, Dad!"

***

The following morning, after packing cases and leaving the house and its glorious swimming pool for the last time, they headed to Tampa airport, dropping off the fantastic Mustang at the Avis depot. Tickets processed, they waited in the lounge until it was time to board the plane home. Although Oliver felt sad that their holiday had now finally come to an end, he also looked forward to returning home to Wivenhoe, his college and his friends. Settling back in his seat in the huge 747, he pondered over how much bolder, more mature and confident he'd become since meeting Sam.

He leant forward to touch the in-flight entertainment screen in front, and was delighted to see that they were being treated to exactly the same selection of programmes as during their flight from Heathrow. So, after first playing some Dwight Yoakam and Tim McGraw, he then relaxed back to watch one of the films. Without hesitation, Oliver knew exactly which one to choose.

PART THREE

OLIVER IN WIVENHOE, ESSEX, UK

CHAPTER 20

(SUNDAY, 12TH NOVEMBER – THURSDAY, 14TH DECEMBER, 2017)

Job Offer

It had been a very busy and active 18 months for Oliver since his holiday to Anna Maria Island. He turned eighteen in August 2015, two months after their return, and really knuckled down to study hard for his A levels, which the following May he passed with a 'B' in Sociology and an 'A' in English. As well as having success with his academic studies, he had also taken driving lessons while at college, self-financed by his part-time job at the busy Co-op supermarket in Wivenhoe's High Street, and he went on to pass his test at the first attempt in December 2015.

Once he was legally able to drink alcohol in pubs, he enjoyed doing precisely that—in any of the four lower-Wivenhoe pubs—The Station, The Greyhound, The Rose & Crown, and the Black Buoy. He concluded, after much research, that his favourite establishment was the latter, and he could often be found there with his dad or with his friends most Sunday afternoons, when they served their very excellent roast dinners with all the trimmings. Usually, he could drink two or three pints without feeling much effect, but just occasionally, and especially if he hadn't eaten much breakfast, the mere sniff of beer could make him light-headed. Oliver wasn't what you'd call a hardened drinker.

Although he was still getting on very well with Sam, and having had a great time with her when she and her parents did come over to London for their Christmas shopping treat, they both recognised that continuing a romance long-distance via the internet wasn't ideal. Besides, Sam, being the attractive girl that she was, was in high demand in her home town near Indianapolis, and she couldn't keep turning down date requests forever.

And Oliver, being the good-looking lad that *he* was, didn't have any trouble attracting members of what his dad described as his 'female fan-club' for dates of his own. Sam and Oliver maturely agreed to cool things between them, for now at least, aware that they would always have a special place in their hearts for each other. They both agreed that, in any case, their affection for one another could be rekindled again at any time in future.

Turning his attention to his life in Wivenhoe, once he'd passed his driving test, Oliver naturally wanted a car. His own Cannondale bike—similar to the one he'd rented in Florida—was all very good for himself to get around on, but totally impractical for escorting girlfriends to the cinema or for romantic meals at his favourite noodle bar in the nearby town of Colchester. Meagre wages from his part-time job at the Co-op didn't exactly enable him to save for anything more than an old heap that would soon end up at the scrapyard. His father wasn't rolling in money either, and Oliver was well aware that the Florida holiday had cost thousands, so he couldn't realistically expect parental financial help.

What he really wanted after leaving college, and like many young people of his age, was to get out into the wide world and find a proper full-time job, earning a reasonable, regular salary. He had been torn between taking any job on offer in any field, or holding out to follow his dream to become a journalist or writer. He soon got a reality check when he discovered there were precious few openings in that preferred profession, especially with his lack of experience weighing heavily against him. However, he was nothing if not a trier.

Rejections, or even no replies at all, to the many letters Oliver submitted, enclosing essays and stories, began to take their toll. The torrent of enthusiasm that Oliver once had, by now had been reduced to a trickle.

All but giving up on achieving his goal, he reluctantly accepted the offer of working more hours at the supermarket. At least he would now have some more cash in his pocket, and maybe he might save enough to put a deposit on a half-decent car. But he certainly wasn't feeling fulfilled—this wasn't the career move he'd been hoping for. All that studying for nothing, he thought. For him, stacking shelves with biscuits and cakes wasn't an option for long.

Even his 'Florida Key' research had fallen by the wayside. He had been hoping to discover the name or names of *who* had been incarcerated in the cell that his key fitted, and at one point he thought he was getting some positive results from his extensive research. But unfortunately, despite him rigorously ploughing through website after website, it turned out to be yet another dead-end. He was no closer to finding any name than when he'd started. With other things in his life now taking priority, at least for the time being, he reluctantly put the key away in a drawer and, very nearly, forgot all about it.

***

There was always a very convivial atmosphere in the Black Buoy, and Oliver soon recognised the familiar faces of the regulars who also enjoyed a pint or two there. Being the affable character that he clearly was, it didn't take him long to get to know several of the regulars on first-name terms, and they weren't necessarily of a similar age to him either. He got on with most people, and most people got on with him.

Two such local characters, Audrey and Bob Needham, well known around the town, enjoyed chatting to any of the pub's patrons, always showing a natural interest in what they were up to. Oliver was no exception, and Audrey and Bob had first met Oliver when he was in the Black Buoy celebrating his 18th birthday.

From that time on, they looked forward to hearing his weekly update on how his life was panning out, but having been so impressed with Oliver's initial enthusiasm for writing, they were dismayed to hear that his chosen career apparently wasn't moving in the direction that he had hoped. He clearly had shown so much potential, and to them it seemed a waste that he was still working at a supermarket.

One evening at home, after *Eastenders* had finished on TV, Audrey and Bob talked about this and that, and eventually their conversation came around to Oliver—the young man they had grown rather fond of. Now comfortably off and in retirement themselves, they were nonetheless still very active in the wider community, and they had their fingers productively in many pies. Bob concentrated now on his activity as a town-crier, but was nonetheless still marginally connected with a number of business associates from his old working days, and he had always made a point of parting company with everyone he'd worked with on good terms. "Treat people decently, and they're likely to do likewise in return," was his philosophy. "You never know when you might like to ask a favour," he'd say, wisely.

After chatting together about Oliver, the Needhams agreed that they wanted to help pull their young protégé out of the doldrums, and after considering a number of options open to them, they eventually hatched a plan. Being fearful of how Oliver might react to some 'old busy-bodies' interfering, they decided to indirectly open a door, and then it would be up to Oliver whether he'd go through it or not. All they needed was to learn the name of one of the publications from whom Oliver had received one of those 'thanks, we'll keep you on file' replies. "You buy him a pint next Sunday," suggested Audrey, "and while you're at the bar, I'll have a word in his ear and see what I can find out."

Sunday came, and as usual Oliver walked up the narrow, steep stairs from the pub's car park and into the rear entrance of the Black Buoy. There was the same welcoming hubbub, as people were chatting, drinking and eating. "Ah, there you are," said Bob, as approachable as ever, when Oliver entered. "Let me get you a pint—what are you having?" While Bob was waiting to be served at the counter, Audrey invited Oliver over to her corner by the window.

"So how's it been going? Any progress to tell of?" she enquired, trying to sound as natural as she could. Oliver gave her a brief synopsis of his latest news on the job-hunt front, which consisted of very little—except that he'd had one more negative reply from a regional magazine.

"So, who was it this time? What did they say?" Audrey asked.

"Well, this one was the *East Anglian Chronicle*, and they just said the normal 'We'll get in touch if anything comes up in the future'. No doubt that'll be the last I hear from them—it's just the usual nonsense to get someone like me off their backs," answered a dejected Oliver, shrugging his shoulders while supping his pint that Bob had by now returned with.

Audrey pretended to be more nonchalant than she actually was. She had managed to casually prise the information she wanted from Oliver, making a mental note which magazine he had referred to as she took another sip of her white wine. "Well, you never know," she suggested warmly. "Don't ever give up hope."

The next day, after breakfast, Bob got straight to work. "Right, I'll make a few phone calls. Let's see if we can set some wheels in motion to help our man." Publishing was one of the pies in which he still had a few fingers, and it was one of those industries where, at the top of the management tree, everybody knew everyone else.

And Bob was one such man.

The following Sunday, the couple were sitting once again in their usual corner in the pub when Oliver came bouncing in. When he spotted them, straight away he went over, grinning like a Cheshire cat. "You'll never guess what!" he exclaimed. "I've been offered a job!" Clearly over the moon, he could hardly get the words out of his mouth quickly enough, as he tried to tell them what had happened.

"Woah, hold on there, Oliver. First let's get you a pint in," said Bob, winking discretely at his wife. "And then you can tell us all about it."

"No, it's my round this time," Oliver said, as he went off to the bar. Audrey and Bob raised their glasses to each other. When he returned with two pints of bitter and a glass of Chardonnay, he proceeded to explain about the job he would be starting as a researcher and columnist on the *East Anglian Chronicle*'s travel section. At his interview with Edward Wright, the editor, he had been asked what countries he'd been to, and Oliver talked about his trip to Florida. After giving it some careful consideration, or so it seemed to Oliver, his new boss offered him a job there and then.

Edward had already made up his mind about the section he would start Oliver off with. So, for his first assignment, the new columnist was tasked with writing a piece about his experience on Anna Maria Island. Although he had been prompted of course by his old friend, the idea of pumping some new blood into the publication's rather tired and staid looking 'Holiday and Travel' pages had actually been on his mind for some time. Being always so busy, he'd just never got round to doing anything about it—until now, thanks to Bob's gentle prod.

Three weeks would go by before Audrey and Bob next saw Oliver, when the young man came in the pub to triumphantly show off the piece he'd written, waving the glossy colour magazine in the air, already open at the appropriate page. 'PARADISE ISLAND—words and pictures by OLIVER MARKLAND', read the heading, with two whole pages enthusing about 'the perfect holiday destination'. "Mr.

Wright said he was very pleased with it; 'it's not bad for a first effort' were his exact words," Oliver elaborated. "And this is only Part One! He wants me to do a continuation in next month's issue. I'd told him about my 'Florida Key' idea, and he's suggested I include something about it as well, and to carry the next issue's section over to *three* pages."

The revamped section had certainly helped to boost the general appearance of the magazine, and Edward was indeed very pleased with the way things looked. It should even help to pull in some ad revenue from tour operators if he played his cards right, he thought.

He even found himself looking forward himself to reading Oliver's next piece—this 'Florida Key' of his sounded quite intriguing. But because he wouldn't be able to devote a great deal of attention to his new employee, what Edward really hoped was for Oliver to get on with his project under his own steam. That would be so much easier and less time-consuming than watching over him every step of the way. He hoped Oliver would be able to pick up the metaphorical baton and run with it, and use his own initiative most of the time. In truth, it was a tough job being an editor. There were never enough hours in the day, always with unrealistic deadlines to meet, and never-ending aggravation with advertisers and sponsors.

***

With his natural enthusiasm for writing now back on track, Oliver's excitement about researching Joliet prison and his Florida Key had thankfully returned. As a result, it didn't take too long before he began to reminisce about his first love, although admittedly there had been more loves won and lost since—Wivenhoe was full of young ladies who had taken a shine to him.

It had been several months since Sam and he had last connected on FaceTime, and he wanted to make contact again. "No time like the present," he reasoned, late one night, clutching his precious iPhone.

He pressed the menu button twice and spoke into it: "What time is it in Indianapolis?" The phone then informed him it was six o'clock there. Oliver smiled at how perfectly his gadget worked. He tapped a couple more times, a few seconds elapsed, and then Sam's broad smile was all over the screen. "Hi!!! What a great surprise! How are you?" answered one very excited girl in Plainfield, Indiana.

Happy, and also very relieved, that Sam had taken his unplanned call so positively, he exchanged some small talk before updating her on all his latest general news, while diplomatically leaving out any mention of his currently healthy love life. He saved his most exciting news about his new job until last. "That's totally awesome," Sam exclaimed encouragingly. "Well, don't forget my parents' offer for you to come over and stay with us whenever you want. That invitation still stands, you know." How could he have forgotten? With wild dreams of maybe returning to America and conducting research for his magazine column, it was exactly the confirmation he was hoping to get.

"Have you heard of the *Indianapolis Daily Times*?" he asked. "I came across it while searching online."

"Sure," replied Sam. "We get it delivered. It's mostly full of ads, but all the local announcements and news are in it too. Why do you ask?" she questioned curiously.

"I can't say yet, but I'll let you know as soon as I know. I'm working on something." Deciding to hold back from saying any more for now, in case nothing came of his plan, he dropped that particular subject and went on to ask what Sam had been up to since they'd last talked, which had been quite a while ago. Now it was *her* turn to diplomatically leave out any mention of other relations she'd had with the opposite sex. Promising each other that they'd stay in more regular contact, after hanging up, they both happily vowed to themselves that they definitely would.

CHAPTER 21

WEDNESDAY, 3RD JANUARY, 2018

Prison List

With Christmas and the New Year celebrations over, this was now the time when the British public looked ahead to sunny holiday destinations, and of escaping the UK's miserable winter weather. The *East Anglian Chronicle*'s fresh new travel section certainly hit home with its readers, and advertising revenues were showing a positive upturn as well.

The results coming in would have far exceeded the editor's business plans, had he actually had the time to formulate any. Nevertheless, he was extremely pleased with the way Oliver was working and, following the success of his articles, he was very glad that his old pal Bob had persuaded him to "give the boy a chance", as he'd put it. His decision to hire Oliver had definitely been a good one, and he felt happily vindicated. His young new writer had a good style and, judging by the many emails and letters being received, readers wanted more of the same. Oliver's mentioning of the so-called 'Florida Key Mystery' in his second month's article seemed to have particularly captured the readers' interest.

The finance men at the publisher's head office in London had also noticed the change, but were still constantly pushing for more digital activity. "Online presence is where the future lies," was a phrase that Edward was often being told by his seniors, but the poor man simply never had the time to even look at 'online presence'. Lack of time was his excuse. In truth, there was another reason: he barely knew what 'online presence' meant, let alone knowing how to execute it. Although the 62-year old had managed to keep up with the changes in printing technology, this new world of social media marketing was so alien to him that it went clean over his head. It was as foreign as the Mandarin language.

Edward Wright also knew only too well that the powers that be in their ivory tower headquarters weren't too happy with the status quo—and they were keen to see social media being used as a marketing tool. But as far as Edward was concerned, it was far too late in the day to start learning how to do tweetings and bloggings and all that. He just wanted to hang on to his job for long enough to get his full pension when he retired.

So when Oliver approached him at the start of the year with an idea, it was music to his ears. His new recruit wanted to write a blog relating to his column, including his 'Florida Key' research that readers could interact with, as well as linking it with Twitter, Facebook and Instagram. Oliver was certainly tech-savvy, far more than he was himself, so Edward readily agreed. That should keep the bosses satisfied, he thought. With only two years and eight months until pension day, Oliver had approached him not a moment too soon. His glory days of being Editor in the old-fashioned way were now over, and gone forever, and he felt too mentally worn out to learn new tricks. Oliver Markland might just be the saviour who would carry him through to his finishing post.

He welcomed Oliver's suggestion. However, when Oliver also proposed to actually go all the way to America for three weeks to do research, and write the blog, tweets and travel section from there, initially Edward couldn't see how he could possibly sanction that. "I'm sorry, boy, but I simply don't have the budget for that kind of expenditure. Return flights, accommodation, car hire, meals...it'll all mount up, you know. As much as I'd like to say yes, if I signed off that sort of cost I'd get my goolies cut off by the City boys, and then they'd serve them up back on a plate to me! You wouldn't want that, would you?"

Oliver certainly wouldn't, but having already anticipated his boss's potential objection, he had come to the meeting well prepared. "But you see, Edward," he began, to the man who had recently instructed him to call him by his first name instead of Mr. Wright, "you've no need to be concerned with accommodation costs—I've got that covered. And I doubt that a hire car will be necessary either—my girlfriend's family have hinted that I could use one of theirs. Also, I'll pay for my meals myself, just as I would if I were here. So really it would only be the flights I'd need financial help with, and I've already found a really great deal. Look!" he continued, shoving his iPad right in front of Edward's nose at the relevant website.

Well aware of the pressure from above to increase the publication's digital presence sooner rather than later, Edward leaned back in his office swivel chair, arms stretched behind his head. The only sound he uttered for the next two minutes while Oliver waited with bated breath was a contemplative, "Hmm," followed by another minute's silence. He guessed that would be excruciating for Oliver. Edward took great pleasure from slowly and softly delivering his verdict so he could watch Oliver's reaction. His new recruit's enthusiasm reminded him of himself from half a century ago when he had begun his own career in Fleet Street. "Well, boy," he began, followed by another long pause, "this 'Florida Key' business had better be worth it. And you'll need to do a heck of a lot more blogging about local East Anglian stories to win me over completely…so get your tickets booked before I think better of it. Now get out of my office!" he said with a broad smile.

With a swift, "Thanks, Edward," Oliver quickly went out of the door. It was all he could do to refrain from punching the air as he ran to the little cubbyhole at the end of the corridor that had become his own workspace. Straight away, he began designing how his new blog pages would look. He also wanted to share his great news, but it would be too early in her time zone for Sam to receive a FaceTime call, so instead he sent her an email that she'd find in her Inbox when she awoke that morning.

Re: Guess what?

Hi Sam. Guess what?! My boss is letting me do more on 'Florida Key'. I'm coming out to research and write! Will tell you more tomorrow.

Oli x

That email was easy. Then, he attempted to compose a second, more involved and elaborate one to someone else. This proved to be much harder, as he struggled with the best way to approach the editor at the *Indianapolis Daily Times*. After the fifth unsuccessful attempt to find the right words, he gave up and decided to return to that task later.

Oliver's head was spinning with excitement, and he found it very difficult to concentrate on any single thing for more than a few minutes.

He went back to his Joliet prison research, hoping to fathom out what the '410A' markings on his key might mean. This time, Oliver approached the puzzle from a different perspective. Instead of scrutinising the many websites directly relating to Joliet prison itself, now he tried a different tack, delving deeper into the actual manufacturer of the key, the Folger Adam Company, 'Makers of the Finest Detention Equipment', according to what he read.

Whenever he held his key, Oliver was sure he felt a sensation compelling him to learn all he could about it. He shuddered. Although it was merely an inanimate chunk of cold metal, it was as if it possessed some peculiar power over him. Certainly, it was true that since beginning this quest for information, he had become somewhat obsessed with the key's history, feeling an uncontrollable urge to discover where and when it had been used, and who it was used to lock behind bars. Get a grip, Oliver told himself. It was he who was in control of the key, not the other way round.

As he continued, trancelike, browsing the internet, he stumbled upon a site specialising in the buying and selling of such penitentiary keys from all across the United States. He learned that the location of each prison was identified by the wording on the key's bow, and enthralled, he read on, eventually coming across an article written by a Folger Adam key collector, offering tips on how to spot a fake in this clearly booming market of prison memorabilia.

Basically, if there were tiny letters or numbers engraved on the key's blade, such as this one's '410A', it was likely to be the genuine article. Reassured, Oliver read on, becoming increasingly engrossed in the information he was gleaning. And then there it was, what he'd been looking for; the meaning of '410A' on his Joliet prison key. According to the website, this particular key was used to open Cell 10 on the 4th floor of 'A' Block. Bingo!

Oliver checked the time. Eager to still present a rough layout of his new blog pages to Edward before the end of the day, he was about to return to his design work. But before exiting the screen he was currently on, he'd just click on one last link; the one that the Folger Adam key collector had included at the bottom of his article.

As the new page gradually opened up, Oliver gasped. Judging by how long it was taking to fully load, this must be a huge file, he concluded. His hand began to shake as it hovered over the laptop's keyboard. Could this be the Holy Grail he'd been searching for? The simple heading at the top of the page indicated that it might very well be: 'JOLIET CORRECTIONAL CENTER: INMATES HELD 1950-1986. A STUDY by Dr. E. J. GOLD'.

Doing a quick search on the author of the report, Oliver learned that Gold had been an historian who had died in 1987 at the age of 98. Clearly, judging by the amount of information compiled, he must have been completely obsessed with his chosen subject. What an unusual obsession to have, Oliver thought, as he held his Florida Key very tightly in his hand, realising that perhaps he was also suffering a similar affliction.

Oliver began daydreaming yet again, fantasising about his key having some strange force over him, compelling him to continue this research–as if he were being willed to discover something. But what?

A cold chill ran through him. He literally shivered. As quickly as he could, he put his key down upon the desk, telling himself to pull himself together.

He focussed back on the historian's website. There were so many pages to digest. There were hundreds of entries, maybe even thousands. Inmates' names, ages, their crimes, cell numbers in which they were held, year of incarceration, year of release, parole, or death—and sometimes even further notes, underlined in blue, presumably because they linked to more material elsewhere. Logic told him that analysing all this information was certainly not going to be quick and easy, and would take an awful lot of studying before he'd have any chance of finding what he was looking for, if indeed he ever would.

Some of the pages had been compiled in date order, alphabetically, or in number order in some cases that included cell numbers. And to make matters even more arduous and intricate, some of the groups of pages themselves were out of order. It was as if poor E.J. Gold had died before he had been able to finish his life's work.

Almost too anxious to begin reading down the various columns of data, in case he met with another dead-end blank, Oliver decided to break away for a short while. He reasoned that by walking away from his desk for a few minutes, somehow any results for '410A' would show up more positively. Yes, he knew it didn't make sense, but nevertheless he did something out of the ordinary. Usually grabbing a quick Pepsi from the vending machine just outside his room, this time he went and made himself a cup of tea in the small staff kitchen half way along the corridor. As he waited for the kettle to boil, he prepared his mug with tea, milk and sugar. Such was his feeling of excitement, he spilled half the spoon of sugar on the worktop, and spent further seconds that seemed more like minutes clearing up the mess. Finally, carrying his mug of sweet tea back to his desk, he reopened his computer and started reading. There were potentially 273 pages to get through.

He scrolled and clicked along, speed-reading each page, one by one. By the time he'd reached page 150 of 273, his eyes were straining to the point of soreness. But then—Eureka! He finally came to a list of inmates held over the years in the cells of Block A, 4th Floor.

Oliver rubbed his eyes and carried on, now almost hysterical with anticipation. Page 150 began with 'Cell 3', went on to 'Cell 15', back to 'Cell 42', and then various other numbers over the next several pages. "Come *on!*" shouted Oliver, exasperated at his computer. He looked up, embarrassed, hoping no one was walking past his open door at the time.

Then, as if the computer had heard him, it presented what Oliver had spent so long searching for. "*Yes!!!*" he cried. There, on his screen on page 157 of the document, were the details of eight different individuals. These were the eight inmates who had spent time locked in Cell 10, 4th Floor, Block A of Joliet prison between 1950 and 1986.

"At last!" exclaimed Oliver out loud, this time not caring whether anyone caught him talking to himself. He sank back into his office chair on castors, clasped his hands behind his neck and used his feet to push himself away from the desk, spinning himself round and round until he felt dizzy and needed to stop before he felt sick.

CHAPTER 22

(WEDNESDAY, 3RD JANUARY, 2018)

Cell Pairing

At the outset, as far as Oliver had been concerned, the information displayed on the computer screen in front of him merely consisted of a list of names—a list of individuals with whom he had no personal connection. But as he thought more about his fascinating internet discovery, he reminded himself that they were names of human beings who had spent years literally only a few feet away from the very door to which his key locked them in or let them out. Oliver began to feel a real connection with them.

Sure, he thought, these people may have done terrible things, committed awful crimes but, to him, the names were more than just statistics. As his computer's cursor moved up and down the screen, Oliver studied the surnames in the year order that they had been jailed. While staring at the screen, he also picked up the key and held it tightly. All of a sudden, he felt a surge of energy compelling him to comprehend as much as possible about at least one of the inmates—and to find out why he had been imprisoned and where he was now. He reread the list so he could decide to whom he should give his special attention:

1950 - Hoffman

1954 - Ryan // 1958 - O'Flannagan

1965 - Trudeau

1972 - Peters

1976 - Flynn

1977 - Emanuele // 1981 - Yakamoto

As Gold's completed study only went up to 1986, one year before he'd died, Oliver wondered whether any other inmates had since been housed in this cell after Emanuele and Yakamoto. It was perhaps by no means a complete and thorough list, but it was the best source of information that Oliver could have hoped for, and he marvelled at the man's dedication in compiling such comprehensive detail. Oliver chuckled to himself. He'd struck gold thanks to Mr. Gold.

Oliver looked across to the additional information that appeared next to each name, and could see that Hoffman and O'Flannagan had been found guilty of armed robbery and had been released in 1980 and 1982 respectively. Ryan, who had committed manslaughter, had died of natural causes in 1985. Flynn had been found guilty of rape, but there was no further information about what had happened to him. Peters and Trudeau's crimes weren't listed, although Peters's notes simply said 'released', and Trudeau's said 'moved'. The last two people on the list had been jailed for homicide–Emanuele's name also had the word 'ASSASSIN' against it, and he and Yakamoto both had the word 'LIFE' written down.

Oliver withdrew his gaze from the computer screen, looked upwards to the ceiling and pondered. He had previously learned that Joliet Correctional Center had been closed in 2002, and most remaining inmates had been transferred to nearby Stateville Correctional Center, just a few miles to the west of Joliet. So, if 'life' did mean life, it was theoretically possible that the last two names on the list could in fact still be residing there.

Bearing in mind how long ago they had begun their sentences, it was also a possibility that either or both could have passed away. There were certainly more questions without answers, and now there was yet another question: why were there two pairs of names listed together? Maybe if he studied every small detail available, he would eventually find the explanation. It was all terribly laborious, and Oliver knew that at this rate he'd never get his blog layouts completed by the end of the day. But this was far more important for the moment, he thought, so he carried on, regardless.

From the top, he began reading the links underlined in blue, leading to further information elsewhere. One of the links against Emanuele's name repeated the word 'ASSASSIN'. "Hmm—how fascinating. Was he *really* an assassin?" Oliver wondered. He read on to discover that M.J. Emanuele had, if what he'd read was true, been hired to kill no fewer than six men over a period of three years. Oliver could only speculate as to who would have paid to have their dirty work carried out. Gangsters? Drug barons? The Mafia? All the other links associated with Emanuele simply came up as 'PAGE NOT FOUND', indicating that they'd been subsequently removed. "Hmm," Oliver repeated under his breath.

After a good deal more work, he stumbled upon the reason for the list's paired names. One of the links against O'Flannagan's entry suggested that increased prison populations necessitated cells to sometimes be shared. Ryan and O'Flannagan had been cellmates together, as had Emanuele and Yakamoto. So it looked like Emanuele had been jailed in '77, having the cell to himself–and then in '81 he had to share his space with Yakamoto. As they were both 'lifers', maybe they had been moved to Stateville in 2002 together, and possibly were still there to this day.

As usual, Oliver's mind wandered off at a tangent. He imagined the scenario of actually meeting these people. Wouldn't it be interesting to conduct an interview for the blog, he thought, and discover what life had really been like, cooped up in Joliet prison, sharing a cell with another prisoner?

Completely captivated, Oliver continued with his cross-referencing. He clicked on the link against Yakamoto's name, hoping to find further information, and he wasn't disappointed. But what on earth could this 'Paris BR Murder' possibly mean? Had the crime been committed in France? Two newspaper clippings were then displayed to reveal the answer.

Intrigued, Oliver read the headlines, both containing the three words 'Bike Radio Murder'. So, that's what the 'BR' abbreviated, he concluded. Fascinated, he decided to put all his other work on hold for the rest of the day. He couldn't resist examining every single word written about the man with the Japanese name—so today's blog designing and everything else would just have to wait until tomorrow, he told himself.

As the articles revealed Yakamoto's full story, a wave of sadness came over Oliver. It had something to do with the fact that this guy was clearly a keen cyclist like himself. And, according to the report, Yakamoto had emphatically maintained his innocence throughout his ordeal, and without fully understanding why, Oliver instinctively believed him to be innocent of murdering Sandy Beach, the reported victim.

Oliver examined the facts: Yakamoto had been crossing America on a pedal bike. Surely, Oliver thought, cyclists don't go around killing people, do they? He felt a strong wave of empathy for the cyclist who had surely just been in the wrong place at the wrong time. It all seemed so improbable that this young man, barely a little older than his own present age, could be a cold-blooded murderer, hitting a woman over the head and killing her.

Oliver read on. A handlebar radio was the weapon? This seemed even more incredible. It was definitely this last entry in Gold's notes that captured Oliver's interest the most, having now made up his mind that Yakamoto surely couldn't have been guilty. Inexplicably, he decided there and then that it would be Yushi Yakamoto to whom he would devote his full attention. "Who knows?" he wondered. "Maybe I might even get to interview Yakamoto and discover the whole truth behind the story of the 'Bike Radio Murder'."

CHAPTER 23

(WEDNESDAY, 3RD JANUARY, 2018)

Welcome Reply

Oliver looked at the time. It was already 5.42p.m. So absorbed in what he was reading, he hadn't noticed the other office staff going past his door on their way home. He got up from his desk and glanced towards the large open-plan space at the end of the corridor. It was empty of people, except for Val, the cleaning lady, busy pulling along a Henry vacuum cleaner to suck up the aftermath of yet another busy day in the life of the *East Anglian Chronicle*.

Deciding it was time to go home too, Oliver bent down to put his cycle-clips on over his jeans. He folded his laptop shut, put it in his satchel and headed outside to where his bike was locked, fastening his helmet straps as he walked. Mentally exhausted from all today's internet research, he decided that enough was now enough, and that tomorrow he really must get back to developing the magazine's digital layouts. Any further Joliet prison research would have to be put on hold until he was back in the United States.

For Oliver, it wasn't too long a ride from Colchester, out of the business park where the *Chronicle*'s building was, weaving along the busy roads and onto the calmness of the Wivenhoe Trail, a flat, gravelled path that ran between the railway on the left and the River Colne on the right. Normally, Oliver would have his eyes on the river the whole way, mesmerised by the sunlight's reflection as it shimmered across the incoming or outgoing tide. But today, he hardly even noticed the water at all, so deep was he in thought about the day's developments.

And what a significant breakthrough he'd made, in more ways than one. Not only with the discovery of Gold's comprehensive study, but also the agreement he'd come to with his boss about the blog—and of course his return trip to America. "That's so awesome!" he guessed would be Sam's reaction when he told her. He also couldn't wait to tell everyone else his exciting news, including Audrey and Bob, but especially his dad. He hadn't seen him in a while and hoped they might be able to catch up later over a quick pint.

But he was also very conscious that he must contact the *Indianapolis Daily Times* as soon as possible, as part of his general plan. Maybe he could pop into the Black Buoy on his way home this evening, have another attempt at getting something composed on his MacBook, and then call to invite his dad round for a drink after he'd finished.

Still thinking hard, before he knew it, Oliver had already cycled past Wivenhoe's railway station, The Station Hotel, and Natalie's Boutique Chic shop in the High Street. If only she sold men's clothes as well as women's, he thought, then he'd have the perfect excuse to go in and say hello to Natalie more often. He admitted to having quite a crush on the woman, especially when she spoke in her delightful Geordie accent.

On he cycled, past Tollgate Fisheries from where they always offered the perfectly cooked portion of chips that Oliver enjoyed at least twice a week.

The pub was only a few metres further down, and soon he pulled up outside, propping his bike against the wall, feeling glad that in Wivenhoe there was no need to lock it. Good, he thought, as he entered and saw that it wasn't yet very busy inside. He knew it soon would be, so the quicker he got his pint and got down to work, sitting in his favourite nook, the better.

He wanted to ask if he might be allowed to operate out of the Indianapolis newspaper's office, write his blog and conduct research from there. But how exactly should he approach this question, he wondered? Should he send a personal email to the newspaper's editor, or directly to the publisher, perhaps? As he already had some journalistic credentials, what with his position here at the *Chronicle*, he hoped that his unusual request would at least be given some consideration.

Oliver mulled things over, remembering advice he'd been given. "Don't only write about what *I* want," he told himself. "Offer them something that *they* might want in return." But what could that be? Maybe he shouldn't send an email at all. Perhaps a posted letter would be better? It may make more of an impact in this age of email correspondence. As he took a couple of gulps of Guinness, he decided he would send them a letter—a neatly handwritten actual note on good Basildon Bond paper—and sent with a British stamp showing the Queen's head on the envelope. Guessing that they must receive hundreds of emails on a daily basis, this unorthodox approach would surely grab the attention of at least someone in authority there.

Oliver tried putting himself in the shoes of the prospective recipient, and considered this would be the best approach. "I bet they don't get that many physical letters, let alone a handwritten one from England," he thought. He'd compose it now on his computer, and write it out the following day in longhand, using a fountain pen—the Parker that his dad had bought him for his sixteenth birthday. Unable to remember the last time he'd used the pen, the thought of it reminded him of his father, so before he began tapping the keypad, he made a phone call inviting him round to the pub in half an hour or so.

"Only for a quick one, Dad," he explained over the phone. "I've got a very busy day tomorrow, but I've also got something very important to tell you." Leslie Markland wasn't used to going to the pub mid-week, but nonetheless he was pleased for the opportunity to meet up with his son. Normally, his boy was so busy talking with all and sundry at the weekends, he now rarely got a look in these days—let alone a proper chat.

"Okay, son, I'll see you around eight," Leslie agreed. For the following 30 minutes, Oliver slogged away, attempting several drafts until eventually feeling satisfied that he'd got the tone of his composition just right. Tomorrow, he'd find out who he should personally address the letter to, and get it posted. He'd also include an issue of the *Chronicle* with an example of his column in it, along with some printed information about Colchester and, for good measure, some pretty pictures of Wivenhoe. That should also help to catch their eye, he hoped. At eight o'clock precisely, Oliver looked up to see his dad come through the door, just as he was typing out a few final words.

After a pleasant couple of pints and a full update from Oliver, Leslie Markland walked home, very proud that his son had so much enthusiasm for what he was doing, clearly relishing his new job. Who would have thought? As he took a shortcut through St. Mary's churchyard, Leslie smiled, realising that actually he had never doubted that one day, sooner or later, his son would fall on his feet. And that was certainly exactly what he had done.

Oliver stayed behind at the Black Buoy for a few minutes longer so that he could reread the draft of what he'd written:

Draft Letter to Publisher of Indianapolis Daily Times

Dear (xxxxx)

I am contacting you in the hope that you may be able to help me with a project that I am working on for our publication, the East Anglian Chronicle. We are based in Colchester, England, the oldest recorded town in the country, approximately 60 miles from London.

I currently write a column and blog for the Chronicle. We've recently been getting a great reaction to an intriguing story about the penitentiary at Joliet, Illinois, and a specific police case from the 1980s, known as the 'Bike Radio Murder' in the town of Paris, Illinois.

I wonder if you may have heard of the case, or even better, if you have any records of it on your files? I am particularly keen to conduct an interview with the man found guilty of the murder, Mr. Yushi Yakamoto, who may by now have been moved to nearby Stateville.

I have been offered accommodation in the town of Plainfield, near Indianapolis, and I will be writing my column and blog from America during my three-week visit to your country.

I would very much appreciate it if I could perhaps do some of my research from your offices. I have full press accreditation, and I am intending to come just as soon as I can finalise my arrangements, hopefully later this month.

For your valued assistance, I would of course give full acknowledgement to your newspaper in everything that is published.

Here at the East Anglian Chronicle, we are keen to extend our best wishes to you all at the Indianapolis Daily Times, and I hope that my request reaches you well.

Good! That was the general gist taken care of, Oliver decided, satisfied. He could add the finishing touches tomorrow, and politely ask for an email response at their earliest convenience.

***

(THURSDAY, 4TH – TUESDAY, 16TH JANUARY, 2018)

The following day, Oliver did as he'd planned and sealed his completed letter to Indianapolis. Then he concentrated on re-designing the magazine's blog pages, writing another column, as well as making contact with Sam's parents. He just wanted to be completely sure that he'd still be welcome to stay with the Dickinson family before finally booking his BA flights. Fortunately, their speedy reply confirmed that he would be—and it sounded like, judging by Sam's FaceTime call, that they were all genuinely looking forward to him coming out. She excitedly told him about the many places she couldn't wait to take him to in her home city.

The Post Office advised him that his letter to the Indianapolis newspaper should take between five and seven days to arrive. So, after the fifth day, Oliver checked his Inbox constantly, at least every hour. Finally, on the seventh day, the email he'd been longing for popped up. Based on his holiday experiences of how Americans communicate, it was as short and to the point as he'd expected. He knew the reply would either be a quick 'yes' or an abrupt 'no'. He began reading, crossing his fingers for the former. Fortunately, he wasn't disappointed:

Oliver – Thanks for reaching out.

We'd be delighted to welcome you. Let us know your ETA. I've checked our records on the 'Bike Radio Murder' story. We don't have much on it here, but our sister paper in Terre Haute covered it extensively. You may wish to write them as well. I copied your letter to the Ed there. Write Ursula O'Mahoney—she's expecting you. Address below.

Best

Steve Borowitz

Publisher

Delighted with the response, Oliver sat back and reread the email, amazed at how well things were coming together. "Right," he thought. "Now all the elements are in place, I'd better book those flights."

After a number of clicks on the BA website, and using the company's Visa card with Edward's permission, it was all done, and he'd be flying out on Tuesday. That gave him four complete days to prepare, and get his new blog design finalised.

Not long later, there was the familiar 'ping' sound as a further email appeared in Oliver's Inbox, the sender using the full name '*Uschi Ne Mathghamhna*'. Was that a real name? He was just about to press the delete button, assuming this to be yet another all-too-common scam email that constantly cropped up from somewhere in Romania or Ukraine. Luckily, just in time, he noticed a few words displayed from the first line of text: "*Oliver, your charming letter was…*".

Maybe it wasn't a scam after all, so he clicked to open and speed-read the content, without fully absorbing everything in the rather confusing format in which the email had been written.

Oliver, your charming letter was passed to me today by my colleague in Indianapolis. I went to London once and loved it. The case known as the 'Bike Radio Murder' was a big deal here in '81, and our paper covered it extensively. Sure, come on over and we can turn things up for you.

Steve B. sent some scans of your quaint little village. My niece is hoping to visit London this fall. Can you help? How far are you?

She doesn't know anyone there. By the way, you won't be able to interview Yakamoto. He was executed in 1996. What's the weather in Wivenhoe? Foggy, I bet, next to a river. He always maintained his innocence, but they all say that. My niece is called Siobhan—bet she'd like to meet you when you're here. You can talk London.

See you in Terre Haute. When?

Ursh

With the sentences all over the place, Oliver was very confused on its first reading. And who was 'Ursh'? He assumed it must be the same Ursula O'Mahoney that Steve Borowitz had mentioned, but Oliver couldn't be certain. He reread it, this time more carefully. Previously he'd missed the part that mentioned Yakamoto. "Wow!" exclaimed Oliver out loud, stunned at the revelation he'd now digested. After quickly looking on Google Maps to see where exactly Terre Haute was, he hastily sent a reply.

Dear Ursh

Thanks for your email. I'm sure I'll be able to help your niece. I'll talk to my boss, Edward Wright. I've just booked my flights and I'll be arriving in the US next week. I'd be very grateful for any assistance you can offer me at your Terre Haute office, and maybe I could sometimes use a desk there as well as at Indianapolis?

I will contact you again nearer the time to advise exactly what day I'll be coming. I see it's only 80 miles away from where I'll be staying, and I'm hoping to borrow or rent a car while I'm over. If not, I could get a bus perhaps? Thank you.

Meanwhile, would you be kind enough to send me any more information about Yakamoto, please? I understand he was a cyclist—like me! But I can't find any further reports on the internet, other than the two I already have (attached); one about the killing of Sandy Beach, and the other about Yakamoto's upcoming trial. I'm intrigued to learn as much as I can.

Best regards

Oliver Markland

***

The following few days went by far too slowly, but Oliver had plenty to do preparing for his trip, what with putting the finishing touches to the *Chronicle*'s online pages, as well as his blog. Edward was over the moon with Oliver's achievements, and was keen for his bosses to see as well. He would of course credit Oliver with most of the work, he decided, but as he was Editor, a fair share of praise from HQ ought to be directed at him. After all, it was he who had hired Oliver, and it was he who had sanctioned the magazine's digital development. At last, he should be able to get his superiors in The City off his back once and for all until pension day, he thought.

Oliver wasn't concerned with any such office politics or point scoring. He was just so excited to be flying out from Heathrow for such a great experience, and to be meeting Steve Borowitz and Ursh. Or should he refer to her as '*Ursula*', or '*Uschi Ne Mathghamhna*'? He had no idea, but he guessed he'd soon he'd be finding out. He could hardly wait to see the Dickinson family once again, and especially Sam, of course.

Tuesday eventually came, and not a moment too soon as far as Oliver was concerned, but far too quickly for his father. After an emotional farewell at Heathrow, Oliver boarded the plane, nervous yet excited in equal measures. As Leslie made his own way back to the multi-storey car park, he felt sick with worry, plain and simple, as he hoped and prayed that his son would be safe during the whole time he'd be away. Despite him now being a young man and no longer a boy, this was still nevertheless the first time he'd taken a flight away on his own. Leslie sighed, knowing full well that he had no choice but to stand aside as Oliver carved his own life's path and got on with what he wanted to do.

Meanwhile, Oliver was now strapped firmly in his seat. With the engines roaring for take-off, the acceleration of the jet thrust him backwards as the plane took off, bound for JFK airport. "New York, New York!" Oliver couldn't hold back from saying the words out loud. The elderly lady sitting next to him turned and smiled, recalling her first time arriving in the Big Apple over fifty years earlier.

Somewhat embarrassed, Oliver explained that he'd never been there before. "I wonder if it's just like I picture it," he elaborated, "skyscrapers and everything!" Not that he'd be visiting the city yet—although for his return trip he may be making a stop-over, depending on available time and funds. If he did, the Empire State Building, Statue of Liberty and Ground Zero were at the top of his must-see list.

The lady nodded her head. "It will be everything you've imagined—and a whole lot more."

Having to pinch himself that this was all actually happening, Oliver thought ahead. On his outward journey, he'd be stopping at JFK for a couple of hours, awaiting the connecting flight to Indianapolis International. From there, Sam and her parents would be collecting him and taking him back to their home in Plainfield. He wondered what their home would be like, and speculated whether his and Sam's fondness for each other would be rekindled. He hoped so.

He also reflected on the fact that, only a few short weeks earlier, he'd been stacking shelves in the Co-op, and now he was an international jetsetter—and writer—on a mission! A mission to investigate the unfortunate case of Yushi Yakamoto, and the 'Bike Radio Murder'. And judging by the second email he'd received from Ursh, his investigation wouldn't only be for the benefit of the *East Anglian Chronicle*. Half an hour into the flight, and after the stewardess had been along offering drinks and snacks, Oliver retrieved his laptop from the overhead locker.

Would he at some point wake up and discover that this had all been a pleasant dream? He studied yet again the number of newspaper clippings dating from 1981 that Ursh had kindly sent him, attached with the accompanying email that he reread for what seemed like the hundredth time.

Hi again Oliver

Please find the attached files of press cuttings. It all happened before my time, but colleagues here tell me this was big news back then.

My niece is so pleased you're coming over, and she wants to pick your brains about London – and Colchester and Wivenhoe. It's incredible that your boss Edward has offered to hook her up with his journalist contacts. He said there might even be a temp job for her at your offices later this year. Thanks so much for running with this.

Why don't you do some writing from our Terre Haute site? We'll be glad to include some in our paper. You'd be our 'Young Sherlock'! We love that TV series over here. Sure, we can find a desk for you. And no worries about vehicles – we have a pool car you can use.

Apparently, a lot of people around here thought Yakamoto was innocent back in '81. Just a cyclist in the wrong place at the wrong time.

I'll get the car over to our Indy office.

See you soon, Sherlock!

Ursh

This was going to be such an adventure, Oliver knew. After closing up his laptop, he flicked through the various video channels on the in-flight entertainment system. Rejecting the latest CGI blockbusters, he settled back for the next 138 minutes to enjoy an old 1970s classic with Michael Caine and Laurence Olivier—*Sleuth*. Oliver loved a good old mystery.

PART FOUR

OLIVER RETURNS TO AMERICA

CHAPTER 24

(TUESDAY, 16TH JANUARY, 2018)

Newspaper Offices

When Oliver walked down the steps of his Delta Airlines plane to the tarmac below, and followed the string of passengers making their way towards the Baggage Reclaim area of Indianapolis International Airport, he had no idea what to expect, and was suddenly hit with a head full of nerves.

What if Sam and her parents weren't there to meet him? What would he do? Where would he go? But then, as he and the other travellers were being funnelled through the crowded arrivals hall and he read the overhead 'EXIT TO STREET' sign, he noticed a silver banner in the distance spelling the words 'WELCOME OLIVER'. There, in front of him stood Sam and Kerry Dickinson on one side of the aisle, and Chris on the other, holding the banner above their heads. All the other passengers that walked under that banner ignored it, but Oliver didn't. As he approached, he almost cried with a mixture of joy and relief. There were hugs all round when he reached Sam and her parents.

As Chris drove them along the freeway to the Dickinson's family house in Plainfield, Oliver spent the whole journey answering a flurry of excited questions from his hosts, especially from Sam, who was clearly delighted to be reunited with her friend. Today was a day to settle into his new surroundings, his home for the next 21 days. Once inside, he was shown to his room next to Sam's, where he unpacked and took a shower. A little later, he was downstairs and seated around the large oak dining table for a meal with the family. This gave him the opportunity to outline his plans, and to also ask a favour.

"Absolutely!" assured Kerry, responding to Oliver's question of transportation. "Sam has her own car, and I'm sure she won't mind getting you over to the newspaper's offices in the morning. Sam nodded enthusiastically.

"But now . . ." Chis suggested, ". . . just relax, eat and rest. You must be tired after those flights. Tell us more about your project. From what Sam's told us so far, it sounds pretty interesting."

For the remainder of the evening, Oliver described, in as much detail as he could, all the elements that brought him to where he now was. He enjoyed elaborating to his captive audience about his recent research into Joliet prison, Yushi Yakamoto, and the 'Bike Radio Murder' story of 1981.

But then, as if being hit by a brick, all of a sudden he became overwhelmed with fatigue. It must have been a combination of his exhausting journey, jetlag, the evening dinner, and the non-stop talking. He excused himself and went up to the room he'd been allocated. After cleaning his teeth, he almost fell on the bed. Wearily pulling the duvet over himself and adjusting the pillows, he very quickly felt himself drifting towards sleep. In his state of semi-consciousness, he dreamed he heard a soft knock at his door. As it turned out, it was no dream. Despite his exhaustion, Oliver mustered up a second wind. He and Sam had a lot of catching up to do.

The following morning, he woke early. His natural body clock was in turmoil, and it took him a while to work out where he was. As he adjusted, he was as excited as he was apprehensive about the big day ahead, meeting his temporary colleagues at the newspapers. Or were they his bosses? As he lay in bed, it felt as though he had a million things competing for his attention.

But it was his late night liaison with Sam that was still firmly on his mind. Where was she? He was expecting her to be lying next to him, but then he vaguely recalled her giving him a final kiss on the lips before tip-toeing out the bedroom, carefully and quietly closing the door behind her. He must have fallen into a deep sleep immediately after she'd left. It was great to be back in her company again.

As he gazed around the large bedroom, Oliver admired his surroundings and thought about his first impressions of the house into which he'd been welcomed. By Wivenhoe standards it was huge—even larger than the house he and his dad had stayed at in Florida. Coming up the drive yesterday after being collected from the airport, he'd been impressed by the mock-Tudor façade, and the topiary hedges shaped like peacocks in the garden. The inside of the house was tastefully presented, and there were rooms in every direction leading off the enormous hallway with its oak-panelled walls and flooring. The Dickinsons certainly liked oak. His own room had an en suite shower room and, as well as the king-size, very comfortable bed, there was a large writer's desk facing the window. That would be perfect for doing his work, Oliver decided. He rose from the bed to look out of the window. As he focussed on the kidney-shaped swimming pool below, he smiled. For the next three weeks, he was sure he'd be extremely comfortable here.

His present surroundings were all well and good, but Oliver reminded himself that this wasn't a holiday, and that he was here for a very specific purpose. His mind raced ahead, anticipating how the day might unfold. Eager to get on with it, he showered and dressed in the lightweight beige suit that he had brought especially, and went downstairs for breakfast. It was in fact his only suit. Kerry and Sam were already there. "Ah, there you are! We thought we'd never see you. Wow, you're looking smart!" said Kerry, with a warm, welcoming grin.

Oliver looked at his phone to check the time. 10.15a.m. His appointment at the *Indianapolis Daily Times* to meet Steve Borowitz was at midday. "Don't worry, it'll take less than half an hour to get downtown," assured Sam, reading Oliver's concern about being late. While her mother turned back to continue preparing Oliver's breakfast, Sam mouthed a sexy kiss at him. He sent one across in return, just at the moment when Kerry turned around. She said nothing, nor did Sam, but Oliver went bright red. He looked down, trying desperately not to make any further eye contact.

***

Sam dropped Oliver off in the street outside the newspaper's offices at five minutes to twelve, and wished him good luck. "Call me if you need picking up," she shouted through the open window of her car as she drove off. Oliver kept telling himself not to be nervous, but he couldn't help it. He brushed down his suit and adjusted the pink tie he'd never previously worn as he entered the building. He approached the unattended receptionist's desk, and wondered what to do.

Just then he heard a man's voice call his name from the gallery at the top of the stairs. "Oliver! You're Oliver, right? I'm Steve. Come on up."

As Oliver ascended the stairs towards Steve's outstretched beckoning hand, he turned back to see two women returning to their posts in the reception area. Did he hear one say to the other "He's kinda cute, don't ya think?" or had he misheard? For the moment, it didn't matter. He followed Steve to his office and took the sofa seat that was offered.

"So, you're our Young Sherlock, are you? Or are you his sidekick Doctor Watson? Ha ha," laughed Steve, rather too loudly at his own joke that made no sense. "Oliver Sherlock or Oliver Watson? Who's it to be?" Before Oliver had a chance to answer, Steve continued. "We like the idea of you coming here. This Bike Radio Murder case was the talk of the town way back when, and I guess a lot of our readers will remember it. We want you to write a column in our paper all about what you are up to here, in our country. It'll be fun, and the readers'll love it! Beef it up, won't you? Make it terribly British, what what? Ha ha." Again, he laughed at the way he mimicked the English accent, before he continued. "See what you can find out about this Yushi guy, huh? Some folks felt sorry for him. Wrong place, wrong time. Always said he was innocent. Maybe he was, maybe he wasn't. Tie it in with your key story, huh? We've got a car here for you. It's nothing special, just a pool Hyundai, but I guess you're used to small cars over there in Blighty, ha ha. Well, I gotta be gettin' on now. Do a good job for us, huh?"

Oliver wasn't able to get a word in edgeways, such was the machine-gun tirade of Steve's quick-fire dialogue. He wanted to ask some questions about the Bike Radio Murder files, but never got the chance. He'd been in the Editor's office for barely five minutes before Steve was standing up from behind his desk and ushering him to the door, and directing another torrent of words at Oliver: "Now go downstairs and get the car key from Tabatha on Reception. She's got it all covered, and no doubt she'll give you some forms to sign. You know the sort of thing—just to protect our liability—and then I'd get on over to Uschi's office in Terre Haute if I were you. She's waiting for you. We call her Uschi, but she prefers 'Ursh'. Or 'Urs'–we never know. Best you call her 'Ursh' to begin. Should take you an hour or so. Take Interstate 70, or Route 40, but I think 70 will be quicker." With that, Steve held out his hand for Oliver to shake, holding open his door. "Do a good job for us, ya hear, Sherlock? This could be good for our bottom line."

Poor Oliver. He exited Steve's office, still open-mouthed as he descended the steps to where Tabatha was waiting for him, his head in a spin. Bottom line? What was that? Interstate 70? And had Steve meant 'Route 40', as in 'root'? Then why call it 'route', rhyming with 'roundabout'? The meeting was over far too quickly for Oliver to conclude whether he liked or disliked Steve, so he decided to just do what he was told, and go to see Ursh over at the Terre Haute office. He hoped he'd find the way. He hoped he'd be able to drive the car okay on the Interstate highway. He hoped Ursh wouldn't be like Steve.

Tabatha noticed that Oliver was looking a little pale. "Take no notice of Steve—he's always like that. I guess that was how he was with you?" she whispered. Oliver nodded, still somewhat shell-shocked from his encounter. Then, in her normal voice, Tabatha asked the other woman to come over with the car keys and papers that needed signing. "This is Dianne," she introduced her colleague. "But don't be having anything to do with her—she's married. But I'm not!" Whether it was just an innocent flirt or not, Oliver blushed red for the second time that day.

Half an hour later, aware that he'd better not exceed the speed limit on his first drive in America, his car jogged along the highway. He couldn't complain about the little silver Hyundai—in fact, he quite liked it. It drove easily, it was automatic, the air-con worked, and so did the radio. Oliver was in his element, wondering what Ursula O'Mahoney would be like, and hoping he'd have a little more time with her than Steve had granted. He dearly wanted to ask more questions about what the paper wanted him to write, and what they had on file about the events from 1981 that he was so interested in. As he drove along, the sexy name of 'Ursula' conjured up all kinds of images in Oliver's mind. For some inexplicable reason, he pictured Jessica from the Bob Hoskins film *Who Framed Roger Rabbit*? Perhaps he was getting carried away, what with his exploits with Sam last night, and the undoubted flirtation from Tabatha and her work colleague a short while ago. And now here he was anticipating that Ursh would be even more sultry and sexy than Jessica Rabbit.

In another thirty minutes, he was being ushered into the editor's office and, incredibly, she and Jessica Rabbit did indeed share similarities. Perhaps not exactly as the cartoon character had been portrayed in the film, but not far off. Ursula's hair was brown and not red, and she was shorter than the cartoon image—more in line with Bob Hoskin's height. But Ursula was just as sexy—perhaps even more so. If this were the aunt, what would her niece be like? Oliver wondered. He reminded himself that he really shouldn't be thinking such thoughts—after all, he already had a girlfriend, didn't he?

The whole situation he was in seemed like a surreal dream, and he struggled to differentiate between what was real and what was make-believe, as he drifted into a semi-trance. He was brought to his senses by the woman who had just greeted him in the *Terre Haute Daily Times* head office.

"It's very lovely to meet you, Oliver, to be sure," Ursula said warmly, with a charming mixture of American and Irish accents. "I guess you have a hundred questions for us, wouldn't you, now? Take your time, and let's go through everything, shall we?" Oliver immediately warmed to Ursula's friendly stance, and breathed a huge sigh of relief that they could actually have a conversation lasting more than a few seconds.

For nearly two hours, they discussed ways in which Oliver's articles could be best presented in the newspaper, and how they could capitalise on the popularity of the *Sherlock* TV series. After their meeting had concluded and Oliver was driving back to Plainfield, a large folder of newspaper cuttings and photographs on the back seat, he was already making plans for what he'd be doing the next day.

He had no idea that he might be stirring up a dangerous hornet's nest.

***

For the past thirty-five years, Marc Ozborn's antisocial behaviour hadn't much improved. In fact, if anything, as he approached his 68th birthday, it had become worse. He'd just about managed to scrape a minuscule living over time with a number of manual jobs here, bar work there, and social benefits in-between that enabled him to occasionally pay his rent on time. But more often than not, the prospect of eviction was never far away.

The 1980s trailer had since been replaced with a newer model with upgraded insulation, thanks to a local government scheme, but it was still parked in unpleasant surroundings. Of course, in Ozborn's eyes, his situation was always someone else's fault. If he didn't spend such a large proportion of his money on Coors, Jim Beams, Marlboros, weed and cocaine, he'd be able to vastly improve his living standards, but that thought never crossed his mind.

In one particular area he never had any difficulties. Because of his undoubted rugged and handsome looks, deep voice and trim body, he always found it easy to get laid. Women found him incredibly attractive, initially at least. Even prostitutes offered their services for free, dreaming that this man might be 'the one' who could lead them to more fulfilled and meaningful lives. But as soon as women grew familiar with his slovenly, unreliable and violent behaviour, they tired of him and let go. Those women, who thought they might tame him, were always disappointed.

The high turnover of relationships didn't bother Ozborn too much—he simply moved onto the next 'victim' prepared to suffer his verbal, emotional, and sometimes, physical abuse. In his eyes, women were there for his pleasure only, and he couldn't see the point in showing any care or warmth in return. Usually, the breakups occurred after a couple of months, but sometimes only weeks, days, or often they were just one-night stands.

One common denominator in his relationships with women was that they ended acrimoniously. Of course, in his mind's eye, the arguments that preceded the break-ups were always instigated by his lady-friends—never himself. Fortunately for most of the women, they were able to let go, move on and eventually forget. Unfortunately, two of them couldn't, because they were no longer alive. Even more unfortunately for Ozborn, the second of 'his' women who'd died, this time of natural causes, had been bringing up their baby daughter, Coldplay.

Just over five years ago, the mother of Coldplay, thirty years Ozborn's junior, had proudly announced to her hero that she was pregnant with their baby, convinced that conception occurred while the British band's 'Fix You' had been playing. Fatherhood was the last thing that Ozborn wanted. While they'd been making love on the floor in front of her log fire, she'd been convinced that he was 'the one' she'd been waiting all her life for, whereas *he* merely saw her as a way to gratify his needs, and maybe he'd enjoy a few good home-cooked meals along the way. One day after her jubilant revelation had sunk in, he went out of her front door on the pretext of buying some cigarettes, and disappeared. She never saw him again.

Tragically, three years and two months after Coldplay had been born, her mother contracted septicaemia. At two in the afternoon she complained of a throbbing feeling in her left arm, and 90 minutes later she fainted, and died in hospital only one day later. During the days leading up to the funeral, all efforts made by Coldplay's rather elegant aunt Melody Goddard and her husband Stephen to track down and make contact with the child's father had been in vain—and Coldplay went on to be lovingly brought up by the couple as the child that they had never been able to have themselves. Melody, a psychologist who had a passion for good clothes, was a kind and devoted substitute mother to the little girl. She also adored her tiny dog, Blaise-Pascal. Often, Melody could be seen around her home neighbourhood carrying Blaise-Pascal in a small leather handbag, with the creature's head just barely peeking out of the top.

On the few occasions he was sober, Ozborn occasionally recognised he ought to take responsibility for looking after his daughter, some at least. But those feelings never lasted long. In his darkest moments, deep down he was ashamed of himself and his life, but mostly he refused to admit those sentiments to himself or the outside world—especially not to Coldplay and her adopted parents. So he blanked his emotions, and any thoughts of his daughter had been locked away. Instead of facing up to his demons, he filtered his guilt and mixed-up feelings through a temper that was liable to flare up at the slightest provocation.

CHAPTER 25

(THURSDAY, 18TH JANUARY, 2018)

Waterbed Experience

The bundled-up copy of the *Indianapolis Daily Times* was hurled over to the Dickinson's house by the boy on his delivery round. Oliver was already dressed, breakfasted and eagerly waiting for its arrival. He'd been told by Sam that the newspaper usually came at around half-past eight each morning, and sure enough, today it did. Had Ursula managed to get the ad to appear in the Terre Haute and the Indianapolis editions like she said she would?

Spreading the newspaper on the dining table, Oliver eagerly turned each page as he stood over it, and let out a small gasp. There it was, what he'd been looking for, about mid-way through! A whole half-page dedicated to the Bike Radio Murder of 1981, including some clippings of old headlines and a grainy photograph of Yushi Yakamoto being led away by policemen either side of him, next to text outlining the main details of the case. As Oliver pulled up a chair, as if being seated would help him to concentrate on the article's contents more thoroughly, he yelled to Sam in excitement. Sam was almost as excited as he was, and she quickly stopped what she was doing and came over to join him as he read out loud the accompanying appeal.

"WHERE WERE YOU IN 1981? DO YOU REMEMBER THE BIKE RADIO MURDER CASE?

This newspaper invites anyone who recalls this notorious crime that took place in Paris, Illinois, to get in touch with our sensational new BRITISH investigative reporter, 'YOUNG SHERLOCK' aka Oliver Markland. You can follow Oliver's progress exclusively every day in our new featured serial, as he attempts to get to the bottom of WHAT

REALLY HAPPENED. Call 555-468-8474 or email NOW, in confidence, to youngsherlock@dailytimesgroup.com"

"Wow! Sensational, eh? You're famous already, Oliver, and you've only been here five minutes!" said Sam, proudly. Oliver couldn't hide his expression of delight at how Ursula had obviously pulled out all the stops to get something printed so quickly. He was more used to the less dynamic and slower approach of the *East Anglian Chronicle*. Checking the system, he tried calling the 555 number from the Dickinson's house-line. Instantly, his own mobile phone rang. So Ursula had also managed to get the redirection set up. Very impressive, he thought. He then tried sending a blank test-email from his iPhone, and immediately it popped up in his Inbox. So she'd got that organised as well. Fantastic!

Oliver was now ready to begin his role as Young Sherlock for the Indianapolis and Terre Haute newspapers, and he crossed his fingers that he'd soon get some leads. Meanwhile, wanting to get a first-hand impression of the location where the victim had been found, he looked up the address from the files and checked on Google Maps to see how long it should take him to get to Paris. "Do you want to come along? It could be fun," he asked Sam.

She apologised that she was unable to accompany him on this occasion, as much as she'd have liked to. "Next time, perhaps," she said.

***

When Oliver pulled up at his Paris destination, he unclipped his iPhone from the car's windscreen holder, turned off the satnav map, then shuffled out of the silver Hyundai, stretched his body and took a good look around. So, finally, here he was, at the house he'd read so much about, where Sandy Beach's body had been discovered by a neighbour. This was *the* house in which Yushi Yakamoto had supposedly killed Beach, using a handlebar radio to hit her with. He wondered how much it had changed during the past 35 years or so.

What were the new owners like? How did they feel about living in a place where someone had met their death? Oliver's mind began wandering as usual. Being such a keen cyclist himself, he *wanted* to disbelieve the recorded facts. He *wanted* to believe that someone else was guilty of such a crime.

It suddenly struck him that he'd never in his life been to the scene of a crime, any crime, let alone a murder. Of course, Oliver didn't believe in ghosts, but nevertheless, even on this cold January day of bright sunshine and blue skies, standing in front of this seemingly empty house, he sensed a kind of eeriness. He told himself not to be so stupid, and courageously decided to knock at the door. The front drive in front of the garage was full of gravel but with hundreds of weeds growing among the stones, the lawn was unkempt, and there were dead tufts of grass in-between the cracks of the paving slabs. The fence around the side of the house had one panel missing, and another had almost fallen down, only being held up by one remaining nail that was about to give way any day. The two front windows had old grey curtains pulled to, so it wasn't possible to see inside, and as he walked up to the front door, one of the steps creaked and cracked under his weight. He pressed the doorbell, without hearing a ring or chime in response, he banged the knocker, waiting at least a minute before knocking again, more loudly this time.

Concluding that there was no one present, he sheepishly began to walk around the side of the house to the back yard. He'd never done anything like this before, and he knew that technically he was trespassing. But he was a journalist, wasn't he? And journalists didn't give up at the first hurdle, did they? Nervously, he arrived at the rear decking. Most of the wooden planks were rotten and split. On its side, beneath a window, was a rusty old barbecue kettle that had seen better days. The gutter and down-pipes had become partially detached from the main wall, and the patio door in front of him was so dirty that it almost looked as if it had been painted black.

Using the palm of his hand, Oliver wiped a section of the glass so that he could peer inside. The sun's reflection on it was too strong for him to be able to make anything out. He found his hand resting on the handle. Instinctively he pressed it downward—and unbelievably, it wasn't locked. Feeling scared, and yet also embracing his role as an intrepid reporter, he pushed the door open, stepping cautiously inside, calling out several tentative 'Hello's. The calls were met with silence, the dusty kitchen was very dark, with the only light now coming in through the open patio door.

Remembering the many newspaper clippings he'd read, Oliver realised that this was where Sandy Beach had last been seen alive. A shiver went through him. He quietly moved through the kitchen and down the small hallway from where there were three doors leading to a bathroom and two bedrooms. One of the bedrooms was empty, apart from one double bedframe and rotten mattress. The next, larger, bedroom had more in it. There was a dressing table, a wardrobe with an open door revealing that it was empty, a mirror, table lamp, and some discarded clothes in the corner. Everything was covered in a thick layer of dust, and a smell of mustiness hung in the air.

A large bed positioned centrally against the rear wall drew Oliver towards it. He prodded it. The surface of the mattress moved in a way unlike any other bed he'd seen. Oliver pressed harder, and he could hear the sound of sloshing water. Could this be one of those waterbeds he'd heard about, he wondered? He'd never actually seen one before, and as his curiosity got the better of him, he sat on the corner of it, his head facing away from the door. It was soft and saggy, and he bounced up and down slightly as the material that held the water in place stretched and moved. All of a sudden, a giant blister appeared on the canvas material, which developed and grew at a frightening speed just to the left of his legs. Within seconds, the blister ruptured, causing a torrent of water to pour out from the gaping hole. The faster the water spilled out, the larger the hole became.

Oliver didn't have a clue what he should do, and in his blind panic, trying in vain to stem the flow of water with his hand, only making it worse, he failed to notice the old lady standing at the door behind him, a formidable double-barrel shotgun in her hand. The elderly lady cocked the gun's latch with a loud click, making a sound that Oliver heard but struggled to locate. As he realised that the sound couldn't have been from the bed itself, he leapt forward from the gallons of water now fast spreading across the floor. As he twisted his body round, he jumped out of his skin at the sight of a shotgun being pointed at his head. He let out such a shout that the lady, frightened out of her own skin, accidentally pulled the trigger just as the cascading water sloshed against her feet with great force. What with that, and the fierce kick of the gun, she lost her balance and fell to the ground. Luckily for both of them, the buckshot missed Oliver, flew through the air, hitting the ceiling light and causing the bulb to explode into thousands of tiny glass pieces, scattering everywhere like rain.

By now, the old lady had dropped the gun, and was floundering around on the floor like a fish, her clothes completely soaked through, as she attempted, without success, to get up. The bed canvas was now a shrivelled up piece of wrinkled material at the bottom of its wooden frame. The water was still flowing out of the room and into the hallway, spreading to every area of the house's flooring. The words that boomed forth from the larger-than-life lady made Oliver obey her command. "Help me up, young man. Help me up before I drown. What on earth are you doing in here? Who are you? You're in *big* trouble!"

"I know," was all Oliver was able to say, feeling faint and almost passing out, before pausing and then telling the lady his name. With each word he spoke, the lady became more certain that she could recognise his accent to be English. She could see he was visibly upset and shaken. She also could tell instinctively that no malice had been intended by the British intruder, and although soaking wet, she began to see the funny side to the bizarre situation, and started laughing.

"Come on, give me your hand, you silly man, and pull me up. Then we'd better go next door and dry off, where you can tell me what you're up to. Come on, I've decided I'm not going to shoot you!"

Much to Oliver's relief, the lady's bark had turned out to be worse than her bite. After assisting her to her feet, he followed her to the house next door where he sat alone waiting while she went off to change into dry clothes. His own clothes were wet in patches, but not as thoroughly soaked as hers were. Despite the shock of having had a gun pointed at him, he thought he recognised the lady's face. Putting two and two together, he wondered—could she possibly be the neighbour from the 1981 news reports?

He didn't have to wait long before she returned to the room. "Well, young man, it's a good job my beloved late husband Daniel hadn't caught you snooping around. I don't think he would have been such a bad shot as me!" she said as seriously as she could, before breaking in to a wry smile. "Okay, now tell me what you were doing."

For the following twenty minutes, Oliver explained his whole story, and the lady—who confirmed her name was indeed the very Mrs. Hannah Toporofski of the old newspaper articles—remained silent. That was until the point when he described his new role as the Young Sherlock, and she then let out a shrill shriek. "What a brilliant idea!" she exclaimed. "I'm sure I might be able to help you!" She went out of the room, and returned a few minutes later clutching a large scrapbook that she then placed on the table in front of Oliver. "Take a look through this!"

Oliver began turning the pages, expecting to see the same newspaper cuttings that Ursula had already provided him with. But instead, it was full of clippings relating to a man named John Moores. He looked up at Hannah, puzzled.

"That man . . ." began Hannah, ". . . is the reason why that poor cyclist went to meet his maker with a lethal injection at Joliet. I'm convinced of it. I told Moores, as sure as I'm talking to you now, that I'd heard and seen another man at Sandy's house around the time of her murder. But did he take any notice? Did he heck! He was a racist bigot, and thank God he got his comeuppance. Unfortunately for that boy with a Japanese name, it was too late, in my humble opinion."

Oliver really wanted to properly digest the whole contents of the book, but now was not the time—he was still traumatised from the events earlier. He wanted to return to the sanctuary of his temporary home at the Dickinson's. "Do you think I could borrow this, please?" he asked, half expecting his request to be refused. But Hannah was already hoping that she might be able to step back in the limelight, if the popularity of this 'Young Sherlock' character took off in the *Terre Haute Daily Times*, the newspaper that she read avidly every day. Hannah could see that Oliver might very well be a mere press writer today, but potentially a TV celebrity tomorrow.

The hairs on the back of her neck stood up as she realised that this young man could be her passport to a second bout of television 'stardom'. "Of course, honey, you take it with you now, and bring it back when you return with the TV crew!" she cooed.

"Huh?" asked Oliver, totally confused.

"Never mind," was Hannah's reply. Apart from the scrapbook, Oliver kept thinking of the watery mess in every room of the house next door. He asked if he should go and mop it up, or call the owner or someone else. "I *am* the owner," Hannah said, before explaining how she'd bought the place from Sandy's parents two years after her murder. The parents could never get over the fact that their daughter's life had ended there, and didn't ever want to revisit the property. Technically, they owned it, but it represented too much sorrow for them. So when Mrs. Toporofski offered to buy it from them for half the market value, they readily accepted. Hannah had every intention of turning the double garage into an antiques emporium—but never got around to it. Year after year went by, until her beloved husband Daniel had sadly passed away, and she knew then that she'd never find enough energy to put the house in order and fulfil that particular dream. And so she let the property go to rack and ruin. Now in her late eighties, she was too tired to care less about whether the floors were wet or dry.

But for the first time she could remember since becoming widowed, she found some fresh enthusiasm emerging, and decided there and then to help the young man as much as she could. After all, she did still care about the opportunity to appear on television again, and any resurgence of interest in the 'Bike Radio Murder' just might give her that chance.

CHAPTER 26

(THURSDAY, 18TH JANUARY, 2018)

Media Interest

During Oliver's drive back to his temporary Plainfield home, his head was in a spin as he continuously churned over the events of the day, and what Mrs. Toporofski had told him before he'd departed from her house. She said she remembered a man leaving the vicinity of the crime scene in a pickup truck, and she also described hearing raised voices the same evening that Sandy Beach had been killed. Or so she thought. Oliver acknowledged that after a period of over three decades, and with Mrs. Toporofski currently in her later years, she may well have got some of her facts wrong. After all, the last thing she had said to him, quite emphatically, was that her memory wasn't as good as it used to be.

But very disturbing was the fact that apparently she'd told the same story to the police chief when he'd interviewed her after she'd discovered the dead body. Surely she should at least have had her statement submitted to the court, or even been called to testify in person, such was the relevance of her information, but Oliver had seen no mention of that in all the case reports he'd researched. Before today, he'd only come across Chief John Moores's name, later to become a Governor, in the various newspaper reports he'd read. But now, according to Mrs. Toporofski's description of him, he sounded like a bit of a dodgy character.

Oliver decided that the raised voices Mrs. Toporofski thought she'd heard *could* have been Yakamoto and Beach arguing, although some sixth sense was telling him that that was unlikely. But if it hadn't been Yakamoto's voice, who's was it? Maybe Oliver's own wishful thinking was now playing a part in his personal summation of what had happened back then. He couldn't tell. Regardless, he puzzled over who the driver of the truck might have been, if indeed there had been one. Was it possible for both men, Yakamoto and the truck driver, to have been present in the house at the same time? Why had Moores apparently ignored Mrs. Toporofski's story? Maybe a copy of her statement still existed. If it did, Oliver knew that he would certainly like to read it.

Pulling off the freeway and into a rest area, Oliver Googled Moores's full name. His search revealed that although being found guilty of racism and corruption charges, Moores had only served a three-month suspended sentence, and was now apparently living freely in retirement in Chicago—about 200 miles from Indianapolis. It seemed, Oliver thought, that money really could buy you a get-out-of-jail card in this country.

Could Moores' conduct have influenced Yakamoto's final fate? he wondered. Already drawing his own biased conclusions, Oliver reprimanded himself. He should remain impartial and stick to the facts. He would dearly love to interview Moores if at all possible—it could make for great reading in his blogs and newspaper columns. But he doubted whether such a request would be granted—so for now he would put that idea on the back-burner. Maybe at some point in the future, he'd attempt to find Moores' email address and send a carefully-worded message. But for the time being, as soon as he arrived home, he really must concentrate on the writing that he was obliged to do. He liked to think that there were people out there eagerly awaiting Young Sherlock's next instalment. After a quick coffee, Oliver returned to the freeway for the remaining part of his journey back to Plainfield.

By the time Oliver arrived home at the Dickinson's, he was thankfully by now much more composed. Everyone was out, so he went straight upstairs, sat at the desk in his room, and began to work. He kept looking at his iPhone just in case emails had come in, answering the appeal that had been published in yesterday's papers—but he was disappointed to see that there was nothing. However, he *had* received an email from Ursula's niece, Siobhan. It was rather gushing with comments about London, England in general, how much she was looking forward to going there, and how much she appreciated Oliver putting her in touch with his boss at the *East Anglian Chronicle*. She was also keen to visit Scotland during her travels, and asked where in England it was. She ended with a request to meet up with Oliver, and buy him a burger and soda as a big thank you. Oliver was shocked at her apparent geographical ignorance, but remembered how insular some Americans could be. He'd heard of some who had lived all their lives never having left their own state, let alone crossing their international border.

There was also an attachment to Siobhan's email. "Woah!" he mouthed in wonder as he saw the accompanying photo of the stunningly beautiful Siobhan. He instantly forgave her for not being more informed about the countries of the United Kingdom. "I wouldn't mind giving her a private lesson in geography," he said to himself with a grin. He ogled her dark, long flowing hair, incredible figure squeezed into tight jeans and clinging white t-shirt, blue eyes and warm smile. For some time, Oliver found it difficult to focus his mind on his writing tasks, especially while he was thinking how he should reply to her last paragraph in which she also offered to help him with his investigations.

"Concentrate, Oliver!" he told himself firmly. He felt certain that if he met up with Siobhan in person he'd find it extremely difficult not to fall for her hook, line and sinker—and that wouldn't be particularly good for his relationship with his hosts. As he continued to work, occasionally gazing out of the window at the garden and pool below, he knew his loyalty ought to remain with the Dickinson family, and particularly Sam, of course. So, his reply to Siobhan became another email he decided to put on hold, for the present at least.

After writing up the day's ordeal for the newspaper column, Oliver was pleased with the way he'd included some comedic value to the waterbed story—although he hadn't seen any funny side to it earlier.

He emailed his column off to Ursula at the Terre Haute office, and also Steve at the Indianapolis headquarters. He then wrote the draft of his blog that he'd finish off and upload to the *East Anglian Chronicle*'s website later. By now he was feeling quite exhausted, and with dinner not for another hour when the others were due home, he decided to take a short nap—but not before checking out Google Maps, in preparation for the following day's planned visit.

Sixty minutes later, he was awoken from a deep slumber in which he had been dreaming that he was floating on an air mattress in the middle of a calm river, suddenly transforming itself into a massive waterfall. The knock at his door, followed by Sam calling him down for the evening meal, roused him with a sudden start, his forehead covered with beads of sweat. "Err, thanks Sam, I'm, err, just coming," he mumbled in response, somewhat dazed.

At the dining table and now feeling much more alert, Oliver related the day's adventures to his captive audience of three. He then informed them that, very early the next morning, he planned to make the three-hour drive to Joliet and visit the old prison building there. "You know it's a tourist site now, don't you?" asked Chris. Oliver did know, but nevertheless he wanted to get a feel for the place first hand. He wanted to imagine how it must have been for Yushi during his time as an inmate, and what better way than to actually go there? He had another plan up his sleeve. While in the same vicinity, south of Chicago, he'd attempt to also go to nearby Stateville Prison, in the hope he would learn more about Yushi's cellmate, referred to in Gold's study as 'ASSASSIN'.

The only information Oliver had about the cellmate was his name—M.J. Emanuele—and Oliver was aware that by now he may no longer be residing at Stateville anyway. He may have been moved to another prison, or released, or indeed may have since passed away. He was sure, though, that it would be easier to make such enquiries in person rather than by phone. For some reason that even he didn't understand, he decided to keep these intentions to himself.

Shortly after finishing their meal of jerk chicken and salad, Kerry left the table to fetch the ice-cream dessert. While she was in the kitchen, Oliver's phone rang. Knowing how rude it was to talk on the phone while a meal was in progress, at first he ignored it, but it kept ringing. Eventually, he discreetly looked at the screen in case it was Ursula or Steve, or someone from back home in Essex. Oliver saw that it was none of those, and just showed up on the screen as a number he didn't recognise. Perhaps it was a member of the public responding to the newspaper ad appealing for information! He was desperate to pick up. Sensing Oliver's anxiety, Chris made it clear he didn't mind the call being taken at the table. "Go ahead, Oliver," he gestured with a wave of his hand. "It could be important."

Kerry returned with a large tub of Ben & Jerry's ice-cream and began sharing it out. Pretending not to eavesdrop, the others continued talking among themselves, while at the same time straining intently to hear Oliver's side of the conversation. They picked up on him agreeing to meet the caller in Paris the day after next, and then they waited patiently for Oliver to elaborate once he'd hung up.

"Was that a lead?" asked Sam, hopefully.

"No, I'm afraid not. Maybe something better though!" Oliver answered, hardly able to contain his excitement, but trying to play it coolly. "That was WTHTV-NEWS10 channel in Terre Haute. They want to do a five-minute piece with me outside the murder victim's house. It will be broadcast live, and again later on the six o'clock news!"

Sam's mouth gaped in amazement. "So not only are you in the papers, you're gonna be a TV star as well! That's fantastic! We can get NEWS10 here," she squealed.

Oliver restrained his glee. "Well, I wouldn't exactly say 'TV star', Sam. I bet they're going to goof me up as some British eccentric pretending to be Sherlock Holmes. But it's worth doing, I guess. You know what they say about any publicity being good publicity.

Perhaps it might increase the chances of getting some public response. One never knows unless one tries these things, does one?" he asked in a self-mocking British accent.

They all laughed, and Sam was super-impressed with Oliver's logic and confidence. This time she *was* keen to accompany him to Paris, and she made it clear. Oliver shifted awkwardly in his seat as he remembered the side of the phone conversation that hadn't been audible to the others. The caller, a researcher from the TV channel, had explained to him that she'd been prompted to call Oliver by a friend, none other than Ursula O'Mahoney, who had suggested that her niece also work as an assistant on the project.

So Siobhan would also be joining Oliver in Paris. "Err, I'm sorry, Sam," Oliver answered slowly, trying to work out a good enough reason why he needed to go alone. "They, err, want me to go to a meeting with the producer after the filming. I'll probably be gone all day. Maybe next time, eh?" Sam slowly nodded in agreement, obviously disappointed. But by repeating the same phrase she herself had used once before, Oliver knew she couldn't really argue. Although pleased that he'd been able to successfully deflect her request without raising any suspicion, he still felt guilty as he questioned his true motivations for not inviting her along.

He thanked Kerry for the delicious meal and said he must now go upstairs to finish off today's blog and get a good night's sleep in readiness for an early morning departure to Joliet. Once the blog had been uploaded, he sent off a quick email to Siobhan, expressing how pleased he would be to meet her the day after tomorrow, and that he was very much looking forward to working with her. She must have been online at the same time, because almost immediately she sent a reply that simply read "*Me too! Goodnight, Oliver*". As he was getting comfortable in his bed, Oliver's heart skipped a beat before he promptly fell asleep.

CHAPTER 27

(THURSDAY, 18TH JANUARY, 2018)

Payment Offer

By the time Marc Ozborn had awoken, it was already nearly midday. Nursing the hangover that had become a daily occurrence for much of his adult life, as well as some of his childhood, the first thing he did was to reach for the jar of instant coffee and put two heaped spoonfuls plus four sugar cubes into the only unchipped mug he owned, still dirty from the day before, while simultaneously switching on the kettle that was half-filled with yesterday's water.

He considered his plans for the day ahead, or at least what was left of it. It was true to say that life had suddenly and unexpectedly become easier for him quite recently, since he'd been left a modest sum of money. His one remaining aunt who had passed away over a year previously at her nursing home in Oregon had never had any contact with her nephew, and had wrestled between leaving her cash to a cats' home, or keeping it in the family. After due consideration, she decided on the latter, and left her savings to her only surviving relative. After her passing, it had taken many long hours for the lawyers at Goode & Harte to sort out the complicated probate. The firm eventually managed to track Ozborn down, two thousand miles across the country, but not without creating a new set of problems.

During the time when such efforts had been made to locate Ozborn's present whereabouts, a newly-employed post-graduate at Goode & Harte had inadvertently alerted Melody Goddard of Ozborn's address by sending out the wrong set of documents to her—the one meant for him. When she opened the package and studied the contents, she wondered whether Ozborn would ever think to financially contribute towards Coldplay's upbringing and, to put it mildly, she was very sceptical. So, she decided that as soon possible in the new year, she'd take the matter into her own hands by paying Ozborn a visit, accompanied by her husband Stephen. Together, they would try prodding at the man's guilty conscience, if indeed he had one.

Eventually, when the firm's mishap had been rectified, and Ozborn's inheritance was finally settled, he found himself to be richer overnight by precisely $56,204.79. He thanked his lucky stars for the best, and only, Christmas present he'd had for as long as he could remember, but he soon found that his windfall hadn't come without some downside.

Within two weeks, Ozborn's bank balance was by now already down to under £20,000, and even he had been surprised by quite how quickly money flowed away with no effort at all. Firstly, there had been a number of debtors who became increasingly riled by his excuses for non-payment, and Ozborn sensed that their hints of violence could very soon become more than the idle threats he'd been so expert at avoiding, so he reluctantly settled up. He also promptly blew a stack of money on some fancy clothes and shoes. Of course, it was about time for some new furnishings for the trailer, including a black leather sofa and, while he was at it, why not get a new stereo system? he thought.

Then, as well as paying for a brand brand-new Ford pickup in cash, he decided he would fix up his beloved old Dodge truck that was parked behind his home, up on jacks for the previous 14 years or so.

Despite the vehicle now being 46 years old, its engine still started after a splutter or two when he turned the key. But the muffler and tailpipe were now completely shot with rust, and the wheels had been removed and thrown in the back, their worn-out tyres showing hardly any tread.

Mice and vermin seeking shelter had made good use of the interior's roof lining and seat padding. To anyone else, the vehicle would have been considered a wreck—but Ozborn, always fond of it, had hoped that one day he'd get it fixed up and back on the road.

Now he at last had the financial wherewithal to do just that, and he was looking forward to getting on with the job—just as soon as he was sober enough. As he finished off his coffee, he thought that perhaps today would be the day he'd make a start.

As it turned out, today was also the day Coldplay's guardians, along with their little dog Blaise-Pascal, decided to pay a visit. And right when he was in the middle of listing the parts he wanted to collect from the local Dodge dealer later that day.

When the strangers first turned up, Ozborn refused to even acknowledge the existence of a daughter. He certainly didn't want to heed their suggestion to do "the right thing," as they'd put it, "for the child". Why should *he* have to contribute to her wellbeing? That was up to the State, surely, and the responsibility of her guardians—not him.

Their suggestion of financial contribution really rattled him, and his anger increased. He even warned them he had a gun and wouldn't be afraid to use it if they didn't vacate the vicinity of his property. They did go to leave quickly after that, but not before slamming down a batch of six colour photographs of the little girl. The top ones pictured her blowing out five candles on a cake at her recent birthday party, and others were taken when she was much younger, although Ozborn wouldn't have known that because he point-blank refused to look at them. Antagonised and angry, the selfish Ozborn made a kneejerk reaction in the slight hope it might ease his inner demons, but mostly just to get the couple off his back and encourage them to go away without any further discussion.

"Five grand," he stated abruptly. "Take it or leave it. That's all I've got left," he lied, just as Melody and Stephen were getting ready to walk away, empty-handed. "Come back this time tomorrow and I'll have the cash—then I don't want to hear from you ever again. Understand?"

"We understand alright," answered Melody. "You're a cold,

heartless bastard, Marc. And one day, you'll realise that $5,000 is diddlysquat. Sure, it'll help with some essential purchases for the poor little cherub, but what that young girl—your daughter—really needs to know, is that she has a father who loves and cares for her.

"Well, I don't," spat the young girl's parent. "Now get the hell out of here before I change my mind about the money. I'll have it for you tomorrow, if you want it. Now, go."

Not expecting to even extract $500 from the man, let alone a promise of ten times that sum, Melody and Stephen, both sobbing as they walked towards their car, were however at least grateful for small mercies. "We'll be back tomorrow, then," shouted Coldplay's uncle, turning his head towards Ozborn one last time before driving off.

Ozborn stormed back inside the trailer, slamming the fly-screen door behind him, creating a loud clatter of metal on metal. Inside, he then paced up and down the cramped space, doing a quick calculation in his head. "Damn! Now I'll only have less than fifteen grand left. And a new set of wheels and tyres are gonna be at least two. Muffler and pipe another one. Shit! Damn the kid!" Ozborn continued talking aloud, frothing at the mouth as he spoke.

Slumping back in rage on his new leatherette couch, piled high with old issues of Playboys, CarMarts and TV guides, he shoved them all off onto the dirty floor, among the cigarette butts and empty beer cans. He caught a glimpse of the photograph of the little girl blowing out candles that lay face up on the coffee table. "Damn kid," he reiterated. "Why did her mom have to go and die? She should be the one taking care of her, not me," he shouted out loud, head held back as he stared at the low ceiling, wrestling with his mixed emotions of guilt and fury.

He began to tear up the pictures, one by one, throwing the fragments on the floor. But when he got to the fourth, fifth and sixth pictures, it was clear that these hadn't been taken at the same time as the first three. These three had obviously been taken years earlier, when Coldplay was only a toddler. Ozborn looked at the images of the little girl being held in her mother's arms.

For a few brief seconds, he paused, and his eyes focussed intently on the beautiful woman cradling the baby girl. He had to admit the mother had been a stunner. Her appearance reminded him of another beauty. Another woman who had been dead for many years. His mind went back to the brief encounter with Sandy Beach in the early eighties. The recollection was not an isolated one. After years of conveniently blanking out their short relationship, Sandy Beach's untimely death had begun to haunt him lately. He'd even suffered a few sleepless nights—and he had no idea why.

He took solace in a swig of Jack Daniels, finishing off the bottle that was propped up next to him on the sofa. And then, true to form, his anger exploded in the usual way. He hurled the bottle as hard as he could at the 40-inch TV in the corner of the trailer's lounge. On impact, the screen shattered, sending an instant spider's web of broken glass to all of its four corners. The endless stream of colourful cartoons that moments earlier had been playing in the background suddenly ceased, as the screen went black with sparks flying, coupled with a loud bang and a puff of smoke billowing upwards. "Fuck! Fuck, fuck, *fuck!*" yelled Ozborn, even more angry now—this time with himself as well as the outside world.

He kicked open the door, not bothering to lock it behind him, stormed out to his new Ford, got in and sped off in the direction of the nearest local bar where he stayed until midnight, talking nonsense to no one in particular—just anyone who had the misfortune to sit on a barstool next to him in the dimly-lit room, while Ozborn became ever more drunk and obnoxious than usual.

Finally, when he was barely able to sit upright any longer, the proprietor instructed Ozborn in no uncertain terms that it was time for him to go. At first objecting, Ozborn then realised how ravenously hungry he had become, having not eaten a thing all day, save for a few peanuts. Shouting some incoherent obscenities as he left the premises, he staggered over to the truck and climbed in. Hardly able to drive in a straight line, halfway home he stopped at a Tex-Mex carry-out for a burrito and slaw to go.

While waiting for his meal to be prepared, he idly flicked through that day's newspaper that was lying on the counter by the window. Unable to focus his eyes properly, on account of his inebriation, as well as his poor eyesight that was worsening with age, he very nearly missed the headline on page 51 containing the words 'BIKE RADIO MURDER'. At first, he failed to register any relevance. It wasn't until he browsed further down the page, past the picture of the guy with the Asian appearance being led away by police, to the portrait of the sexy dental assistant in her tunic, that old memories of her were stirred for the second time that day. So many years had gone by since that April evening in 1981, but to Ozborn it seemed like the events had occurred only yesterday.

"What the *hell*?!" he exclaimed, paying no attention to the other customers turning round to stare at him, as he unsuccessfully strained to read the small print. He would have to look at the newspaper again when he was less drunk, so he tore the page out and crammed it unfolded and screwed up into his pocket, ready to read another time. As he did so, he heard the restaurant's new assistant, proudly displaying her one gold star on her lapel badge, call out his order.

"Burrito and slaw to go!" she announced, rather timidly. Ozborn rudely snatched the brown cardboard box out of her hands and swayed out the door, climbed back in his truck, and sped out of the parking lot and into the street, tyres screeching. A few seconds later, a loud claxon sound alerted him to glance up, only to see the red flashing light that had seemingly appeared from nowhere in the rear-view mirror.

CHAPTER 28

(FRIDAY, 19TH JANUARY, 2018)

Cell Discovery

Oliver had become used to his little Hyundai, and now that he was familiar with driving on the 'wrong' side of the road, he positively enjoyed the experience. He slotted one CD after another into the built-in player, as he made his way to Joliet, Illinois. Thanks to the efficiency of the route selected by his iPhone satnav, he reached his destination well before the time he had anticipated.

Pulling up at the entrance to the old prison, he felt the memory of watching *The Blues Brothers* film come flooding back, and here he was at the very place depicted in that film, but this was now no movie—it was the real deal. Oliver followed the signs that read 'VISITORS PARKING', got out of the car and took in his surroundings. The building in front of him was like a scene from a horror movie, a huge, four-storey castle with towers at each corner and a protruding grand entrance—all built in yellow sandstone. To the right, a long wall that adjoined the castle-like building extended the entire length of the car park.

There were a number of placards dotted around, informing visitors of interesting facts and figures about the prison—as well as one stating the opening hours, the location of the gift shop, and another apologising that, because of the dangerous state of repair, only limited access would be allowed to the cell blocks. Oliver was very disappointed, especially when he looked up at the large black-and-white photographs mounted along the wall showing inside the building from when it was a working penitentiary. They were fascinating.

With the photographs giving him some idea of what it had been like inside, Oliver walked in the direction of the entrance turnstile, as indicated by the signage, hoping to get a full-blown guided tour. Sadly, he soon discovered that would not be the case. In fact, whether he had visited last week, this week or the following week, he would have only been able to gain access to a limited number of communal spaces, and only the ground floor of Cell Block B. Of course, the authorities had made sure that the cafeteria and the gift shop were fully open, aiming to extract as many dollars as possible from the eager public.

Once he'd paid his $20 entrance fee, Oliver set foot in the main section of the building. Directly in front of him, he found the kitchens to be accessible, still with their stainless-steel vats that had once been used to cook gallons of stew and rice for the hundreds of inmates. The massive eating area was to the left of the kitchen, with long wooden tables running the entire length of the room. Further down the corridor, the library was open, with many books still strewn across the floor for effect. Oliver was saddened that they hadn't been picked up and put back on the shelves. Maybe it added to the authenticity, in the eyes of the franchisee responsible for the tourist attraction, but as far as Oliver was concerned, disrespect shown to books was a crime in itself.

He continued to wander around, coming eventually to the quadrangle where prisoners would have been able to exercise and play basketball as part of their daily routine. Following the throng of visitors as they were being guided into the dark and dingy 'B' Block, he looked upwards at the peeling paint hanging off the walls and ceiling.

The photographs on the walls cleverly integrated image and reality, with a soundtrack playing in the background of the general din, clanking of keys and doors, and shouts, moans and groans from the inmates and guards that would have been heard back then. The dim lighting and dank indoor air enhanced the eerie atmosphere. Oliver felt a chill run through him, and it wasn't only from the cold temperature. But, as much as all this was without doubt of great interest, where Oliver *really* wanted to go was cell 10 on the 4th floor of 'A' Block. "No, that's off limits," was all the security guard would say when asked.

Oliver had seen enough. What a shame, he thought, that he'd come this far and wouldn't be granted access to Yushi's cell. He exited the building and dejectedly made his way back across the car park tarmac, only to suddenly stop dead in his tracks, possessed by a sudden thought. No! It was wrong to give up so easily, he told himself. He'd come to Joliet with the specific intention of visiting Yushi Yakamoto's old prison cell. He was a journalist, was he not? He was here on a mission. Reaching into his bag, he pulled out the key—his actual 'Florida Key'—, turned 180 degrees and headed right back to the turnstile where he'd entered previously. He'd have another attempt.

"Excuse me," he began to the man dressed as a prison guard, but more likely to have been hired just to look the part and offer basic information to visitors. "Can you tell me where Cell Block 'A' is please? You see, I've got this key and I want to see if my key fits the lock."

Despite Oliver demonstrating his best English accent, his request fell on deaf ears. The make-believe guard was having none of it, and engaged in no conversation at all. Looking straight past Oliver, he merely offered a shake of the head and a few words. For the second time, Oliver was informed that Block 'A' was 'off limits'.

Clearly making no progress, but determined not to give up, Oliver politely turned and left, with a meek 'thank you', and began heading back towards his car so that he could work out his next move. As he walked parallel to the red-bricked wall, he went past a small door halfway along. Although he hadn't paid particular attention to it previously, now he examined it much more closely. If he wasn't mistaken, he thought it might be slightly ajar. With the sun's shadow cast between it and the surrounding woodwork it was difficult to be certain—the only way to find out would be to go over to it and take a closer look.

After checking over his shoulders, he was alone as far as he could make out, and neither could he see any CCTV cameras. Without spending a second longer to consider what he was doing, he ran across the dry grass to the door, illogically bending down just like in the movies, as if that would somehow make him more invisible. There was no time for hesitation, and as soon as he reached the door that was indeed open an inch or two, he pulled it further, took one final look around, and quickly sneaked inside.

Aware that he really oughtn't to be doing this, Oliver was spurred on by some spontaneous energy that he'd never experienced before. With his heart thumping, he found himself in a long corridor, with nothing to indicate whether he should go left or right. He got out his iPhone and typed some relevant words into Google. When a diagram of the prison quickly appeared, based on where he assumed his location to be, his instinct told him he should turn right, which he did.

At the end of the corridor, which was dark, cold and smelt musty, the space opened up to a larger area with wide staircases and yet more corridors. In the far distance, he could just about make out another, narrower, set of metal steps. Oliver looked up, down and all around, excited—but also more scared than he'd ever felt before in his life. It appeared that he was in a central hallway, with signs for various locations pointing in all directions. This must have been one of the central thoroughfares, he thought, and it reminded him of being in the main reception area back home at Colchester Hospital. Here, as well as there being boards pointing to 'MEDICAL', 'CHAPEL' and 'PUBLIC RESTROOMS', there were signs to 'BLOCK B', 'BLOCK C', and 'BLOCK D'. Oliver looked for one marked 'BLOCK A'. There wasn't one. Could that mean that he was in fact already in it? If so, he now just wanted the 4th floor, and that was indicated by the sign pointing to his left.

He hesitated. Dare he venture up there? He stood still and listened. There wasn't a single sound. Feeling momentarily brave, he ventured up the steps, trying desperately to contain any noise from his footsteps to a bare minimum. Going past the next two floors, he eventually reached the top one, with a sign confirming he was on the fourth. He peered down the long corridor. If it had had carpets, wallpaper and lighting, it would have been akin to a Travelodge, Oliver thought. He crept along, past the first steel-barred door on the left, marked with the number '1' above it. As he went on, past numbers 2, 3, 4, and so on, he felt certain that anyone listening would be able to hear his heart actually pumping the blood around his body. He continued by the numbers 7, 8, 9—until he finally reaching the all-important number '10'.

Like all the others, the door wasn't completely closed. He wanted to step inside, so began pulling the door open towards him. Its hinges squeaked, the sound echoing all around the cavernous building. Not wanting to bring any attention to himself, even though he was sure of being completely alone, he opened the door just a fraction at a time so that no noise emanated. Oliver was surprised at how even darker it was inside the room compared to being outside in the corridor. It took him a while to adjust his eyes to the very minimal light that came in from the only source–the skylight that partially ran along the length of the main block outside the cell.

Oliver couldn't quite believe that, finally, here he was, standing in the cell that had been the subject of his intense interest for so long. The very cell that, according to the research he'd been able to carry out, used to be 'home' to two inmates whose names he was now so familiar with—Emanuele and Yakamoto. He looked down at the key held tightly in his hand, and wondered if it would actually fit into the lock of the door. He couldn't resist the temptation to try, even though he was afraid the clanking sound of metal might resonate throughout the building.

As carefully and with as much precision as he could, he slowly put the key into the slot, managing to muffle the sound as much as possible. Yes! It *did* fit—but now Oliver wondered whether it would actually operate the latch. He tried to turn it. At first it didn't budge, but as he applied more and more force, gradually the key became unseized and rotated very slightly. He wiggled it back and forth, his action further freeing up the mechanism. He tried turning it fully once more. With an unexpected clunk, the thick metal plate shot forward from the lock housing, causing a deafening noise that rippled throughout prison block A. Oliver jumped in shock, and with an almost comical action, tried to deaden the sound with his bare hands, even though it was obviously too late. The damage had been done.

Inside the cell, he stood motionless for only a few seconds, although it felt like minutes. During that time, he cast his eyes around the cold, barren room that he guessed must have been about twelve feet by ten. At the opposite wall to where he was standing, the iron bunk bed had been stripped of any linen, but the mattresses were still there, stained and torn. Next to the bed was a white porcelain sink with a crack right across its bowl, and one single tap. At the far end of the room, offering no privacy, was a toilet with no seat.

As Oliver's eyes gradually adjusted to the dim light, he noticed a number of graffiti markings scratched on the brickwork next to the lower bed. He moved closer to take a better look, but unfortunately wasn't able to make out any of the words or letters—it was simply too dark. Just as he was staring at the markings, trying to decipher anything at all, the electric lights outside the cell in the main building suddenly came on. Oliver was scared witless. The light shone through the bars of the door, illuminating the area of the wall that he had been looking at. Torn between getting the hell out of there without delay, and examining the wall for a few more seconds, his curiosity got the better of him. While he studied the markings, he thought he could hear distant footsteps far away, reverberating throughout the prison building.

"Bloody hell. I'd better get out of here, now!" thought Oliver. He took one more quick look at the wall, now that his eyes had become fully adjusted to the dull lighting.

This time he was definitely able to make out the etched words, just as he could now hear two men's voices in the distance. "You check this floor and Two," said one. "Okay, and I'll do Three and Four," replied the other. A short while later, the heavy sound of boots stomping up the main staircase grew increasingly louder.

Still intrigued by what he had read on the wall, as quick as lightning, Oliver pulled his iPhone from his pocket and took one quick snap, knowing that even in the dull light it would work. Unfortunately, he'd forgotten that the camera's auto flash was switched on, and an instant bright light went off.

Petrified that he'd now given away his location, he was thankful that he was wearing his Converse baseball shoes with soft soles. Without another moment's hesitation, he darted through the partly-open cell door without making a noise. "Bugger!" he almost said out loud, when he saw his precious Florida Key still protruding from the lock. He had no choice—he *had* to remove it. Keeping an ear for the rhythm of heavy boots coming up the steps, he managed to pull the key out exactly in time with the man's down-step, shielding the sound the key made as he whipped it from the door.

Oliver quickly and stealthily ran to the stairs at the far end of the corridor, away from where he could hear the man's boots coming, keeping himself as close to the cell walls as possible to avoid being seen. He just managed to catch a glimpse of one of the men in a security uniform, and he waited until the guard had reached the end and disappeared down the corridor, out of sight. "Good", thought Oliver. "If I can't see him, he can't see me." Still clutching his key, Oliver made his next move, leaping with hardly a sound down the steps two at a time to the floor below. With speed and agility on his side, he continued down to the second level, and then to the safety of the ground floor.

Running as quickly as he could, his sense of direction enabled him to retrace his steps back to the doorway through which he'd entered, and it was luckily still open. He escaped through it to the bright sunlight outside, where there were a number of people walking, some towards the official main entrance, and some in the direction of the parking area. Without drawing undue attention to himself, he slowed his pace to blend in, and joined those people returning to their cars.

By the time Oliver reached his own silver Hyundai, he thought he was going to be sick. Hand shaking, he fumbled around in his pocket for the central locking remote key, and pressed the button. Combined with the welcoming blip-blip sound, the door became unlocked and, once sitting within the confines of the driver's seat, he felt like he could at last breathe again. Letting out a huge sigh of relief, he rested his head back, and hesitated before starting the engine.

Oliver was able to remember exactly what he'd read on the wall of the cell. But still, before driving off, he flicked through his phone's photo library to the most recent picture, and stared at the image he'd captured. The scratched surface had read: 'ASK MJ. YY. 6.14.96'. He racked his brain, trying to figure out the meaning.

He studied the letters and numbers. Could 'YY' be Yushi's initials? That was surely likely. And what about the numbers? Of course! They could be a date perhaps, written the American way with the month first. The 14th of June 1996.

With all his recent research still so fresh, Oliver immediately recognised that particular date's significance as being the day of Yakamoto's execution. And what did 'ASK MJ' mean? Could it be an instruction by Yushi to 'ask MJ' about something? But who could MJ have been? he puzzled.

He leant behind and grabbed his satchel off the rear seat, lifting it over to occupy the space next to him, and began rifling through the file full of papers, trying to find something—anything—that might give him some clue. He came to the recorded list of all occupants in the cell since 1950—Hoffman, Ryan, Trudeau, and so on, glancing quickly at all the names.

And there it was, in black and white! Emanuele's initials were 'M' and 'J'. Oliver tapped his iPhone and went on to E.J. Gold's web page and clicked on the link against Emanuele's name to refresh his memory. Mark John Emanuele, known as '*The Assassin*', had been sentenced to life imprisonment in 1977. If 'life' meant 'life', then presumably he would have been transferred to Stateville when Joliet had ceased operating as a working prison in 2002.

Straight away, despite his tiredness from all the excitement so far, Oliver knew for sure that he must now go ahead with his planned second prison visit of the day. It was, according to his satnav, only six miles across Des Plaines River to Stateville. Exiting the main gates of old Joliet prison, he headed west to the place where, he hoped beyond hope, Emanuele was still residing.

Concentrating hard, Oliver drove along without any music so that he could think. Would he actually be able to meet Emanuele, he wondered? And if he *were* to be allowed, would Emanuele still remember Yushi from such a long time ago? And even if he *could* recollect his old cellmate, would he understand what Yushi had meant by 'Ask MJ'? That was always assuming the letters 'M' and 'J' meant this guy Emanuele. But Oliver had a suspicion they did.

Fifteen minutes later, Oliver pulled up at the entrance to Stateville Prison, apprehensive and nervous. "Come on," he lectured himself. "Rise to the challenge. Pull yourself together and get on with it!"

Unlike Joliet, this was a fully-functioning prison, with all the appropriate security in place. It was by now mid-afternoon, and Oliver was feeling very weary. Nonetheless, he had a real sense of purpose when he entered the administration office and walked over to the reception area. He decided to adopt a bold approach and come straight to the point in a forthright and assertive manner, somewhat out of character.

"Can I help you, Sir?" asked a rather overweight official in uniform, getting up from behind his desk and blocking Oliver's movements any further.

"My name is Oliver Markland. I'm over from England, writing for the *Terre Haute* and *Indianapolis Daily Times*, as well as the *East Anglian Chronicle* in Britain, and I'm researching an inmate by the name of Mark John Emanuele. Would it be possible to tell me whether he is here, and if I could interview him, please?" Oliver had noticed that as soon as he'd mentioned the name Emanuele, the security man had raised a quizzical eyebrow.

"All the way from England, huh? You mean ol' M.J.–'*The Assassin*', as we like to call him?" asked the man in authority as he loomed over Oliver, but hardly letting Oliver get a word in to reply. "My, oh my! Man, of course M.J. is here. But he ain't had nobody of any importance pay him a visit in years! And I should know, man—*I've* been here longer than *he* has, so I'd say I'm more of a prisoner than him! He's sure better off than me. Man! Is he in for a surprise when I tell him he got a visitor from Great Britain, that'll be for sure! He's lived here since Joliet closed down, and I guess he'll be here until the day he dies. By rights, they say he should have fried years ago, but rumour is he had connections in high places. Nowadays, he's a tame pussycat who found the light in Jesus."

"Fantastic!" exclaimed Oliver, hardly believing his ears. But then, the security officer continued with some less positive news. "But, I'm sorry Sir, visiting day was the day before yesterday. You'll have to come back next week now. Monday morning at ten. But there's still no guarantee he'll see you, although between you and me I doubt he'll turn down the chance to show someone the finger. Come over here, and I'll take down your details and register you. Name and address please? Plainfield, huh? Well, I'll need to inform M.J. of your intention to meet him, but you can phone before you make the journey just to be sure it's okay."

Feeling overcome with tiredness, what with the security man's non-stop monologue, Oliver now just wanted to get back in his car and drive home to Plainfield before the Friday evening rush hour became too heavy. Disappointed that he'd have to make a return trip, he was nonetheless delighted to have had such a positive outcome. He gladly gave the man his full details, said goodbye and left the building.

It wasn't until he was halfway home, this time with the radio blaring at near full volume, that he wondered what on earth the comment about 'the finger' could have meant? Oliver knew the normal meaning of '*giving the finger*', but why would Emanuele want to *show* 'the finger', especially to someone he'd never met before? No matter, Oliver thought—he'd hopefully find out next week. What now excited him even more was tomorrow's appointment with the TV crew outside Sandy Beach's old house. And oh yes, he also remembered he'd be meeting the beautiful Siobhan as well—another reason to get excited!

CHAPTER 29

(FRIDAY, 19TH JANUARY, 2018)

Bungled Arrest

There had been gap of sixteen years since Katie Copeland had last worked on a forensics case. Back in 2001, she found that while constantly searching for minute clues in the goriest of places, the aftermath of homicides and suicides had become too stressful, and her general happiness was being affected. After she had discussed this with her husband Paul, they both agreed that he was by then earning enough to support them both and their two children, and it was time for Katie to tender her resignation. After twenty years in the job, she'd become too weary, and she no longer had the same passion for the career that had begun in 1981.

Since retiring, Katie had been contentedly getting on with what she described as a normal family life, bringing up the children and making a home. Back then, Issey had been ten and Max only six, and Katie enjoyed spending increased time with them and also taking more of an active role in their school's PTA. Her former job hadn't completely been forgotten, and she liked to keep abreast of developments that occurred in the world of forensics, especially in the field of DNA, the area that had always fascinated her. DNA science had come on in leaps and bounds since first being used in mainstream crime detection in the late 1980s, and she'd begun to feel a yearning, when family circumstances would allow, to return once more to work, in some capacity at least. With Max backpacking his way across the Far East, and Issey working in Pennsylvania as a media account manager at Hershey's Chocolate World, Katie was ready.

Not wanting to return to the pressures of a full-time job, even if, at her age, there had been a vacancy, Katie had decided to try her hand at working freelance. She'd offered her extensive knowledge and expertise to Police forces to help them catch some of the 'bad guys', and she'd been welcomed back with open arms. Her phone never stopped ringing.

It was the best of both worlds for Katie—she'd be invited to join an investigation team, without any obligation to do so. She could pick and choose which cases she thought would be interesting, and turn down the ones she didn't fancy. When submitting her hourly-rated invoices, she soon found that her income was at least triple what it used to be. And she was also allowed access to all the lab and data facilities just as if she were still on the Police payroll.

Being the fastidious person to the nth degree that she was, Katie had always kept a comprehensive file on every single crime she'd worked on, initially in hard copy, even right back to her first cases since graduating in 1980. During her self-imposed retirement period, her 'hobby' had been to transfer all her old case files to digital. She also scanned every relevant photograph as well, and updated the files with any subsequent news reports that she came across. She didn't know why, but she supposed it was 'just in case' one day it would come in useful. Paul knew it was simply a symptom of her being an obsessive-compulsive person. Everything in his wife's life had to be in order. Everything neat and tidy. Everything in its place. That was how Katie liked to live, and he didn't mind at all. He loved her whatever.

Katie had spent most of the morning clearing up after a rather lively dinner party held the previous evening at home. By the afternoon, she was worn out and feeling a little the worse for wear, probably on account of the large bottle of exceedingly delicious caramel vodka that one of her friends had brought for her to try. Only now, after finally putting away the last stack of plates from the dishwasher, did she allow herself to put her feet up and relax.

Ogling the lifestyles of major celebrities, Katie idly flicked through the latest issue of *Star Life and Style* magazine, while, for the time being, setting aside the *Terre Haute Daily Times* on the coffee table, with the intention of reading it after dinner that evening. For now though, gazing casually at glossy magazine pictures was about all she was able to manage. Maybe the hair of the dog would help tame her mild headache, so she poured herself just a small glass of white wine. Illogically, it did the trick.

By the time Paul had come home from work, Katie's one glass had already led to one or two more, and she was now in no mood to cook a meal, even if she'd been capable. "So, I guess I should order a Dominos?" suggested her sympathetic and kind husband. "Do you want your usual?" he asked. Katie nodded, half asleep, but roused by the anticipation of her favourite meatball pizza with extra onion topping being delivered by the man on his motorbike.

An hour later, cosy in her pyjamas, and pizza devoured, Katie could hardly keep her eyes open, and announced she'd be going to bed. "You get some rest, darling", Paul smiled, affectionately. "You just can't handle these heavy nights anymore, can you? Go and get some beauty sleep and I'll join you later after I've watched the game," he suggested. While his wife dragged herself upstairs, Paul tidied away the cardboard pizza cartons and then settled down in his favourite armchair to watch the Dodgers compete against the Boston Red Sox on TV. He smiled at how his wife, usually so full of beans, had clearly overdone it the previous evening.

Enjoying a little 'me-time' to himself during the sponsors' announcements, he casually turned the pages of the newspaper that was in front of him. When he reached page 51, the article about the Bike Radio Murder caught his attention. Wasn't that a case that his wife had been involved with ages ago? It had been a big deal at the time, and he was sure he remembered Katie mentioning it on various occasions as being one of the first cases she'd ever led.

Knowing how she liked to update her files, he tore out the article before throwing the rest of the newspaper in the bin, and would show it to her later if she was still awake. Fat chance of that now, he thought, and he was right. By the time he went up to join her in the bedroom, the only responses he got were snores. He smiled with affection yet again at how, every time he ever dared bring up the subject of her loud snoring, his wife denied any responsibility for creating such a din.

***

When Marc Ozborn woke up, he struggled to recognise his surroundings. He'd spent a most uncomfortable night in the Terre Haute police station, lying on a cold, hard bench with only one grey blanket and a single pillow on which to rest his head, awaiting a decision that would determine his fate. He would either be cautioned for drink-driving, or he would be charged. If charged, as this was now his third offence, it was more than likely he'd be serving a custodial sentence.

Very fortunately for Ozborn, the newly-recruited police officer had bungled his arrest procedure, resulting in the evidence against Ozborn becoming technically null and void. Without this fact being disclosed to him, Ozborn was offered as his one final chance, the opportunity to attend a three-day workshop, relating to alcoholism and the dangers of driving under the influence. Ozborn, thinking that he had to choose between either accepting the workshop or being charged, didn't take long to make his decision, even though he had little intention of attending the first workshop on the following Sunday morning.

He was released without charge and told to attend the local Community Center at 2.00p.m. the following day. Before leaving the police precinct, he needed to sign for the return of all his personal belongings taken off him at the time of being taken into custody. The releasing officer placed a metal box on the desk in front of Ozborn and proceeded to call out its contents while simultaneously checking them off his list, one by one.

"Timex watch with cracked glass, one brown wallet containing $17, one set of keys, one torn and crumpled newspaper page," at which point, out of curiosity, the officer uncrumpled it and looked at both sides. "One side with an advertisement for Travers Nissan Dealership, and this an article about the Bike Radio Murder. Hmm, I remember that one. It was big news at the time. Sign here, Mr. Ozborn, and let's hope we don't see you here again in the near future."

Ozborn did what he was told and signed the document that was placed in front of him, put the wallet in his back pocket, clipped the watch clasp around his wrist, grabbed the bunch of keys and selected the one for his truck. He'd forgotten all about the newspaper cutting, or why he had it. He was just about to screw it up and chuck it in the bin, but the officer's words reminded him of how he'd tried to read it last night in his drunken stupor, and had kept it for when sober.

Once out of the door and walking towards his truck, he glanced down at the piece of paper in his hand. When inside the cab he sat there and fully read it before driving off to his trailer. After such a bad night, all he now wanted was to get his head down and catch up with some sleep, but what he'd read didn't exactly help to calm him. In fact, his mind churned. His first, and, for him, common, reaction was anger. But there was a second reaction. He had to admit to feeling quite unsettled. As he drove, mulling over the contents of the article, he wondered whether he'd actually get any sleep at all.

After believing that, for so many years, he'd gotten away with a murder that he must surely have committed, the last thing he wanted was some young kid playing detective and stirring up a hornets' nest now. Glancing down while driving, he scanned the article for the kid's name. This guy Oliver Markland shouldn't be interfering in business that needn't concern him, he thought.

Ozborn decided that, for the time being, his best course of action would be to do nothing. He'd keep his ears open and nose to the ground, and hope for no further developments. With any luck, this idiot 'Young Sherlock' guy would get no responses to his ridiculous appeal, give up and go back to where he came from, and that would be the end of it.

So engrossed in his thoughts when he turned into the trailer park, Ozborn hardly noticed the car parked in front of his door and almost crashed right into it, causing a look of great alarm on the faces of its occupants. "*Shit!*" Ozborn shouted, once he recognised the car as belonging to Melody and Stephen from the previous day, and having completely forgotten they were due back today. He really was in no mood for a friendly discussion. He stormed out of his pickup, went up to the closed window of the car and banged his hand hard against it. Blaise-Pascal, the little dog sitting quietly and contentedly on the rear seat, yelped in fright.

"I don't have the money," Ozborn shouted. "Something came up. I'll have it tomorrow evening. Come back then. Now, get lost." His voice was so loud with rage that the nearby sleeping dogs began barking.

Stephen lowered his window and began protesting. "But you said . . ."

"Are you deaf?" Ozborn retorted. "I know what I said. But something came up, okay? Now you can come back tomorrow or not. I don't care. But I ain't got the money today."

Melody began crying. "Come on Stephen," she said. "Let's go before I get to do something to the bastard that I'll regret."

Stephen started the engine and began driving away. "We'll be back at six tomorrow. You'd better have the money then!" he called out as his window closed.

"Oh yeah! Or else what? Damn! Get outta here!" Ozborn called after them as they exited the trailer park gates. He kicked the ground, sending a shower of small stones into the air and creating a plume of dust.

"Damn!" repeated Ozborn as he entered his home through the flimsy aluminium door that slammed shut behind him. "Oh, fuck!" was the next thing he said, as he was greeted by the sight of the smashed TV screen and shards of glass, still on the floor since yesterday. At least he could afford to get a new one, but for now it was as much as he could do to crawl under the sheets of the bed at the rear, and fall asleep. But sleep did come almost immediately. He didn't awake until the middle of the following morning, and for the first time he could recall, it was with a clear head.

CHAPTER 30

(SATURDAY, 20TH JANUARY, 2018)

Information Appeal

Sober for once, that Saturday morning, Ozborn was able to think much more clearly than usual. He pulled back the curtain to a crisp winter's day with bright sunshine and a cloudless sky, then opened the window to allow some fresh air in.

He got up, got dressed, made himself a strong coffee and looked around. What a mess, he thought. He'd never really taken much pride in his surroundings before, and as he began clearing things up, he experienced a minor epiphany. With a new sense of clarity, he knew what he wanted to do today, and in what order. Finish his coffee was first on the list. Second, was to go shopping for a new TV. Then he'd buy a muffler and a new set of wheels for the old pickup, and he'd get to work on it fixing it up. All of a sudden, Ozborn felt he had a glimmer of something to live for, aside from the cocktail of booze, weed and cigarettes that he was used to.

Oh yes, and the third thing to do, he remembered, was to get the money for his daughter. There! He at last acknowledged her existence, but then quickly shut off any emotions he felt for her, vowing not to become distracted by them again. Maybe one day in the far future he might want to see her, but not yet. So, for now, he'd buy away any tiny amount of guilt he felt and simply make it disappear with a visit to the First State Bank to withdraw $5,000.

But along with the euphoria of his life's wake-up call came an uneasy threatening sensation from the Bike Radio Murder newspaper article that played heavily on his mind. He'd have to deal with that threat somehow if it became necessary to do so. But for now he'd concentrate on going to the bank, along with Joe's TV Depot and

Supreme Custom Wheel Mart. After dressing a little more smartly than usual, he went off into town, stopping for a hearty breakfast of waffles and bacon on the way.

By the early afternoon, Ozborn returned to his trailer with a thick wad of cash crammed into his wallet, and the latest large-screen Samsung that he staggered inside with. In the back of his Ford, ready to be fitted to the old Dodge later, was a set of four gleaming chrome wheels with new tyres, as well as a very expensive stainless steel muffler and tailpipe system.

Beginning to feel mildly happy with his new-found assertiveness, he took the TV from its box, replacing the smashed one that he'd find somewhere to dump later. For now, he chucked the old one outside the trailer door, hearing it crash to the ground, and then began flicking through the various channels once he'd connected up the new one and switched it on.

The Bruce Springsteen song '57 Channels (And Nothin' On)' came to mind as he ploughed through endless advertisements, cartoons and keep-fit instructors flogging their latest DVDs. On some stations he found 1960s B-films, as well as old *Dallas* episode re-runs that were being shown back to back with yet more ads, weather and news reports. He had no interest in any of them and began to wonder why he'd bought a television set at all. Until, that was, when he happened to come across the WTHTV-NEWS10 channel, coming from Terre Haute.

On the screen, shown standing outside a house in Paris, Illinois that Ozborn still had etched in his memory, was a young man being interviewed by the channel's reporter. Standing next to him was an elderly lady with long, silver hair, obviously relishing her time being on the television. Ozborn reached for the remote control in order to increase the volume, just in time to catch the tail end of the lady being interviewed.

"Yes, of course," she said. "I was the one, on that fateful day, who discovered the body of the young woman lying in a pool of her own blood." The woman raised her hands to her face, and her voice quivered as she continued. "It may have been over thirty years ago, but I remember it just as if it were yesterday. I don't think I'll ever get over it, you know!" And with that, she tossed her head sideways, and then down, dabbing the corner of her eye with a tissue before looking up once more at the camera.

The reporter then turned to the young man, and as he did so, a caption reading 'OLIVER MARKLAND FROM ENGLAND ('YOUNG SHERLOCK')' scrolled along the bottom of the screen, while he answered the reporter's question. "So, Oliver, you're known locally as the journalist 'Young Sherlock'. Can you tell us briefly what it is about this particular case that has brought you all the way from the United Kingdom to investigate it?"

Oliver looked confidently at the camera. "It's true that Yushi Yakamoto was found guilty of murdering Sandy Beach in 1981. He'd been cycling across your great country when he was apprehended for the brutal killing that took place in the house behind me. It was big news at the time, and I'm sure many of your viewers will still remember it. But, you see, I'm just not convinced that justice was done all those years ago. The more I've researched it, the surer I've become that the whole truth hasn't yet come out. Yushi Yakamoto was an American citizen with a Japanese name, held securely in a prison cell for fifteen long years. He was locked in tightly by this very key," Oliver said, holding up his Florida Key for the viewers. "That was until he was, I believe, unjustly executed."

Ozborn continued watching, not quite believing what he was seeing, as the lady standing at the young man's side interjected. "Yes, and I'm *certain* I heard raised voices that fateful night when poor Sandy, my dear neighbour, was killed. I'm sure there was more than one man present. And what's more, I saw someone *drive* away from the scene early the following morning. What bothers me is that I told all this to the police at the time, but they chose to ignore me. And now I'm really hoping our British friend, with your help of course

. . ." Mrs. Toporofski continued, staring directly at the camera. ". . . might be able to uncover the whole truth."

The cameraman focussed the lens back on Oliver as the reporter spoke into his hand-held microphone: "Mr. Markland, you've become kind of a local celebrity around these parts, haven't you?" he asked. Oliver smiled, turning slightly red with embarrassment. Clearly, he was enjoying all this new-found attention, yet concerned that, at the end of the day, it was all because someone had actually died. He tried his best to steer the interview back on track, with a more sincere and serious slant.

"That's not really the point here," he began, in his most exaggerated English accent. "What's important is for anyone who has *any* information about what happened that night in 1981, to please come forward and contact me." As Oliver continued to speak, a telephone number and email address appeared on screen. "It could mean that there's someone still roaming these streets of your country. Someone who thinks he's gotten away with murder for all these years. I appeal to anyone who has information, no matter how apparently insignificant, to get in touch with me. I pledge to do my best to uncover the truth."

The camera turned back to the reporter. "Well viewers, you heard it here. This is Oscar Peters, with the Young Sherlock and Mrs. err– Mrs . . ." as he looked down at his notes, ". . . Mrs. Hannah Toporofski, coming live from Paris, Illinois. And now back to you Davinia, in the studio."

"Damn!" said Ozborn softly to himself, trembling with a mixture of acrimony and worry. He very nearly punched the TV screen and broke the second one in as many days, but stopped himself in the nick of time. He retrieved the crumpled newspaper article from the trash, sat back on the couch and read it once more, considering what he should do. "Damn Brit! Who the hell does he think he is, coming over here, stirring things up?"

The unusually positive emotions Ozborn had begun experiencing earlier that day quickly evaporated, and he felt his hackles begin to rise.

Hoping that doing some work and having a few beers would calm him down, he stormed from the trailer and yanked down from the back of the truck the four new wheels that he'd bought earlier, and chucked them furiously one by one to the ground. The second of them narrowly missed a stray cat that had been befriended by one of his neighbours who, of course, Ozborn didn't get on with, and it shot away. By the time he picked up the fourth wheel, the cat had returned, and this time Ozborn deliberately hurled the heavy object right at it, this time clipping its tail and causing it to squeal loudly in pain. Ozborn smiled and wished he had a fifth wheel to throw.

He was right. Getting stuck into some work on his old truck did help to soothe things a little. And he reasoned that at least there were no reports on the news of the Bike Radio Murder case being re-opened officially by the police. But the work therapy only worked until Coldplay's guardians returned at six o'clock, just as they said they would. By then, the light was fading fast and Ozborn had already consumed several Buds. As he heard the crunch of their car on the gravel, he was just lowering the jack after fitting the last of the four wheels. He looked up and peered through the gap in the row of bottles perched upon the pickup's hood.

Ozborn approached his visitors, swigging from yet another bottle and holding a monkey wrench in his left hand. He didn't care that his stance looked so aggressive. "I s'pose you better come in while we get this done," he growled in a deep drawl. Stephen followed Ozborn into his trailer while Melody leaned into the rear of their car to pick up Blaise-Pascal.

"Come on, my little darling," she said lovingly to the tiny dog as she carried him, following Stephen inside the trailer where the TV was still on.

Ozborn's eyes were glazed and distant as he pulled out the batch of high denomination banknotes from his wallet, throwing the money down on the table. "There! Count it. It's all there," he instructed Stephen, coldly.

In the background, while Stephen counted the notes, the main six o'clock news headlines were being read out relaying President Trump's latest rhetoric. "Yeah, go man, go! That's just what this country needs," Ozborn declared, to the utter dismay of the other two adults. Blaise-Pascal growled, sensing the negative atmosphere in the room.

Stephen was about to interject and contribute his own opinion as a Democrat, when he felt a firm nudge against his foot. He looked at Melody, her face telling him to shut up, get the money and leave. They both then noticed Ozborn suddenly stop and stare at the screen as soon as the commentator announced they would soon be continuing with local news.

"Join us after the break," said the newsreader. "We'll be right back with our report on the British Young Sherlock hoping to get to the bottom of a murder that happened thirty-seven years ago."

"That damned son-of-a-bitch," exploded Ozborn. "That kid needs a lesson taught!" Coldplay's guardians were then even more shocked to see Ozborn reach down behind the cushions of the sofa and pull out a handgun. They had no idea why Ozborn had reacted this way to the item on the TV, and they didn't want to stick around to find out.

Without delay, Stephen gathered together the money as quickly as he could, pulled his wife to her feet, and almost shoved her towards the door in front of him. "Come on, Melody, it's time for us to be going." Melody didn't argue.

Ozborn shot at the ceiling, creating a hole in it large enough to see the moonlight through. The noise was deafening and startled Blaise-Pascal so much that, without warning he leapt from Melody's arms, yapping in fright before scampering to the open door and jumping down the steps.

Melody screamed and Stephen grabbed her by the hand, eager to get away as soon as they could. Turning to look behind her, Melody caught sight through the open tin door of Ozborn still holding the gun and firing it randomly. Dogs from all over the trailer park began barking and more stray cats meowed. Stephen opened the passenger door of his car and pushed his wife in, then ran round to the other side and got in as quickly as he could, fumbling with shaking fingers to locate the ignition key slot. "But where's Blaise?" hollered Melody.

"I dunno. It's too dark to see," answered Stephen, scared out of his wits and more concerned for his wife's safety than the dog's whereabouts. With a roar of the engine, he selected reverse gear and put his foot down hard. The tyres skidded on the loose ground as their car shot backwards through the trailer park gates, clipping the rear bumper against the post as it sped through the gap. With Stephen using his rear-view mirrors to guide him, Melody strained her head around, looking for any signs of her dog.

"*Stephen!*" she shrieked, just as she caught sight of two wide eyes reflecting the car's reversing lights in them. Stephen slammed on the brakes and the car skidded to a halt just in time, only an inch from one terrified animal. "Oh, thank God!" Melody shouted, as she leaned over and pulled the lever of the car's rear door so it opened just enough for Blaise-Pascal to jump in. "Oh, thank God you're safe, my little darling. Now Stephen, let's get *outta* here!"

Stephen put his foot down again, and steered the car onto the dark road, only lit now by the moon. "What the hell happened there?" Stephen yelled, adrenalin pumping through his body as the car's speed increased. "Something spooked Ozborn for sure. As soon as that Young Sherlock report came on, he went crazy. What the hell?"

Melody, although clearly shaken, was more concerned that she had her precious little Blaise-Pascal back safely with her. "I don't know, Stephen. But we got Coldplay's money, didn't we? That's all that matters."

A few miles out of town, Stephen slowed the car to a more respectable level as they headed home to collect Coldplay from her friend's house where she'd gone after school, and gradually calmed down. "I guess you're right on that, I do guess you're right. Let's go see if our favourite little girl has had a nice time, shall we?"

CHAPTER 31

(SATURDAY, 20th JANUARY, 2018)

Caller Response

To say that his first meeting with Siobhan had gone well was an understatement. "You were magnificent!" she said enthusiastically as she leant across to kiss Oliver on the cheek. Oliver had been looking forward to making the acquaintance of Ursula's niece ever since receiving the photograph she'd attached in an email to him, and he was not disappointed. With long dark hair, bright blue eyes, and a perfectly smooth complexion, she was every bit as beautiful in real life as she had been in the picture.

Oliver blushed. "No, I wasn't. I was just doing what I had to," he replied, with a certain degree of false modesty. "The proof will be in the pudding, as we Brits say." Having already decided that he fancied the pants off his new work colleague, he thought that mentioning anything remotely associated with England might enhance his chance of her feeling the same way about him. False modesty or not, he also believed his TV appearance had gone rather well. Now it was just a matter of waiting to see if any responses were forthcoming as a result of its broadcast.

It was seven o'clock in the evening, and Siobhan had invited him to go back to her aunt Ursula's house for dinner following the filming of his interview earlier that day. It had been Ursula's suggestion, not only to be sociable, but also to discuss how best to progress the newspaper's story that was rapidly gaining the public's interest and imagination. They'd sat around the television, watching the latest re-run of the local news bulletin just after the six o'clock main headlines. Ursula couldn't help but be impressed by Oliver's performance on TV, as well as his captivating writing style, and she knew that she and her newspaper were on to something potentially big. She wanted to encourage Oliver all she could to continue with his campaign. It was good for business—plus, she liked him, and could tell that Siobhan did too.

"I think we should celebrate. Let's break open some bubbles!" Ursula suggested as she unwrapped the foil from a bottle of her favourite French Limoux—so much more refined than Champagne, she thought. She proceeded before waiting for an answer.

"I'd love some, but . . ." replied Oliver, politely shaking his head and placing a hand over the flute that was being handed to him. ". . . I've got to drive home later, and the last thing I want is to get caught being over the limit."

"Nonsense!" argued Ursula. "Call the folks where you're staying and tell them you're having to make an extended business meeting here. Don't forget, I'm your boss! And I'm sure Siobhan won't mind putting you up on her sofa for the night, will you darling?" she said with a wink as she turned towards her niece. "Her condo is only a short walk away from here, or if it's too cold you could always call an Uber cab."

"But I don't have my overnight things with me," Oliver protested, but not too emphatically. There was nothing he would like more than to spend the night at Siobhan's. Anything might happen, and he definitely hoped it would.

After Oliver had finished texting Sam, informing her not to expect him because of his unplanned business meeting, Ursula proceeded to raise a toast. "That's settled, then!" she said. "To our Young Sherlock!"

Siobhan beamed as she raised her glass and repeated affectionately: "To our Young Sherlock!" It was becoming a habit for Oliver to blush, as he did so one more time.

More wine flowed throughout the evening over dinner. When Ursula's husband John came home later, he was also in a fine mood. He'd been at his local tavern watching a satellite stream of his beloved West Ham United play soccer against Arsenal, winning two goals to one. All in all, Oliver was enjoying immensely what had turned out to be a great evening with his new work associates, now friends.

And the great evening was just about to get better still when the hospitality at Ursula and John's ended, and started at Siobhan's. After saying goodbye to Ursula and John, he and Siobhan walked the mile or so down the road in the clear evening, lit by the moon, both relaxed in each other's company but not entirely sober. Half way, Siobhan linked her arm through Oliver's and tugged him closer so she could kiss him, and not just a little peck on the cheek this time.

Oliver responded positively, and looked forward to getting even closer to her. Ten minutes later, the couple were indoors, and Siobhan made a beeline to make them both a filter coffee, put some relaxing music on and adjust the lighting. Everything was clearly set for a night of passion as she gently took Oliver by the hand and led him to a huge sofa that occupied a large portion of the living room. Oliver's head was in a whirl, partly as a result of the alcohol consumed earlier, but more with anticipation and excitement as he watched Siobhan lift off her top and unhook her bra, to reveal the most exquisite breasts he'd ever seen.

"Come on," whispered Siobhan in her beautiful half American, half Irish accent that sent quivers through her guest. "Don't keep a girl waiting!" As Oliver began to also undress, at first removing his shoes and socks, he felt a tingling from within his trouser pocket. He'd previously turned his phone to 'vibrate' while having dinner earlier and had meant to return it to ringtone, but had forgotten. Although full of the moment's excitement, he was suddenly brought back to earth as he realised that this could be a response to his television appearances.

He checked the phone and didn't recognise the number displayed. At least it wasn't Sam calling—that could have been awkward. He looked across at Siobhan with raised eyebrow asking for her approval to take the potentially important call. Siobhan thought it would be funny to flirt with him while he was doing his best to maintain a cool and calm voice when he answered, and nodded for him to go ahead. As Oliver began to speak with a tentative "Hello?" Siobhan proceeded to strip off her skirt and dance naked, except for some skimpy panties, only a couple of feet in front of him, while at the same time reaching over to unbuckle Oliver's leather brown belt. The second time Oliver said "hello?" his voice was considerably higher. His appreciation of Siobhan's performance was quickly showing an effect, much to the delight of his hostess, while he did his best to concentrate on listening to the caller.

Much to Siobhan's disappointment, Oliver then sat bolt upright, and the reaction she'd been successfully creating thus far disappeared. Oliver turned his iPhone slightly away from his ear so that she could also eavesdrop in on the conversation.

"Listen up, y'hear," they heard a gruff, deep voice say to Oliver. Before Oliver had a chance to respond, the voice continued. "You're the Young Sherlock, yeah? Well, I got some information for you that'll lead you to the real killer. If you wanna know more, meet me on Monday at The Old Parlor on Main Street. You got that? Capeesh?"

Oliver was alarmed but thrilled. Not knowing where The Old Parlor was, he raised his eyes quizzically at Siobhan, who was now reaching for her blouse in order to cover up. She exaggeratedly mouthed back the word "Paris" at him.

"Is that in the town of Paris?" Oliver asked the caller.

"Man, you're smart," the voice answered. "At noon. Don't be late!" the caller demanded.

"Okay, I won't. But what's your name? And how will I recognise you?" Oliver asked.

"You won't," came the response. "But I'll recognise you from the TV. Don't be late," he repeated. And with that, the phone call was ended abruptly. Oliver stared at the phone, then looked at Siobhan, not at all comfortable with the formidable tone of his caller.

Siobhan wanted to get the atmosphere back on track and began unbuttoning her blouse once more, but Oliver's feeling of unease prevented him from responding in the way she had hoped. Instead of being in the present moment, his mind was racing ahead to Monday. He was sure that something was meant to be happening on Monday and he was desperately trying to recall what. He looked at the calendar app on his phone. "Oh, no!" he cried out. "That's when I'm going to Stateville to meet with Emanuele at ten in the morning. I'll never be able to get back in time."

He tapped the key on his phone to get back in touch with the caller. After two rings it answered. "Err, I'm sorry," began Oliver, apologetically. "I'd forgotten that I can't make Monday. Can we meet Tuesday instead please?" Despite his politeness, the request fell on deaf ears.

"Look, Sherlock. I ain't in no mood for games. It's Monday or never. And if you're smart and wanna know the truth, I'd suggest you be there." The red phone button then appeared on screen, indicating that the man had again terminated the conversation.

"Oh, no!" was, once again, all Oliver could think of saying.

CHAPTER 32

(SUNDAY, 21ST JANUARY, 2018)

Case Review

Realising that their evening's romantic activities were unlikely to be resumed, Siobhan disappeared to the kitchen to make them both a chamomile tea to replace the coffee that had by now gone cold. While waiting for the kettle to boil, she had an idea, and called into the living room. "Well, *I* could go," she suggested. Oliver looked through the half open doorway at the skimpily dressed beauty as she was pouring the hot water into two red mugs.

"No, I couldn't possibly let you do that," Oliver answered, after carefully considering her suggestion. "I didn't like the tone of his voice, and besides, he also made it clear that *I'd* have to meet him, and no one else."

"No, not to meet Mystery Caller, silly," Siobhan giggled. "I meant *I* could go to Stateville in your place. Now that you've made the arrangements for Emanuele to be visited, we mustn't pass up such an opportunity. If you cancel now, there may not be a second chance before you return to England, so I suggest we strike while the iron's hot."

Oliver was bitterly disappointed at the prospect of not meeting Emanuele himself, but he also knew Siobhan was correct. At the end of the day, he concluded, he had to do what was right for the overall story—the big picture, as they liked to call it in America. "Hmm, well…err… he started, very slowly at first, dragging out his words for what seemed ages to Siobhan as she brought the hot drinks through. "… Well, I suppose you're right. I guess I would have to call the Stateville office first thing in the morning and inform them of the change of visitor, and I'll just have to hope it will be okay with them.

But don't forget it could all be a wasted journey for you—the officer did say there was no guarantee that Emanuele would actually meet me, let alone you. That's his prisoner's right."

"Well, it's still worth a shot!" Siobhan began. "Okay then, that's settled. Now, we should drink our tea and get some sleep. I've got a busy day lined up for tomorrow, helping Aunt Ursula at the office. Sundays don't count when you've got a newspaper to bring out. And now I think it'll be best if I travel up and stay at a motel tomorrow evening somewhere near the prison, so that I've got no worries about driving north in the Monday morning rush-hour traffic."

"Crikey! I'd lost track of the days," exclaimed an alarmed Oliver. I forgot that today is already Saturday. Oh blimey, it's a good job one of us is on the ball. What would I do without you?"

"Oh '*blimey*'!?" Siobhan repeated Oliver's expression, accentuating it, then added, with a laugh, a mock Dick Van Dyke '*Cor blimey, mate, luv-a-duck!*' "I do love your English sayings. Come on, let's get some rest." Having no intention of making up the sofa bed in the lounge, with their teas finished, she led him by the hand upstairs. Before falling asleep, she hoped she might reawaken his interest in at least having a romantic bedroom cuddle.

Despite the late hour, Oliver was unable to resist Siobhan's charm, and by the time they fell asleep in each other's arms the two individuals had now become a couple.

The following morning they repeated their energetic activities of the previous night. After dressing and going downstairs for breakfast, Oliver reached for his phone and called Stateville prison.

The administration secretary was very helpful.

"So you want to alter the visitor from yourself to Miss Siobhan O'Mahoney, your colleague? Alright then Sir, we'll be expecting her tomorrow morning, then. We'll inform Mr. Emanuele. He won't believe it—he hasn't had a visitor in ages."

***

Across town, Paul Copeland had already left for work by the time his wife had woken. As he was a realtor, Sundays were often one of his busiest days of the week. Katie got up and greeted the morning like she normally did with a hot shower followed by 'putting on her face', as she called it—rummaging through the countless jars of make-up strewn all over her dressing table before settling on her old faithfuls, Nivea moisturiser and Avon foundation.

Every day, Katie picked up the Avon jar and every day she sang the doorbell chimes of the advertisement, and every day that amused her. Then, her little luxury would be to dab a tiny amount of her very expensive Prada perfume behind her ears. Perfume was never something that her husband thought to buy her—so she would buy it herself, but without complaint. She found it gave her a feeling of pleasure and self-empowerment that she rather enjoyed.

As she sought the correct bottles among the many others that had been previous birthday gifts from her children, she glanced down and noticed the newspaper cutting that had been left on the chair by her husband. She almost missed it as it was gradually becoming buried under the pile of clothes that she'd picked up off the floor. Sitting on the end of the bed to read it, her mouth opened in astonishment to see that the old case she'd worked on was once again back in the news all these years later.

After applying her fragrance, she decided to cancel the shopping trip planned for the morning, and instead examine the old files that related to the Bike Radio Murder. She was sure that she'd transferred the details digitally, and when she turned her iMac on, she found that indeed she had. Studying the documents, the recollections of her forensic investigation gradually resurfaced. There had only been a handful of her cases where Katie hadn't been totally convinced that all the facts had emerged. And this, she remembered, had been one of them.

At the time, Katie had had her suspicions that there might have been another male present in the murder victim's house around the time of the killing, but having no positive evidence with which to prove her hunch, she'd hit a dead-end. Of course, she had verbally discussed her thoughts with John Moores, the police chief at the time of the investigation, but without firm facts upon which to act, he had gone ahead and charged the one person they were unanimously certain *was* present. That person had been charged, prematurely in Katie's opinion, but by then she was off working on the next case. The chief, Katie remembered thinking then, had been too keen to close the investigation and add another tick to his list of successful prosecutions. To this day, it was an opinion she still held, and would soon share again.

Further immersed in the files on her iMac, she then came across her own personal 'off-the-record' notes that she'd written in 1981, a couple of weeks after the murder. They reminded her of the utter frustration she'd experienced working with a man so much more senior than herself—but, at the time, had she been too weak to speak out against him?

Katie's still perfectly-clear pencil-written notes to herself gave the same uncertain feeling now as they had done when she had scribbled them down so many years ago:

Sandy Beach Murder Case

1. Fingerprints found on fragments of the plastic pieces (cycle radio) match Yakamoto and Beach, plus there are other prints from person unknown. Moores says this could have been anyone, such as from where it was bought.

2. Based on print clarity and relative freshness, possibility that cycle-radio had also been held by person unknown with some force. Moores suggests extra pressure used when radio was fitted to handlebar at the shop that sold it in Allentown, and he would investigate. I'm still waiting to hear from him.

3. Semen found on waterbed mattress and on Kleenex found at side of bed possibly came from two different men. Moores suggests one sample could have been much older from a previous boyfriend but I believe they were both recent.

4. *Hair strands on clothes in bedroom and in blood pool in kitchen was brown in colour. Yakamoto's and Beach's hair colour was black. Moores says this could be from anyone coming into contact with victim over time, e.g. at dentist where Beach worked.*

5. *Beach's blood found on front door threshold in small dots approx. half an inch diameter—likely to have come from a shoe sole partially stepped in blood on floor where victim was found. Trainers worn by Yakamoto when arrested had similar pattern but dots were slightly larger in size, and were more hexagonal than round. Moores didn't have an explanation and says he would investigate further, and this was left with him. I have heard no more from him.*

I believe that someone else could have been at the scene, and possibly at the same time as when the murder had been committed, but I don't have the evidence to substantiate that theory. I also think that Moores was too ready to explain away my findings.

Katie Copeland, April 29th, 1981

Katie recalled her emotions of frustration as if they were yesterday. This had been one of the early cases she'd worked on after graduating, and she had been too timid and inexperienced to challenge the chief's assertions. Had he undermined her work? She remembered him saying in no uncertain terms that she should move on to her next case and leave the hard work now to him. How patronising! He had also hinted at how much influence he had over her career path, a career, he'd pointed out, that had only just begun.

Belittled by Moores, she had vowed never to let that happen again, and fortunately with each subsequent case she worked on she had become stronger. She looked across to her bottle of Prada and acknowledged that a psychologist would have a field day analysing her.

Katie's empowerment had been gradual, but the dabs behind her ears had somehow kept the Chief Moores of this world at bay ever since.

The thrill of working on such cases came flooding back, and Katie remembered just why she'd studied so hard for the qualifications to do the job she was so proud of—it was something she'd wanted to do from as far back as she could remember, even as a young teenager watching detective stories on television.

She liked the fact that in the world of forensics there was either right or wrong—no in-between. Of course, there would often be an element of speculation and supposition with any case, but what she loved was the possibility of getting to the truth with the use of science.

Looking back over her personal notes, Katie knew she *had* to check out the DNA of the hair samples and the semen samples. Now that there was someone else, coming all that way from England, who was also keen to get to the truth, she *had* to act. She made a quick call to her friend David at the lab, guessing that on a Sunday morning he wouldn't be too busy to grant her a favour—especially if she put on some extra charm in the way she knew he'd find hard to resist. David, it had to be said, adored his food.

"David. Hey there, darling. You know how much I *love* working with you," Katie joked. "I've got a little something I'd like you to help me with, and I'll make it worth your while. If you could pull out the box from Stores marked 'Beach, 1981', I'll bring in your favourite Caramel Latte and two Crispy Cremes. No, I'll make that *three!*" With such an incentive, Katie knew she had David like putty in the palm of her hand. "I'll be there in half an hour," she said before quickly hanging up, not giving her foodie friend any time to protest.

Katie's head buzzed with excitement. How thrilling that the science of DNA had moved on at such a pace in recent years. And with modern technology she knew it would take less than a couple of hours to get some test results—especially if David pulled out all the stops for her, and she'd do her best to make him want to.

She picked up the newspaper article again, and called the number written in italics at the bottom of the page. "Hello? Mr. Markland?" she asked boldly. Without waiting for an answer, she continued. "I may have some information for you."

***

After having successfully arranged for Siobhan to visit Stateville prison in place of himself, Oliver had gone upstairs to take a shower, leaving his iPhone on the breakfast table next to the packet of Cheerios. After it had rung several minutes later, Siobhan picked it up, but before she'd had any chance to say a word, the woman caller obviously thought she was talking to Oliver.

"Woah! Hold on!" Siobhan stopped her. "Hang on a second. This *is* Mr. Markland's phone—but *not* Mr. Markland himself. Can I get him to call you back in a minute please? He shouldn't be long." Just then, Oliver appeared in the room, his hair still wet and with just his underpants on. Siobhan swooned as she turned round and caught a glimpse of his near-naked body.

"Who is it?" he mouthed. Covering the phone with her hand, Siobhan told him it was a woman with some information.

"Great!" said a delighted Oliver as he was handed the phone. This was just getting better and better by the minute. While Siobhan looked in admiration at Oliver's physique, she also listened intently to a series of 'Oohs', 'Aahs', and 'Reallys?', as well as a few 'goshes' that amused her greatly. However, because she was unable to hear the other half of the conversation, she could hardly wait for Oliver to give her the full lowdown on what the call was all about.

As soon as he'd thanked the caller and said goodbye, Oliver slumped into Siobhan's soft sofa, pulling her with him so he could give her a kiss square on the lips. "I can hardly believe it!" he said.

"*What is it?*" Siobhan cried out, impatiently.

Oliver tried to explain, but he was too excited to formulate his words in the right order, so he gave up and simply asked: "Can you come with me to meet Mrs. Copeland later?"

"I can if you want me to, but who exactly is Mrs. Copeland?" Siobhan asked, quite reasonably.

"She's only *the* forensic scientist who worked on the Bike Radio case, that's all!" answered Oliver. "She's on her way to the lab to check out some things now, and wants to meet us after."

"In that case, I definitely can come. I'm not going to miss *this* meeting for anything!" Siobhan said as she went upstairs to get ready. Oliver following closely behind, worried that his jeans and t-shirt, the only clothes he had with him, weren't totally appropriate for a meeting with such a professional person.

CHAPTER 33

(SUNDAY, 21ST JANUARY, 2018)

Radio Interview

Guessing that Oliver, being British, preferred tea over coffee, Katie Copeland had some Lipton's English Breakfast sachets all ready in the cups for when her guests arrived. Siobhan and Oliver were invited to take the bench seat at the large pine table in the centre of the kitchen. After the initial introductions and pleasantries had been conducted and hot water had been poured in the cups, Katie got down to business.

"It was my husband who initially brought your story to my attention," she began, unfolding the newspaper cutting and placing it on the table by way of an explanation. "I've been semi-retired for some years now, but I remember this one well," she continued, jabbing her pointed finger at the headline. "At the time I always felt that something didn't quite add up, and I still think that today."

Oliver was particularly pleased to hear this, knowing that his own feelings were probably based more on wishful thinking than facts, given his empathy towards Yushi, a fellow cyclist. And now here was someone, with much more of a scientific brain than his creative one, thinking along the same lines.

Katie continued. "I've just come from doing a little research. You see, I still do some consultative work for the Police from time to time, and they allow me access to their laboratory and storage facilities. It's a huge place, with racks filled to the ceiling with every piece of evidence from all the crimes dating back to the sixties, and everything is recorded and logged, quite easy to find so long as you know where to look for it. And . . ."

As interesting as Katie's monologue undoubtedly was, Oliver

wanted her to steer away from *how* the archive system worked, but what was *in* it, relevant to the Bike Radio Murder case. Katie sensed his impatience, and came back on track. "Anyway, DNA testing wasn't around back in 1981, but now that it is, I've been able to check out one or two anomalies I was unsure about during my initial investigations."

Good, thought Oliver. This was what he wanted, and he leaned across the table to show Katie that she had his full attention. She went on. "The semen stains found on the waterbed and Kleenex were from two different males, of that I'm now certain. The fingerprints found on the plastic remnants of the radio weren't *only* Yakamoto's and Beach's. There were hair samples found where their DNA didn't match that of Yakamoto. And not only all that, there was a partial footprint of blood from a shoe sole near the front door of the house, and I don't think it came from the same shoe that Yakamoto had been wearing. So, in my opinion, there had definitely been someone else present in the house, and I *think* probably at the same time. I'd say that at the least, not all this circumstantial evidence had been taken into account at Yakamoto's trial. And at worst, I'd say that the truth had been obstructed from coming out."

This was music to Oliver's and Siobhan's ears, as Katie continued: "I'm afraid I can't *prove* the presence of another person *at the same time*. But if, in fact, there had been someone else there, it *could* mean that Yakamoto's constant claim of innocence to the day he died *was* true. Perhaps they did get the wrong man after all. I'm sorry, but perhaps I've been more of a hindrance than a help by even suggesting this."

"No! Not at all!" Oliver exclaimed, raising his arms in the air. He assured Katie of their extreme gratitude for her help, and that her expert opinion was indeed very welcome.

Katie had prepared a small folder of notes relating to her findings and handed it to Oliver. "I'm afraid this is about as much as I can offer you for the time being," she said, apologising that she couldn't do more, before continuing. "But if I find anything else you can be sure I'll let you know."

"I wish you the best of luck with your investigations," Katie said while standing up to show them to the door. "*I'd* like to see you find out what really happened to Sandy Beach just as much as I'm sure *you* would. You know you're gaining quite a reputation around here, don't you? But be prudent. If in fact Yakamoto didn't do it, that means someone else did—and whoever that person is, they're not going to be very happy to discover you on their trail. After all, they think they've escaped justice all this time. So just take care, okay?"

With Oliver now in a rather reflective mood, as he drove away with Siobhan at his side, he thought about when he'd first bought his key from the Florida flea market. He couldn't have possibly imagined in his wildest dreams that it would have led him on this journey, and up until now, this whole affair had just been one great adventure. It had so far been nothing but fun, and such an incredible experience. But Katie's words of warning were right, of course. If Yushi hadn't done it, someone else out there had. It suddenly dawned on Oliver that if the wrong person had been convicted, the real killer might have been watching when he'd made his 'Young Sherlock' TV appearance. For a second, Oliver felt frightened, and for a very brief moment of weakness he considered dropping everything and heading back to the sanctuary of Wivenhoe where he felt safe and secure. Katie's words had been a wake-up call.

But he soon told himself not to be such a cowardly fool. "I've come here to do a job, and I'm going to follow it through!" he spoke out loud to a considerably startled Siobhan.

"What on earth are you talking about?" she asked.

"Sorry, Siobhan. I was just day dreaming," he explained. She was still none the wiser.

A short while later, just as Oliver was dropping Siobhan off at her place, his phone rang. It was a local radio station calling to ask if he could do a short pre-recorded interview that would be put out just after the main news at the top of the hour later that afternoon. "Why not?" agreed Oliver, turning to Siobhan and explaining what was happening. Very impressed, she stayed in the car to listen to the proceedings.

"Okay then," said the programme's producer. "Please stay on the line, Oliver, while I put you through to David Roberts, the show's presenter." Oliver waited a few seconds, listening to a series of clicks and pops while preparations were being made in the station's studio. Then he heard the same voice come through again. "Putting you on in three," said the producer. "Three, two, one. Okay Oliver. You're now through to David."

"Good afternoon, Young Sherlock . . ." Roberts began, in an exaggeratedly jovial tone. Siobhan sat silently in the car for the duration of the interview, dismayed at how the DJ was somewhat making fun of her man.

"I didn't care much for his tone," she said after it was all over. "Did you?"

Oliver shrugged, admittedly feeling he'd been stung. "Well, I suppose any media coverage is worth having," he answered thoughtfully.

"I guess you're right," agreed Siobhan as she leant across to give him a parting kiss, about to go indoors and pack a bag for her evening's two-hour journey up to Stateville.

Just before saying one final goodbye to Siobhan, even though Oliver knew he should find The Old Parlor in Paris using his satnav without too much difficulty, he still asked her for the directions. Her warm voice somehow helped to calm his nerves. He then wished her good luck for the following day. "Try to find out as much as you can about Yushi, and give me a call as soon as you can. I think your visit will be limited to an hour, so you should be finished before I meet Mystery Caller at noon."

Oliver was jealous that Siobhan would be the one going and not himself, but he also knew how important it was for him to meet the man who claimed to have information about the 'real' killer. It could of course be a total red herring, thought Oliver, but he had an inkling that this could be a lead worth checking out. But recalling the brash tone of the man's voice, Oliver felt more apprehensive than he knew why.

When he'd taken the phone call, Oliver had possessed a certain bravado, possibly aided by the cocktail of seeing Siobhan's rather exquisite body swaying in front of him, as well as having consumed quite a few flutes of her aunt's fine sparkling wine. Monday had seemed such a long way off then, but now the day was nearly upon him, and he wished someone could accompany him.

Perhaps when he got back home to the Dickinson's later, he could invite Sam to join him. Or even better, Sam and her father as well. Chris Dickinson was a big man, tall and strong, and nobody in their right mind would mess with him.

CHAPTER 34

(SUNDAY, 21ST JANUARY, 2018)

Déjà Vu

It hadn't been too difficult for Marc Ozborn to get his old Dodge truck to fire up again, despite it having lain dormant for a good while. He knew a thing or two about the workings of the internal combustion engine, and a thorough clean of the points and spark plugs, plus an overnight charge of the battery did the trick. With the hood still hooked up, he pumped the gas pedal a few times while turning the ignition key, listening intently to all sounds coming from the engine bay.

At first the motor only cranked over, then he heard the glimmer of life come back into his old pride and joy. A few more turns, and then came a triumphant roar as the V8 spluttered into glorious motion, the growl sounding exactly as Ozborn remembered it, with exhaust fumes spewing in a cloud of thick smoke from the newly fitted tailpipe. The muffler could wait, for now. The old one was just louder than it ought to be but shouldn't affect the truck's general performance too much, he thought.

It was getting late in the afternoon and the low sunlight was making Ozborn quite drowsy. Of course, that could also have been from the three or four Buds he'd been drinking while peering into the engine bay and making various adjustments to this and that component. Despite the tiredness, he was keen to give the vehicle what it really needed—a good run to blow out all the old cobwebs. So he lowered the hood with a loud clunk, climbed in the cab and revved up a few more times before slowly driving out of the trailer park and onto the open road. Without considering where to go, he automatically turned left towards Paris, and hit the gas.

Despite the inevitable few initial misfires, Ozborn felt over the moon to discover how well the truck was now running. It still looked as it did back when he'd last driven it—rusty, scratched and dented—but he cared little for its appearance. And although it had for sure seen better days, he was getting far more driving pleasure from it than his new Ford. They just don't make 'em like they used to, he thought with a smile on his face, proud that he'd got his 'old favourite' running again.

Once out of his home town of Marshall, the ten-mile straight section of road to Paris would be perfect for opening up the throttle and cruising along at nearly a hundred miles per hour, maybe over the ton if the wind was behind him. It was Sunday afternoon and, with not much going on, Ozborn knew that many of the traffic cops would be taking a breather back in their precinct. So, after filling up with a tankful of new, clean gas at the local Mobil station, Ozborn put his foot down, feeling confident that he wouldn't get caught on the trip there and back.

It seemed that before he blinked, he was already approaching the outskirts of Paris. Slowing down and enjoying listening to the low rumbling sound coming from under the hood, he just cruised around the town that he hadn't had cause to visit for some time. He turned on the radio, and caught the tail end of some Jay-Z rap song—if 'song' was the right word to describe the crap, in Ozborn's opinion, before presenter David Roberts went on to introduce a Sam Smith track, fresh from the singer's latest album. "Far more like it," Ozborn muttered under his breath. Paying more attention to the music on the radio than to where he was going, an accidental touching of the kerb startled him back to reality. He looked around and realised he was near the street in which Sandy Beach's old house had been.

Ozborn had not been back there since he'd awoken naked on the rear patio decking early that April morning in 1981. The scene that he'd played over and over in his mind hundreds of times suddenly came back with a vengeance. The memory of how he accidentally trod in some of the congealed blood surrounding that woman's lifeless body always made him feel nauseous and sick—and today was no exception. He vividly remembered how his shoe had slid off the gas pedal a number of times when he'd driven away and how he'd scrubbed the blood away from the metal, and burned his boots in an old oil-drum incinerator as soon as he'd got home.

For more than three decades, those horrible flashbacks had haunted him, despite being so blurred now that he was unable to distinguish between reality and fiction. But now, everything was finally becoming as clear as the bright sun shining in the sky today—and he didn't like it one bit. Perhaps, Ozborn thought, by revisiting the property, he might be able to banish some of those awful memories to oblivion. "That damned Sherlock boy!" he muttered again. "Why'd he have to drag this whole thing up all over again?"

Pulling up outside the house, Ozborn gazed at the rotten timbers of the bungalow, then at the loose roof tiles and unfastened guttering. The whole place looked a very sorry state of affairs indeed. He sat there for five, maybe even ten minutes, with the engine idling and the worn old muffler rumbling. For a moment, he contemplated stepping out the truck and wandering around. But what would be the point? As a shudder ran through him, he decided not to hang around any longer. Now in an uncharacteristic contemplative mood, he lit a cigarette and adjusted his hat, letting his pickup truck crawl along slowly towards the end of the road, with its low-revving engine producing a deep hum that vibrated all around.

***

Hannah Toporofski had just sat down in her living room with a tray on her lap containing a bowl of Polish sausage and sauerkraut. She'd been looking forward to eating it ever since that morning when she'd been to the new East European deli that had opened recently in the town's Main Street. She pressed the button on the TV remote that was lying on the sofa next to her, and got ready to watch whatever was on, hoping that there might be a repeat of the interview she'd appeared in with that nice young man from England.

Alas, there wasn't, for that was now yesterday's news. Instead, she settled on watching an episode of *Frasier*. Shifting her plump bottom to get as comfortable as she could, she became more and more irritated with the low rumbling sound from outside that was spoiling her eating and viewing experience.

For what seemed ages, this irritation continued. After a few mouthfuls of her food, exasperated, Hannah placed the tray at her side and stood up to find out wherever the noise was coming from. She looked out of the window, just at the moment when an old rusty truck was crawling slowly away from the house next door towards the front of hers. An uncanny feeling of déjà-vu swept over her, and she physically shuddered. Convinced that this whole scenario had already been played out once before in her life, Hannah shook her head in disbelief. As she watched this strangely familiar vehicle edge very slowly past her window, she even thought the driver, whose outlined silhouette she could just about make out, was adopting the same position as before—with his left arm half resting out of his open window and cigarette hanging from his mouth.

For Hannah, it was quite the most bizarre experience. She had never been able to recognise any car on the road—in her opinion they all looked the same—and yet she was certain she'd seen this particular one previously, as well as the man behind the wheel. Maybe it was just the familiar colour of the vehicle that triggered this reaction, she couldn't be certain. She knew it was illogical to do so, but nonetheless she grabbed her digital camera and took a few snaps of the vehicle before she watched it slowly turn right towards Marshall at the end of the road.

With an audible sigh, as well as a few out-loud tut-tuts, she then returned to the comfort of her sofa, determined to finish her now cold meal. It had cost, after all, $5.99, and money didn't grow on trees. So she carried on eating it regardless, all the while contemplating what a silly old fool she was being.

But the more she thought about it, the more she felt compelled to act, in some way or another. After much deliberation, she decided she needed to tell *someone* about the inexplicable sighting. Instinctively she knew it was *somehow* connected to her neighbour's murder, although she had no idea how. She'd be considered crazy, she knew that, but at least her conscience would be clear as long as she did *something*, no matter how much folks might laugh at her.

After clearing away her tray and rinsing the bowl under the kitchen tap, Hannah decided to phone the young man who she'd been interviewed with by the television reporter. Picking up the card carefully placed by the phone in the hallway, she pressed the numbers. When her call went straight through to a 'please leave a message' request, Hannah nervously became tongue-tied and hung up. She so much hated answering machines. So, next she searched around for the other card that she'd been given. "Now, what was that pretty girl's name?" she asked herself. "Where did I put it? Ah, yes, here it is. Siobhan O'Mahoney." This time, her call was answered.

"Hello dear, it's Hannah Toporofski. You came here yesterday when the TV people were doing that interview with me," she said, emphatically.

"Of course," replied Siobhan. "I remember. What is it? How can I help?" She chuckled to herself at how the caller had built up her role in the TV interview with Oliver. Nevertheless, Siobhan had rather liked her, and once Mrs. Toporofski had explained the reason for her call, obviously embarrassed and feeling foolish, Siobhan did her best to put her at ease. "Any information, no matter how unusual it may seem, could be of great interest, Hannah, so please don't worry. Now, would you be able to email the photos of the truck across to me?"

The very mention of the word 'email' sent Hannah into a state of panic. "I'm so sorry, honey, but I can't do computers very well. I can manage to turn one on and look at the pictures of antiques, but I'm afraid that's about all I can do. I use the computer for researching and valuing the items. Some are worth quite a lot of money, you know," Hannah went on, beginning to go off topic. "I'm afraid you'll have to come back here if you don't mind, Miss Siobhan," Hannah explained, rather demandingly.

Siobhan didn't mind. Knowing that she'd be driving near Hannah's house on her way to Stateville later that evening, she agreed to call by, deciding that even if it were only to pacify the elderly lady she'd taken quite a liking to, it wouldn't be too much trouble. "Thank you, dear," said Hannah, gratefully. "I'll see you later, then."

***

Oliver had just pulled up in the Dickinson's driveway when Siobhan called to tell of this latest development. "All leads are potentially important," Oliver responded with enthusiasm. "We may as well follow this one up, as long as you're sure you don't mind stopping off in Paris. It's turning out to be a busy time for both of us, isn't it?"

"Sure is," replied Siobhan. "But I rather suspect that Hannah's just looking for any excuse to get back on the TV—so I'll have a quick chat with her, get the pics she took, and then get on the freeway to Stateville. Quite honestly, I don't mind a bit. It's all very exciting." What Siobhan really meant to say, but was a little too shy, was: "It's all very exciting doing all this *with you, Oliver*."

Siobhan then pensively thought a moment before continuing, her eyes a little moist. She'd not realised until this moment that she'd actually fallen head over heels in love with the handsome young Brit, and the thought of going away now, just for one night without Oliver made her feel quite sad. With a quiver in her voice, she spoke softly into the phone: "And you take care, y'hear? Look after yourself while I'm gone."

Feeling rather embarrassed that she'd let her emotional guard down a little too soon in their burgeoning relationship, she cheered herself up before finishing the call by making a suggestion. Speaking in a more chirpy tone, she continued: "I've had an idea! Let's meet up tomorrow around two o'clock for lunch at The Old Parlor and we can compare notes. I should easily be back by then, and even if your meeting hasn't finished, I could get to see Mystery Caller as well. It'll give us both something to look forward to, and the place does terrific surf 'n' turfs as well."

"Great idea!" said Oliver, although not sure what surf 'n' turf was. "Tomorrow at two it is, then. See you there." He hung up, amazed that such a stunningly attractive girl was so keen to spend time with him. And now he was about to go back to the Dickinson's house for a Sunday evening with the equally beautiful Sam. He suddenly felt awkward, especially knowing that if he were to ask Sam and her dad to accompany him to The Old Parlor tomorrow, things could become difficult if the meeting with Mystery Caller went on too long and overlapped with Siobhan's arrival.

"Hmm," Oliver pondered. "Probably best to keep the two girls in my life separate, for now, at least." Choosing between whether he should risk the possibility of Sam meeting Siobhan, or just taking the easier option of going to The Old Parlor alone, he decided on the latter.

CHAPTER 35

(SUNDAY, 21ST JANUARY, 2018)

Police Warning

Apart from the doom and gloom of the national headlines, the rest of the radio news was local—and made up of quick bullet points, catering for the short attention span of the majority of the station's listeners. But so as not to depress the audience too much with the current state of the country's affairs, DJ David Roberts always tried to follow the news bulletin with some light-hearted relief. So, despite the seriousness of the subject matter on this occasion, the presenter had had some fun with the pre-recorded interview he'd made earlier with the British 'detective' who was gaining notoriety as 'Young Sherlock'.

"Good afternoon, Young Sherlock. So, Mr. Holmes . . . that's not your real name, is it?" Before Oliver had had the chance to answer, more questions kept being fired at him. " . . . How do you like investigating a *moider* over here in the US? What's it like being a detective here, compared to Baker Street in your own London Town?"

Oliver took the jokes at his expense in good humour and began answering with a very exaggerated British laugh, then proceeded to get serious for the next 45 seconds before the interviewer wound things up with a standard "well, that's all we've got time for", and: "Good luck with your investigations, Sherlock. Keep us posted with any developments. Oh, and please pass on our best wishes to Doctor Watson, won't you?"

Roberts rounded off the very one-sided interview with a jolly "Ta ta for now", and cut off Oliver's response. He then played a record with a famous opening riff of saxophone. How corny, thought Ozborn. Even *he* got the 'Baker Street' reference, as he turned down the volume of the Gerry Rafferty song, and negotiated his way through Paris's residential area towards the open stretch of road home.

Slumped behind the wheel of his pickup, Ozborn reflected on the interviewee's 'serious' 45 seconds of prime-time radio that he'd just been listening to. The 'Young Sherlock' had very briefly told of how his associate investigator would soon be meeting Yakamoto's cell mate, and that he himself had just come from seeing the forensic scientist who had originally worked on the Bike Radio Murder case. And as if that wasn't enough to wind him up, Young Sherlock had then gone on to say that the scientist was aware of 'certain discrepancies' in the case files she had been reviewing.

Whatever did that mean? Ozborn was deep in thought contemplating what discrepancies they could be. As far as he was concerned, he just wanted old sleeping dogs to be left alone. But if this guy Markland, Ozborn thought, kept insisting on uncovering these 'discrepancies', he would have no alternative but to put a stop to this nonsense. For sure, the Markland guy was getting on his nerves, and Ozborn knew he needed to be halted in his tracks. The only question was how would be the best way to do that. He didn't *want* to resort to violence, but if that was the only option left open to him, then what else was he supposed to do?

To relieve his rising anxiety, as soon as Ozborn had reached the stretch of road outside Paris where he could let all the horses from under the hood loose, he did just that, pushing the metal hard to the floor. It was just his bad luck that his speeding pickup caught the attention of eagle-eyed Sergeant Lorraine Mills, whose patrol car was stationary at the side of the road, waiting behind some trees in her favourite ambush spot. Bored with the evening's inactivity, the most exciting thoughts that had entered her mind thus far had been what to feed her cats, Max and Monty, when she'd get home after her shift. Then after that, she may well spend an enjoyable hour or so sorting through her extensive collection of shoes, perhaps rearranging them in order of colour, instead of style. Yes, that's what she'd do later, but for now she'd have to sit and wait for some action. She chuckled to herself as she thought of the many times her husband Lee would ask the same old question time and again about what can she possibly do with such an extensive collection of footwear. She knew he would never understand, so she'd given up trying to explain that it was what women do.

But, seeing the speeding vehicle, her thoughts were brought sharply back to the here and now. Good! For her, this brightened up what would otherwise have been a very dull Sunday evening.

Mills adjusted her shoulder-length blonde hair tied up at the back, put her police hat on and donned her Ray Ban sunglasses, ready to pull out on to the road.

Once she had managed to catch up sufficiently to read the fast-moving Dodge's license plate, she was able to obtain enough information on the police's system to tell her all she wanted to know about this particular motorist.

Blissfully unaware that he was being followed, Ozborn slowed down as he neared the outskirts of Marshall. Thinking he was being smart, he didn't want to alert any eagle-eyed law-enforcement officer that he was driving a vehicle currently registered for Non-Use, and that it didn't have any valid insurance. So he drove nice and slowly through the streets all the way to his trailer park.

Unfortunately, so did Mills. "Damn!" exclaimed Ozborn when he spotted her police car in his rear-view mirror, just as he pulled up to his trailer. "Won't they just leave me alone?" Ozborn dejectedly slumped back in his car seat and waited to be approached by the woman in uniform now walking towards his open window.

Assuming the fines he'd no doubt be facing for not having the correct vehicle documentation in place, Ozborn hadn't realised that his high-speed drive from Paris had also been caught on the police car's on-dash camera. But instead of being reprimanded about his speeding offence, it was something else that was brought to his attention. "Mr. Ozborn, I think we're in a little trouble, aren't we?"

began Sergeant Mills. "Weren't we meant to be attending a driver's workshop for alcohol and substance abuse this morning?"

Ozborn had completely forgotten the course he should have gone to following his other arrest late the previous week. And things didn't improve when the policewoman then continued: "And we know Sir, don't we, that as well as your vehicle being unregistered for road use, it's a crime to drive it without the appropriate insurance? Not only that, impressive as it is for a vehicle of this age, I have to say, we really oughtn't be driving it at nearly double the legal limit, ought we?"

The peculiar manner in which the officer spoke really grated on Ozborn's nerves, and it took all his reserve to keep cool. He was too old for all this hassle, he thought. As the officer then began talking into the radio that was strapped to her shoulder, presumably to headquarters to get yet more detrimental information about him, he wished she'd just disappear and leave him to get on with the rest of his life. He'd already had enough of her damned overbearing style.

But, suddenly, everything changed, and with it Ozborn's luck for the better. The officer hurriedly re-approached his truck and continued to talk, this time much more rapidly: "We're fortunate aren't we, Sir, and apparently for the second time in the past few days?" she said, referring to Ozborn's recent arrest. "I've been called to an urgent incident on the highway. Make sure we get our papers and licence plates in order without delay, and don't drive the truck again until we do. Do we understand?"

Totally bemused, Ozborn just sat there and nodded open-mouthed, watching the officer run back to her patrol car, then jump in and speed off.

He raised his eyes to the heavens and thanked his lucky stars, having been convinced that this time he was going to be taken away for longer than just one night behind bars.

***

It was about six o'clock that evening when Siobhan pulled up at Hannah Toporofski's house in Paris. Even before she reached out to bang the knocker, the door was opened. "Come in, do come in, honey," invited the eager lady. "I know I must sound so foolish, but, honestly my dear, when I looked out the window earlier, it was just as if the whole scene from 1981 was being re-enacted—as if it were only yesterday. And I'm the last person in the world to distinguish one car from another. I don't know a Chrysler from a Ford, but I simply *knew* I'd seen this one before," she went on, continuously talking as she led Siobhan through to the study. She handed over her camera with the image of the pickup truck already displayed on its tiny screen.

Siobhan took a look at the blurred pictures through squinted eyes. "Okay, Hannah, let's see if we can upload these to my laptop. We never know, do we? They might well turn out to be relevant." Siobhan said, trying very hard not to sound patronising. The truth was she was beginning to think that Mrs. Toporofski might have lost some of her marbles.

Computer gadgetry was second nature to Siobhan, and after a few minutes fiddling around with a USB cable and her own Toshiba laptop, she was done, much to the astonishment of her host. "There! I was able to see the picture much clearer while I was uploading them. Oliver and I now have got something definite to go on, Hannah, and we both really appreciate you calling us. We'll certainly let you know if anything turns up as a result of this. Well, I'd better be on my way—I have a long drive ahead of me. Thanks so much again, Hannah."

Hannah Toporofski was rather disappointed that her guest didn't want to stay longer to ask her some questions. As she said goodbye to Siobhan at the front door, she decided to ask a question of her own, and she came straight to the point. "Do you think, honey, that you'll be able to get another TV crew to come here? You know, I could do a piece-to-camera about my déjà-vu experience, couldn't I, honey?"

Siobhan desperately wanted to hit the road, but tried to be as polite as possible. After all, Mrs. Toporofski was a lovely old lady, but was definitely eccentric, to say the least, and even a little crazy, in her opinion. "We'll certainly be in touch, Hannah, if the TV people want to do something. But I'm afraid it's them who call the shots, not us," was how Siobhan decided to leave things.

She held out her hand to shake Mrs. Toporofski's, but instead of shaking it, the old lady leant over and kissed Siobhan on the cheek and whispered, as if she could read Siobhan's mind: "See what you can do, honey. I know that you must think me a little silly, but really my dear, I'm not completely loopy—I know what I saw."

Rather startled by Hannah's action, Siobhan withdrew as respectfully as possible while trying not to cause any offence. "Goodbye for now, Hannah, and thank you for all your help. I'm sure the pictures will be of great use to us," Siobhan said, crossing her fingers behind her back. Then, remembering one of Oliver's colloquialisms, she added a good-humoured: "Cheerio, then!"

As she exited the door and got in her car as quickly as she could, Siobhan waved goodbye from her car window as she headed to the end of the road and then, unlike Marc Ozborn before her who had turned right towards Marshall, she turned left—towards Stateville.

As she drove along the freeway for her hoped-for meeting with M.J. Emanuele the following morning, all Siobhan wanted now was to reach the motel where she'd booked a room, have a hot shower, and collapse into bed. It had been an exhaustingly-full two days, not to mention the long night in-between. And tomorrow was likely to be equally busy.

Fortunately, the traffic wasn't too bad, and thankfully for Siobhan it wasn't long before her wish came true. After checking into a cosy room and performing her ablutions, she pulled back the freshly made bed cover. As she adjusted her pillows and made herself comfortable, she suddenly remembered that she should have sent Hannah's pictures to Oliver.

The images of an old pickup truck surely couldn't be all that important, and besides, in her opinion, this was probably all just a ruse for an eccentric old lady to get back on the TV. Deciding that she'd send the images to Oliver in the morning, Siobhan drifted pleasantly into a deep sleep.

CHAPTER 36

(MONDAY, 22ND JANUARY, 2018)

Middle Finger

On Monday morning, Marc Ozborn began another day with a fresh sense of purpose and, unusually, without a hangover. Not quite believing his good fortune of the day before in only having his knuckles wrapped, he decided to follow Officer Mills's instruction and get the old truck legalised. That morning, he would go into Paris to the vehicle licensing office to get the license plates renewed—they would be open until noon. And then, at midday, he'd be meeting the kid from the TV in The Old Parlor. Ozborn made a strong coffee, sat down and thought about how he proposed to stop the boy poking his nose where it wasn't welcome.

At long last, he thought, things in his life were finally coming together. It had only taken him nearly 70 years! He now had a little money—not much, but certainly enough to afford things like sorting out his car insurance, buy wheels for his beloved truck, and even pay the rent on his trailer on time without getting hounded regularly by his landlord. He'd also managed to deflect the intrusion by Coldplay's guardians, and one day he might even actually want to see his daughter. One day, although not yet. But what he certainly did not want was this Young Sherlock guy getting in his way and spoiling things.

For over 35 years, he'd carried around the unclear memory of what happened at Sandy Beach's house, and he thanked his stars that he'd never even been remotely linked with her death. If he had, he wondered, he might have ended up the same way as the guy with the Japanese name.

Young Sherlock, indeed! Who the hell did this kid from England think he was, coming over here and upsetting things? As usual, Ozborn could feel his hackles rising, but aware of his own anger-management issues, he was determined to keep his emotions in check from now on. He'd have to be careful not to lose control when meeting the kid, he thought. Unwelcome attention from the crowd at The Old Parlor Tavern was definitely something to avoid, if at all possible.

Ozborn needed to work out a plan that would scare Oliver Markland off and get him wanting to take the next plane home. He'd devise something threatening. Something that would frighten Markland away, never to return. That shouldn't be too difficult, thought Ozborn, as he recollected Markland's appearance on TV. He looked kinda weedy, in his opinion.

As he clasped his mug of strong black coffee, watching the steam rise from it, he decided what he had to do. The old, disused timber sawmill at Flatrock Creek should be a sufficiently formidable place, he thought, to give Markland the message to put an end to his investigations, and get lost.

It had been a long time since Ozborn had been out to Flatrock—since the days he'd go there with his gun and let off steam. That was one of the ways he used to take control of his temper—setting up cans and bottles along the cross-timbers of the old building structure, walking a hundred paces, turning around and letting rip. Even if he said so himself, he was a respectably good shot, and watching the bottles explode their fragments of glass in the air usually calmed him down.

That's what he'd do. No need for violence, not unless it was called for—just the mere hint of what *could* happen to Markland if he didn't 'capeesh'—Ozborn's favourite word. He formulated an idea to lure Markland to Flatrock on the pretext that there was something related to Sandy Beach that he wanted to show him. Then, when they got there, a small demonstration of his shooting skills would follow, along with a few choice words—and that should be enough to persuade Markland to abandon this damned crazy Young Sherlock alter ego, period, and stay the hell away.

Ozborn was aware that his strategy to silence the boy was, perhaps, ill-conceived. He knew that he didn't know enough about Markland to be certain he'd scare Young Sherlock back to England, but he didn't care. An ill-conceived plan was better than no plan at all, and Ozborn was blinkered. A lesson needed to be taught.

He went on to think that he may even leave the boy there and make him walk back—it's only sixteen miles or so, so it wouldn't exactly kill him. Pleased with his plan, finishing off his coffee, he then gathered the necessary documents together to take to the vehicle office on Grandview Street. If he got that sorted nice and early, he could then get to The Old Parlor before midday and have time for a couple of Buds before his 'special guest' arrived.

***

Oliver Markland was nervous that morning. It was 9.37a.m., and in less than half an hour Siobhan would be meeting M.J. Emanuele. In less than two and a half hours he would be meeting the man who had some information for him. He thought back to the phone call he'd received from that man, and a shudder went through him as he replayed the caller's gruff voice in his mind. But, would it be an important lead? Oliver felt compelled to follow it up.

On holiday in Florida, and now that he was here in the Midwest, everyone he'd met couldn't have been nicer. But the man he was due to meet didn't sound like that. In fact, he sounded the downright opposite, Oliver thought. Still, they were going to meet in a public place and there would be plenty of people around, so everything should be okay, shouldn't it? He may even get there a little early, sit in a corner watching out for everyone entering the pub, or tavern, as they called them. He'd try to identify Mystery Caller from a distance, and if the guy looked too shifty, Oliver could simply slip out—or just stay sitting in the corner keeping his head down until the man got fed up with waiting and decided to leave.

But first, he wanted to speak to Siobhan and find out how she was. As if Siobhan had read his mind, she too was anxious to call Oliver, also feeling nervous about her imminent meeting with Emanuele. She had just pulled into the parking lot at Stateville Prison and, having made good time from her motel, she turned off the car's engine. Before calling Oliver, she rummaged around in her handbag.

Although certain that she did have her notebook and biro, she just wanted to double-check. It would be so embarrassing if she wouldn't be allowed to use her phone to record the interview, and then find that she didn't even have the means to write an account of proceedings either. Relieved to find her pen and paper lurking at the bottom of her bag, she then checked that her phone had enough battery life. Siobhan saw that it was 87% charged, and was satisfied that it would be enough to last the whole interview, if its use were granted.

There wasn't much time to speak to Oliver but she desperately wanted to hear his calming voice. "Hi. It's me," she said hurriedly as soon as Oliver picked up after only one ring.

"I'm glad you called," Oliver replied. How was your evening? How was the drive? How was Hannah?"

Siobhan had completely forgotten about the previous evening's meeting with Mrs. Toporofski, which had been a monumental waste of time, in her opinion. "Oh yes, I was just going to text you her pictures," Siobhan white-lied, wanting to sound on the ball. "It was all pretty much nothing of interest, I'm sorry to say—I think she's rather lost the plot. Just wants to be on TV. And she's only got a few blurred photos of an old truck anyway. There are probably thousands of them on the road, all looking the same, but I'll send the pics to you in a jiffy, no problem. Listen, I'd better go now. I just wanted to hear your voice and wish you luck at The Old Parlor. Gotta go now. See you later. Bye!"

Siobhan hung up and then quickly sent the pictures to Oliver, as promised, before getting out of the car and walking to the building's reception area.

Before Oliver had a chance to say anything, he found he was staring at the red 'CALL-END' button on his iPhone. A second later, his phone bleeped, indicating that a text had come through. The time displayed told him that Siobhan only had a few minutes before her allotted meeting time, and he visualised her now going into the same reception area at Stateville that he himself had been inside a few days previously. He decided to look at Mrs. Toporofski's pictures later.

Siobhan was approached by the man in uniform, and she was asked for her ID, nature of business, and name of whoever she was visiting. When she declared it was M.J. Emanuele that she'd come to see, the man's eyes lit up. "Ah yes, Miss. He's been expecting you. First it was gonna be Mr. Markland. It was he who came here the other day to make the appointment in person, right? But I see that you're much prettier—and I guess that'll be a nice surprise for ol' M.J." he joked.

Siobhan laughed apprehensively, but then realised she didn't quite know what was funny. "What do you mean?" she asked.

"Well, he's a bit of a ladies' man, if you know what I mean, Ma'am? I'm sure it must be frowned upon in the Bible that he's so fond of quoting, but we've been told to turn a blind eye to his habits, Ma'am, if you get the picture."

"I'm sorry, but I still don't understand," Siobhan looked at the man quizzically. Then, as if it were an explanation, she was told that Emanuele had become a born-again Christian since his days in Joliet.

"To this day he's been carrying a Bible around with him everywhere he goes," chuckled the administration officer as he handed Siobhan an identity tag to hang around her neck. Siobhan still wondered what the man was talking about.

"Anyway, Ma'am, it's a special day for our man today," continued the officer. "We don't think he's had no visitor for years. Not the normal kind, that is. Plenty of lady visitors, you understand, but they don't really count, do they? Anyways, the Governor says you can have full access—even visit his room if you want, just like the others. But don't worry—we'll be keeping an eye out for you, and besides, you're not like one of them. We don't ask no questions around here—we just do what we're told, but we do know what's what, if you know what ah mean. The word is that, in the past, he mixed with some pretty high-on up people in his days on the streets. Just his bad luck that he got caught. Just his good luck that he never got fried."

Siobhan gulped, still none the wiser about what was being said to her. As she was being led through the security door, she wondered where she was being taken. Would she be going to sit at a table in a large room with Emanuele? Would there be other prisoners present at the same time, meeting their own respective visitors? Or would it be like on the TV shows where she would have to sit in front of a glass screen with the inmate on the other side, talking through a round speakerphone?

Hoping she would be having a one-to-one conversation, with no physical barrier between them, she tensely followed the officer along a lengthy corridor. "He'll be here until the day he dies," said the officer, making conversation. "We guess that won't be too long on account of his cancer. The drugs are looking after him well for the time being, but when the time comes, the truth is, we'll all miss him. He's as gentle as a soft pussycat nowadays—wouldn't even swat a fly."

Siobhan gulped harder, as they came to an empty, high-ceilinged, hall-like room. This whole situation was surreal, she thought. Seated at the desk in the middle of the room was an immaculately-dressed, bald man wearing smart, designer glasses. He was reading a book that he closed when Siobhan entered, and then stood up and outstretched his hand to greet her as she walked towards him, while he still held the book in the other. "Well, this is indeed a pleasure," said the man in a most charming manner that took Siobhan completely by surprise. In fact, everything about the man took her by surprise—especially his voice, so mesmeric that she could quite easily have fallen into a trance just listening to it.

"Well, you are quite the picture, aren't you?" Emanuele smiled. "Please take a seat and tell me what I can do for you," he continued, ushering her to the chair on the other side of the desk, pulling it out ready. In doing so, he put the book down. As she expected, based on what the officer had told her, it was a Bible—but not the old-fashioned type she was used to seeing in churches, or her motel room the previous night. This was a modern, line-illustrated version for colouring in. Glancing at it, Siobhan almost wanted to find religion herself so that she could have a go. She loved those colouring books that had recently become so popular.

But it wasn't just the Bible that caught her attention, as Emanuele pulled the chair from the desk. The middle finger of his left hand was missing. Embarrassed that she may be staring at it a little too long, she quickly turned her gaze away and sat down. "I see you've noticed my little injury," remarked Emanuele. "I might show you how it's coming along later. But first, let's get down to business and talk about why you're here. I asked Patrick in Administration to fill me in, but all he would tell me was that it's something to do with Sherlock Holmes. Now there's a good mystery for me."

Siobhan tried to play things cool, but was struggling not to be constantly distracted by Emanuele's hand—or the strange hushed way he spoke. She placed her handbag on the table and began rummaging through it. "Would you mind if I get my note pad?" she asked. "And if it doesn't bother you too much, perhaps I could put my phone on to record our conversation, please?"

Her host was equally mesmerised by his young visitor's big blue eyes. "Of course," he replied. "Go ahead. As you wish."

After Siobhan had made herself comfortable, she began explaining the whole story, as clearly and concisely as she could. At the point when she mentioned Oliver Markland, Emanuele's expression was emotionless, but when she explained his 'Young Sherlock' persona, he became excited, and suddenly interrupted. "Ah, I see now! This is all about poor Yushi, isn't it? I've been watching your boyfriend on the TV. Very good, isn't he? If I'd have known, I would have come here better prepared. Never mind, we'll just have to go back to my room, won't we? Don't look so alarmed, my girl, I won't assassinate you! That's all in the past now." He giggled. Siobhan squirmed.

"Why do you think he's my boyfriend?" Siobhan asked curiously.

"Come now!" Emanuele answered. "I'm right, aren't I?" Siobhan blushed, not knowing what to say.

"Come on. Let's get out of here," suggested Emanuele. "I'd better tell the guard what we're doing," he continued, nodding towards the uniformed man sitting on a stool by the door, reading a newspaper. "Just going back to Headquarters, John. Taking my guest with me. I have something rather interesting to show her." The guard stood up, and followed them out the door.

"Not the finger, surely, Mr. Emanuele?" the guard whispered out of Siobhan's earshot as Emanuele went past. "You don't want to distress the young lady, do you, Sir?"

Although she wasn't able to hear what was being said, the scenario Siobhan found herself in was becoming a little too bizarre for her to absorb, and she wished Oliver were with her. Boyfriend, huh? She rather liked hearing that. But for now, she was 'in for a penny, in for a pound'—another Oliver colloquialism that she loved hearing him say. So off she went, following the two men down a corridor, up some stairs and in through a door that the guard unlocked and held open for them while he stood aside as they entered. Emanuele held up his hand to halt the guard from following them. "A little privacy, please, John," Emanuele said, mischievously.

"Alright, Sir. Ten minutes," replied John, who proceeded to sit on one of the chairs outside the cell door.

Inside, Emanuele's 'room' was nothing like Siobhan expected. The first thing she noticed was that it was carpeted. Nothing grand, but carpet, all the same. The bed looked comfortable, and apart from it being single-sized, it wasn't too dissimilar to the one she'd slept in back at her motel. There were pictures on the wall, not the distasteful pictures of nudes with large breasts that she'd expected, but nature scenes that were as beautiful as they were calming. The modern, flat-screen TV was switched off, and the wooden desk was neat and tidy, pens and colouring pencils all laid out in a row in order of their shades.

An attractive, modern wardrobe and chest of drawers were in the far corner, next to the open window that let in a cool but pleasant winter breeze. Siobhan took a peek behind a brick-built screen jutting half way into the room that revealed a toilet, sink and shower, with a white plastic shelf above the sink that contained several toiletries, soaps and other bathroom items. She stepped back and her eyes scanned the row of classics on the bookshelf above the desk. All in all, it was a room in which Siobhan thought she could have stayed in quite comfortably, and she could hardly describe it as a prison cell.

Emanuele was proud of his surroundings and took delight in the expression of surprise shown on Siobhan's face. "Not what you anticipated?" he asked. "It wasn't like this in Joliet, you know," he went on, as if that explained everything. She didn't know what Emanuele must have done to receive this special treatment, but although she was curious about it, his accommodation wasn't exactly what she'd come to ask him about.

"No, it's not what I expected at all," Siobhan answered, slowly and quietly, as her host reached up to the shelf and took down a different Bible—this one more traditional. The hand in which he held the book displayed his thumb and three remaining fingers more prominently than before, so much so that Siobhan stared even harder. Emanuele knew this, but wanted to save his best surprise till last. Siobhan was puzzled why another Bible was being brought out. It wasn't long until it all became clear.

"As you know, I used to share a cell with Yushi," began Emanuele. "Dear, charming boy he was. A bit mixed up, but a real sweetie. I had a lot of time for him, you see. Bipolar, I think they call it, these days. Right up until the day before he went to meet his maker, he'd been insisting his innocence for that terrible killing. That wasn't very nice of him, was it? But I can't really talk, can I?" continued Emanuele. "Then again, my many exterminations, as I like to call them, were just paid contracts. His was down to a deficiency of the mind."

Damn! Thought Siobhan, as she suddenly realised she'd forgotten to turn on her phone recorder. Without asking again, she switched it on, and then looked at Emanuele, very confused. "What do you mean—'*that wasn't very nice of him*'? He didn't do it, did he?" she added. "It was someone else, wasn't it? So, you mean . . ." she carried on with her questions in quick succession, not giving Emanuele any chance to answer.

But Emanuele calmly held up his forefinger to his lips, and then opened the old Bible about half way through. Folded up and held between the pages was a piece of faded, yellowing paper that he took out and handed to his visitor.

As Siobhan unfolded the document and began to speed-read it, her jaw dropped.

While she was reading, Emanuele went over to the bathroom and took a look at one of the jars on the shelf, adjusting it so it was in a more prominent position. He then returned to sit on his bed while Siobhan continued examining the paper. To this day Emanuele hadn't shown Yushi's handwritten confession note to any other living soul. After all, no one until today had ever asked about it.

It began, addressed to '*MJ*', with two powerful sentences: '*I did it. I killed Sandy Beach*'.

"Oh my God," thought Siobhan. She read on, quickly skimming past some sections of the handwritten note. Legibility was a problem but she focused on a few key points:

'I heard her call him by name – something like Mike, Mart or Mark . . . '

'One minute he was violently hitting her . . . '

' . . . I "wasn't a real man like Mark".

I heard his name better that time . . . '

' . . . she deserved what she got . . . '

' . . . I smashed her head . . .

'I guessed he'd be caught and would take the rap, while I was well away from there.'

Siobhan was so startled by what she was reading, she began hyperventilating. She desperately needed a drink of water, but also knew how important it was to get this note over to Oliver as quickly as possible.

"Can I have this?" she asked Emanuele.

He pondered a while, then shook his head. "I'm real sorry, Ma'am, but I really think I'd like to hang on to it, if it's all the same," he answered.

Siobhan was very disappointed, but asked another question: "Then could I photograph it, please?"

This time, Emanuele nodded. "I don't see why not," he confirmed.

As Siobhan laid it out on the desk and got her phone ready, she noticed that its battery level had already gone down to only 19%.

She hurriedly took some pictures of the note that had been written on both sides, but the auto-flash blurred every image, so she took them again, this time with the flash off.

Eventually, the photos looked satisfactory, and sufficiently clear for Siobhan to text the best ones across to Oliver—she guessed he'd probably be at The Old Parlor by now, getting ready for his meeting at noon.

The phone's battery was now at only 16%, but she also wanted to get some shots of Emanuele himself because she thought they might be useful for Oliver's blogs as well as for her aunt's newspaper. She frowned as she realised that more pictures would mean an even greater drain on the battery. Still, it had to be done, she thought.

By the time she had finished, she was now desperate for some water, and asked if she could wash her hands, and whether the tap water in his 'bathroom' was suitable for drinking.

This was exactly what Emanuele had been hoping to hear. "Why of course. Please help yourself," he said, gesturing with his hand for Siobhan to go behind the screen.

At first, she approached the sink, bent down, and turned on the cold-water tap, so that she could splash her face to freshen up. She lifted her head up to dry her eyes, and looked at herself in the mirror above the shelf.

Then she noticed a jar with something unusual in it, but it took a while to towel her face dry, before she was able to examine it closer.

Horrified at what she saw, she let out a deafening scream that had the guard come rushing in. Emanuele looked at him and nodded towards the bathroom.

"Have you been at it again, Mr. Emanuele? You know that's not a nice thing for the young lady to see, don't you?" said the guard in a firm, but jovial manner. Luckily for Siobhan, as her stomach muscles lurched, she had a toilet pan just behind her in which to vomit.

"I'm so sorry, my dear," apologised Emanuele, rather insincerely. Knowing exactly what must have caused his visitor's reaction, he reached around to remove the jar from the shelf, and in doing so held it up to the light, pleased with how his missing finger's thick hair was continuing to grow so well in the watery substance that covered it. And the nail, also nourished by the liquid, was now at least two inches long. "You see, I'm left handed, and it was my trigger finger," he began, as if that were enough of an explanation for his grotesque keepsake, but he went on: "I chopped it off myself as penance for all those bad things I did. When I found God, I had to show my sorrow to Him."

Having decided she'd spent quite enough time in the company of the peculiar man, Siobhan told the guard in no uncertain terms that she wanted to leave "right away", quickly gathering up her things and walking towards the door.

The guard winked behind him at Emanuele, as he accompanied the young lady back to the prison's Reception.

Still shaking, Siobhan ripped off her ID tag and threw it on the desk. "He's sick!" was all she could say to the uniformed man.

"Have a nice day, Ma'am," she heard the man reply as she pushed against the rotating door and exited the building.

In his room, Emanuele continued laughing with the guard who had by now returned. "We've got to do *something* to pass the time, haven't we?" chuckled the inmate.

"We do, Mr. Emanuele, we surely do," confirmed the guard. "It gets 'em every time, doesn't it?" Emanuele nodded with a wry smile. But despite the rather cruel entertainment he had enjoyed at his visitor's expense, there was something else that had given him a great sense of satisfaction—that at last someone had asked him about Yushi, and had learned the truth about what had happened in 1981.

Emanuele sat down and mulled over how Yushi, during his last hours on earth, had turned to him and begged to be forgiven for his sins. Although Emanuele was not a man of the cloth, for Yushi, he had been the closest thing to any God with whom he felt comfortable enough to disclose all. Emanuele had sworn on the Holy Bible that he would look after his confession note, and only share it when the right person came along. He'd spent many years behind bars, with very few visitors, and Siobhan, with her beautiful big blue eyes, was, in his opinion, that right person. And with his cancer gradually spreading, he was relieved that he'd been able to pass on what appeared to be Yushi's confession before it became too late.

PART FIVE

THE KIDNAPPING

CHAPTER 37

(MONDAY, 22ND JANUARY, 2018)

Ozborn Sets a Trap

According to Google Maps, his journey to The Old Parlor in Paris would take Oliver around 90 minutes from the Dickinsons'. Ideally, he'd thought it would be best to arrive early so that, while waiting for Mystery Caller to arrive, he could catch up with some writing. It had been a couple of days since he'd sent anything over to the *East Anglian Chronicle*, and it was about time he updated his blog. And, if time permitted, he could take a look at Mrs. Toporofski's pictures, the ones that Siobhan had sent across.

Once he pulled off Route 70 near Marshall, it wasn't long before Oliver found The Old Parlor. It looked like a typical bar, with neon signs inviting clients to 'DRINK COORS', and 'Try The Best Surf & Turf For Miles'. Ah, yes, he remembered that he'd be doing just that when Siobhan was due to join him later. That was something to look forward to, and the anticipation of having a nice meal with her helped to quell the nerves he was feeling about his imminent appointment.

As planned, Oliver arrived half an hour early at the establishment, which, on entry, was much darker in contrast than the bright sunshine outside. Spotting a perfectly-positioned, empty table in the far corner, once his eyes had adjusted, he went straight to it, out of sight from the few lonesome looking men on stools at the bar, cradling their ice-cold beer bottles. Enticed by the neon sign he'd seen outside, and thirsty from his drive, when the waitress came up to him he ordered a Coors Light. The waitress raised her eyes as he spoke. "Cute accent," she remarked as she turned towards the bar.

Oliver was well used to this sort of comment by now. "Err, thanks," was all he said. While he waited for his drink to be brought over, he checked his phone for Siobhan's text, but there was no signal. He then began thinking about what to write in his blog.

"One Coors Light for the cute Brit over there," called out the waitress to her colleague behind the bar. One of the patrons on a stool, wearing a Stetson hat, looked up, his gaze following the waitress as she returned to the man in the dimly-lit corner, carrying the tray containing Oliver's beer bottle and glass. Although it was too dark to see properly, Marc Ozborn recognised the man's profile from the TV pictures he'd seen. He climbed down from his stool, picked up his own bottle off the bar and sauntered over to where Oliver was sitting.

In turn, Oliver also instantly recognised the gruff voice, and looked up when he heard the man in the hat speak. "So, you're the Young Sherlock, are you?" Mystery Caller said, more as a statement than a question.

"Err, yes, that's me," Oliver responded, caught off guard by the early arrival of the man who then picked up a chair from a neighbouring table and swung it round and sat down next to him. It was a little too close for comfort, in Oliver's opinion, and he already didn't like the guy—his odour was stale for a start, and his breath reeked of alcohol.

Having already worked out his tactics, Ozborn leant towards Oliver and gave a smile. Although he did his best to come across sincerely, Oliver was sceptical. But when the man went on to say how much he'd been interested in the Bike Radio Murder story, and how he'd been so pleased to watch his Young Sherlock persona on TV and read the pieces in the papers, Oliver was, despite his misgivings, just a little flattered.

"Well, it's real nice meeting you here like this, Mr. Markland," continued the man. "I sure do admire what you're doing—and I think I can help. There's something I'd like to show you later—but I left it in the pickup. We can get it later—I didn't expect you to be so early." Again, he gave a smile that had the desired effect and put Oliver at ease. Maybe it was the Coors helping to relax him, but Oliver was slowly beginning to warm to the guy's rough way of talking. "But first," continued Ozborn, "let's finish our beers and enjoy the music," he said, cocking his ear to the speaker system on the wall.

The song playing happened to be one of Oliver's favourites—'Everybody's Talkin'' by Nilsson. "Man, I just love this song," stated the man, who still hadn't introduced himself.

"Yes," agreed Oliver. "Actually, I do too, Mr. . . . I'm sorry. I don't know your name . . ."

Oliver didn't realise it, but he was walking into a trap. Ozborn held out his hand. "Actually, you can just call me Marc. How do you do?" Ozborn said, trying not to sound like he was mocking the British accent, but of course he was. The comment went over Oliver's head anyway as, with each sip of beer he drank, he mellowed a little more.

After retracting from a handshake that Oliver thought was akin to rubbing sandpaper, it was now his turn to lean closer towards the man. "So, you have some information for me about the Bike Radio Murder, then? I think that's what you said on the phone. I'd be very grateful for any lead, no matter how small. You see, I'm not entirely convinced that they got the right man. After all, as far as I can make out, the guy they caught was just a simple cyclist passing through the town. Can you tell me anything about the case?"

"I sure can, Oliver. I sure can," Ozborn repeated. "Come on. Drink up and I'll show you. As I said, it's outside in the truck." Without waiting, the man who was still wearing his Stetson, stood up and began walking to the exit. Oliver took the last swig of his bottled beer, and followed. He thanked the man who was by now holding the door open for him, and they both walked to Ozborn's old Dodge truck that was situated across the lot, near the road. Once outside, Oliver's phone that was on silent picked up a signal, and he felt the familiar vibration in his pocket indicating that some texts had come through. "Door's open," Ozborn said, with false politeness that Oliver didn't pick up on. "Climb in. We can sit and talk some more, and I'll show you something I'm sure you'll be interested in seeing."

For a moment, Oliver hesitated. But the prospect of maybe learning something to help him with his investigation was too much to walk away from. So, he opened the rusty door with its pitted chrome push-button handle and got in, sitting on the large bench seat, wide enough for three, maybe even four adults, while he waited for this man he only knew as 'Mark' to get in the driver's side. When Ozborn did get in, his whole character changed noticeably, as he turned to Oliver and, with a menacing grin, said: "Ready?"

Before Oliver could answer, Ozborn had already turned on the ignition, and with a roar of the engine, he lifted the column-shift into gear. The acceleration forward was such that Oliver's head was thrown back, startled. Without a headrest, the force cricked his neck and it sent a twinge of pain right down his back. Immediately, Oliver could tell that something wasn't right. He turned to look across at the man behind the wheel, who remained staring straight ahead as he drove at speed out of the parking lot and onto the road.

"Ya know what time it is, Sherlock?" Ozborn barked, frowning, his false, charming demeanour having disappeared in an instant. Oliver took his phone out and looked at the screen that showed 12:03, also enabling to see that he'd had two texts from Siobhan. "It's just gone midday," he shouted over the noise of the engine.

"No, it ain't," replied Ozborn. "It's time you got taught a lesson, you goddamn Limey, foolin' around playing detectives like it was some game. Well, I don't appreciate that too good."

Oliver listened to the words being spoken with such venom

that spit was being projected from the man's mouth as far as the windshield.

The truck was being driven far too quickly for Oliver to jump out. He would have sustained much more of an injury than a cricked neck. Despite the pain he was in, he shifted his body and cowered as far towards the door as he could, looking around the cab. "Where are we going?" he asked, scared and confused.

"You'll see. I suggest you just sit back and keep quiet," was all Ozborn would say, as he drove out of town towards the open landscape.

Ozborn appeared transfixed. He was intent on getting to Flatrock Creek without saying another word. Oliver was, by now, genuinely frightened. Still holding his phone, he slowly and subtly moved it over to his right side, out of view from the crazed driver, wondering whether he would be able to send a text message to someone for help. He discretely looked down at the phone's screen that was now displaying one of Mrs. Toporofski's pictures, sent by Siobhan. The vehicle in the picture looked very similar to the one he was in now. Admittedly, he hadn't paid particular attention to the vehicle a few seconds earlier when walking towards it in the parking lot, but it was definitely the same make and colour. Oliver was certain of that.

Oliver kept his head motionless and forward facing, while moving his eyes around, trying to see something, anything, that would give him some more information about this man who had now become his captor. In front, folded up untidily and stuffed into the shelf beneath the dash, was a bundle of official looking documents. The top one that Oliver could see was headed 'DEPT. OF MOTOR VEHICLES – LICENSE PLATES'.

It was easy for Oliver to read the large font at the top, but he had to screw up his eyes in order to make out the smaller words in the address box beneath the heading. It was tremendously difficult to focus as the truck bounced up and down on the uneven road. Eventually, when they reached a smooth enough section, Oliver was able to make out the name at the top of the form—'M. OZBORN'. That was a start, he thought. At least he now knew the full name of the person who, to all intents and purposes, had kidnapped him.

As the truck roared along the road at around 60mph, as discretely as possible, Oliver held his iPhone at his side, out of sight from Ozborn. Squinting downwards at the screen, while appearing to stare straight ahead, Oliver rapidly moved his right thumb, and tapped out a message. He then pressed the 'Send' button, and hoped to goodness that Siobhan would get it.

CHAPTER 38

(MONDAY, 22ND JANUARY, 2018)

Siobhan Gets The Message

Siobhan was by now more than two thirds back to Paris, and she expected to arrive comfortably by the agreed time of 2.00p.m. to meet Oliver. She was hungry, and was looking forward to her surf 'n' turf meal with him, and also discussing the revelation of Yushi Yakamoto's confession note. She'd only had a chance to speed-read it while she was in Emanuele's cell—or rather, his room—and was eager to reread it and absorb its contents more thoroughly in Oliver's company.

She couldn't imagine how the strange bald man had managed to get himself such relatively luxurious surroundings. And how on earth could she have initially enjoyed listening to him talk? What a creep! But that was all irrelevant now. What *was* relevant was the information Emanuele had been keeping to himself all these years.

There was now a whole new dimension added to the murder scenario. Yushi's note, if authentic, confirmed that there indeed had been another man present at the time of Sandy Beach's murder. What was his name again, she asked herself, trying to remember. Mark? It was something like that, according to Yushi. Yes, it was definitely Mark, she remembered, recalling that Yushi had later confirmed that in his note, further on. He certainly didn't sound like a very friendly guy, did he? In fact, he sounded downright dangerous, if he's taking drugs and having violent mood swings like Yushi was suggesting. She wondered what had become of 'Mark' these days.

'I guessed he'd be caught and take the rap . . .' was one of the extracts

from Yushi's confession note that Siobhan couldn't quite figure out. Who was Yushi referring to? Could it be this same Mark guy?

Having left Stateville prison in such a hurry, Siobhan was now desperate for a bathroom break, and began to look out for a freeway rest area, and hopefully she'd find one with a Starbucks too, so she could also get a cappuccino to go. Fortunately, she noticed there was one coming up in two miles, according to the highway sign that she'd just gone past. Not a moment before time, as she felt her bladder getting closer and closer to bursting point. She sped up to get there even quicker, parked up and dashed in to the ladies' bathroom, getting a rush of euphoria once she'd begun to feel human again.

Waiting in line at the counter for her coffee, she instinctively picked her phone out of her handbag and began scrolling through her various messages. While she was doing that, a new one pinged through from Oliver. She opened it straight away, curious to know how things had gone with his meeting.

"One skinny cap to go," called out the assistant. But Siobhan didn't hear, so shocked was she with what she read.

"Oh, my God! Is this real? Is this an example of her friend's British sense of humour?" she wondered, optimistically waiting for the punch line that didn't follow.

"Madam! One skinny cap to go," the assistant repeated, this time a little louder.

In a total daze, Siobhan completely ignored her order and walked out into the sunshine towards her car. "Oh, my God," she muttered to herself again. Hurriedly climbing in, Siobhan read Oliver's message again and again.

"HELP. KIDNAPPED. SAME TRUCK MRS T SAW. MARK OZBORN. HEADING NORTH ON 150. DON'T CALL. WILL TXT WHEN POSS"

For a second, she was confused, especially when she read the name Mark Ozborn.

Siobhan had a hunch. She couldn't be certain, and she knew it was a long shot, but there were too many coincidences mounting up.

What with Oliver's reference to the 'same truck' that Hannah had seen, and now the same first name, Mark, being referred to in Yushi's note, and now in Oliver's text.

She felt as though, in slow motion, she was watching a one-arm bandit machine in a casino. The more fruits that aligned the more worried for Oliver she became.

Had Oliver been referring to the photo of Yushi's note that she'd texted him earlier? What should she do? Realising the potential severity of the situation, and that this was indeed no joke, she knew she had to call the Police. Her hands trembled as she tapped the numbers on the dial screen, and initially got no response whatsoever. "Come *on*!" Siobhan shouted at her phone. Damn! She'd pressed '811' instead of '911'. She tried again, and waited for what seemed like an eternity.

Eventually, she heard a click, and then a woman's voice. "911. What emergency service do you require?"

"Police. Please hurry," said Siobhan, realising that she'd never in her life called Police, Ambulance or Fire. More clicks, and then another woman asked her a series of questions about her identification, address and location. It was all taking far too long, thought Siobhan, as she noticed the battery indicator on her phone turn red, informing her that she only had 5% charge left. At this rate, it would go dead before she'd even had a chance to tell them about Oliver's situation.

She began to shout, while at the same time doing her best not to panic. "Look, my phone's going to cut out at any moment. Please, just listen. My friend's been kidnapped. He may be in danger. He . . ."

The woman interrupted in a firm manner. "Ma'am, please do your best to keep calm. I know it may be difficult for you, but we must get all your particulars before we proceed. And what is the name of your friend?"

Exasperated, Siobhan gave her Oliver's full name, and then began trying to explain, without getting too tongue-tied, about the potential danger he might be in. But infuriatingly, the woman kept stopping her. "Ma'am, it's very important you speak clearly and concisely. Where and when did you last see Mr. Markland?"

Siobhan could feel herself about to explode. "Yesterday afternoon. But that's irrelevant. It's today that he was due to be meeting someone in Paris . . ." The woman, who could have been operating out of anywhere in the country, and obviously not familiar with the towns of Illinois, cut in yet again: "What, Paris, France? In that case Madam, you need to . . ."

At that moment, Siobhan could hear nothing more, and she found herself staring at a blank screen as her smartphone finally ran out of power. "Oh God!" she cried out. "Now what do I do?" she asked herself. She thought for a moment, remembering that she'd noticed some phone accessories in the shop next to the Starbucks franchise inside the highway services. She ran back to the building and began searching for the correct charger for her Samsung Galaxy among all the various gizmos displayed. There! She found one for her particular model and grabbed it off the hook before darting across to the pay booth, searching through her bag trying to quickly find her purse and Visa card.

She looked around in case there was a payphone, but unfortunately there was only one, and it was occupied. That's a sign of our times, Siobhan thought, remembering that only a few short years ago it would be normal to see a whole row of them. For once, as she rushed back to her car, she resented the modern age of fast-developing technology.

Back inside the car, after undoing the overcomplicated plastic wrapping, she then plugged the charger into the cigar lighter and connected her phone to it. Impatiently, she had to wait a few excruciatingly long minutes before her phone finally burst back to life. While leaving it on charge, she tapped 911 once more.

Incensed, poor Siobhan had to go through the whole calling process yet again, wasting precious moments when all she wanted was to alert the powers-that-be about Oliver's plight. At long last, once she'd been able to explain everything sufficiently enough for the authorities to take proper notice, and not before time, she was asked for the exact message that Oliver had sent her. Fortunately, her brain was sharp enough to be able to recite it precisely.

At the point when Siobhan said, "*SAME TRUCK AS MRS T SAW*", she suddenly remembered that she had the pictures from Mrs. Toporofski on her own phone. When she told the woman at the 911 call-centre this fact, Siobhan also tried explaining who 'Mrs. T' was, but ended up confusing things more. "Madam, I'm afraid you've lost me," the woman said curtly. "Please just wait with your vehicle at your location and we will send a patrol car to you."

Very thankful that she was now being taken seriously, Siobhan said goodbye and then, while waiting for the Police to arrive, called her aunt at the newspaper.

Ursula answered straight away, but only managed to hear half the story before her niece told her that she had to go because, what seemed like after no time at all, she could see a police car pulling into the busy highway services area. Ursula was left bemused, while Siobhan assumed the car was the one that had been dispatched to meet her, got out of her own car and waved her arms in the air to attract attention.

Two officers approached her. "Siobhan O'Mahoney?" asked one of them, an overweight black male. His colleague, a white female as thin as her colleague was fat, didn't say anything to begin with and let her colleague do the talking. "So, there's been a kidnapping? A Mr. Oliver Markland? And you've got pictures of the kidnapper's vehicle, you say? Can we see, please?"

"Sure," replied Siobhan. "But you'll need to sit in my car. The images are on my phone, and that's charging right now. It's got zero power at the moment, so if I unplug it, it will die again." As if it were a scene from a Keystone Cops movie, the man squeezed with great difficulty into the passenger seat of Siobhan's tiny Honda. While the policewoman got in back and leant her head forward, they both looked on as Siobhan found the images on her screen of a rusty old pickup truck.

"You don't see many like that anymore," the policeman said, admiring the distinct lines of the old model Dodge V8 that, as a car enthusiast, he recognised easily.

"Now, wait a minute," said the woman, screwing up her eyes so she could see the screen better. "If we're not mistaken, we followed this vehicle back to the trailer park in Marshall for speeding recently—it may even have been only yesterday. The guy had no insurance and no current licence plate, and should have attended a drink-drug course. We gave him a warning as we got called away pronto. Rough looking son of a . . . What's your man's name? Ozborn? Hang on, let's check this out."

She went back to the patrol car and began punching some details into the on-dash computer. Her male colleague stayed and talked with Siobhan in order to get a clearer understanding of the whole story, since the incomprehensible message from the call-centre had been far from clear. "Man! I don't believe it!" he exclaimed. "Young Sherlock? You don't say! I seen him on the TV." He struggled to get his large frame out from Siobhan's small car seat, and called across to the patrol car. "We're only dealing with that doggone English detective here! The one that's been on the TV recently. You betcha! Well, I'll be damned."

Lorraine Mills, being the more senior of the pair, spoke firmly to her colleague. "Thank you, Officer," she said, while continuing to check things on the police's database. This was the first day the patrolman had gone out on duty with her, and she was so far not overly amused by him. Maybe they'd just got things off on the wrong foot. "That may as well be, but we sure would appreciate you not cussing like that," she called back. Feeling embarrassed about having his language reprimanded while in the presence of Miss O'Mahoney, if it hadn't been for his dark skin, the poor man would have gone red.

It didn't take Sergeant Mills too long to receive a more

comprehensive picture of Marc Ozborn, the owner of the pickup, based on his previous behavioural records. She liked to put two and two together and make four. She was better at doing this in real life than when she watched the latest whodunit mystery on TV. Despite her love of detective books, Lorraine could never quite manage to work out who the killer was, much to the amusement of her husband Lee. "You'd think with all your reading, and being a policewoman an' all, you'd be better at playing TV detective," he'd say. She'd laugh.

But today Mills was firmly in the real world, and knew exactly how to conduct herself in the pursuit of her professional duty. Added to that, due to Ozborn's more recent misdemeanours and scuffles with the law, she was able to establish that he needed apprehending at the earliest opportunity. She returned to Siobhan's car. "If it's correct that he's heading away from Paris along Highway 150, we shouldn't find it too difficult to spot him. We've already checked with The Old Parlor, and the waitress remembers serving a young man with an English accent—and she later saw him leave with an older, rough looking man, probably in his late sixties, early seventies, at just around midday. So, we guess that was them."

"We've just put out an APB," Mills continued. "So, for now, we gotta just wait and see. And maybe Mr. Markland will try to contact you again too. Ma'am—try not to worry unduly. Nine times outta ten, this kinda thing gets resolved real quick, and usually there's nothing sinister involved." The policewoman handed Siobhan a card, and then continued: "But keep your phone close to you at all times, and call this number immediately if you get any news from your friend. Your call will come through direct to me, see?"

"I see. I will," agreed Siobhan. "I guess it's okay for me to head off now? I just want to get back and go to see my aunt in Terre Haute."

Sergeant Mills nodded. "Are you sure you'll be okay?" she asked with compassion. "We can follow you if you wish, Ma'am."

After Siobhan reassured the police sergeant that she'd be fine, she re-joined the highway and drove off in the direction of Interstate 41,

Terre Haute and the offices of the *Terre Haute Daily Times*. As worried as she was for Oliver, this was indeed a news story that her aunt should be told about first hand, and Yushi's confession note added an incredible possible postscript to the whole sorry affair of Sandy Beach's last night in Paris.

CHAPTER 39

(MONDAY, 22ND JANUARY, 2018)

Oliver Leaves His Tracks

Oliver felt so tense, he tried to do some breathing exercises that he'd once read about. Apparently, he understood, if you breathe in slowly through the nose and out through the mouth while visualising you are in a peaceful place, like a running stream or a field of bluebells, you could slow down your own heart rate. So that's what he tried—and after a while, thankfully, it seemed to work. Instead of the panic he'd felt a few minutes previously, now he was able to at least think clearly about what he could do to help himself.

Although it was hard to check, he felt pretty sure his text would have successfully reached Siobhan. Could he risk another, without his captor noticing, he thought? He made a decision to glance at his phone screen again and was rewarded. He had a text message. He prayed it was from Siohban.

In order to pacify the man next to him, whose name he had presumed to be 'Mark Ozborn', he asked, again, a perfectly innocent question: "Where are we going?"

"That's for me to know and you to find out," was all Ozborn would say, as he stayed fixated on getting to wherever their destination was. Oliver tried keeping his head casually towards his side window, while secretly looking downwards at his phone. The possessed man next to him continued to drive in a straight line along Route 150, listening to country music that was now blaring out of the radio at full volume.

And then Oliver had a brainwave. GPS-tracking! If only he'd

downloaded that app for locating the whereabouts of your phone if it's lost or stolen. Berating himself for not having done it before, he pondered whether he'd be able to manage downloading it now, but without being noticed. And, of course, there was also the content of Siobhan's text document that he hadn't yet read. What if it were significant? He really ought to try to read at least some of it, he decided.

"Okay, eyes down, here goes," he thought, as he did his best to view Siobhan's message that accompanied an image of a hand-written note.

Her message read: "Oliver—there were two of them there! Yushi and another guy called Mark. But Yushi finished Sandy off after the other guy had passed out! It's all here in the note that Yushi wrote and gave to Emanuele."

What the . . .? Oliver was totally confused, and frantically tried to work out what Siobhan had meant. Did that mean that the man next to him in the truck could in fact have been present at Sandy Beach's killing? If indeed he was the same guy. He did say that his name was Mark. And the license document in front of him says 'M. Ozborn'. Now, Oliver was even more scared. There was only one thing for it—he'd have to open the image and read as much content as he could—hopefully it would explain everything. Trying his very best not to obviously look down at his phone, he managed to open the attached picture of Yushi's note.

Damn! It was impossible to read. The image was far too dark, it was written in scrawly handwriting, and the road was too bumpy for Oliver's eyes to focus. He would have to read it later as soon as he got the chance. Meanwhile, he'd do his utmost to set up the tracking app.

Click! Click! And another gentle click. Then, just a few more seconds to go before the app loaded. Done! Open! Now it should be possible for Siobhan to track him, inform the police, and that would be the end of this whole terrifying ordeal.

All he had to do was text Siobhan without Ozborn noticing, to let her know what he'd done. With a few movements of his thumb his message was completed, and now all he could do as they sped along the road, was to wait.

***

Siobhan was just pulling up in the street outside her aunt's office when she heard the phone go 'ting'. She looked at the text message that Oliver had just sent. Oh my God! He's so clever, she marvelled. She ran into the building, past the receptionist and up the stairs to the door marked 'Ursula O'Mahoney–Editor'. Without knocking, she stormed in while what looked like a board meeting was taking place.

Ursula, at the head of the table, and the other six people seated, all looked up and stared at the sudden intrusion. "Siobhan!" she exclaimed, alarmed by her niece's grave expression. "Whatever's going on?"

"I'm sorry Aunty. It's Oliver!" she began. "He's in grave danger. He's been kidnapped! But I can track his phone now! I've got to call the police!"

Ursula turned to her colleagues. "Ladies and Gentlemen, I think we'd better adjourn this meeting. But by the sounds of it, we are in the middle of an unfolding news story. You know all about our new investigative reporter, Young Sherlock, don't you? I think we'd better get our news teams on to this straight away. Stick around so we can get a briefing from Siobhan after she's called the Police. Siobhan darling, do what you have to do, and then tell us all what's happening."

Searching for her purse in which she'd put the policewoman's card, Siobhan nodded. She found it at the bottom of her handbag and began calling the number—this time more controlled than before. In seconds, the call was answered. "Oliver's set up a tracking device on his phone!" Siobhan blurted out to Sergeant Mills.

"Brilliant! Where is he?" asked the Sergeant. "No, wait. Where are you?"

"I'm at the offices of the *Terre Haute Daily Times*," Siobhan answered.

"Stay there!" instructed Mills firmly. "Someone will be right over." The phone went dead, and just as Siobhan began explaining everything to the board members, they all heard the sound of a siren in the distance that became louder and louder. Siobhan, standing near the window, was able to see clearly down to the street below. She saw an unmarked car stop outside, and what she imagined must be a plainclothes officer come running up the steps and through the front door.

"Siobhan O'Mahoney, please," the man shouted, showing his police ID to the receptionist on the ground floor. She pointed upstairs, and the man bounded up them, two at a time. Siobhan was now standing outside her aunt's office, in the corridor waiting for him to appear as he came up on to the landing.

"In here!" she called out, just as a news reporter was also walking quickly along to the Editor's office from the other direction.

Before Siobhan could speak to establish whether the officer had good or bad news for her, he introduced himself. The policeman spoke with authority, as he shook hands with her and entered the room. "I'm Detective George Hardy. Luckily, I was in the vicinity when Sergeant Mills radioed me, and she briefed me about Oliver Markland and his kidnapper. According to his truck licence plates, the owner of the pickup is one Marc Ozborn. I understand your friend had managed to activate a tracking app on his phone. Let's take a look now, can we?"

Detective Hardy exuded an air of capable confidence, and Siobhan was glad to have him on side. She assumed that once he took control, Oliver would soon be rescued and everything would get back to normal.

Thank goodness, she thought. Feeling momentarily relieved, she even began imagining what a great scoop this story would make for her aunt's newspaper, as well as Oliver's blog and his magazine in

England. But her feelings were short lived when she then checked herself and remembered that first, Oliver had to be rescued from the bad guy by the good guys. What if he were already in deep trouble?

CHAPTER 40

(MONDAY, 22ND JANUARY, 2018)

Hardy Races to the Rescue

Within the confines of Ozborn's truck's cab, Oliver had perhaps become a little over-confident with the use of his phone at his side, as he glanced down at it once more. Unfortunately, on this occasion, he was less discreet, and it was more blatantly obvious what he was doing. Ozborn clocked him. "You little shit! Give me that!" Ozborn shouted. Oliver retracted further and pushed himself right up against his side of the cab, too far for Ozborn's right arm to reach.

"Don't you dare try any funny business with that, y'hear?" Ozborn growled. Unaware that Oliver had actually been using his phone already, Ozborn's gaze returned to the road ahead. Nearly there, he thought. One more mile or so, and they'd reach the turning to Flatrock Creek up ahead on the left. Oliver continued cowering, when a minute later, without warning and hardly slowing at all, Ozborn swung sharply left onto the dusty stony track leading towards some hills in the distance.

Bouncing along at great speed, Oliver began feeling ill. "Can you slow down, please? I think I'm going to be sick," he pleaded with Ozborn.

"You'd better not throw up in my truck, for your sake," was Ozborn's angry response, as he continued driving at the same speed, following the track as it weaved past the various trees and shrubs along the way.

Probably caused by constantly looking downward at his phone, and the beer he'd consumed earlier, Oliver felt worse than ever with every bump the truck's wheels made, and his face turned noticeably pale as the sensation of nausea engulfed him. When they got closer to the hills, he could make out what looked like an old timber building up by a river, about a mile away.

Ozborn drove the truck fast down a dip in the track, and up the other side, swerving left and right. At the top of the mound, the vehicle actually took off and landed with an almighty crash as it careered along its way. This was the final straw for Oliver. Without warning, vomit projected forth all over the interior of the cabin, on the seat between him and Ozborn, on the dashboard and up to the windshield. Ozborn was incensed. "*Fuck you*!" he hollered, and slammed on the brakes, causing the truck to skid side to side before eventually halting right next to some large bushes.

Seizing the opportunity, Oliver grabbed the door lever and tugged it upwards, then put all his weight behind the door itself. As it opened, still feeling faint and dizzy, he literally fell out of the cab and into the bush. Dazed but fully conscious, he knew instinctively that this was his moment to escape.

Fuming with anger, Ozborn began to slide his way across to the passenger side to get out after Oliver, then realised that his hands were now covered in the mess created moments earlier by his passenger. "Oh, Christ!" he looked down. "You better get back here boy. *Now*!" he called, madder than ever. Not wanting to cover his jeans with the vomit on the seat, Ozborn decided to slide back and get out of his side and run around the rear of the truck instead.

Despite it being January, the heat of the bright afternoon sun bore down on Oliver, making him feel even worse. But he knew this was his only chance to make a run for it. Those precious extra seconds gained could mean everything, and it was now or never. There was no telling what Ozborn was capable of doing in his fury. With youth on his side, Oliver darted behind a bush and ran to the next one, scrambling on all fours to the next and the next, all the time out of sight from Ozborn. Ozborn could be heard shouting and swearing, completely enraged as he tried in vain to see which way Oliver had headed.

Taking a few seconds to catch his breath, Oliver crouched down low and didn't move a muscle as he planned his next move. The old timber buildings he'd seen in the distance were likely to afford him better protection than being out in the open, so that's where, he decided, he'd aim to get too. It looked like the trees and shrubland continued all the way up to his destination. Once there, he could try calling for help, assuming there was a signal on his phone.

"Oh, no!" he sighed. As he reached down he realised the phone was no longer in his pocket. He must have dropped it when he'd freed himself from the cab, he guessed. He had a quick look back towards the first bush, but there was no sign of it. As he heard Ozborn's frightening yells and shrieks, the adrenalin pumped through Oliver's system, enough to overcome his dizziness. He made a dash for it, using all the stamina and strength in his legs that his frequent cycling had developed. He ran as fast as he could, scratching himself to pieces as the shrub branches caught against his clothes and arms. He was gaining precious ground on Ozborn, who could still be heard shouting some way behind.

Looking in every direction, Ozborn couldn't see Markland anywhere. There was less ground cover back towards Highway 150, so he guessed the old buildings up at Flatrock Creek were where the boy was headed. Probably familiar with the old sheds better than most, Ozborn reasoned that he had a good chance of finding his quarry in whatever hiding place he chose. He was not a man who liked to be beaten.

With cold and calculated determination, he gave up trying to run after the boy—his ageing body wasn't up for that sort of exercise, and was no match against someone more than three times younger. Instead, he walked assuredly back to his truck and got in. With the engine still running, before putting it in gear, he casually lit a Marlboro. The boy would be caught, no problem.

Initially, his plan had only been to give the boy fair warning that he should get the hell back to England, and maybe offer him some extra encouragement with a demonstration of his shooting expertise. But it hadn't taken him long to realise that this Young Sherlock had connections. He presented a real serious danger and a more permanent solution was needed to take care of the problem. The mess in his stinking cab had been the final straw. The boy, through his own stupid fault, had now changed the game plan. "I'll teach the young son-of-a-bitch a lesson," Ozborn ranted away to himself. "He'll wish he'd never even heard of the name 'Young Sherlock' by the time I'm done with him!"

It took Oliver only six minutes to reach the first of the buildings, sprinting as fast as he could all the way. In the distance behind him, he heard the low rumbling sound of Ozborn's truck, gradually becoming louder by the second. Then he heard a deafening '*Crack*' as the vehicle must have been only two hundred yards away. "I'm coming to get you!" Ozborn shouted through his open window while he pointed his gun and shot randomly upwards in the air. That should scare the boy, he thought.

"Shit. This is getting deadly serious," thought Oliver, now petrified, as he entered the first building through a large, rotten barn door and into the dark and dirty interior.

***

Back at the *Terre Haute Daily Times* office, Detective Hardy watched on as Siobhan worked her phone and waited for it to pick up a GPS signal. There was a total of nine other people present in the room, all leaning forward to watch as well. Wherever Oliver's location turned out to be, they all wanted, but without stating yet, to join the reconnaissance mission. Especially Peter and David, the News and Photographic Editors, respectively.

Everyone stared at Siobhan's phone, watching for what seemed ages, as the little wheel on the screen went round and round. Then, slowly to begin with, a map began to appear. "It's working!" Ursula proclaimed, excitedly. Secretly, she was already imagining the next morning's headline: '*KIDNAPPED YOUNG SHERLOCK BRAVELY RESCUED BY OUR TEAM*'. She hoped she wasn't getting ahead of herself.

The map continued to load, and then, as if by magic, a small red dot also appeared on the screen, indicating the position of Oliver's phone. "He's north of Paris, near Georgetown. That's almost an hour from here." Hardy stated, straight away making a call. "Get all available units over to the vicinity of Georgetown. This is an emergency. Approach with caution. We have a young man's life potentially at risk."

Then, while still on the phone he turned to Siobhan. "Can you zoom in any further?"

Not familiar with the app, she quickly touched the screen with forefinger and thumb to expand the map. Horrified, she watched as the screen suddenly went blank. She must have done something wrong. Detective Hardy didn't hide his frustration. "Jesus Christ, girl! What are you doing?" he said, curtly.

His attitude certainly didn't help the situation, and Siobhan began to feel her eyes well up with tears, not helped by the emotional day that she'd already endured.

Ursula intervened robustly in no uncertain manner. "I'd appreciate you not talking like that to my niece, Sir. I'd remind you we're dealing with her—*our*—friend, so Siobhan is understandably stressed enough as it is, without you making things worse."

She turned back to Siobhan who was now shaking, and spoke calmly to her. "See what you can do, dear. Just do your best."

Siobhan snivelled and sniffed as she composed herself again and reloaded the app. This time, she was more careful, and cautiously touched the 'plus' icon on the screen. That did it! The red dot remained in the centre as the map grew larger and more legible around it, enabling Hardy to read the location. "He's at Flatrock Creek!" he shouted into his phone. "Repeat: Flatrock Creek. All available units."

"Good job, Siobhan," he said. "And I apologise for earlier. Let's get going, shall we? You coming?"

Siobhan turned to her aunt, who nodded her approval. "Be careful, sweetie." Ursula then turned to two of her colleagues. "Peter. David. Grab your cameras and you follow too. Safety is paramount, but don't forget, getting a good story and pictures is a very close second. Go!"

Detective Hardy raced out of the room and down the stairs, followed closely by Siobhan, Peter and David. "Peter—you go ahead and bring the car round to the front while I go back to my office and grab the cameras," instructed David.

"Be quick!" commanded Hardy, as he and Siobhan ran to his car. "Every minute counts." He pulled out a magnetised blue light and attached it to the roof of his car. Siobhan jumped in the passenger side, and they both waited a few seconds before Peter's car pulled up behind. David came running down the steps and jumped in.

Hardy revved the engine and sped off, tyres squealing. "Hold on tight!" he called out. The acceleration pushed Siobhan firmly back in her seat as they sped towards the highway, with Peter and David not far behind.

"God, I hope Oliver's all right," shouted Siobhan above the noise.

"So do I," said Hardy. "So do I."

CHAPTER 41

(MONDAY, 22ND JANUARY, 2018)

Oliver Hides from Danger

Once inside the timber building, it took Oliver a minute or so before his eyes adjusted from the brightness outside, so much so that momentarily he thought he'd gone blind. The sickness feeling had thankfully gone, but he did feel very thirsty, with the dusty atmosphere not helping. When he could eventually see properly, he took in his surroundings and ran forwards towards the large space ahead. It was empty except for some old sawing machinery, a rack of rusty hand-tools and a collection of picks and axes, brooms and poles. Further over and propped up against the right wall was a large wooden ladder, wide at the bottom and narrow at the top. Up above, Oliver's gaze settled on a first-floor landing and the remains of a staircase. Only the uppermost two stair-treads still existed, hanging precariously by some nails attached to the underside of the landing. The ladder would be the only means of reaching the next floor, but not in its current position.

Oliver didn't know what he'd find up there, but he did know what was down on the ground—not much. There was nowhere to hide and there was only one other room adjoining the large one that he was in, but it was locked. However, he *was* able to see up above that at the end of the landing was a passage leading along a narrow corridor. It looked like the corridor was running above the position of the locked door below. Maybe there were also three closed doors up there as well, Oliver thought, but his view was restricted and he couldn't be sure. What he *was* sure about was that in the distance outside he could hear the rumble of Ozborn's truck engine, idling away. All then went quiet as the engine was switched off, and Oliver heard the familiar-sounding click when the car door was opened, and then a loud clunk when it was slammed shut.

With no choice but to try to get to the landing before Ozborn entered the building, Oliver prayed he might find some refuge if in fact there were further rooms up there. He ran to the ladder so he could move it and gain access to the landing, but it was much heavier than he imagined, and impossible to carry. He tried shifting it along but it was too much for him to manage. All he could do was to slowly walk it, one upright rail at a time, in a near vertical position.

All was going well, until the left rail hit an uneven mound of loose ground. Oliver struggled to hold the ladder in place, but it was simply too heavy. As he lost control, the whole thing began to tilt, and the more it tilted the less control he had of the weight. Although Oliver did his best to hold tight, it was no use. He had to let go and leap backwards as the ladder became top-heavy and came crashing to the ground.

Any moment now Ozborn would reach the entrance, and the noise of the ladder falling was a sure giveaway of his location, Oliver was in no doubt of that. Looking back across to the barn door he'd just come through, he noticed a solid timber bar attached on the inside that could be moved across and engaged in a housing at the door's side, like a huge latch. If he could just close the door and slide the bar in place, that would give him some valuable time to have another attempt with the ladder.

"Sherlock! You in there? I'm coming for ya," called Ozborn from outside, having been alerted, as Oliver anticipated, by the sound of the crashing ladder. Oliver darted over, pushed shut the door and pulled the bar across, securing it from inside. There! That would keep Ozborn out, at least for a while. Then, rushing back to the ladder, Oliver thought out his next move.

It was imperative to get up to the landing. The only way he would be able to raise the ladder would be to drag it against the wall, lift one end and prop it sufficiently to crawl underneath and push upwards with all his might. Inch by inch, he managed to get it almost upright. Then, with one final burst of strength, he managed to push it across so that the top fell against the edge of the open landing. The top of the ladder only just reached, but it would be enough for Oliver to climb up.

"*Sherlock*!" boomed Ozborn again, even louder than before, as he banged on the barn door. Oliver was confident that Ozborn wouldn't be able to get in, and he felt a little safer. That was until he heard Ozborn call out some more: "You think you're smart, Sherlock, don't you? But I'm smarter than you because I know another way in." Was he bluffing, Oliver wondered? Without waiting to find out, Oliver clambered up the rickety rungs as far as possible. When he reached as high as he could, he rested his stomach on the landing floor, grabbed at some heavy timbers lying on the floor, and pulled himself up with his hands.

At last, he was relatively safe, he thought. Exhausted, Oliver rolled across the old floor that was inches thick with years of dust and pigeon droppings, and took in his surroundings.

If indeed there was another way for Ozborn to get in the building, Oliver assumed it must be on the other side of the locked partitioning door on the ground. The timber of the door had looked rotten, and Oliver guessed that, with one hard kick, Ozborn would probably be in and then he'd be able to get to the ladder as well. With that in mind, Oliver decided to push the old ladder away from the landing so that it crashed to the ground again. It might mean that he couldn't get down, but it would certainly make it more difficult for Ozborn to get up.

It was unhelpfully dark up on the landing, with the only light coming through the cracks between the exterior slatted wall and a couple of small holes in the roof, probably where birds could find their way in. But the illumination was sufficient for Oliver to find his way along the narrow corridor, where his assumption of there being three closed doors turned out to be correct. He tried each of the doors as he went past. Luckily, they weren't locked, but the first two opened into completely empty rooms, about twelve feet square, and offering absolutely no hiding place whatsoever.

At the end was the third door. Oliver tried the handle and found this to also be unlocked, opening into another space almost identical to the one he had just come from at the top of the ladder. He guessed he must now be in the area of the building above the other side of the locked door on the ground floor.

Now he was standing on a landing area that went all the way around the four walls, just like the previous space. Oliver could see that this one also had a non-existent staircase, except for the few treads hanging from the landing's underside. From his position, Oliver commanded a clear view of the whole area below, including more saw-cutting machines and other tools. He could also see what must be the second way in to the building, to which Ozborn had referred.

Stacked against the walls were several old crates and boxes, and many planks of wood of all lengths and thicknesses piled on top of one another. Oliver crouched down behind the pile of timber, so that he could just about still see everything on the ground level. All was silent, and at last he had a chance to catch his breath and rest. He was sure his heart could be heard a mile away, it was pumping so hard.

Oliver tried to calculate his chances of rescue. The longer he could keep this guy Ozborn at bay, the better, he reasoned. If only he still had his phone. It's at times like these, he thought, weighing up his predicament, that he could really do with phoning a friend. Who'd want to be a millionaire if you're dead? His mind raced ahead, thinking all sorts of ridiculous thoughts. The intensity of the situation he found himself in brought out a bizarre sense of British humour, and he allowed himself a slight grin.

But when the potential danger he was facing sank in, he felt terrified, so much so that he literally began to shake with fear. The Co-op job in Wivenhoe might have been less exciting, but it was certainly far safer than this, he thought.

***

According to the inbuilt satnav computer, Detective Hardy's car should reach Flatrock Creek in 32 minutes, the device indicated. Hardy had hoped that some other Police units might have already arrived at the scene, and begun dealing with the crisis. But en route he'd learned via police radio that today was a particularly busy one, what with a serious accident on Interstate 74 further west, and the baseball playoff in the nearby town of Effingham later that evening, where crowd control preparations were underway. Most local forces were already tied up attending to their duties, and it meant that only one other unit was available.

Police driver Theresa Ashley, and her colleague William Wheatley were the first to pull off Route 150, and they began driving along the same dusty and bumpy track that Ozborn had travelled along a while earlier.

The two of them had been assigned as a unit for the past four years and two months, having joined the force on the same day. After their initial training, their Captain had recognised they made a good team, and decided to put them together. The duo gelled, to the point where they became not only good friends, but their families also got together regularly for barbecues, wild-camping vacations and fishing trips.

"Better turn off the siren and take it steady, now," William suggested.

"Sure. You're right," Theresa agreed. "We don't know what we're going to find," she said. "Let's not give this guy Ozborn any pre-warning that we're coming. Who's the guy he's taken captive?"

William looked down at his notes. "Oliver Markland—a British guy. Ha ha! You and he can talk cucumber sandwiches together when we get him freed," he joked. Officer Ashley, like the guy they were trying to rescue, was British born, having left her home town as a teenager. Until Theresa had joined the police, she had been a well-respected owner of a cab company, but her work hadn't given her the fulfilment she was craving. So, she sold the business and decided to work at driving of a different kind. Now, at 53, becoming a policewoman, she knew she'd found her true vocation, and loved every minute of the job.

Her partner became more serious as he continued briefing his driver, taking a last drag of his cigarette before stubbing it out and flicking it from the window. "They say Markland's got a tracker on his phone. But unfortunately, we can't access it until the other party gets here. A woman by the name of O'Mahoney is on her way now with Detective Hardy."

"I see. The big gun's coming out to play, is he? We're honoured!" Theresa said with a smile.

"Yeah. But George is alright," answered William. "I guess they should be arriving anytime soon. But let's see if we can wrap this up before they get here, shall we, and add another to our list of triumphs?"

"Right on," answered Theresa, with her usual enthusiasm for getting a job done. William looked up from his clipboard. "Wait a minute—I think I know this place. I came fishing here once—up at the river near the old saw mill. I guess I would have come at it from the north, and that's why I didn't recognise it straight away. Look. There's the old woodshed up ahead a mile. Maybe that's where they're at. Come on, partner—let's get to it. Drive real nice and quiet and park behind those bushes up there in the distance, and we'll go the rest of the way on foot."

"Right on," William repeated. The two of them liked being cops, putting the world to rights. For Theresa, it was more exciting than picking up fares for a living, and the ever youthful-looking tall and lanky William, with six young children to provide for and grateful to have a job, thanked the Lord each day it was this one. He couldn't imagine doing anything different.

***

Inside the woodshed, Oliver crouched down on the landing floor in complete silence. He was out of sight from the point where Ozborn entered the building, but capable of viewing everything on the ground below.

Oliver was now looking down at a man who appeared like he was possessed, with his face red with rage, unkempt hair and eyes focussed and menacing. At first, Ozborn stood motionless and looked all around, noticing the broken staircase as well as the collection of poles next to the saw-bench. Sherlock must be *somewhere*, he knew, perhaps in the next saw-shed that he remembered was on the other side of the door. He approached the door and turned the handle, not expecting it to be locked, but it was. He took a few steps back and tried to ram it with the left side of his body. Ouch! Surprisingly, despite its rotten timbers, it didn't budge. All he managed to do was to cause a spasm of pain to go down his shoulder. Damn! What with the remnants of Sherlock's vomit still on his hands, he wasn't in the mood for this. He called out.

"I know you're in here. Why don't you make this easier for both of us and come out? I only wanna talk to you. I'm not gonna harm you." Ozborn listened to the silence for a few seconds before stepping away from the door, raising his right leg to kick it in. The door still didn't open, but this time he managed to jar the whole of his right side. More pain. Now his patience really snapped and he decided to escalate proceedings to a higher level. He pulled his gun out.

Aiming at the metal lock, he took a shot. A loud crack rang out, almost deafening Oliver as he watched on from above. But even more alarming than the sound was the ricochet of the bullet as it bounced away from the door, whizzing past Ozborn and embedding itself in the bench. "Fuck, that was close," mumbled Ozborn. "But it looks like it did the trick," as he examined the lock casing to see that it was now hanging off the door by a single screw. He gave the door one more kick, and it swung open on its rusty thick hinges, revealing the other saw-shed next door that he knew from memory was located there.

Ozborn looked around. Unaware that the two officers outside in their car had also heard the gunshot, he went over to the ladder that was lying on the floor. "Well, the son-of-a-bitch came in," he reasoned, "and he ain't nowhere to be seen down here, that's for sure. So, there's only one place he can be, Ozborn determined, and that's up on the landing."

"Come on, Sherlock," he called out, trying to sound reasonable. "You're up there somewhere, I know it. Let's talk, shall we? We can work this out now, like civilised human beings." Oliver had difficulty not passing out with fear, especially now that Ozborn was out of his line of sight, and he could only hear the sound of Ozborn struggling to drag the heavy ladder along the ground.

Outside, Ashley and Wheatley, whose vehicle was now quietly creeping along near to the saw-sheds, had just heard through their open windows what they knew instinctively was a gunshot. "Did you hear that?" asked Ashley. "It sounded like it came from inside the building." Ashley drove the car to a patch of ground shrouded by bushes, and halted. They both got out and closed the car doors as quietly as they could behind them, then ran, heads down, to the barn door, the same one that Oliver had pulled the bar across.

"Probably locked on the inside," whispered Wheatley. Wanting to keep the element of surprise on their side, they deftly moved along with their backs against the building's wall, looking for another entrance. Both had now taken their guns from their holsters, holding them primed and close to their chests.

CHAPTER 42

(MONDAY, 22ND JANUARY, 2018)

Siobhan Reveals Yushi's Note

Just as officers Ashley and Wheatley were searching for an entrance to the barn, Detective Hardy and Siobhan were approaching the highway turnoff to Flatrock. With their blue light flashing and siren wailing, they were making good time, but anxious to get to Oliver and Ozborn as soon as they could. They were closely followed by newspaper staff, Peter and David, who were doing their best to keep up.

During the journey from Terre Haute, Siobhan had taken the opportunity to properly reread Yushi Yakamoto's note and convey its contents to the detective as he drove, explaining its background complexities as they sped along the Interstate highway. Hardy went over the story.

"So Yakamoto said he *did* kill Sandy Beach all along, then, even though he maintained his innocence right up to the end as far as everyone else was concerned?" Hardy asked.

"Yes," answered Siobhan. "Until us, Emanuele had been the only person who knew the whole truth, according to Yushi, about what happened that evening she was killed."

"But this guy Mark also hit the woman as well? Before Yakamoto interrupted their little sex game?" Hardy went on, trying to get his head around the details of what had happened.

"According to Yakamoto's note, yes," confirmed Siobhan. "According to his confession note that he wrote by hand and gave to Emanuele, Yakamoto turned up and witnessed Beach getting roughed up by Ozborn, with her consent, and felt embarrassed, upset and sickened. Not to mention jealous and confused."

"So Sandy Beach and 'Mark' then carried on with their sordid sadomasochistic activities that Yakamoto wanted no part in, until Mark staggers away and falls asleep outside? And then Yakamoto totally loses it, and clouts Beach on the head with his bike radio?" Hardy continued. "Yakamoto was uncontrollably furious that Sandy Beach preferred the other guy more than him, and something inside him just flipped?"

"Exactly! You know the saying 'Hell hath no fury like a woman scorned'? Well, I guess it was like that, except Yakamoto acted like he'd taken on the role of the scorned woman," said Siobhan, looking again at the image of Yushi's note on her phone. "He must have been deluded into thinking that she loved him. See, it says here: "*I finally got a girl to show me love, or so I thought. How could she have been so cruel as to lead me on*?" Siobhan read, verbatim.

"But what does the part about 'CFNM-DOM' mean? What's all that about?" Hardy asked. "I don't get it."

"Well," began Siobhan, feeling a little embarrassed, having to talk about a sensitive subject with a man double her age, who she barely knew. "I'm no expert, but I believe 'CFNM' means 'Clothed Female, Naked Male', where the woman—Sandy in our case—takes control over the man, Ozborn, and *DOM*-inates the sexual proceedings, commanding him to do whatever she tells him. The game is that he obeys."

"Including, in this case, getting this guy Mark to treat her roughly and slap her about?" Hardy asked, his eyes rolling upwards in disgust. "But if Yakamoto was so sweet and innocent at the time, how did he know about all that stuff?" he puzzled.

Siobhan guessed the answer. "Because he'd discussed all that had happened in detail with Emanuele while they were sharing their cell together. It was Emanuele who'd educated him in the ways of the sexually-deviant, sordid world."

Siobhan was uncomfortable discussing the subject, but was glad that the online research she'd undertaken had proven useful. Hardy kept quiet, concentrating on the road ahead, while listening intently as Siobhan went on: "For Sandy, the physical pain from being knocked about by this guy Mark, bizarrely, was what turned her on, how she got her kicks, excuse the pun. I guess she got hers from a dominatrix sex game, while the guy got his from the booze and drugs. She egged Yakamoto on even further when she noticed he had returned to the house while she and Mark were doing their thing. Perhaps being watched really got her going. Only she knew that Yakamoto was there. The man was too out of his head to be aware of his presence."

"Hmm, I think I'm understanding," said Hardy, slowly. But being totally honest, he wasn't sure that he really was.

Siobhan continued interpreting Yakamoto's note for his benefit: "Mark hit her hard and she fell to the ground, concussed but conscious, still infatuated with the man's slaps and wanting more. The man's intake of weed, and God knows what else, then got the better of him, and he goes outside completely drunk and drugged up, passes out, naked, remaining there the whole night. Meanwhile, Sandy is on the floor, frustrated as hell, and apparently begins teasing Yakamoto for not wanting to join in the fun. I kinda feel sorry for the guy at this point. He was being ridiculed by the woman he mistakenly thought was in love with him. He certainly had massively misguided feelings for her."

"Then Yakamoto finally lost his cool with Sandy, who was continuing to tease him," Siobhan carried on. "Instead of him helping her up, an argument between them developed when she upset him further for not being, in her words, a '*real man like Mark*'."

"And that finally pushed Yakamoto over the edge?" asked Hardy.

"That would have done it for sure!" Siobhan confirmed, interpreting the confession note as best as she could. "I think you got it," she agreed.

"So, incensed beyond words, Yakamoto picks up the bike radio that he'd noticed in her kitchen—the same one that the guy Mark had stolen off his bike—and hits Beach with it while she's laying on the kitchen floor?" surmised Hardy. "And kills her."

"Mr. Hardy, what if 'Mark' and 'Marc, spelt M A R C, Ozborn' are one and the same man?" asked Siobhan, slowly. If it's the same pickup truck, according to Oliver's text, it all makes sense!"

"Please. Call me George," he said, thinking hard, and trying to breathe a little light relief into such an intense conversation.

"Okay, George," Siobhan went on. "Yakamoto must have stood over her and whacked her with such venom that the radio smashed into fragments, knocking her out. Then he kicks her in the side for good measure, before coolly taking off and riding his cycle to the motel that Sandy had kindly booked for him earlier, as if nothing had happened."

Hardy had worked out the rest for himself without Siobhan's help. "So, he knew that Ozborn, if that's who it was, was asleep on the patio and would likely be the only suspect, knowing that he also had his fingerprints all over the radio," he said, turning to Siobhan with a matter-of-fact expression, before concluding his reading of the situation. "But what Yakamoto hadn't reckoned on was for Ozborn to wake from his stupor and disappear well before Sandy's body was discovered by the neighbour. Gee, what a psycho!"

"Yeah," agreed Siobhan. "It was as if he simply blanked his mind after the event, and assumed that Ozborn would get the blame. Whether around the time Yakamoto's bipolar state that Emanuele had referred to meant that he genuinely didn't remember what had happened, or simply chose not to, is something we'll maybe never find out. We only know that he finally confessed to Emanuele years later in his note, addressed to '*MJ*'."

Siobhan reread the beginning of Yushi's note:

MJ

I did it. I killed Sandy Beach.

"Perhaps his memory came back. Perhaps he suffered diminished responsibility. Or perhaps he was a cold-blooded killer all along. We'll probably never know," said Siobhan.

Detective Hardy and Siobhan now only had a few more minutes until, according to the satnav, they'd shortly be turning off Route 150 to go along the track to Flatrock, just like Oliver and Ozborn, and Ashley and Wheatley had covered earlier. It was good timing because Hardy had only one final thought that he wanted to air before they arrived at the scene.

"Okay, I have one last question for you," Hardy began, turning to Siobhan and choosing his words thoughtfully. "So . . . we've established that Yakamoto had returned to the house *without* Ozborn noticing, and then not long after that, Ozborn had gone to the patio and passed out, right?" he asked. Siobhan nodded.

Hardy continued. ". . . and then if Yakamoto had left Beach's, and had cycled off to the motel that evening, long *before* Ozborn had awoken in the early hours of the following morning . . ." Siobhan frowned, desperately doing her best to follow Hardy's line of thought.

This time, Hardy spoke even more slowly than before. "So, *if* Ozborn had then seen Sandy's body on the floor, dead . . . and he remembers hitting her during their, game of—what did you call it? CFNM? —then surely that means that all this time, since 1981, Ozborn's been believing that he himself had been Sandy's killer, not Yakamoto!"

"Hmm, yes, I guess so," agreed Siobhan, cautiously. "That hadn't occurred to me. Ozborn must have been carrying a heavy burden around all these years, if that's the case." Then a frightening thought suddenly occurred to her. "Oh no!" she uttered suddenly. "What if Ozborn's now thinking that if 'Young Sherlock' keeps delving deeper into the Bike Radio Murder case, his cover will be blown? If he thinks he's been able to get away with one murder, he may be thinking he can get away with a second!"

With an even greater degree of urgency, Hardy was determined to get to Oliver's location as soon as they could—every second could count. His car tyres skidded and squealed as he braked hard, took the turning sharp left off Highway 150, and then sped up again along the uneven track, red dust and stones spraying in a cloud of dust.

As he leaned out the car's window and cut the siren and flashing light, he glanced at his passenger who looked deep in thought. Siobhan prayed that by now Oliver must have read Yakamoto's confession note from her text message, and had put two and two together. She desperately hoped he might be able to negotiate with Ozborn and convince him of the futility of his actions.

Detective Hardy brought Siobhan out of her deep thoughts with a start. "Okay now. Have we still got a signal from Oliver's tracker app?" he asked. Just then, a voice came across the radio. "Is that you, Wheatley? What can you tell us?" asked Hardy, urgently.

Wheatley took it upon himself to relay the grim news that they were certain they'd heard a shot fired from inside the building.

CHAPTER 43

(MONDAY, 22ND JANUARY, 2018)

Ozborn Pulls His Trigger

"Yes, we still have a signal," answered an ashen-faced Siobhan, looking at her screen. "According to this, Oliver should be right *here*!" Hardy slammed on the brakes, and looked around. His car's sudden stop almost caused the car following to smash into it.

"Woah! That was close," called out Peter, as he just managed to bring his own car to a stop, the two vehicles only inches apart. "Where's Oliver? I don't see him." asked Peter, stepping out the car and going up to Siobhan. "Are you sure that thing's working?"

"Well, yes, I am. Look!" Siobhan handed her phone to him. Peter glanced at it before getting out and looking around the area. Up ahead in the distance, he could make out the timber buildings, and these were clearly marked on the map that was showing on Siobhan's device. Next to their cars was a mass of undergrowth that continued all the way to the sheds, but the dot that indicated Oliver's position wasn't showing the sheds—it was right where they all stood.

Siobhan looked over Peter's shoulder at her phone and took it back, almost snatching it from his hand. "He should be right here!" she said, incredulously. "Maybe he's hiding in the bushes!" She raised her hands in front of her mouth to form a human loudhailer, and was about to yell out Oliver's name when Hardy stopped her.

"Wait!" he commanded with authority. "Let's look around first. Everyone split up and check this area thoroughly. And quietly."

They all moved apart from each other, their heads bowed down, scrutinising the ground. It was Siobhan who spotted Oliver's iPhone lying on the ground between the track and one of the bushes. She picked it up and looked at it. It was still switched on and showing a number of texts and emails that hadn't yet been opened—including the one she'd sent attaching the image of Yushi's confession note. "So, Oliver doesn't yet know what we know," she thought, alarmed. She returned to the cars, holding the phone in the air, and when Hardy reached her side, she began crying.

"Show me exactly where you found the phone, please," Hardy asked, compassionately. She took him to the spot, and he looked around nearby. A few feet up ahead, in the direction of the sheds, a small piece of distinctive red and white cloth was dangling from a shrub and blowing slightly in the light wind.

"I'd swear Oliver had a shirt like that!" Siobhan sobbed.

"Now then," Hardy tried to reassure her. "It looks like he's caught his t-shirt on the bramble, and he's made a run for it up to those sheds, I'll bet ten bucks. Get back in the car. Come on Peter—you and David come with us and leave your car here. Everything will be okay. We'll find him, don't you worry." Hardy's apparent confidence calmed Siobhan, and she smiled at him. He smiled back, trying to be reassuring, and wishing he was as confident as his smile suggested.

Hardy proceeded to drive slowly and stealthily up the track towards the river and the woodsheds. As they got nearer, with David the photographer forever snapping away, they noticed Ashley and Wheatley's police car tucked away in the bushes. Hardy parked his car next to it, and the four of them silently got out.

"Stop," Hardy said in a loud whisper. "This is my job to do, and it could be dangerous."

He reached back into his car through the open window and, retrieving his gun from the compartment under the dash, made it clear that the other three could stay behind in the safety of the car if they preferred.

"No way!" Siobhan, said softly but emphatically.

"Okay," Hardy conceded. "I can't stop you. But *be careful*. Stay behind me and don't do anything until I say. We don't know what to expect, and we don't even know whether Oliver is actually in there."

"But you bet me $10 he was," Siobhan reminded him, trying to make light of such a serious situation.

"So I did, young lady. So I did," comforted Hardy, as he put his muscular arm around her shoulder.

***

Moments earlier, inside the shed, Oliver had been keeping very still on the landing. He had listened a few moments earlier to the sound of Ozborn moving the ladder into position. Somehow, Ozborn must have been able to manoeuvre it more easily than Oliver had done earlier—or perhaps it was simply that Ozborn's arm muscles were that much stronger. For a few seconds, all Oliver could hear was deafening silence, followed by the faint, far-away sound of footsteps and creaking floorboards.

"Oh God!" thought a terrified Oliver. Ozborn must be on the landing of the other shed now, and he guessed it wouldn't take him long to come down the corridor. Oliver imagined him checking the two empty rooms before entering the third, the room in which he was now crouching, waiting . . .

Oliver had to do something, move somewhere else, but where? He was too high up to jump to the ground and escape. He considered a slim chance that he might lower himself, by holding onto the broken stair treads, as low as possible, then let go and drop—but the noise would attract too much attention. Plus, he'd probably break a leg and wouldn't be able to move away quickly enough. Ozborn would have clear sight of everything below, including him. And also, Ozborn would have a clear shot too. Oliver quickly discarded that idea.

Now that Oliver had become accustomed to the dim light from the cracks in the timber and the hole in the roof, he looked around more carefully upwards. The roof looked like it might be his only chance of escape, if there was any way he could make the hole bigger and squeeze his body through and out on to its surface. But he guessed he wouldn't be able to do that in the small amount of time he had available. Anyway, he had a fear of heights, and just the mere thought of clinging to some slippery roof tiles almost made him pass out.

But then, as he studied the roof area more thoroughly, he thought he could make out the outline of a small trapdoor in the wall, under the eaves. It was barely large enough for a human to get through, so it may only be a cupboard—but it was better than nothing. He knew that if he stayed where he was, Ozborn would certainly see him behind the stack of timber within seconds of entering the room. He believed that the trapdoor was his only chance of escape.

The trapdoor was high up on the wall, but fortunately there was a crate beneath it that might help him, Oliver thought. He decided to try it. He did his best to not make a sound, but just as he heard his pursuer coming closer, he caused the floorboards to creak, enough for Ozborn to be alerted. With only seconds to spare, he clambered up on the crate just high enough to push open the trapdoor, but its hinges had rusted with time so badly that they had firmly seized. Oliver knew that it *had* to budge if he was to have any chance of escape, and he pushed harder. Gradually, the door moved an inch, and then another and another, just enough for him to squeeze through.

Had Oliver remained in his spot behind the stack of timber, he would have clearly seen the two uniformed police officers entering the building, and he could have alerted Ashley and Wheatley of his whereabouts, and the whereabouts of Ozborn. But now that he was away from his viewpoint, he was oblivious to their presence, in the same way that they were oblivious to his. All they could hear was the creaking floorboards coming from somewhere up above.

At the exact moment Oliver managed to push open the trapdoor and tightly squeeze through it, Ozborn entered the landing area, catching a brief glimpse of Oliver's body as it disappeared into the void on the other side. Without thinking, Ozborn's instant reaction was to fire his gun. The bullet pierced the flimsy wooden wall between the landing and the void.

Down below, officers Ashley and Wheatley, on hearing the gunshot instinctively took cover while simultaneously looking upwards in the direction of the loud bang. But their view of Ozborn was obscured by the crates and stack of timber. Outside the building, Siobhan gasped and covered her mouth with both hands. Peter and David ran back and crouched on the ground behind the car. Detective Hardy kept his cool and edged his way inside the barn door, holding his Police-issue Colt revolver firmly with both hands. He insisted with a motion of the gun that Siobhan stay where she was.

The void behind the trapdoor was larger than Oliver had expected. It was more of a room than a cupboard, and at the far side there was a wall with a window, but to get to the window he would have to jump across three missing floorboards, underneath which was a fifteen-foot drop to an area directly above the building's barn door entrance. He had to make a dash for it, so, feeling dizzy with fright, he took a run-up and leapt across the gap. As he did so, he caught a glimpse of someone below. It looked like a woman with long dark hair, but as he only saw the person for a split second, he couldn't be sure.

Reaching the window, he tried to see if it would open. "Damn!" he muttered. It was a fixed type that had four square panes of glass, all of them broken with corners missing, making the remaining glass lethal and impossible to climb through unless he could knock the broken panes out. As he looked around for an implement he could do that with, he felt his dizziness increase. It wasn't only through fear. Unaware that he'd been shot, he was leaving a trail of blood that oozed from the wound in his upper right arm.

Ashley and Wheatley looked at each other when they heard the shot ring out, and courageously ran through to the other woodshed, acknowledging the presence of Detective Hardy when they noticed him for the first time. Without a thought for her own safety, Sergeant Ashley began climbing the ladder. Hardy stayed where he was and looked up, just in time to see some movement from behind the stack of timber as Ozborn moved towards the trapdoor.

"*Ozborn! Stop*!" Hardy shouted, with his gun poised to shoot at an unseen target. But Ozborn ignored him. By now, he could think only of silencing the boy, without considering the consequences.

Inside the void, Oliver had found a stick of wood that would enable him to break the remainder of the windowpanes. He was about to take a swipe using all his rapidly dwindling strength when Ozborn appeared at the trapdoor and peered inside. With the wood in his hand, Oliver leapt back over the missing floorboards and hit Ozborn square across the face. It was enough to daze Ozborn, but not to stop him. Siobhan, looking up in the direction from where the noise came from, moved into a position which afforded her a perfect line of sight through the hole in the ceiling at the two men above.

A semi-stunned Ozborn staggered backwards with the shock of having the stick whacked across him. Having lost all ability to think clearly and logically, as if on autopilot, he fired two shots randomly in the air, as he staggered towards the trapdoor for a further attempt at reaching Oliver.

Now very weak, Oliver looked down at the pool of blood at his side, realised he'd been wounded and willed himself not to faint. Siobhan watched in horror from below as Ozborn raised his gun again, ready to shoot at Oliver through the open trapdoor. Hardy was also standing underneath the missing floorboards with his gun poised, but his position was such that Oliver was between him and Ozborn, making it impossible to take a shot at Ozborn without risking hitting Oliver as well.

Siobhan decided that she had to do something. She had to trust her hunch that this was the same guy Yushi had referred to in his confession note. She had to shout out something that would break his concentration. "*You didn't do it*!" she yelled. "*You didn't kill Sandy*!"

Caught off guard, Ozborn was baffled enough to momentarily stop in his tracks and look around to ascertain where the woman's voice had come from. Through the gap in the floorboards, he saw Siobhan. "What the hell are you talking about?" he shouted.

"You think you killed her, but it wasn't you—it was Yakamoto all along," she continued, playing for time.

Ozborn was surprised by what Siobhan was saying, and very confused. "Yeah, sure. I know your game," he countered. "The little shit's out to get me, and I may as well finish him off now. Whether I go to jail for one killing or two ain't gonna make much difference now, at my age."

"But, you needn't go to jail for either killings," shrieked Siobhan. "I'm telling you, you didn't kill Sandy Beach—it was Yakamoto who hit her with the bike radio while you were out cold on the patio. I've got his confession note all on here," she continued, waving her phone in the air, trying to look convincing. "Why don't you drop the gun and come down peacefully?"

Just then, Ozborn heard the familiar 'click' sound of a gun's safety catch being pulled back, followed by the sensation of a cold hard object being pressed against his head from behind. "Drop the gun, Ozborn," demanded Ashley, with Sergeant Wheatley standing close by, a pair of handcuffs at the ready. Weighing up the dramatic scene as best as he could, Ozborn decided on doing what he was told, and let loose the grip on his gun. It dropped to the floor and Wheatley kicked it through the hole to land at Detective Hardy's feet on the ground.

"Good work, you two," Hardy called out. "Oliver, it's safe now. You can come on down."

Siobhan expected to see Oliver's cheery face appear at any moment, but instead there was no answer. "Oliver!" she called out again. Still there was silence. While Wheatley proceeded to handcuff Ozborn, Ashley moved forward slightly to take a look through the trapdoor, and was met with the sight of Oliver lying still and flat across the timber floor, with a large amount of blood next to him. As the pool of blood gradually found its way through a gap in the boards, it dripped down in front of Siobhan.

"*Oliver!*" she cried out, hysterically.

Theresa Ashley, who was less emotionally attached and had professional training on her side, got straight on her radio that was strapped to her shoulder, and spoke calmly and concisely. "We have one male casualty, at Flatrock Creek woodsheds. Ambulance required urgently. Gunshot wound. The victim is unconscious. Copy?"

CHAPTER 44

(MONDAY, 22nd JANUARY, 2018)

Moores Shows Remorse

Peter and David had been listening intently as best as they could. When they deemed it safe to do so, they then appeared at the shed's barn door, furiously writing notes and taking an abundance of photographs. Remembering what Ursula had said about safety being paramount, they'd heard the proceedings and decided they could now begin doing their respective jobs on behalf of the *Terre Haute Daily Times*. This sure beat covering the latest ball game, or violent arguments in overcrowded shopping mall car parks, they concluded. This was a real news story. If they played their cards right, they might even be in line for next month's journalistic awards in Chicago.

But more important than any newspaper story, was Oliver's condition. Directly following the horrendous incident at Flatrock Creek, Siobhan and the four officers had to endure an excruciating four minutes before they could even establish whether Oliver was alive or dead. Thankfully, he was alive, but there would then follow a further 48-hours before Siobhan's young friend would regain consciousness.

***

(TUESDAY, 23rd JANUARY, 2018)

Detective Hardy wanted to tie up the loose ends of the case, and the next day he had been working hard to extensively join all the pieces of the jigsaw together—present and past, with the help of

Siobhan and the many files on Oliver's laptop computer. The whole Bike Radio Murder story, from 1981 up to Oliver's current-day investigations, was extremely well and cohesively documented, but there was one particular loose thread that bothered him—that of former Police Chief turned corrupt Governor, John Moores. What had happened to him? Hardy wondered. It didn't take very long to make some enquiries and come up with the answer, and Hardy decided to take a drive north east to find out more.

Wheelchair bound, Moores now lived comfortably at the Greenacre Care Home in East Chicago, in his own palatial apartment overlooking Lake Michigan, with warden-assisted care on call 24/7. Ironically, some of his carers were of Japanese descent. During his working life he would have considered it unthinkable that he'd be allowing such people to give him a daily wash-down, let alone occasionally wipe his arse when it became necessary.

Moores had clearly been able to hang onto a lot of his ill-gotten fortune, but Hardy wasn't interested in looking into the financial aspects of Moores' life. He just wanted to know whether Moores had deliberately perverted the course of justice regarding Yushi Yakamoto's case.

When Moores agreed to receive his visitor that day, George Hardy arrived at the main reception area and was taken by the warden to Moores's apartment room, where a sad and lonely figure was sitting in his wheelchair staring out at the water. Without turning around to greet Hardy, the old man spoke with a voice that was almost inaudible. "I've done my research, and I know who you are, but I can only guess why you're here. Yushi Yakamoto, yes?" Hardy nodded silently, and even though Moores wasn't looking at him, he knew that his assumption had been correct.

"I'm tired now, Mr. Hardy. Tired of living," continued Moores. "I doubt that I've got a lot of time left on this planet, and there's little point in me pretending that I haven't done some very bad things in the past. God only knows I'm now paying for the errors of my ways.

But there's still something I should admit to. I *need* to admit to. What you decide to do to me after I've told you, that'll be up to you entirely. I won't try to change your mind one way or the other."

"Go on," Hardy then encouraged. While Moores was speaking, it was clear to the detective that despite it being well documented that in the past Moores had been a racist, especially against the Japanese, it appeared that he might be leading up to a confession. Although he seemed to be exhibiting signs of genuine remorse, could it be that Moores was simply saying what he expected Hardy wanted to hear? Was it all a clever performance? Hardy couldn't be sure, although he was certainly intrigued.

"But I don't understand what you had against Yakamoto." stated Hardy. "Whatever your past thoughts of foreigners might have been, hatred even, Yakamoto wasn't even Japanese—he was born and bred in the United States. You knew that at the time, just as you were also well aware of someone else in Sandy Beach's house at the time of her murder. That's true, isn't it? And yet you chose to ignore some of Doctor Copeland's forensic evidence, as well as the neighbour's witness statement. Yakamoto might well have been spared the needle if Ozborn's presence at the murder scene had been taken into consideration—after all, his actions *had* been a contributing factor to Beach's fate."

This time, Moores swivelled around in his chair and looked up at Hardy. Moores' eyes were moist. "Not a day goes by when I don't think about that. I did bad, I know that—but my feeling against all foreigners back then was so strong, and especially the Japanese on account of what they did to my poor father. I accept now that I was wrong, but at the time I couldn't help it—the hatred and contempt I felt was so ingrained. Thankfully, I'm a reformed man now, Mr. Hardy, although I don't expect you to believe me, even though it *is* the truth. But I'm afraid I did even worse than ignore evidence or witness statements—I'm only glad that things didn't work out the way I'd planned."

"I'm afraid you've lost me," Hardy said, puzzled.

Moores went on to explain. "I wanted Yakamoto dead. That's terrible for me to say now, but at the time it was a fact. And when he was sent to jail, I celebrated the fact there was one less Jap on our streets. How shameful was that? Please, you don't have to answer that question, because I'm well aware of the answer." Moores paused for breath before continuing. "I didn't know back then that one day, Yakamoto would in fact be executed. I had hoped for it, shame on me, but I couldn't be sure. So, I tried to organise an execution of sorts myself!"

"Go on," whispered Hardy, hardly believing what he was hearing.

"No doubt," continued Moores, now with tears visibly formed in the corners of his eyes. "No doubt you've heard of M.J. Emanuele? *The Assassin*? Of course you have. It wasn't by accident that he ended up sharing a cell with Yakamoto. When I became Governor, I had a lot of power in the running of Illinois prisons, including Joliet. You see, I could influence all the prisoners' locations—who went where, who shared cells with whom, you know, that sort of thing."

Hardy continued listening, second-guessing what was coming next, and hoping that he was wrong. But he realised that he wasn't when Moores continued: "First, I got Yakamoto and Emanuele put together in the same cell on the pretext of solving some overcrowding situation. And then I gave Emanuele one final contract to carry out. I thank the Lord now that he refused to go through with it, otherwise that would have been another burden I'd have had to bear for the remainder of my days."

This latest revelation filled Hardy with horror, if he understood correctly. To think that such a thing could happen in a prison in modern-day America beggared belief, as far as he was concerned. Moores carried on with his guilt-ridden tale: "Luckily for me, and Yakamoto, Emanuele had found religion by then, and didn't go through with what I'd ordered."

With his hands shaking visibly and clearly very upset, Moores went on: "I heard from sources still loyal to me that your, err, friend Miss O'Mahoney recently paid a visit to Emanuele, and was a little, err, upset—yes that's the right word—upset, to discover his trophy from our alliance in a jar. He tells everyone that he cut off his own 'trigger' finger. But who uses their middle finger to pull a trigger, I ask you? That's a load of baloney, for sure." The conversation was becoming more and more difficult to stomach for Hardy, especially when Moores then tried to bring some light relief to his disclosures. "Ha, ha! A load of baloney for O'Mahoney!" Moores joked, without smiling.

"Cut to the chase, Moores. I'm feeling sick of all this," demanded Hardy, now very irritated by Moores' mixed signals—boastfulness on one hand, and sadness and regret on the other.

"Okay, okay," conceded Moores, as he got the message, with his weak voice faltering. "I was the one who dismembered Emanuele's hand as punishment for not doing what I'd asked!"

A shudder went through Hardy as he listened to Moores tell his guilty secret. "There! I've admitted it now for the first time," said Moores. "You're the only living soul who knows, apart from Emanuele himself of course."

"I'm honoured," replied Hardy, sarcastically. Moores went on to elaborate further: "I'd got Emanuele alone in the kitchens at Joliet, picked a meat cleaver from the rack, held him in an arm-lock from behind and simply chopped the finger off that I'd forced him to splay upon the stainless steel work bench. I threatened Emanuele I'd get his life sentence moved up a notch to the death penalty if he ever let on, so he made up a story about doing it to himself. And this is now the first time I've admitted my actions to anyone."

Moores continued. "Even when I was in jail myself, I was still able to call upon so-called friends to pull certain strings for me, so when I could I tried to redeem myself by making Emanuele's remaining life behind bars considerably more comfortable. A token of my sorrow, an apology if you like. That's why when Joliet closed and he was moved to Stateville, he ended up living in more of a hotel room than a cell. He was lucky—he went on to find God, didn't he? Maybe he even found happiness, whatever that is. I never found my God, or happiness, and I doubt I ever will. I'm now truly sorry for my actions, Mr Hardy. And now my fate rests in your hands."

Without saying another word, and without making further eye contact with Moores, Hardy got up, walked slowly and deliberately to the door, and left the apartment. As he walked along the hallway towards the care home's exit he reflected on his highly irregular meeting, his mind in a spin. He'd heard some weird and abhorrent stories during his career, but none quite so bizarre as this.

During his drive home, he considered what he ought to do next, wondering what advantage anyone would gain if he were to instigate new proceedings against Moores. Hardy was satisfied that Moores appeared genuine in his remorse, although he accepted that that fact alone was an insufficient reason for whatever action he decided upon taking.

Hardy concluded he should wait till the morning after a good night's sleep, just like his mother had raised him to do whenever there was a difficult decision to be made. This afternoon, for now at least, he would concentrate on simply getting home and taking a relaxing bath with a strong Bourbon whiskey by his side.

CHAPTER 45

(WEDNESDAY, 24TH JANUARY, 2018)

Mitori Feels Compelled

After Oliver had been shot, the situation thankfully had been quickly brought under control, and he was efficiently collected by air-ambulance and flown for specialist medical attention at Terre Haute's Imperial Hospital. It was touch and go though, and the quick actions of Ashley and Wheatley, as well as of the air-ambulance crew, had almost definitely saved his life. The rapid loss of blood, coupled with the shock to his body's system, had meant it was a close-run thing.

It had been a whole 48 hours before Oliver became conscious again, while lying there in his hospital bed. When he did come round, at first, numb and unsure of where he was, it gradually dawned on him that he wasn't actually dreaming—that in fact this was all very real. The last thing he had remembered was being inside the small room at the woodsheds, and the terror he'd felt at being pursued by Marc Ozborn.

Now that he realised he was in the safety of a warm and comfortable hospital bed, he came to the conclusion that the whole scene could so easily have turned into a nightmare. He was aware, without being told, that he could easily have been killed.

Once his grogginess had dissipated, his mind soon sharpened when he could hear that he was not alone. Luckily for him, he thought, the two girls present in the room hadn't noticed the flickering of his eyes, squinting open very slightly, first the right one and then both. Oliver decided to shut them tight again quickly and to remain very still. The pattern on the machine to which Oliver was connected began oscillating in a different rhythm, but to the untrained eye that meant nothing. To the nurse in the other room who could monitor the machine remotely from where she sat, it meant that her patient was ready to be seen by the specialist to assess his wellbeing and undergo various tests.

This could be a very awkward moment, Oliver realised, as the potential gravity of his situation sunk in, specifically his domestic situation concerning the two women at the side of his bed. Of course, it wasn't as bad as being shot at by a crazed man, he knew that, but not far off. While listening very intently to the conversation going on around him, he tried to work out exactly how much Sam knew about Siobhan, and how much Siobhan knew about Sam.

"He could have died, you know," said the voice that Oliver recognised as being Siobhan's. "It was so awful waiting for the ambulance to arrive, and the amount of blood he lost was staggering. Before the paramedics got there, we'd torn up every bit of rag we could find to wrap around his arm, but still it kept bleeding."

Oliver listened intently while Siobhan continued to describe to Sam what had happened at the saw-shed, leading up to Ozborn's arrest.

"Thank God!" Sam began, somewhat in awe of Siobhan. "Thank God you had the brilliant idea to shout out to Ozborn that he wasn't the killer." Thinking back, Siobhan was rightly proud of what she'd done. By following her hunch, she may well have saved Oliver's life, and she was looking forward to talking through the sequence of events with Oliver when he regained consciousness.

Oliver just lay there in the hospital bed, eyes still shut tight, making a mental note to thank Siobhan for her quick thinking at the next opportunity. After all, he thought, how many Marks must there be in the world? It's not exactly an uncommon name. He reiterated Sam's sentiment under his breath. "Thank God!"

Just then, as Sam looked towards Oliver with grave concern, the nurse entered the room. "Hi there, girls, I'm going to have to ask you to leave us now. The Doctor wants Mr. Markland over for an MRI scan right away."

"Okay," responded Siobhan, standing aside to let the nurse through. "I've got to get over to my aunt's newspaper to write today's update," she said to Sam.

"And I need to get home now, anyway," replied the other voice who Oliver knew to be Sam's. "It's been real nice meeting you, Siobhan, even though the circumstances haven't been good. I sure am looking forward to Oliver getting back home with us—my mom and dad and me. Especially me, to tell the truth—he's recently been so preoccupied with all this Bike Radio Murder stuff, that we really haven't had much time for each other, and I can't wait to have him back to how things used to be before all this started."

Siobhan raised a quizzical eyebrow, but decided this wasn't the time or place to delve deeper into what things Sam was referring to. She'd be bound to find out later. Both girls turned towards their man, who they assumed was fast asleep, and blew invisible kisses through the air to him. "He will be alright, won't he?" asked Sam to the nurse, looking at her expression for any signs of reassurance.

"Please tell us he's gonna be okay," pleaded Siobhan. Without making any commitment, the nurse just did her job, and with positive compassion simply said that it was for the doctor to assess, and that was where she was now taking the patient.

For now, Oliver made sure he kept his eyes closed until he was safely half way down the hospital corridor. The nurse pushing his bed was clearly a very perceptive lady. "You can open your eyes now, Mr. Markland," she said, checking behind her in time to see Oliver's two visitors walking towards the exit in the other direction. "But I think you might potentially be in a spot of trouble there later, young man, if you don't mind me saying."

"I think you may be right," Oliver agreed, rolling his eyes. Half an hour later, he was being wheeled back to his room following what he was told had been satisfactory test results, with a doctor reiterating how lucky he had been to survive the shooting. Oliver looked up to the ceiling and contemplated what he ought to do next with his life. The contemplation was easy, although coming to a conclusion was a little more difficult. Nevertheless, he made a decision, one that both his head and heart agreed on.

During the previous week's dinner with Siobhan at her aunt Ursula's, it had been bandied around by Ursula that they might be able to find Oliver a permanent position at the newspaper, and Oliver had been very excited about exploring that prospect further. But, what with the traumatic events of the past few days, the thrill of remaining in America had lessened somewhat, and the return to the comfort and safety of Wivenhoe, as soon as he was able, was now a much more appealing proposition.

But for now, he knew that as soon as he was well enough, he had work commitments that he was obliged to fulfil, contractually and morally. In fact, as it happened, he decided he was feeling well enough right now to get on with them. No time like the present, he thought, so with a burst of energy that surprised him, he reached down to the side of his bed and opened the cabinet's door to retrieve his laptop that he knew Siobhan had thoughtfully brought in with her. Making himself comfortable by propping three pillows behind him, he began writing. He knew his readers at the *Terre Haute Daily Times* and the *East Anglian Chronicle* would be waiting, and he had an awful lot to tell.

Despite his tiredness, a whole three hours went by before he typed the final full stop of the last paragraph, fired off his work by email, and closed the lid down on his MacBook. Seconds after he'd safely returned the machine to the space inside his bedside cabinet, and even before flattening the pillows down, Oliver fell fast asleep, exhausted, while still in his sitting position.

***

(SATURDAY, 27TH JANUARY, 2018)

Being the sports fan that he was, Paul Copeland had once again been flicking through the *Terre Haute Daily Times* in the way he usually did from the sports pages at the rear towards the news pages at the front. It was when he'd eventually reached page 3 that he gasped and called out to his wife. "Katie! Take a look at this!"

Katie was in the kitchen preparing their evening meal, with a pot of Bolognese sauce on the stove and a glass of crisp Chardonnay in her hand. "What is it?" she asked, as she came through to the lounge, enjoying a few sips of wine along the way.

Paul had folded the newspaper to the appropriate section and handed Oliver's 'Young Sherlock' report to her. She took it, sat down and began fully digesting its content. "That poor young man. He was so nice when he came here with that girl. What was her name now? Siobhan? She was a beauty if ever I saw one. Thank goodness Oliver survived. What an ordeal he must have gone through! I wonder if she was his girlfriend." she went off at a tangent. "It certainly looked that way."

"Yes," said Paul, amused at how his wife's scientific mind mingled with her romantic one. "But have you read the piece at the bottom? Look!" he pointed over Katie's shoulder while she was reading. "They're really going to town with this. It says there will be another instalment in the Sunday supplement tomorrow, along with a full pull-out section. And he says he'll be working on writing a book about the whole Bike Radio Murder story. You're bound to feature in it. You'll be famous!"

"Hmm, we'll see about that. I can't imagine anyone being interested in reading about me," said Katie with a smile. "But for now, I'd better get back in the kitchen. We need food, and the sauce needs stirring."

***

(MONDAY, 29TH JANUARY, 2018)

It was a little past six in the evening when Phil Booth rode home from work on his most recently acquired Harley Davidson, a superb 2004 Super Glide Sport, up the drive outside his house near Cincinnati, Ohio. This was the model he'd wanted to own for many years, and now, nearing retirement, he'd finally got one. He still enjoyed his job as a traffic cop, and today was excited to tell his wife Lou about the talk of the precinct that day.

As usual, she heard the bike coming towards the house a mile away, and switched the garage door open so that he could ride straight in as he turned onto the drive.

"Hulloo, little Lou!" Phil said, as he took off his helmet and leant down to give his wife a kiss. Their current dog, Bert The Third, came bounding up, slobber dripping from its mouth as usual. Phil, who rarely read a newspaper, especially now that he had become elected to sit on the local community council and had even less free time than previously, surprised Lou by taking a copy of the *Cincinnati Herald* from his luggage box. "Look at this!" he exclaimed, waving it in the air. "I've got something to show you. But it's all over the internet as well, so let's go inside and I'll show you online."

Puzzled, a curious Lou followed her husband indoors to their study and pulled up a chair next to him while they waited for their Dell table-top computer to come to life.

A short while later, she watched on as he scrolled up and down the website pages that Phil's colleagues had told him about at work. "It was all such a long time ago," Phil began to explain. "But after the boys at the precinct helped to prod my memory, everything came back to me."

"Lou, do you remember me telling you about a guy with a Japanese name who I picked up for riding his cycle on the Interstate? I don't expect you to, as it was over thirty years ago now. But anyway, I'd let him off with a warning, and gave him a lift with his bike over to

Cincinnati. His handlebar-radio fell off in the trunk, and I took it over to his youth hostel on the way home from work."

Lou nodded, slowly at first, then faster. "I do remember, vaguely," she said. "What of it?"

"I'd helped them catch the guy back in '81 . . ." Phil continued explaining. ". . . when it turned out they'd got the wrong surname. Well, look, it says here he's been in the news again with some English guy calling himself 'Young Sherlock', coming over and reporting on the whole story. "I remember now that the bike radio had been used as the murder weapon." Lou grimaced while Phil continued: "And they're talking about making a movie about it now. Who would have thought? I wonder if they'd like to use the Harley in it!"

"Come on," laughed Lou, ever the realist, and affectionately bringing Phil back down to earth. "I think you might be getting a little ahead of yourself, don't you? Come on—Bert needs taking for a walk. That's more important right now."

***

It was certainly true that Oliver's column had escalated in readership far beyond the local confines of Indiana and Illinois states, ever since Ursula O'Mahoney had convinced her boss, Steve Borowitz at the *Indianapolis Daily Times*, to syndicate the articles nationwide. It had been a great suggestion, thought Borowitz, and had definitely paid off. His media company had quickly become the talk of the publishing world. Hints of books and films may have been a little hyped up, he admitted, but other newspapers all across the country were now clambering to jump on the 'Young Sherlock' bandwagon.

It made entertaining reading for the majority. But 700 miles across to the east in Allentown, Pennsylvania, for one particular family—that of Yushi's sister Mitori—there was only sadness and sorrow as the media coverage continuously brought the name of her beloved late brother to the fore.

Mitori felt compelled to write a letter to the man behind the 'Young Sherlock' pseudonym.

CHAPTER 46

(WEDNESDAY, 31ST JANUARY, 2018)

Zac Drops a Bundle

"Are you sure I've done the right thing in writing to him?" Mitori Jarvis asked Jerry, her husband, as she churned over in her mind the contents of the letter that she'd neatly addressed to Oliver Markland and taken to the Post Office a couple of days earlier. On hearing Jerry's comforting reassurance, she nuzzled back into his arm that reached strongly around her shoulder as they lay together on the sofa. "At least I've said my piece, and explained about Yushi, and I hope now that all this can soon come to an end. Yushi didn't deserve this treatment. What do you think, Jerry?"

The truth was that Jerry was sick to the back teeth of listening to his wife going on and on about her 'dear beloved brother'. He was stressed out enough as it was, thinking about the three jobs he was doing his best to hold down. When he wasn't running a local radio station, he was fitting venetian blinds at clients' homes. When he wasn't doing that, he was selling and installing telecommunications equipment to anyone who wanted the fastest and most up-to-date internet connection. It was a booming, important and pressured time for him, and the last thing on his mind was a man who he never knew personally, and had been dead for over twenty years.

But he daren't let on that by now he'd absolutely had enough. While rolling his eyes from his safe position out of sight from Mitori, sprawled out on the sofa behind her, he muttered with as much sincerity as he could muster: "I think you've done *exactly* the right thing, MJ," he answered with words he knew she would appreciate hearing. "For the sake of Yushi's memory, darling" he added for good measure.

"But you know everything I wrote in my letter was completely the truth," Mitori retorted abruptly, almost confrontationally, despite her husband's empathy.

He rolled his eyes yet again before finishing. "I know, my darling. I know."

***

The offices at the *Terre Haute Daily Times* were becoming quite chaotic—not only since the increased activity caused by the recent Bike Radio Murder coverage, but generally. Advertising was on the up, and because of that, the size of the paper grew to an enormous 128 pages. Circulation was growing healthily and, all in all, business was booming. Ursula was pleased, and so was her boss in Indianapolis. For some while, it had been on Ursula's mind to take on a new member of staff to help with the increased workload.

Zac Brightmore, on the face of it, had all the right qualifications for the job that didn't require any—none. Ursula had wanted to put something back into the local community by offering a position to someone who hadn't been fortunate enough to go to university and get a degree. She advertised, and Zac, along with thirty-four others, applied. In the successful candidate's role, tea-making and Post-Room duties wouldn't require proof of higher education, and for the time being, Ursula wanted Zac to start at the bottom anyway. As he was the least qualified out of the 35 hopefuls, she offered him the job. She thought that once he'd gained some experience, she'd then see what else he could do within the organisation to contribute towards its, and his own, progression.

Likeable as he was, always happy to engage in conversation with anyone who had the time, and with his cutely rounded, sometimes red face expressing unbounded enthusiasm, Zac did appear to be initially lacking in some basic skills that would be useful in his job. Being somewhat accident-prone, he would occasionally drop things.

And sometimes he would get the coffee and tea orders mixed up, other times he might forget altogether to collect the outgoing mail from the staff writers until he was reminded a few minutes before his shift was due to finish. Neither of these crimes were serious enough for him to be reprimanded, and Ursula had the patience to stick with him while he developed his proficiency. The main thing was that everyone liked Zac, and that's what Ursula saw as his most important attribute. A happy ship leads to good results, she always maintained.

On the day Mitori's letter had arrived, addressed to 'Oliver Markland, c/o Indianapolis Daily Times, 3420 East Street, Indianapolis, IN.' and had subsequently been forwarded to the Terre Haute office, it was among a batch of ten or so others that Zac had unwittingly dropped off the trolley.

There the batch fell to its temporary resting place between the fridge and the stationery cupboard, and there it would remain for quite some time.

***

At the Dickinson's household, Chris, Kerry and Sam had pulled out all the stops to welcome Oliver home. A banner had been tied across the front door, so that when the car, kindly organised by Ursula, had collected Oliver from The Imperial Hospital, at the point of arrival he would get an eyeful of the message: 'WELCOME HOME TO OUR SPECIAL YOUNG SHERLOCK'. Chris and Kerry had decided not to grant permission to the local TV station for Oliver's homecoming to be filmed, but they did allow a photographer to be present to take some pictures for the following morning's newspaper.

Oliver was feeling physically very well, having recovered faster than the doctors had expected. His arm wound was also healing nicely, and the sling and the bandages would be removed in a couple of days. After careful consideration, he had made up his mind that it was now time to return to England. Drinking a pint or three of Guinness in his favourite pub, the Black Buoy, was the first thing he promised himself he would do on his return to Wivenhoe.

Although he'd had a lot of fun in the States, Oliver wanted to put his life-threatening experience behind him and move on—or rather move back. But what that practically meant job-wise when he returned to England, he didn't know. Maybe, he thought, he could continue writing his blog and column for the *East Anglian Chronicle*, or perhaps he really would write that book that had been suggested in one of the recent newspaper footnotes—the one that had also been seen by Paul and Katie Copeland.

As to a movie being made, mentioned in some of the online reports that he'd become all too aware of, and the subject of much jovial teasing from his newspaper colleagues, Oliver was wise enough to recognise made-up sensationalism when he saw it. It would be fantastic if there were ever any truth in the rumours, though, he daydreamed.

Before allowing his mind to wander too far into the realms of fantasy, for now he concentrated on getting through the Dickinson's front door, and showing gratitude for the trouble the family had obviously gone to with their welcome. As Oliver entered the house, Kerry was in the kitchen and came towards him, her arms out wide. She was genuinely emotional as she hugged and greeted him. "Don't you ever go and do something like that again, will you?" she said with mock scorn as she held him close for a few seconds longer than Oliver felt comfortable with. He thought he was going to suffocate while his head was squashed close to her bosom. For a moment he enjoyed the fullness of Kerry's ample breasts before checking himself. When he was eventually let go and he stepped back, he found himself looking at her in a whole different light!

A pang of guilt at enjoying Kerry's embrace rather too much ended as he turned to Chris, who was standing with a pint glass of Guinness ready to hand to their house guest-turned-family member.

"Welcome home, Oliver. Good to see you," he said.

Oliver took a sip from the glass, and raised it in the air. "Cheers!" he exclaimed emphatically, in the most English accent that he could muster.

Chris, Kerry and Sam laughed and copied him. "Cheers!" they replied.

Then it was the turn of Sam to step forward. Saying nothing, she just put both arms around Oliver, and swung him left and right as if she were doing the waltz, lifting him off the ground as she did so. He winced a little as he felt some pain shoot up his slinged arm, but for the sake of not causing Sam any embarrassment, he took it in his stride. She was ecstatic that her friend had survived such a serious ordeal, was ecstatic now that he was safely in her arms, and ecstatic that he was at home to spend time with her now that his investigations had finally come to an end.

Chris eyed Kerry in a way that said, 'let's leave them to it for a while, shall we?' and they both sneaked off to the TV room. Sam whispered in Oliver's ear. "I'm so happy you're back here with us again. We can be together properly now, can't we?" Without Sam noticing, Oliver squirmed, knowing that soon he'd have to break the news to her that he'd already booked his BA ticket to Heathrow, and that his flight would be on the approaching Saturday. He only had two full days left in which to say goodbye to Ursula at Terre Haute, return the pool Hyundai to the Indianapolis office and say goodbye to Steve Borowitz, although he guessed that would take all of ten seconds if indeed he were able to get a word in edgeways. He also needed to update his blog, newspaper and magazine articles, pack his bags—and of course to see Siobhan. So much to do, so little time.

But for now, he decided on focusing on what was clearly on Sam's agenda for this evening. He doubted whether his arm in a sling was going to present too much of a problem, and as it turned out later, it didn't.

CHAPTER 47

(THURSDAY, 1ST – SATURDAY, 3RD FEBRUARY, 2018)

Ursula Makes a Presentation

"You make sure you keep in touch with us, y'hear?" demanded Ursula, as she presented Oliver with a farewell gift—a token of her gratitude on behalf of all the staff at the *Terre Haute*, and the *Indianapolis Daily Times*. "We'll surely miss you." Judging by the thunderous applause given by the crowd squeezed into her boardroom-office, it was obvious that she wasn't far wrong.

Oliver looked down at the wrapped object he'd just been presented with, and tore off the paper to reveal a genuine 1980s bike-handlebar radio, presumably very similar to the one at the centre of the Bike Radio Murder investigation. Constructed from red and black plastic, it had two silver knobs that Oliver instinctively twiddled. The one on the left operated the 'on', 'off' and 'volume' functions, while the one on the right was for the tuning. Someone had thoughtfully fitted some batteries. And with a turn of the left knob it sprang to life. In between the two knobs was an orange-coloured rectangular button, with the word 'HORN' embossed above it.

He looked around at the gathered group before settling his gaze on Ursula, sitting next to Peter the photographer and David the journalist—or was it the other way round? Was Peter the journalist, and David the photographer? Oliver couldn't remember, but no matter, he thought, as he pressed the button to the delight of the crowd, and himself.

Reacting to the loud buzzing noise by jumping backwards in mock surprise, he looked around at the people in the room, every one of them laughing. About to make a few light-hearted quips expressing his gratitude to his colleagues for their support and friendship, Oliver suddenly became overwhelmed by the heavy emotional impact of the afternoon's gathering. Holding the radio tightly in his hands, he realised that the object represented a snapshot of his life ever since buying a key in Florida when on holiday with his dad. It also represented the more recent traumatic events he'd been through in which he'd had a narrow escape from death.

Oliver found it necessary to turn around quickly, hiding the emotion that engulfed him. After he'd heard a series of schmaltzy 'Oohs' and 'Aahs', he wiped his eyes and took up his position once more to face everyone. His attempt to regain his composure was this time successful, and he just about managed to coherently thank all his temporary colleagues for their kind wishes and generous gift.

"I will never forget my time in *your* great country. Thank you, all of you. And especially Ursula, and Siobhan," he said, turning to the two ladies next to him. Although Oliver thought he'd been discreet about his relationship with Siobhan, it was nevertheless blindingly obvious to everyone else. A cheer erupted, making Siobhan go red when she sensed all eyes focussing upon her.

Ursula was conscious of her niece's discomfort, and called an end to the proceedings. "Come on, you guys," she commanded, with a smile in her eyes. "We have a newspaper to bring out in the morning. Now get back to work!"

After all the assembled personnel had left the room, including new recruit Zac Brightmore, she turned to Oliver and said sincerely: "You've done us proud here. I hope that Siobhan will do your folks proud when she comes over to your great country. Look after her, won't you? She's very precious to me."

Oliver had almost forgotten that Siobhan was due to work at the *East Anglian Chronicle*, but he was very pleased to have been reminded. He looked forward to welcoming her and showing her around Wivenhoe, his village on the river estuary that he loved so much. He also looked forward to working further with her at *The Chronicle*, and eagerly anticipated introducing her to his friends and dad at the Black Buoy. He looked forward to being with *her*, full stop.

***

Oliver woke early, on the day of his journey home. His last night in America had been something of a non-event because by the time he'd returned his car, got back to the Dickinsons' home in Plainfield, prepared everything for his early morning departure, had a shower and dinner, it was already 11.30p.m., and everyone was tired, including Sam and himself.

That night, there had been no farewell party, no last supper at a local restaurant, and no 'after-midnight delights' with Sam. An all-too-brief hug and kiss in front of Kerry and Chris was to be their rather unsatisfactory farewell. All in all, as far as Oliver was concerned, the evening had been an anti-climax, but by the time he crawled into his Indiana bed for the last time, he was too worn out to care. He just about had enough energy to run a last couple of thoughts through his mind.

The first was to go over his travel arrangements. Chris had helpfully offered to take him to the airport for his early-morning check-in. The second was a little deeper, and involved him questioning his own morals. Had he been slightly using Sam? he wondered. Maybe more than just slightly? Had he been taking advantage of her friendship, and that of her parents? A wave of guilt swept over him. But perhaps there had *also* been an element of Sam enjoying his Young Sherlock adventure. Oliver recalled that she had told him how exciting it had been to witness his progress with the Bike Radio Murder story, so just maybe she had also taken advantage of him too, in her own way.

While Oliver mulled these complex thoughts over and over, he was unable to prevent a losing battle with sleep as his eyelids grew heavier by the second until he could fight no longer. Soon after drifting off, he entered into a dream in which he was drinking in the Black Buoy with Siobhan, and not Sam, at his side. Oddly, as is the case with most dreams, the most important aspect is often the most trivial. This one involved the Guinness, which instead of being served at ice cold temperature like they did in the States, had to be at room temperature, just the way he preferred it.

The following morning, Oliver awoke feeling refreshed. He pulled back the curtains and viewed the sun just allowing a peek of its glow above the horizon. With Sam and Kerry still fast asleep and Oliver deciding to have breakfast and coffee at the airport, he got dressed and went quietly downstairs and out of the front door, carrying his bags that he'd already packed the previous evening.

Taking in the final few moments that he'd be spending in his now-familiar surroundings, he stood by Chris's car and waited for him to appear, which he did ten minutes later, when Oliver heard the familiar crunching sound of footsteps upon the shingled driveway.

"All ready?" Chris asked, quietly. Oliver nodded, as the car doors unlocked when Chris pressed his key fob. The early morning cool mist hovered just above the lawn. It was going to be another pleasant day in Plainfield as the sun began to rise rapidly higher in the sky, with the trees casting horizontal shadows in the distance. For Oliver it was going to be a *brilliant* day—he couldn't wait to get home.

As the plane carrying him back to England left the tarmac, he breathed out, scratched his now unbandaged arm and let the waves of anticipation and excitement engulf him.

PART SIX

BACK IN WIVENHOE

CHAPTER 48

(WEDNESDAY, 4TH JULY, 2018)

Return

Poor Zac Brightmore. He'd been keeping his head down, doing his best to get on with his job. Five months had gone by since he started at the newspaper, and he'd finally managed to get the tea and coffee orders right. Not only that, he now managed to collect the outgoing post in plenty of time on a regular basis. He also handled the incoming packages and mail, delivering them to their intended recipients with proficiency. He was pleased with his work-performance, and Ursula was relieved that her protégé had finally turned the corner.

But on one particular Wednesday morning, Zac was filled with horror when he bent down to pick up his marker pen that had fallen between the fridge and the stationery cupboard, and noticed a bundle of envelopes laying there, covered in dirt and dust. Merely puzzled at first, he used a thin ruler to pull the bundle towards him. Once the letters were close enough, he picked them up to make a closer examination, looking for any date stamps. Most of the letters had no obvious markings, but two of them did.

Zac looked at the calendar on the wall and turned back the pages to the date in early February shown on the two particular envelopes.

He went into a cold sweat when he realised that the date was from *after* he'd begun his job. So, he reasoned, it must have been he who had dropped the bundle without realising. What should he do? he wondered. Own up and feel humiliation and embarrassment at best, or run the risk of being fired at worst. Ursula did seem like a very reasonable and fair employer, but maybe he was taking too much for granted by assuming she'd let this error go. And he needed this job. What if any of the letters were of crucial importance? Zac made himself a cup of herbal tea and stewed about what he ought to do for the best.

He looked through the bundle, and noted who the addressees were. He knew for a fact that three no longer worked at the newspaper, so he would bin those letters. Another four looked obviously like junk mail, so they followed, straight into the waste-paper basket. That left another three to be dealt with. Should he confess to his error, he asked himself? Three remaining letters were preferable to ten, but zero would be an even better number, so maybe he could just accidentally-on-purpose lose them all over again, and no one would be any the wiser.

Yes, that's what he'd do, he decided—except for one particular letter that stood out because it was written in precise, neat handwriting, and addressed to 'Mr. Oliver Markland'. Zac thought back. He recalled that, soon after he'd commenced his employment at the newspaper, he had attended Oliver Markland's leaving presentation, and the man in question had seemed like a very nice guy, and if his memory served Zac correctly, Mr. Markland had left his forwarding address in case he received any future correspondence. Yes, that's right, Zac recalled after an anxious minute or two. Markland had definitely left a forwarding address, and it was in England.

In fact, the harder Zac thought, the more he vaguely recalled sending on one or two letters very soon after he'd joined the *Terre Haute Daily Times*. And now, here in his hand was one more letter to be forwarded. Never having set foot out of his own country, he found it difficult to imagine just how far away England was—but he guessed it must be an awfully long way. This long-distance letter would just take a little longer to reach its destination, he thought, trying to excuse his mistake and banish his feelings of guilt.

He looked up the address and put the envelope into a new International Post bag, slipping in an accompanying note that read: '*Dear Mr. Markland. This just arrived for you. Judging by the post-mark, I guess it must have been lost in US Mail system. Best. Zac*'

"Phew!" thought Zac, relieved that he'd come up with a solution to his dilemma, and pleased that he would be able to continue with his work without anyone being any the wiser. He finished up the herbal tea that he'd been letting brew to perfection, and then went off to collect his colleagues' afternoon drinks orders.

***

During the past five months since returning to Essex, Oliver had settled back into Wivenhoe life, and was very glad to be home.

His blog for the *East Anglian Chronicle* had continued to be a great success, and after his welcome return he had been asked by the magazine editor not only to take overall control of the burgeoning travel section, but, under instructions from the parent company, to also become Editor-in-Chief of the entire online presence for the whole publishing group.

While Oliver had been away in America, regularly submitting blogs, articles and pictures by email, the readership of the *East Anglian Chronicle* had been captivated, and advertising revenues had gone through the roof, especially from tour and travel operators. This fact hadn't gone unnoticed by Adam Hellinger, the CEO of the publishing group behind the *Chronicle*, and it was he who suggested to editor Edward Wright that Oliver be given a key role within the company.

This had now become a 'proper job', and Oliver was happy to

recognise it as such, as well as relishing his new upgraded role within the organisation. He knew that his promotion was mostly due to the way he'd handled the Bike Radio Murder story. But he was very happy with the way things were now panning out for him, and equally happy with his increased salary, sufficient to help him afford something rather better than his current old banger of a car.

So wrapped up in his writing and publishing career, Oliver had almost forgotten the disappointment he'd felt when Yushi Yakamoto's confession note had come to light. It was true that until Siobhan and he had gone over it in fine detail while he'd been recovering in his hospital bed, up to then he'd been convinced that Yushi had been innocent of the crime he'd been executed for.

Oliver admitted to himself that, despite Yushi's eventual fate, all along he'd very much hoped he might have been able to clear Yushi's name. He didn't know why he'd felt so compelled to do this. After all, Yushi had been a complete stranger to him, from a period many years before Oliver had even been born. It was too lame a reason simply to suggest that it was because both Yushi and he had shared a passion for cycling. He knew there was more to it than that but, whatever the reason, Oliver couldn't quite put his finger on it. It was as if the purchase of his Florida Key had somehow drawn him towards Yushi, and it had then become Oliver's mission to prove that Yushi hadn't been a murderer.

Having studied the whole story so thoroughly and intently, Oliver felt like he had come to know Yushi personally, and had been able to understand the cyclist's mindset. It was like Yushi had become a friend, and a friend whose passing Oliver now grieved.

CHAPTER 49

WEDNESDAY, 4TH JULY, 2018

Book

Although he'd been deeply saddened by the end of Yushi Yakamoto's story, Oliver had benefitted enormously from the whole affair. Newspaper CEO Mr. Hellinger had called for Oliver to go to his office in the City where he made a proposition that he was sure would benefit the business, as well as Oliver himself.

Mr. Hellinger had suggested that Oliver's story would make a terrific book, and that if he wrote it, Hellinger's company would publish it. He even went as far as suggesting a title for the book —*The Bike Radio Murder.* It was fairly unimaginative and quite a mouthful in Oliver's opinion, and Oliver felt sure it could be improved upon. But not wishing to introduce any negativity to such a positive meeting, he decided to keep quiet—for the time being—at least until he could hopefully come up with a better alternative at a later stage.

Now back at his office in Colchester, Oliver glanced down at the large Joliet prison key that he was now using as a paperweight on his desk.

He reflected for a short while on the unbelievable journey he'd been on, and the new one he was about to embark upon as a book author. He couldn't wait to get started.

As he sat there, staring at the ceiling, he thought about his time in America. Of course, he missed the friends and acquaintances he'd made there; Ursula O'Mahoney had obviously played a key role in helping him, as had Steve Borowitz for being receptive to Oliver's initial handwritten correspondence. That had been a smart move to send a letter in that way, thought Oliver, and he gave himself an imaginary pat on the back. Katie Copeland had been a real help too, and the TV news crew who'd filmed him outside Mrs. Toporofski's house had been a great thrill to work with.

Ah yes, Mrs. Toporofski. How could he forget her? She had certainly proved herself to be a larger-than-life character, and Oliver laughed out loud when he remembered the time he flooded the house with a waterbed and was almost shot by the lady. And then of course there was the time when he really did get shot.

As Oliver continued to mull over the events that had occurred at Flatrock Creek, he shuddered. It had only been thanks to the professionalism of Detective Hardy and Police officers Theresa Ashley and William Wheatley that he was still alive. That had been a very narrow escape, and he owed the emergency services a huge debt of gratitude.

"Perhaps one day I'll return to Illinois and Indiana to pay a visit, and thank them personally," he thought, because the last time they had seen him he was unconscious.

There was one person though who Oliver very definitely would not be visiting unless he were to be surrounded by at least half a dozen armed police to protect him—Marc Ozborn. At least Ozborn would be behind bars for another seven months, he thought.

While reflecting on his horrific ordeal at the hands of Ozborn, what Oliver didn't know was that, thousands of miles away, the old man was being called into the prison Governor's office. Ozborn sat and listened to what was being said, hardly believing his good fortune on hearing that he'd be released on parole within just three weeks. By that time, he would have only served six of his twelve-month custodial sentence, and the Parole Board had clearly deemed him fit to re-enter society. Politely thanking the Governor, Ozborn was unable to wipe the smug grin off his face as he walked back to his cell.

***

Presently, back in Colchester, England, Oliver looked at his iPhone. It was 5.30p.m.—time to pack up and go home from work. He shuffled and tidied the documents on his desk, all prepared and ready for the next day. For the whole day, he had been looking forward to trying out Bambu, the Vietnamese restaurant situated by the River Colne on the outskirts of the town, later that evening with a special friend who he expected any minute. As he stacked the final bunch of papers and placed them under his Florida Key paperweight, a beautiful young woman appeared at his office door.

"Ready?" she asked, looking truly radiant in a dark pencil skirt and smart light blue blouse. How does she manage to look so good after having been at work for the past eight hours? Oliver wondered, looking up at her admiringly.

"I am indeed, Siobhan," replied Oliver, locking his desk drawer and grabbing the jacket from behind his chair. He hadn't seen Siobhan all day, and with a broad smile stretched across his face and a glint in his eyes, he looked forward to telling her the news about his book-writing project.

"Whatever's got into you?" Siobhan asked, when she noticed he looked like the cat that had got the cream.

"I'll tell you soon," smiled Oliver.

Oliver felt enormously grateful for the hospitality offered him by Chris and Kerry Dickinson. He probably wouldn't have gone ahead with his trip to America if they hadn't so generously offered accommodation for him. But although he still thought very fondly of Sam, he recognised that the special place in his heart actually belonged to the girl he was now with, here in Essex. They walked hand in hand to the car park where the red-and-white paintwork on a sharp-looking new Fiat 124 was gleaming in the evening sunshine, Oliver having picked it up earlier that morning.

The sports car was on loan from a local dealership for a three-day test drive, and going by very favourable first impressions as he sped along Clingoe Hill towards Wivenhoe, Oliver decided that he'd soon be signing up to keep it. At yesterday's meeting in London, his boss's boss not only told Oliver to expect a further pay rise the following month, but also that the company would provide him with a generous allowance for a lease car of his choice, within certain parameters, of course. Oliver was delighted to discover that the new 124 fell within those parameters and, knowing how his dad Leslie Markland owned and had such a passion for his own classic 1968 model, he couldn't wait to take him out for a spin in this latest 2018 version.

After arriving back in Wivenhoe, and before going for the meal that had been booked for eight-thirty that evening, Oliver had made an earlier appointment to see a dear old friend he'd known for years, and for moral support he was pleased that Siobhan would be with him. He was sure that with her American-Irish charm, Siobhan would help soften Miss Alberta Louise Baudet to be receptive to a specific request he had in mind.

Miss Baudet had moved south from the county of Yorkshire a few years previously, and had always followed Oliver's progress with enormous interest and enthusiasm, helping him in any small way that she could. She'd become a kind of mother figure to him, and Oliver cherished their very special relationship. Since settling in Wivenhoe, Miss Baudet had bought and now owned a lovely old river-cruiser, moored in its highly-desirable position directly outside the popular Rose & Crown pub on Wivenhoe Quay. Since purchasing the boat from a local man by the name of Watson, she'd meticulously looked after it, having it regularly painted and cleaned by the previous owner. It now looked newer than the day it was built, some forty years ago, and Alberta Louise was very proud of it.

Oliver knew how much Miss Baudet loved her boat, and hoped she'd agree to his proposal. On the way to meet her, Oliver told Siobhan that he had some very exciting news to tell, but she'd have to wait until they got to the boat before he'd say any more.

Oliver parked his glamorous car on the quayside, drawing some degree of attention from the crowd sitting outside and enjoying a pint in the evening summer sun. Siobhan, as she did every day since arriving in England, thanked her lucky stars she'd moved to such a wonderful riverside village. Initially scheduled for a three-month period, her work experience at the *East Anglian Chronicle* had been extended to a whole year, and she was grateful to Oliver for finding her such a perfect and adequately sized apartment only a few hundred yards from the riverfront. Siobhan absolutely adored living there.

Oliver and Siobhan walked along the wooden pontoon that Alberta Louise had especially commissioned to be built alongside her boat. This was the first time that Siobhan had seen the boat close up, and she smiled when she noticed the boat's name emblazoned on its sides—*MISS BAUDET.*

"Welcome aboard!" called out the boat's owner from the rear deck. Her two young guests stepped off the pontoon and clambered inside. As soon as Siobhan met the real Miss Baudet, she instantly felt a warmth for the person, who was perhaps fifty years her senior. She seemed a straight-talking lady, full of charm and character. After a few initial pleasantries had been exchanged, Miss Baudet got straight to the point: "So, Oliver, what's so important that you couldn't wait to come and see me?"

Oliver was glad that he could now broach the subject that he was bursting to talk about. "I've been asked to write a book called *The Bike Radio Murder* about my time in America! It'll be published just as soon as I can get it finished."

Most impressed, and excited for their mutual friend, both Siobhan and Miss Baudet looked at each other and beamed. "That's fantastic! I think this calls for a celebration," said Miss Baudet, as she stepped down to the small galley kitchen just inside the main cabin, soon emerging with a bottle of Champagne and three flutes. After she'd finished pouring the drinks and the three of them chinked glasses, she continued: "That's great, Oliver, but what has that got to do with me? What is it you wanted to ask me about?"

"Well . . ." Oliver began, elongating the word a little too much.

"Come on, Oliver. Spit it out," demanded the boat's Captain.

"Well, Miss B., I need somewhere to work. Somewhere to write in peace and quiet, and your boat would be just the ticket." Siobhan chuckled at Oliver's very British expression while he continued. "I know you like straight talking, so I'll just come straight out with it. Could I please come down to the quay and use the boat as my writing space—my own 'Writers' Retreat'? I might have evenings where I'd be working quite late, so sometimes I'd like to sleep here too, if you didn't mind."

It was Miss Baudet's turn to make Oliver wait as she responded with a repeat of Oliver's artificially stretched word. "Well . . ." she began, relishing the expression on Oliver's face as he waited with bated breath for her answer. ". . . Of *course* you can!" she said emphatically. "In fact, I'd be honoured if you did. Actually, I *insist* that you do! Start whenever you like."

***

Later that evening at Bambu, where the loving couple enjoyed a delicious shared platter, Oliver moved his hand across the dining table. He took Siobhan's in his and gave it a squeeze. "That went rather well, I thought. And I'm sure there will be many nights on the boat when I may need a little company," he said with a mischievous inflection. Siobhan smiled at the prospect of spending romantic evenings and candlelit dinners with Oliver while the rising tide gently lapped at the boat's sides.

"But there's something that's bothering me about the book," she said cautiously, not wishing to sound critical.

Oliver raised his eyebrows. "What's that, darling?" he asked.

"I don't think the title's right," Siobhan said slowly and thoughtfully. "*The Bike Radio Murder* just doesn't have the right ring to it. That's only my humble opinion though, and I hope you don't mind me saying."

Oliver was relieved that Siobhan's concern wasn't overly serious, and in fact echoed his own thoughts. "I'd been thinking exactly the same thing, but I haven't been able to come up with anything better yet," he replied.

"I have," responded Siobhan instantly. "How about calling the book *Florida Key*?"

How it all Ended

by Oliver Markland

WIVENHOE

(MONDAY, OCTOBER 8TH, 2018)

That fine summer's evening in July had been very special. Siobhan and I enjoyed Bambu such a lot. Miss B., as I affectionately like to call her, was at a loose end and we invited her to come with us to the place, but sadly she was busy and couldn't join us then.

However, during the following few months since that evening, Siobhan and I would revisit the place several times, cycling along the Wivenhoe Trail by the river towards Colchester, always ordering our favourite shared platter. Occasionally we would increase the size of the shared platter for three, or even four, when we welcomed Miss B., and sometimes also my dad, to join us.

Still, being by ourselves on that particular evening did give us an opportunity to seal a few personal arrangements of our own. One arrangement in particular meant another visit to Miss Baudet and to Dad the very next day.

You see, on that evening in question I had asked Siobhan to marry me. I'm delighted to say that she said yes, and at the time of writing this account we are currently organising our wedding that will take place next year in her home town, Terre Haute. *The Terre Haute Daily Times* have offered to contribute toward the cost if they can include a section about it in their Sunday supplement, and I have to pinch myself to quite believe our good fortune.

In attendance will be Siobhan's maid of honour, Alberta Louise Baudet herself! She certainly has the right organisational qualities to perform such a role. Ursula and John will both give my bride away, and my father has agreed to be my Best Man.

As you can probably tell, Siobhan and I like to do things a little differently.

You may be wondering how Sam took the news when I finally summoned up the courage to tell her. Initially not too well, I have to say. At first, during our FaceTime conversation, I was as nervous as I'd ever been, and her reaction couldn't have been worse. In fact, I found our line of communication suddenly going dead, and that was the last time we had spoken until I received a call from her only last week.

I'm so pleased to say that Sam has now come round positively to the news. She offered us her congratulations, which I'm so pleased about, and I'm bowled over that she accepted our invitation for her and her parents to attend the wedding. I had no right to expect her blessing, but I had really hoped for it. Actually, she asked if she could bring a guest of her own along—her boyfriend.

I admit that I felt a pang of jealousy when she told me about him, probably because I remember having met him. He was one of the guys we all played volleyball with on the beach at Anna Maria Island. Far too muscular, tanned, and good-looking for his own good was how I remember him from back then, and when Sam sent me a picture of the two of them I could see that not much had changed. I reprimanded myself for being so shallow. I am now very much looking forward to seeing them, as well as Chris and Kerry, on the big day. I believe that Sam and I will be forever soulmates. I do hope so.

Needless to say, I enthusiastically got stuck into writing *Florida Key* the day after my marriage proposal to Siobhan, and I'd been hard at work on it since then, until last month.

Of course Siobhan was right about the book's title, and I'm currently waiting to see if the publisher agrees. That's another thing I'm hoping for.

***

The story you are now reading has been my own account of what happened. I am truly grateful to you for following it this far. I may have spiced up the facts a little for the purposes of my novel (I think they call it 'artistic licence'), but I did in fact go to Florida on holiday, and I did purchase an old key at a flea market, and it did indeed turn out to originate from Joliet prison, Illinois.

It was the Florida Key that had fuelled my ambition to return to America after the holiday, and investigate what had happened to any one of the inmates of Cell 10 on the 4th floor of the 'A' Block, how they came to be there, and what their reason for being there had been. Why had I been attracted to Yushi Yakamoto? Could there have been some parallel force at work guiding me towards him? I like to think so, however bizarre that sounds.

To learn all I could about Yushi and his fate, and turn it into this story, I've been on an incredible journey, mentally and physically. Talking of the *physical* journey that I very nearly didn't return from, I appreciate absolutely how fortunate I was to survive my shooting. Therefore, as well as one particular person who I will soon be mentioning, I dedicate *Florida Key* to all those who were involved in getting me to safety and helping me fully recover to good health. You know who you are, and I would like to say a huge and sincere *thank you.*

And finally, I'll quickly explain why the book is dedicated to one other important individual. Having assumed that I'd managed to tie up all the loose ends associated with Yushi Yakamoto, I received a package that in effect turned everything I'd come to accept on its head.

On that late July day, I'd gone in to the *East Anglian Chronicle*'s Colchester office so that I could catch up with submitting my blog, write up a feature for the next Travel Section, and collect my post. Nearly all of my mail came in electronically, but sometimes I would also receive press releases, formal invitations to various black-tie functions, mailshots, and a few hand-written or typed letters from readers. These were few and far between, but by far the most interesting.

On this occasion, there was one particular item that stood out, attracting my attention more than any of the others. Contained in an International Courier pack, I could clearly see it had come from the United States. Closer study revealed that it had been sent by Zac Brightmore, the new recruit who had started his job at the *Terre Haute Daily Times* shortly before I'd returned to England.

Inside the strong polythene pack was an envelope very neatly handwritten and addressed to me. It was post-marked from months previously, and included a covering note from Zac explaining how the letter had been delayed in the US Mail, and how he'd sent it on to me immediately once it had shown up.

With my curiosity getting the better of me, I quickly tore open the envelope to reveal the letter contained within, and I instinctively turned to the end to discover the identity of the sender. Then I went back to the beginning and started reading, and on doing so I felt ashamed.

Ashamed because during the whole of my adventure I had been so engrossed, obsessed even, in my investigations, my bloggings, newspaper articles, and not to mention radio and TV appearances, that it had completely slipped my mind to consider the feelings of Yushi's remaining direct family member, Mitori. I'd briefly learned of Yushi's sister, from Allentown, Pennsylvania, while conducting my research.

In truth, I felt more ashamed that perhaps I'd become convinced of my own self-importance.

I sat back and read the letter comprising three numbered sheets of paper.

(1)

863 Camelot Road, Allentown, Pennsylvania

FAO Mr. Oliver Markland,

Indianapolis Daily Times Group

1/19/18

Dear Mr. Markland,

I understand you have been investigating the circumstances surrounding my late brother's premature death. Not a day goes by without me weeping because of him. He and I were incredibly close, and although he was my elder sibling, it was I who looked out for him when we were growing up together.

When the news of your research reached Pennsylvania, I read all your on-line blogs thoroughly. To begin with I was upset by the way you appeared to 'sensationalize' my brother's life and sad death, with 'The Bike Radio Murder' story and your 'Young Sherlock' persona. I'm afraid that, at first, I didn't much care for your popular style of writing. But I guess you wanted as many readers as possible, and that was your way of getting them.

However, you appeared to genuinely care about Yushi, and for that I thank and applaud you. The more you wrote, the more I concluded that you were 'on Yushi's side', and that you very much wanted to clear his name.

Towards the end of your writings I sensed your disappointment at not being able to do that, when you reluctantly concluded that my brother was guilty after all.

(2)

I am absolutely certain that he was not. He could not deliberately kill even a small insect, let alone a human being. The importance of all life had been instilled in him by his beloved grandfather, whose wise words Yushi worshipped. I am absolutely certain that my brother's only crime was to be on a bicycle ride that he thought would remove the demons from his unusual and perhaps immature mind, and that he found himself to be in the wrong place at the wrong time. That was all he had been guilty of.

You see, Mr. Markland, when we were growing up, my brother would always falsely confess to anything and everything that I myself had done wrong—and he was like that with everyone else we knew as well. He would make up such elaborate stories so convincingly in order to take the blame for others' wrong-doings.

I used to warn him not to but still he continued, creating intricate tales so that anyone, including our parents, would believe him. I never could work out why he did that—perhaps it gave him some strange satisfaction to shift attention towards himself. Perhaps it was something to do with his condition. It's now recognised more commonly as bipolar disorder, but back then less was known of the condition. Only my parents and I (and of course he) were aware of it. We shall never know what his true motivation was for making up these tales—and I can only guess it. I so wish he were still with us today so that I could ask him.

For years, Yushi had had the good sense to recognise the seriousness of this crime and that he should not falsely confess to it. We had been so close that I am certain that, during my visits to the prison, if he had been guilty, he would have told me.

Thankfully he had so strenuously maintained his innocence, which I am certain to have been the truth, and this may have contributed to the postponement of his execution, prolonging his life for a few extra years. But, unfortunately, in the end and when he knew of his imminent fate, he gave up and defaulted to his normal way of behaviour. Doing that must have somehow made the inevitable outcome more bearable for him—and so he thought for me, too.

I'm sure that Yushi had been trying to make me feel better by his concoction of a hoax story, just like he always had done in the past. He thought that if I could be convinced that his death was in fact lawful and justified, then I would be more able to cope. Unfortunately, he was wrong, and I have not coped. Since his death, I have merely existed.

I was invited by the prison Governor to attend and witness his execution in June, 1996, and to have one last visit with Yushi the hour before.

How could I possibly do that with my heart already broken? The thought of going there to watch him die was so abhorrent that I could not possibly go. But I cannot express how much I now regret not having visited him.

I took a moment's break from reading, my heart going out to this poor woman. It was a very difficult letter for me to stomach, but I continued to the last page.

(3)

I am one-hundred per cent certain that my brother was not guilty of killing Sandy Beach. I couldn't have hoped for anyone else to comprehend my reasoning—until I learned about you.

You were the only person intent on discovering the truth about Yushi, and you nearly got there. Unfortunately, because of his false confession, the true culprit will soon be a free man again, going on to enjoy the rest of his life. Yushi no longer has that luxury.

When I first discovered your work, I had hoped so much that you would be able to restore Yushi's good name. It is impossible to turn back time, but at least I am able to share this information about my brother with you. You are the one person in the world who I hope will believe me.

I think Yushi's confession note that you described, was intended for me. When I didn't go to see him that last time, he instead gave it to his cell-mate Mr. Emanuele, and I only learned of some of its contents from reading your blog. I would so dearly love to have that document, the last thing he ever wrote, but I doubt if that would ever be possible. Unless you could somehow get it for me? If so, I would be eternally grateful.

Sincerely,

MJ

Mitori Jarvis—née Yakamoto

I read the letter yet again—three times in all. But as well as focussing on the contents, something else engaged me: Mitori's full name—*Mitori Jarvis*.

Of course! '*MJ*'!

All along, I'd been assuming that Yushi's scratching I'd discovered on the prison cell wall at Joliet—that day when I'd sneaked in past the guards—meant 'M.J. *Emanuele*'. But '*ASK MJ. YY. 6.14.96*' didn't mean 'ask M.J. *Emanuele*'. It meant 'ask *Mitori Jarvis*'—his sister! Yushi had thought and expected that Mitori would be visiting him that day, the day of his execution. Once he learned that Mitori wouldn't be coming, he must have left his confession note to the one and only person he could—M.J. Emanuele.

Emanuele must have been elsewhere in the prison, perhaps working in the kitchen or the library, when Yushi hurriedly wrote out the note. The poor guy, knowing that he had only a short time left, must have been unable to think straight, and left the note somewhere in the cell for Emanuele to find, maybe on his bunk. On returning to his cell, Emanuele would have assumed the note was for him, and kept it folded up in his Bible all that time, not realising the note was actually meant for Yushi's sister.

I thought about Yushi's confession note yet again. Remembering his scrawled handwriting, I knew it looked like it had been written in a great hurry, and although it was guesswork on my part, I was convinced that my summation of the situation was likely to be correct.

I felt numb with mental exhaustion and anguish—and it was only half past nine in the morning. I had no idea what I should do for the best. I felt a huge sense of sorrow for Mitori.

I considered my options. Did I have the energy to return to America and somehow attempt to convince the police to bring some sort of fresh challenge against Ozborn? Could I retrieve Yushi's original handwritten confession note from Emanuele? I understood completely why Mitori would like to have it, and I remembered that Siobhan had asked him for it, and her request was declined, but maybe I'd have better luck. I could at least try, and I decided to write to Stateville Prison and request a meeting with Emanuele on the occasion of my next trip to the States, when I go there to marry Siobhan next year.

I certainly didn't want anything to do with Marc Ozborn. Even after nine months, I'd still suffer anxiety attacks when recollecting being chased by him. But receiving Mitori's letter had definitely made me consider whether I had done enough to make sure of the right and proper outcome of the whole affair.

Had I fought hard enough, for the sake of Yushi's memory, and now for the sake of Mitori's wellbeing, whose remarks I believed wholeheartedly—perhaps naively, perhaps foolishly—but I believed them nonetheless?

I had come to the conclusion that I should reply to Mitori, but not until *Florida Key* had been published. I weighed up the fact that when I had received her letter it had already been mislaid in the post for five months, so I reasoned that a further delay wouldn't make any significant difference. Besides, nothing I could do would alter the sad history regarding her late brother.

But there was something I thought I *could* do to help ease Mitori's pain a little, after all she had suffered over the loss of her brother. So, in addition to the emergency services personnel who saved my life, I had an idea that I might also dedicate *Florida Key* to her.

Just to be sure I was doing the right thing; I decided to retrieve the computer file containing the digital image of Yushi's confession note one more time. Although it was only a photograph that Siobhan had taken when she was in Emanuele's cell, and Yushi's handwriting had been atrocious, I was able to decipher every single word after stringent and thorough examination. I read it carefully, trying hard to visualise the scene that he had been attempting to describe:

MJ

I did it. I killed Sandy Beach. Sandy ridiculed me when I returned to her house for the barbecue, and I watched her making out with that guy. I finally got a girl to show me love, or so I thought. How could she have been so cruel as to lead me on? I heard her call him by name—something like Mike, Mart or Mark, I couldn't be sure. She saw me come back in the kitchen while the guy's back was to me. Sandy beckoned me over for me to join them. No way!

The guy didn't know what he was doing, clearly out of it. One minute he was violently hitting her, the next he was calm. He was wearing nothing and must have been on drugs or something. I just stood there watching him slapping and striking her but, rather than try to move away, Sandy just stood there and seemed to like it.

CFNM-DOM is what they call it, I've since learned. She was egging him on, and he was slapping her harder—but then after she fell to the ground, he suddenly stopped and staggered off outside, not noticing I was there. Sandy was concussed but still conscious. She looked at me and asked me to finish off what he'd started, and she teased me when I refused, saying I "wasn't a real man like Mark". I heard his name better that time. "Is that what 'real' men do?" I asked. That was so cruel of her, especially as she must have known my feelings for her. It was so disgusting what they were doing, so she deserved what she got, wouldn't you say?

This guy must have been the one who stole my bike radio from outside the diner. How else could it have got there, in Sandy's house? I wanted out. But not before that woman got what was coming to her. It's ironic that I smashed her head with the thing that I'd just been into town to try and replace. After I'd finished with it, it was in pieces that were scattered all over the place, and with his fingerprints everywhere. I guessed he'd be caught and would take the rap, while I was well away from there.

You know what I was like, but you see, they had the right man all along. So, weep for me no more. I finally got what I deserved for the crime I committed.

Yushi Yakamoto

Having previously been certain that Yushi Yakamoto hadn't been guilty of killing Sandy Beach and that Marc Ozborn had, directly after receiving Mitori's letter I had been even more convinced that my hunch had been right.

Of course, I doubted I would ever be able to prove it, and as I was writing these words I could have only hoped that you, the reader, would come to the same conclusion.

But something was now puzzling me. In my mind I'd re-enacted, time and time again, what I'd imagined had occurred that night when Sandy Beach had been murdered. But there was something that simply didn't add up if Mitori were to be believed about her brother's confession being false. All along, I'd hoped that Yushi had been the innocent party; wrongly accused, convicted and executed, and I guess I'd enthusiastically clung to the notion that her letter collaborated my theory.

According to Yushi's confession note, the one that Mitori was convinced was false, Yushi had described how Ozborn—high on cocaine and alcohol—had left the kitchen. But, if that were to be the case, how could Ozborn have smashed Sandy on the head with the bike radio? I read the relevant part of Yushi's note again: '*I guessed he'd be caught and would take the rap, while I was well away from there.*' If Yushi *had* concocted the whole scenario, he hadn't reasoned that it would have been impossible for Ozborn to smash Sandy's head with the radio if he were already out cold on the patio.

And there was another part of the note that now made more sense. The third sentence from the end; '*You know what I was like, but you see, they had the right man all along.*'

"You know what I was like . . .", I repeated to myself. That must have been a reference to Mitori being aware of Yushi's tendency to make up stories. But in this case, it hadn't been a story.

So, surely it *had to be* Yushi who'd done it. It had to have been Yushi who'd killed Sandy Beach in cold blood. Yushi's so-called 'false' confession note to his sister, MJ, wasn't false at all. It was the plain truth.

'*. . . but you see, they had the right man all along*', I read again. Yes, I reluctantly concluded that they had.

With a heavy heart I pondered my next move. The biggest concern now was how to respond to Mitori's letter. I couldn't possibly send her a copy of Yushi's full confession, let alone return to America to try and retrieve the original for her. It would surely upset her far too much, and in my opinion she must have suffered enough already. After careful consideration, I concluded the best thing was to let sleeping dogs lie. After all, Mitori had posted her letter to me several months ago. She must have thought by now that it had never reached me—or that she'd given up all hope of receiving a reply.

I had, until this moment, been thinking that Yushi had become something of a posthumous friend; a troubled friend, that my $17 purchase from a flea-market had led me to. And I'd almost decided to dedicate this book, the book that tells the story of my Florida Key, 'In Memory of Yushi'.

But how could I possibly do that, if he was Sandy Beach's killer?

I couldn't help thinking, wanting to think, that I'd perhaps got things wrong. That Ozborn *had* been the killer all along, instead of Yushi. Perhaps it was more likely that I would never know absolutely for sure what really happened on that fateful day in 1981. Or perhaps one day I would return to do some more digging, and come to a different conclusion, maybe in Yushi's favour.

There I'd go again: wishful thinking. I decided to stop tormenting myself about something I couldn't alter. The facts were the facts; Sandy Beach had been murdered. Rightly or wrongly, Yushi Yakamoto had been found guilty.

Enough was enough. I had a book to bring out. And a girl who I was in love with who I'd be marrying next year.

I decided to forget about what had happened in the past, and to concentrate on what was going to happen in the future.

Oliver Markland

Wivenhoe

2018

ABOUT THE AUTHOR

In 1981, bored beyond words with my job, I decided to pack my bags and go. The day after my 21st birthday, I found myself sitting on a Laker Airways jet, bound for Los Angeles. In the hold was my trusty racing bike that I'd had for my 13th birthday. Two years earlier, I had ridden it across France, so I felt confident that, with L.A. to New York being only four times the distance, cycling from one coast to the other shouldn't be a problem. It wasn't. Once I'd exited the sliding doors at Los Angeles airport and asked a stranger in the street, "Which way is New York?", the journey became a game-changer for me, and I often wonder how differently my life might have turned out had it not been for Freddie Laker and his no-frills ticket price that I could just about afford.

Thirty-seven years later, I'm glad to say I'm still in touch with some of the warmest and kindest people I could have met on that journey. One of them, Chase Kimball, who I met in Salt Lake City, gave invaluable help with this book. His attention to detail is to be commended. When I sent him an early draft of *Florida Key*, he soon came back with observations like: "They didn't have Marlboro Lights back then–just Marlboro Unfiltered", and "'Burger and chips'–Americans don't talk like that. It would be 'burgers and fries'."

My own journey across the States inspired me to write about a fictional bike ride. Half way along a straight 500-mile stretch in Kansas, I met a Japanese guy also cycling solo but in the opposite direction. It was quite surreal, standing in the middle of nowhere with only our bikes and rucksacks. I'm sure he wasn't a potential murderer. Even so, I thought I'd best not use his real name in the book. I recently attempted to track him down through social media, but to no avail. So, if anyone knows the whereabouts of Yoshichika Shida, please get in touch.

Later, my working career comprised a succession of jobs in sales, marketing, and publishing. I had a stint in the music business, championing two great musicians, one of whom went on to international stardom, the other developing huge respect as a world-class singer-songwriter whose silky-smooth voice can tear your heartstrings with a single note. Nowadays, when I'm not busy authoring, I'm decorating. It's the ideal environment in which to conjure up my next novel's sub-plot, while watching the paint dry.

Fast forward to the present: In France, I had a wake-up call. A friend asked me what I did. I replied with the usual 'painter and decorator' answer, with the footnote 'and I also write'. She wisely went on to enquire: "But are you a painter who writes, or a writer who paints? It's not what you do to earn a living, it's what's in your soul."

So, on that basis, I can now include 'writer' in my list of jobs.

My wife, Jane is a brilliant artist *(www.janewatsonart.com)* who does gardening (not a gardener who does art). My daughter, Laura has more talent as an illustrator in her little finger than she knows, and my son, Oliver, whose computer skills overtook mine when he was 15, is currently exploring Asia and Japan. Probably meeting as many warm and kind people as I did when I was his age.

I have many interests and several passions. My interests include our ancient motorhome we call Tallulah (it's a 1978 Hymer on a Bedford CF chassis, in case you're interested), food and wine appreciation (particularly enjoying a full-bodied Corbières), writing a blog (search 'a boat for my potplants') and listening to music on a good hi-fi (especially vinyl–thank goodness they're all the rage again).

Passions include my lovely poor man's classic, a 1968 Fiat Coupé (1438cc, 4-speed, right-hand-drive, and only a few left now), the life and music of Harry Nilsson (Harry who? You know. 'Without You', 'Everybody's Talkin'', 'Coconut'–"You put the lime in the coconut, and drink it all up"–now you remember, don't you?).

And the biggest passion of them all is our piece of heaven in France, our '*Writers' Retreat*' *(www.writersretreatinfrance.com)*. Jane does her art there, and it's where most of this book was written. Situated near Carcassonne, 'our' adopted village of Montolieu is also known as the Village of Books, on account of its 15 independent bookshops catering to just 850 inhabitants. The perfect location for creativity.

I'm now imagining having driven to Montolieu in the Fiat, sitting on the terrace and writing my next book, *Mr. Tap*, with a glass of wine poured from a bottle just purchased from Adrian's shop opposite, with Nilsson playing through the speakers. Hmm–a lovely thought.

ABOUT THE CHARACTERS

Florida Key has been partly crowdfunded, enabling this author to take time away from clients' halls, stairs and landings, and concentrate on completing the project. Without a hefty advance that Stephen King or JK Rowling can command, you have to think of all the ways you can to make ends meet.

Friends asked me if they could join the fun of being in this book, and the creative challenge of how to include them added a hugely positive ingredient to the mix.

There were those whose true name was so delicious, I just had to create a character in which their persona could exist. An example of this is Mrs. Hannah Baltzwinik-Toporofski (yes, she is real). Pure gold, I thought, and I loved writing any parts of the story that she could crop up in.

Another example presented itself when I met Melody and her tiny dog Blaise-Pascal. They were renting our *Writers' Retreat*, and Melody found a copy of *Muddy Water* there. Inspired by the concept of buying her way into *Florida Key*, she asked to be included. Bearing in mind that by this time the first draft was almost finished, I gulped. How could I turn her down, especially with her dog having such a charming name? I couldn't, not least because there was a cash offer on the table. Not a lot, but enough to persuade me to do a rewrite and find a way in for them.

I'm such a cheapskate, and I know it, but it did lead me down a creative path I enjoyed travelling.

I love the Black Buoy pub in Wivenhoe, just like real-life characters Audrey and Bob Needham do in the book. I also met Lorraine McTear for the first time there. Lorraine was instrumental in providing another of the characters–Theresa Ashley. Lorraine had told me about the charity event she co-organises every year, and I promised to donate a signed *Muddy Water* as well as give a part in what was then the future *Florida Key*. Theresa won that auction, the charity became considerably richer as a result, and I had a lot of fun including Theresa as a policewoman in a small town in Illinois, USA.

Miss Alberta Louise Baudet had the honour of making her second appearance, playing the same character in *Florida Key* as she had done in *Muddy Water*. As I wrote the dialogue for her character, I could almost hear the words being spoken by her over my shoulder.

Another cash-for-character addition was Katie Copeland, who I included as a forensics expert. Not knowing much about Katie, I described her in the book as being a bit OCD. I wanted to check that she didn't mind this portrayal of her, and I also mentioned, "by the way, you're a forensic scientist." Not only did she then inform me that she'd always, since she was a young girl, wanted to do that job, but by her own admission she was obsessed with being ultra neat and tidy at home. "Everything absolutely *has* to be in its right place," she elaborated. In the story, I had also written that her husband Paul loves watching sport on TV, and that he reads his newspapers from back to front. And that's exactly what he does in true life. I had no idea. Spooky.

ABOUT THE PUBLISHER

I'd like to give a special mention and thanks to David Roberts at Hornet Books. When I began writing *Muddy Water*, it was David, previously an editor at Guinness World Records, who encouraged me to go on my metaphorical writing journey. It turned out to be far more than that–it became an exciting adventure.

Our paths had first crossed because he was the author of the fabulous *Rock Atlas*, a book featuring significant music-related places throughout the country, and I wanted a signed copy. If, for example, you're intrigued to learn where the pub that Robbie Williams grew up in is, look no further than page 177. By the way, it's the Red Lion in Burslem, Staffordshire.

Little did I know at the time, David was busy forming Hornet, and soon I was being offered a contract to become their first published author. Talk about luck!

Hornet is a thoroughly excellent publishing house, and they are a real pleasure to work with. It may not be the size of Penguin or HarperCollins–yet–but you know you're in good company and safe hands with them. They genuinely care about their growing stable of authors.

Every week, David and I would meet up to talk books, music, this and that, eat dinner (taking it in turns to provide a ready meal) and drink wine (also taking it in turns to provide the bottle(s) of red). Five years on, we're still carrying on this tradition, still chewing the cud and still putting the world to rights.

And we'd also discuss books–*Muddy Water*, *Florida Key*, and hopefully my next, *Mr. Tap*.

Not only is David the publisher, he is also the editor, and the cover photographer and designer. He's also become a great friend.

ABOUT THE WRITING PROCESS

To all fellow novelists–this is not recommended, but it worked for me. It helped me free my mind, allowing me to go down a track that perhaps I wouldn't have otherwise ventured on. Had I always been stone-cold sober, I'd probably have thought: "No, I'd better not write that, better not go there." But, while working on *Florida Key* during a warm February day in Montolieu, I had a phone conversation with David, my editor. I'm sure it was he who encouraged me to do this, but he might now deny it, being the responsible publisher that he is.

You see, my routine would go like this: I'd get up early, have coffee and breakfast, then begin working at around 8am. By 1pm, it was time to open some of Adrian's wonderful wine from his shop opposite. By mid-afternoon I would be cranking up the music as I wrote all sorts of, some might say (including me), wine-induced nonsense, letting the story take on a life of its own. I'd stop 'work' at around 5pm, and turn the music higher, leaving a trail of LPs scattered all over the floor. The following morning, after coffee, I would clear up the records and put them back alphabetically on the shelf, reread what I'd written the previous afternoon, scratch my head and think of the Talking Heads song, 'Once In A Lifetime'. Just like in the song, I asked myself: how did I get here? My God! What have I done?

Then I'd set to, throwing out some of the ideas that I considered too crazy, even for me. And I'd keep some of the good ones, and work on turning them into something I was happy with, good for the plot, and hopefully entertaining for the reader.

For the full list of titles and more information visit
www.hornetbooks.com
and Facebook at www.facebook.com/HornetBooksPublishing/

Visit author Neil Watson's blog
www.aboatformypotplants.blogspot.com